THE GIFTS OF PANDORA

TAPESTRY OF FATE
BOOK 1

MATT LARKIN

INCANDESCENT PHOENIX BOOKS

The Gifts of Pandora: Eschaton Cycle
Tapestry of Fate Book 1
MATT LARKIN
Editors: Sarah Chorn, Regina Dowling
Cover: Felix Ortiz, Shawn T. King
Map: Francesca Baerald

Incandescent Phoenix Books
mattlarkinbooks.com

THE WHISPER

It starts with a whisper, a haunting intimation of a World askew. That we are, in the end, caught in a death spiral, time nearly played out, whilst entropy tugs ever harder upon the Wheel of Fate.

Looking now into the dying embers, we at last apprehend Truth, and in it the revelation that the vaunted tales of old were not what we thought ... And neither, in fact, were we.

For if we have lived before, might not all we've dreamt be but our souls' memories of Worlds become dust ...

A QUICK NOTE

For full colour, higher-res maps, character lists, location overviews, and glossaries, check out the bonus resources here:
https://tinyurl.com/hw52dzss

And if you liked this book, be sure to check out my offer for a free novella at the end.

PROLOGUE

2400 Golden Age

Fulminating clouds encircled the peak of Mount Olympus, every flash a testament to the power and self-aggrandisement of its new lord. Rough-hewn steps sliced the mountainside, weatherworn and slick, a remnant of the Time of Nyx. Oh, but Prometheus had seen them restored. In pyromantic visions, he had beheld the grandeur Zeus would erect upon his new home. Time and again, Prometheus had walked here in his prescient trances, half-aware of the marmoreal temples and grandiose Olympian halls that would limn this peak.

When the time came at long last, he would walk, half in a daze, as oft happened when an Oracle fulfilled his visions and lived in actuality a moment he had lived in prescience too many times. Thus, accordingly, he'd seen his own bemused steps.

Now, though, Titans passed him by, both ascending and descending, and so many pausing to gape at Zeus's coruscating display upon the summit. Perhaps the self-styled god vented thus to announce his victory to the World, though the storm remained, even in Prometheus's visions of distant days to come. If Zeus created this now in celebration, it would endure in perpetuity as a symbol.

Prometheus paused, halfway up the winding staircase, just before a raging cataract. A cool brume rose from where the fall hit the rocks, and he tried to revel in the way it tingled the bare flesh of his arms and shins. He wished he could luxuriate in the beauty of this place, but he could not suppress the shudder that wracked him at the fore-knowledge of what fate would one day befall him here. So very like what awaited Kronos high above.

Zeus would not enact his father's vile sentence until Prometheus and the others had gathered to witness it. The new king sought an exhibition to titillate and horrify, and he would have one, though he surely did not begin to grasp the import of all he had done.

An approaching woman yanked his attention from the cataract as she descended the peak. Zeus might want his spectacle, true, but many would not wish to watch what he intended for Kronos, Nike among them.

She paused before him, dark hair flapping in the wind.

"Did he say aught?" Prometheus asked, raising his voice to carry over the fall.

"He said a great deal," Nike answered. "Not all of it made sense. Some of it made too much sense." A hesitation. "Will you speak with him?"

Prometheus found his fists clenching. He wanted to refuse, but he owed Kronos at least the dignity of a final word. "I must."

Nike frowned, looking like she wanted to say more. Like she was none too pleased at having helped Zeus begin his reign. Nor was Prometheus. Maybe none of the Titans who had sided with him were much pleased. But then, Fate had forced their hand.

With a nod of understanding, Prometheus left her and continued his unpalatable ascent. Flickers in his mind hinted at locations where an agora would one day rise, and beyond, upon the summit, where Zeus would erect his ostentatious palace. About that spot Skystones orbited, an archipelago of hovering rock islands, held aloft by their Otherworldly nature.

The fulgurations from the storm burst amid those floating isles, leaving them in turn radiant or tenebrous. Not so unlike the Titans claiming this place as their home, when even Kronos had not possessed the hubris to think he could dwell among such energies and remain himself.

Finally, Prometheus reached the summit. Here, snows lingered upon the rocks and flurried in the wind.

Others emerged from a cave that bored into the mountainside, hollowed out long ago, in the Time of Nyx, when Men touched something they ought to have left alone. And Zeus would build his throne upon a bed of cancer eating away at the foundation of the World, drunk on its poisons.

Upon the cave threshold, Bia waited for him. Auburn-haired and incarnadine-eyed, the Titan was, perhaps, the most violent of all Styx's brood, and her visage held a sickening glee at what she knew impended. "The king sends for you, Firebringer." The Titan licked her lips, her eyes gleaming. Was she actually aroused by these proceedings? Or perhaps she wished to discomfit him for her amusement.

Either way, Prometheus ignored her salacious airs. "Take me to him."

From the corner of his eye, he saw Bia's expression turn into a glower that persisted even as she guided him downward. Like the stairs rising from the base of the mountain, these were rugged, though in better shape for not having endured millennia of wind and rain. The path led them deep inside the mountain, past the chamber that housed the Oracle Mirrors that had, in their own way, helped ensure the damnation of Kronos. The quicksilver mirrors had shown more Truth than even one such as Kronos was prepared to handle.

Oh, Prometheus knew all too well the agony of foreknowledge and the anguish of unvarnished Truth—the Ontos of the World held no whit of pity. While Men toiled, suffered, and died, they did so in ignorance, and for that, were at least able to sleep at night.

No doubt unaware of his musings, Bia led him onward without the least slowing of her pace, the slap of her sandals echoing upon the stone. Further down, they came to an open cavern, and here, some dozen Titans had gathered to watch the spectacle.

There, off to the side, stood Leto and Helios's twins, Artemis and Apollon, enmeshed in furtive whispers. Across from them, other siblings, Hera and Poseidon, both grim-faced and watching the Titan in the centre of the chamber.

Platinum-haired Kronos, bound in orichalcum fetters, struggling to stand while his captors circled around him like sharks. Kratos and Zelus, Bia's own siblings, snickered as they stalked their prey. Noticing his sister's entrance with Prometheus, Kratos grinned and slammed his fist into Kronos's kidney. Kronos's knees buckled, but Zelus caught him, her hands around his neck.

Prometheus set his jaw, refusing to let Styx's brood take further pleasure in his discomfort at how they treated his erstwhile friend. Still, he could not entirely suppress the visions he'd seen of what they would do to *him*, as well. Perhaps that would be his punishment for failing to stop what was happening to Kronos now.

As if Fate cared about giving anyone what they deserved.

Just outside the circle, bound Arke whimpered, the ichorous ruins of her severed wings still flapping. Someone had gagged her, perhaps tired of her pleas. Hand on her shoulder—though his wrists, too, were fettered—Prometheus's self-proclaimed brother Atlas stared daggers at him. Atlas was not gagged, though he said naught, perhaps knowing neither pleas nor recriminations would avail him here. Or perhaps pride had him denying Zeus even the satisfaction of a word.

"Enough," Zeus's voice boomed from the back of the chamber. There, he stood, hair a platinum mane so like his father's, and eyes ice blue.

At once, Kratos and Zelus stepped aside, the latter dropping Kronos and giving way so that Zeus might confront his father.

Prometheus, though, found his gaze drawn from Kronos to Hekate's haunted visage lurking in the shadows. He had heard others call her Zeus's attack dog, and the king perhaps could not have managed to harness the Tartarian Gate without her. Yet still, from the look of her, this sat little better with her than with Prometheus himself. Or had Kronos said something to her? Certainly, the fallen oligarch cast a withering glance her way before looking up at his treasonous son with defiance.

And of the gate itself, it lay at the far side of the chamber, cut into the stone as if naught more than an archway leading into another tunnel. The Supernal sigils carved into the stones of the arch shone with lurid effulgence that churned the gut to look upon, and the air beyond the gate undulated as if one looked at it from beneath the flowing sea. The tunnel where it led was not a place, in the strictest sense, but the very terminus of the World, for Tartarus bounded the cosmos, both holding back the taint within its walls, and encouraging it to fester.

"You strove against me and you lost," Zeus bellowed at his father, his voice booming through the hall. "For this, you are hereby *damned*. Have you any last words, Father?"

With a grunt, Kronos rose, and looked about the cavern. His gaze settled on Prometheus. "You betrayed me! You and your spawn, the both of you betrayed me! I am here because of what you told me, Fatespinner!"

Prometheus winced. He owed Kronos this confrontation and could not deny the accusations levelled against him. Words failed him, though, and all he could do was stride forward and offer Kronos the chance to look him in the eye. Almost, he wished he could tell Kronos he would one day join him in this torment. As if that might excuse Prometheus now, for failing to end this.

Kronos leaned in close. "I know what is writ upon the Tablet of Destiny," he grated, words pitched so as not to carry across the whole of the cavern.

It was so hard not to waver. So hard to stay the course, even knowing Fate afforded him no choice in the matter. "Destiny is not always what it seems, old friend."

Kronos spat upon Prometheus's sandals. "If there was ever truth to your friendship, it long ago turned fetid."

Zeus's fist snared in Kronos's hair, and, with a twist of his wrist, he sent his father careening along the floor toward the accursed Tartarian Gate. "Bring forth the prisoners!"

At his words, Kratos, Bia, and Zelus lurched into motion, glee writ plain across their features as each of them hauled up one of the condemned. Zelus seemed to take particular delight in Arke's squirming, pointless resistance.

And it was futile, for the orichalcum fetters rendered the bound Titans utterly impuissant, unable to draw upon their Pneumatikoi and thus no stronger than Men, while their captors retained their superhuman strength.

Zelus dug fingers so deep into Arke's shoulders Prometheus saw golden ichor trickle down them, commingling with the still weeping wounds upon her back. A twinge of sympathy shot through him, but she had made her choices, and he could not save her from them.

Kratos, meanwhile, had hauled Kronos to the gate by his ankle.

Zeus stood at the forefront, taking it all in with a manic exuberance that threatened to choke Prometheus. "For crimes of treason against your true king, I condemn you all to eternal torment at the edge of the void, where you shall be scoured down to the piths of your souls." The king chuckled, as if aught amusing lay behind his words. "Justice be done."

At his command, Kratos strode through the gate. His passage took a breath longer than it should have, and Prometheus imagined the viscous resistance that threshold must pose. The Titan dragged Kronos along behind him. Both forms seemed distorted behind the barrier, as they descended the tunnel's path, in the moment before Bia followed with Atlas.

Prometheus wanted to look away, for witnessing this cleaved his soul in half, and not only because he knew he would follow in their wake many centuries from now. He wanted to turn, to leave, even, rather than bear the torment of those who had trusted him.

Betrayer, indeed.

But then, that was all the more reason he owed it to them to look on and bear witness. Fate had forced him to this moment, even as it had damned these people.

It forced him. And it would carry him onward, toward yet worse agonies.

PART I

With all due respect, I find myself compelled to raise the question as to the origins of the term, 'Nymph.' Why, exactly, do we have a word for female Titans of lesser status and not for our male counterparts? But then the answer is obvious, is it not?

— Thalia, Dialogues of the Muses

1

PANDORA

1570 Silver Age

*T*he scents of wine and olives mingled with a tinge of vomit emanating from some corner of the palace courtyard. Laughter, heated discussions, and passionate moans punctuated the silences between the chords of Pandora's harp, and she took it all in, though wine warmed her face and dulled her senses. Being half-drunk helped, too, with whatever meagre hint of modesty she might have still had at sitting here, playing with her breasts exposed.

Such things kept the symposium guests jovial, though perhaps more of them leered at the entirely nude flute girls across the court-yard than at Pandora. Either way, the Pleiades expected as much from hetairai like Pandora, and they paid her far more custom than she'd make seducing any of these men on her own.

So she paraded herself, she strummed her harp, and she sang. This night, she chanted Adonis's almost forgotten epic of the Ambrosial War, her voice soaring as she reached the bit about the death of Okeanus and how his mournful lover named the very ocean itself for him.

And yes, indeed, by the end of the song, nigh every eye in the courtyard was upon her, even those of some few of the Pleiades themselves, the very Queens of Atlantis. When the song at last finished, Pandora rose and offered a bow to her scattered applause, surreptitiously shrugging her khiton back over her shoulders as she stood.

She'd barely had time to grab a bowl of wine—the drinking rules of the symposiarch only applied to the guests, not the entertainment —when the men came sauntering over. They always did. Drunk and brazen, as if she ought to revel and swoon in their favour and attention. Queen Kelaino saved her from idle chatter with a pair of them, though, deftly stepping around them. Graceful, despite the fact that, like any Titan, she stood half a head taller than the Men.

The queen grasped Pandora's elbow lightly and led her away from the garden courtyard, into a paved colonnade that ran through the central palace. "You have a gift for music, Pandora," the Titan said, not looking at her. "You have, in fact, a great many gifts, I am given to understand."

For a glorified whore, she meant. Ah, but much as Pandora oft found it hard to hold her tongue, there were some things one simply did not say to a queen, and certainly not to a *Titan* queen. With a word, Kelaino could shift Pandora's fortunes from free hetaira to *actual* whore owned by some brothel. That the Titan took any interest in her, that she occasionally hired her for these functions, was a boon. A chance to make something of her life on Atlantis, even though Pandora held no citizenship here.

"I am honoured you think so."

Kelaino snorted lightly. "Your false modesty is quaint."

Oh, Pandora could feign modesty or most aught else, given the need, but here, she saw little reason to do so. The sharpest mind in the World was not always a blessing, not for a woman whose intellect might threaten the fragile egos of the men around her. Kelaino, though, clearly felt no threat. Titan pride scraped the very firmament, brushing the stars and claiming them as their due. In a Man, a fraction of such would be called hubris, but amid Kelaino's kind, it was simply a fact of life.

They came to a second courtyard beyond the colonnade, this one home to an artificial lake fed by dolphin-shaped waterspouts three times her height. Within the pool swam great rays and skates and other fish. Once, Pandora had seen this place in daylight and gawked at the myriad splendour of the collected sea life. Now, though, as in most times she had seen the palace, with the shallow lake lit only by moonlight and braziers, the effect became muted.

Across the pond, she caught sight of the guest of honour, King Sisyphus of Korinth, here for his betrothal to Kelaino's sister Merope. At the moment, though, he walked the grounds with an entourage of men, no doubt all drunk and debating the finer points of civic philosophy or some such thing. These days, men liked to quote and debate Urania's dialogues, though most of them probably understood very little of the Muse's actual points. Perhaps they realised their ignorance and feigned comprehension for the sake of saving face, or perhaps they were too self-absorbed to grasp their blindness in the first place.

"I wonder," Pandora said, knowing the wine made her tongue too free but not quite able to stop herself, "if they're on about Utopia once more."

"It has been a favoured topic at symposiums all year," Kelaino said, seeming more intent on watching the fish than Pandora, despite having brought her out here.

"And do you think any one of them apprehends Urania's subtext? That a society oppressing half its population must ever wallow in discontent, even if few among the populace ever recognise its source?"

Now Kelaino's gaze fell upon her like a blow. Here was a woman sharp enough to catch Pandora's meaning. The Pleiades escaped the patriarchal chains that bound mortal women and most other Nymphs, at least to some extent. Save that they ruled merely at the sufferance of the King of Olympus who had destroyed their father and, over the years, forced himself on more than half of the seven queens.

But then, the queens were but a few of his victims.

Pandora felt her jaw hardening. The urge to give voice to such a grievance bubbled inside her like a boiling cauldron, almost more than she could contain. It felt she would overflow from the need to speak of what she'd seen, so long suppressed.

Had it suited her, the queen could have simply slain Pandora then and there. No one would question a Titan, least of all one who ostensibly ruled the polis and island, both. In theory, the Pleiades were all equal, but Pandora had long suspected Kelaino held more than her share of the power. Now, with Merope bound for Korinth and Elektra spending so much time in Minos's court in Knosós, that would only increase. Taygete and Sterope were weak, and Maia, from what Pandora had heard, had never quite been the same once Zeus had finished with her.

Pandora raised her gaze to meet the Titan's own, offering up a challenge. Despite it all, despite all that had befallen her, Pandora refused to give in. She would not surrender to the ravages of circumstance, and she would not allow the facade she wore with clients to became authentic.

"The World is how it is, Pandora," Kelaino said after a moment more. "Your best chance at happiness may lie in accepting that. To defy the foundations of society is folly."

"Which is easy to say when one reigns as queen of the most powerful polis in the World."

Now those Atlantid eyes—so dark as to seem almost black—hardened further. Yes, Pandora so oft crossed lines. For the very existence of such lines deeply offended. "My sister will wed tomorrow. See to it her betrothed gets other women out of his system tonight."

Perhaps Pandora's look of distaste showed plain upon her face. Oh, it wasn't as if she expected to get through a symposium without servicing a guest or two, nor even minded overmuch. Pandora was twenty-five and had been doing this since her bleeds had started. Shame over such things had become a distant memory, given way to practicality and the realisation her choice lay only in how she responded to the throws of Fate. "Shall I point out that the idea that a man who needs to sate himself upon other women on the very eve of his wedding would ever get over such a need is so patently absurd as to offend reason?"

The Titan grabbed her elbow, this time with a grip that felt like it could have torn chunks of the marble fountain clean off. "Vex me, and you may sacrifice more than a night's pay." And given that Kelaino tended to offer a half dozen tetradrachmae for these events, it was a hefty sacrifice. "My protection of you may expire as well."

Protection? As if the queen was an actual patron to her. Pandora had never sought any permanent patron, and she didn't recall any such offer from Kelaino. She studiously forced her face to neutrality. Titan arrogance always tended to shine through, as if even the smallest of kindnesses shown to mortals deserved obeisance and eternal gratitude in return. "I'd not dream of allowing this to become a dull party."

"Splendid." Her voice struck like a whip. "I'm told your cunt sings even more beautifully than your voice." With that, Kelaino spun on her heel.

Pandora winced. Clearly, she had pushed a little beyond the bounds of wisdom with the queen.

For a moment, she steadied herself, watching the dark play of fish swimming around a stingray. If stepped upon, such creatures could unsheathe spines in their tails laced with oh-so-painful venom. Only a fool tromped among them without a care. How she longed for such a stinger herself, with toxin enough to fell even an Olympian. To fell all the Titans who thought themselves so far above Man, and then, perhaps, no few of the men who thought themselves above women.

When the moment passed, she affected her most sensual sashay, circumnavigating the pool in order to place herself ahead of Sisyphus and his entourage. With an expression of half-lidded eyes—one she had spent much time practicing—she made her way close to the demigod king. "I'm told my king will soon depart these lands and belong to but a single woman?"

"'Belong' might be a stretch," the man intoned, eyes roaming over her like he surveyed a newly purchased field.

Oh, she'd known a hundred men like him. More, perhaps. She'd affected arousal by them, played whatever role they needed of her, moulded like clay in their hands. Yet this time, the thought of his intrusion inside her felt vile. Perhaps it was Kelaino's words. Perhaps it was that Pandora had so wanted the queen to sympathise, to share her views, when so few other people even seemed capable of apprehending her meanings. The Nymph might have followed Pandora's reasoning, but she spurned it, and Pandora remained deserted.

Whatever the case, she found her words for Sisyphus ran dry. The moment stretched on, and she considered walking away, payment and supposed protection be damned. But to do so would earn her a foe upon the acropolis island. Most hetairai had short careers, no matter their talents. Men always wanted young companions, and if she had not acquired enough wealth to live on before her age began to show, Pandora might be forced back into real slavery or a brothel. Kelaino could speed Pandora's journey in either direction she chose.

Glowering, she slipped to her knees and reached up under the king's khiton, until she could find his manhood. Some of his followers guffawed, but she ignored them. Why feign romance in such circumstances, when it was so clearly naught save animal lust that drove these brutes? The king ushered the others away as she took him in her mouth, finishing him as quickly as she could.

Without a word, she walked away, spit, and washed her face in the lake. Godsdamn it all! She trembled as if she were some ceramic ready to shatter into a hundred pieces. Why couldn't she have a damn stinger? And why this feeling, now? Self-pity was indulgent and useless, a resort of those without the will or intellect to improve their circumstances.

That would not be her. That had *never* been her. Not when Titans took her from her home as a child. Not when they sold her as a slave. Not when her master learnt she bled and took her as his bedmate. Not when he vanished and she'd been forced to become what she was now to avoid brothel life.

A metic, they called her. A foreigner, trapped on this island, scraping by with only what little she'd managed to steal from her master's estate before she fled. And in nine years she'd become the most famous hetaira in Atlantis.

She looked up from the pool. Across it, Kelaino was now strolling with another man. Just tall enough he might have been a Titan. Yes ... that looked like Prometheus, though she'd only caught a few glimpses of him in the past. He was uncle to the Pleiades, brother to their murdered father Atlas. According to the tales, he'd helped Zeus win the Titanomachy and claim Olympus, as well as given Man pyromancy and the Art of Fire.

She had not known the Titan to attend these symposiums, so what did they discus now? It was not her business, of course, and yet ... Surely only something of import would bring him to Atlantis. Something of greater import than the marriage of his niece?

Before she even knew what she was doing, Pandora found herself slinking along the water's edge until she came up behind one of the marble dolphin spouts and caught their words. She pressed herself flush against the dolphin's pedestal and slipped down, watching the water in case anyone caught sight of her.

"... Because Zeus no longer trusts you," Prometheus was saying. "His paranoia grows ever deeper, feeding upon itself as such things inevitably do, until even the lack of evidence of a conspiracy reaffirms its existence in his mind."

Kelaino groaned and clucked her tongue. "But why now? It's been nigh sixteen centuries since he bound Father and let us rule here."

"He thinks you complicit in the Nectar propagation." Nectar. Pandora had heard of the substance. It was some kind of Ambrosia counterfeit mortals had begun taking, trying to mimic the benefits of the real thing. According to rumour, it could heal almost any ailment, extend life, and dramatically enhance sexual encounters. She'd had a couple of clients surreptitiously inquire if she could get it for them, but Pandora had never dared.

She had also heard the stuff was feverishly addictive and, taken oft enough, might drive one to fits of madness. Her clients—always wealthy men—forever denied any experience with it, though Pandora had her doubts about a few of them.

"Neither I nor my sisters have aught to do with that blight."

"Be that as it may, Zeus sees this polis as the focal point of the worst abuse, and thus, in his mind, the source of it. He cannot imagine this happening under your rule without your knowledge or perhaps even your involvement."

"It is without either!" Kelaino blurted. "Surely you can talk to him, make him see reason."

Pandora shook her head silently, now almost pitying Kelaino. Zeus would not have seen reason if it was carved onto the very mountainside of Olympus outside his bedroom window.

"He will not listen to me," Prometheus said. "You must think to your defence with him. Prepare to offer him proof of your cooperation. Better still if you offer a culprit."

"We offered him Tantalus, nine years ago." Tantalus? Pandora's former master? She barely stifled a gasp. Was that how he disappeared?

"And the Nectar continued to spread. Someone else is behind it, Kelaino, and if you do not find them soon, the king will hold you to account for their crimes."

They broke apart, and, instead of continuing in the direction they had headed, Prometheus doubled back, walking past Pandora. For an instant, an unreadable expression flickered over his face. Then the Titan cast an intense gaze her way, holding her in place as her heart hammered and her breath caught. His eyes were blue as crystals, seeming to sparkle, unlike those of any of the genē. Oh, Kroniads and Tethids both most oft had blue eyes, but not like those.

"Strange," he said, "how oft a single trait may prove both blessing and curse. Curiosity can serve as both the hallmark of wisdom—and discovery—and as the precipitator of the most painful of falls."

Pandora found it hard to swallow under his scrutiny. "Some prices are worth a tumble."

"Some," he agreed, offering her a polite nod, before heading on his way.

His departure seemed to release a pressure from her chest, and she drew in a deep breath. Titans!

And if he was right, Zeus would soon return to Atlantis. The very thought of him had her fair trembling with rage and terror and a host of emotions she could not name nor afford to indulge in.

Pandora had rather had enough of this symposium.

2

PYRRHA

211 Golden Age

here was a special peace along the seashore at sunset, and Pyrrha had taken to wandering on the beach most nights, her dog Sharvara loping along beside her. Well, beside her unless he caught scent of a seagull flying by, then he'd dash off, rushing even into the Aegean. No matter how many times he chased the birds, Sharvara didn't seem to realise he'd not catch prey in the air.

His predictability had her smiling. One could count on dogs. They never changed. They certainly never abandoned their families. For the moment, he stuck by her side, and she nuzzled the back of his neck.

Looking at the waves, the sun was behind her, glinting off the water so vibrantly it stung to stare too long. Still, she watched, waiting for twilight to seep in. Twilight was the best and worst time.

At dusk, an invisible weight sloughed off her ten-year-old shoulders and she could breathe more deeply than any other time. She'd leave the bustle and crowds of Thebes behind and walk for hours. Here, she could feel the lines of the World, threading through the land and sea and sky and into her. Sometimes, though, she could see too much in the gathering dark. Shadows on her periphery would grow so thick they seemed almost solid. Or perhaps, sibilant whispers would carry on the wind like a chorus of nonsense.

Papa told her not to listen, but she could have sworn, a few times, someone was actually speaking to her. But he didn't understand. If there was someone out here, addressing her, didn't she need to know who?

Well, she had come far enough. She plopped down on the sands, and Sharvara immediately lay down beside her, head on her knee. "Somebody needs his ears scratched, huh?" And who was she to deny such an important need?

For a long time, they sat like that, listening to the waves lap upon the beach, even after the last light of the sun had winked out. It was a new moon tonight, and with the lamps of the harbour district so far off, an extreme darkness had settled upon the shore. Papa would not have approved of her going so far out on a night like this, but Pyrrha couldn't stand another moment in that stuffy court.

Oh, sure, Lady Tethys had given them a place to stay after they'd lost her mother. Pyrrha had a home in the court, and Papa told her to have gratitude for that. She *tried*. But Tethys's children were ... She snickered. "Well, they're mostly horrible wretches who deserve to be gobbled up by Cyclopes, don't they, boy?" Papa would have castigated her for saying such, but it was true. "If they didn't want to be scorned, maybe they shouldn't act like they shit gold." She shuddered. "And that Hera, bleh!"

Sharvara whimpered in what Pyrrha chose to take as agreement, and she nuzzled him more. Perhaps they should head back. Papa would worry, after all. This close to the polis there wasn't much fear of bandits, but tripping in the dark and breaking an ankle wouldn't do, either.

Before she could rise, Sharvara lurched to his feet, casting about sharply, ears pricked. A moment later, the dog tucked his tail between his legs and whimpered.

"Who's there?" Pyrrha demanded, climbing to her feet. She peered into the gloom but couldn't see more than five feet ahead. She glanced up at the stars for a brief moment, willing them to offer more light than they did. "Is someone out there?"

The sensation of a figure moving through the shadows to her left seized her, and she spun. Neither the sliver of moon nor the stars cast enough illumination to make out whatever had drawn her attention.

Sharvara had begun to tremble beneath her palm. The hair on Pyrrha's neck and arms stood on end. "Go away ..." she whispered.

She knew she needed to move. Staying here—whether something was out there or not—was a fool's option. But her feet wouldn't respond.

A gasp, as of pain, ushered out from behind her. Pyrrha spun around and saw a fleeting glimpse of a man in the darkness, clad in full battle panoply, his feet dragging in pained shuffles. But he was gone too far in the gloom before her eyes even had time to focus on him.

She expected Sharvara to growl at the figure, but the dog continued to whimper, not seeming to have seen the man. Finding it hard to swallow, Pyrrha forced herself to back away a few steps. Sharvara did not move. "Come on," she grated, tightening her grip on his fur and pulling.

The dog yelped and broke into a wild run, scampering back toward Thebes.

"Sharvara!" Pyrrha shouted after him. Then she clapped a hand to her mouth, realising she had just given herself away to whoever was out there.

Where was Papa when she needed him? Where was anyone? Pyrrha wanted to scream, to weep, but could not afford either.

Not daring to run, Pyrrha continued to back away, toward the harbour. Finally, when she had put enough distance between herself and the site where she'd encountered the soldier, she turned. Behind her stood a bushy-bearded figure too tall to be a Man. He too wore a full panoply, his breastplate encrusted with a dolphin.

Pyrrha stumbled backward, fell on her arse, and shrieked.

The Titan gazed down at her, seeming confused by her presence. He opened his mouth to speak, but only a wheezing moan came out. A gaping wound opened out of the back of his throat. A hole, clean through him. The Titan began to reach trembling fingers toward her.

Shrieking, Pyrrha half ran, half crawled until she managed to gain her feet and break into a dead sprint away from the figure. Tears stung her eyes, further blinding her. Hot wetness ran along her legs. It took her a moment to realise she'd pissed herself.

Unable to stop her sobs, she blundered back into the harbour, gasping for breath. What in the depths of the Underworld? What had she just seen? She flung herself at the first sailor she came to, a rancid man lounging on a pile of rope, a bowl of wine in his hands.

"Help me," she wailed.

The man looked her up and down and crinkled his nose before shoving her away. "Pissant, I'm trying to drink here."

Dazed, Pyrrha found herself wandering the boardwalk, not even knowing what she was about. Only half-aware of herself, she spied Hera and Styx, two of Tethys's children dangling their legs off a pier. Styx noticed her first and elbowed her elder sister. The pair of them sneered at Pyrrha but rose.

"I saw a dead man," Pyrrha yelped.

Hera snorted, and Styx chuckled. "Just one?" Hera asked. "During the war, hundreds of men died here. They brought them into the city by the cartloads."

"H-h-he was still walking," Pyrrha objected.

Now the sisters exchanged a glance. "Then he wasn't dead yet, you dolt!" Styx said and moved to loom over Pyrrha. Styx was twelve and well larger than Pyrrha, while Hera was a woman grown at eighteen. The elder sister folded her arms, denying Pyrrha's silent pleas to intervene. Pyrrha's stomach dropped. No one was going to help her, were they? They would watch while this happened?

Styx shoved Pyrrha. "Did you leave a man to die out there? Didn't think to call for help?"

Pyrrha couldn't get her words to form. "He had a hole in his mouth."

"Aye, that's for eating." Styx pushed her again. "Little Nymph still doesn't know what any of her holes are for?" Her voice had taken on a singsongy tone. "Maybe someone can explain it all to her?"

"Stop it!" Pyrrha shrieked and ducked under the Titan's arms.

Or tried. Styx grabbed her, and for a moment they struggled. Pyrrha stomped on her toes.

"Gah! Bitch!" Styx grabbed her by the hair before Pyrrha could get away. The Titan jerked her backward, sending Pyrrha stumbling off the pier.

For one horrifying instant she was weightless, flailing. Then the black waters smacked her in the back and obscured even the lamplight from the harbour. Pyrrha thrashed her way to the surface, coughing and sputtering, only to hear Hera and Styx laughing.

"Maybe the Telkhines will have a use for her," Hera said.

"Not even Pontus needs someone as useless as—" Styx began.

She was interrupted by a snarling bark, and Sharvara collided with Styx, bowling the Titan over onto the pier. A thrill of vindication shot through Pyrrha on hearing the girl scream and shriek.

Pyrrha swam to the nearest ladder and began to climb. Styx's cries had grown so pathetic she was wincing before cresting the top. "Sharvara, enough!"

But she was too late. Hera had seized her dog with Titan strength. While Pyrrha watched, Hera slammed Sharvara down over her knee, snapping the dog's spine. Then, with one hand, Hera tossed Sharvara out into the waters like her precious pet was a dirty rag.

"No!" Pyrrha gasped.

It was too late, she knew, but she dove into the sea once more, grabbing her beloved companion. Sharvara was still by the time Pyrrha managed to get him onto the dock. The dog offered up a last trembling breath, and then no more.

Throwing herself over the animal, Pyrrha wailed. The lamplight around her flickered and dimmed, and colour seemed to bleed out of it. The lamp's orange warmth faded into a cold aquamarine colour, and before Pyrrha's eyes, the World warped, angles becoming too sharp. The buildings in the harbour twisted, as if doubled over in pain. A mist wafted in over the waves, though she had not seen it before now.

A fell chill seized her, had her shivering.

Beneath her, she felt Sharvara move once more.

Alive? Could he be alive?

As she rose, some translucent vapour flittered out of the animal and seeped into the ground.

Now, looking about, she saw soldiers here, their armour and weapons stained with blood. Some had empty, hollow eyes and moved as if dazed. Others rushed about, seeming intent to engage an enemy she could not see.

What was happening to her? What in the whole vile Underworld was happening?

Another figure ran toward her, shadowy and indistinct, as though viewed through a curtain of water. The figure vaulted crates then made an impossible leap from one pier to the next, to land beside her. He grasped her face, but his touch felt subdued, as if through a woollen blanket.

"Pyrrha ..." Her name was almost incomprehensible, an echo carried to her from far away, borne upon a whispering wind. "Pyrrha ..."

The grip tightened, became more substantial. Slowly, his features solidified into the face of her father, his crystal blue eyes glinting in the returned light of the hanging lamps. The chill faded with the return of light, and Pyrrha slipped into her father's arms, wracked by sobs. "Sharvara ..."

His comforting hand stroked the back of her head. "I'm sorry. I'm so sorry about him, Pyrrha."

Pyrrha pushed away to stare at his face. "Hera murdered him!"

While she expected him to blanch at her accusation, Papa instead just nodded in understanding. "Are you all right?"

Oh. Oh ... "I-I saw ... I don't even know, Papa." First the terror at the beach, and then ... She swallowed, realising she had begun to tremble despite the return of warmth to the night. "Everything turned grey and blue and so very cold, Papa."

Something—pain, maybe—washed over his face for a bare instant, then he hefted her up in his arms as though she were still a tiny thing. Pyrrha couldn't remember the last time he'd carried her thus, but tonight, she cradled her head against his warm chest and shut her eyes.

When next she opened them, Papa was laying her down in her own bed. The room was dark, lit only by an oil lamp out in the hall, and she could almost swear the shadows moved once more. Flickers of what she'd seen raced through her mind, and Pyrrha snatched Papa's hand rather than let him go.

"Am I going mad?"

"No," he said, settling down on the end of the bed beside her. "Though those of narrow minds may not be able to tell the difference, and that is a burden you will forever bear."

She refused to release her grip upon him. "What's happening to me?" He knew something, that much was clear. Sometimes, she thought Papa knew everything. Maybe all Papas did.

Papa glanced at the door and held up a finger in silent promise of his return before extricating his hand. He grabbed a candle and slipped outside a moment to light it. When he returned, he shut the door behind him. His words were meant for no ears save hers, and a flutter of excitement raced through her chest at the thought.

How she loved secrets!

He set the candle down on a shelf beside her bed, then settled back into his spot on the end. The urge to cuddle in his arms, as she had done for his stories since she was a babe, it came upon her, but something in his stiff posture seemed to forbid it.

"What is it, Papa?"

He sighed, rubbing his brow. "Some people have very special minds, Love. These people can catch glimpses of the greater Truth of the World, what scholars call the Ontos. Some can use this to see into the future, and we call them Oracles. But the ability, the Sight, it can manifest in many ways. Others, Mediums like you, can see through the Veil that separates our world from the next."

A fresh surge of panic welled up in her, tightening her stomach into knots. "T-the Underworld?"

Her father nodded grimly. "The edge of that Realm we call the Penumbra, for it is like a shadow of this one. And, it seems, you have looked into it."

"It was ... horrible." And yet far too thrilling. "I saw dead men."

Papa frowned, taking her hand. "Perhaps you saw mere phantom echoes imprinted upon that Realm by strong emotion. Or perhaps you beheld actual shades, wandering in torment. If so ... Pyrrha, if you can see them, they too can see you. That is why you must avoid looking across the Veil. You are not prepared for what you might draw to you."

See her? Yes, it certainly seemed the ghost had seen her too. The one on the beach had actually reached for her. But this ability made her special, different than the others, and Papa wanted her to *ignore* it? Wish it away?

"What is the Veil?" she pushed.

"An Etheric membrane that impedes beings from the Otherworld from entering the Mortal Realm."

That sounded like a bunch of nonsense words, and Pyrrha withdrew her hand just so she could fold her arms over her chest and make her dissatisfaction clear. Papa could always tell, anyway, but sometimes a girl had to make her point.

"Love, listen to me, I beseech you. You cannot begin to imagine the danger you invite in when crossing between Realms, even with just a piece of your soul." Her soul? "Leave the dead be and remain tethered in this world."

Pyrrha huffed, but reluctantly nodded. Papa clearly wasn't going to support her nurturing this gift, which meant she'd need to conceal any further investigation from him. Tethys had a library, and perhaps that would hold more information about ghosts and the Underworld.

But let it go? No, that was impossible. All her life, Pyrrha had been a small child, harried by the princes and princesses of Thebes. Alone save for poor Sharvara.

This Sight, as Papa called it, however terrifying, meant she mattered. A person couldn't give that up.

Not for the World.

3

PANDORA

1570 Silver Age

*T*wo days had passed since the Pleiades' symposium, and, even pacing about Dardanus's estate, Pandora found herself haunted by those crystal blue eyes that seemed to glimpse into her soul. She saw their echo in the fountain in the atrium, glinting in the sunlight. She picked up hints of them in the vibrant fresco that decorated the back wall beyond the columns encompassing this atrium. She found herself, on more than one occasion, glancing about as if that Titan might yet be looking upon her.

"Well?" Dardanus demanded. She'd been hired to teach him rhetoric, though the bastard son of Zeus and Elektra spent almost as much time ogling her arse and tits as he did focused upon logic. A fact clearly not lost upon his young wife, Bateia, who perpetually *happened* to stroll by the atrium so she might cast withering glances upon Pandora.

Or perhaps the Ilian princess merely resented the freedom afforded to hetairai. Bateia had probably never even been allowed to leave her house grounds since her marriage, so Pandora could not judge her too harshly. Even if her ire grew tedious.

"Well what?" Pandora asked, mind racing to catch up with whatever Dardanus had just said. Alexis's supposed refutation of Urania's Utopia. "You're still stumbling over the fallacy of the converse. The breakdown of social class systems is a *necessary* condition of her ideal state, not a sufficient one to satisfy Urania's requirements. More generally, that sort of verbal trickery may convince the mob, but anyone looking at your arguments dispassionately will eviscerate you in debate."

The man actually glared at her, his father's arrogance shining through his convivial facade. As if it were her fault he lacked the wit for debate while fancying himself a scholar. Elektra herself had hired her—Pandora knew her own reputation—on one of the Pleiad's visits to the polis. 'Teach my son languages and philosophy and mathematics,' she'd ordered, and—though Pandora would have loved to reject her given Dardanus's father—she could not afford to say no.

Not so unlike her dealings with Elektra's sister.

But, though her mother wanted the best possible tutors for her son, Pandora suspected that, not unlike many in his position, Dardanus chafed at learning aught from a woman.

"Let's try something else for today," Pandora said, suppressing a sigh. One simply did not express disappointment to the aristoi. One did not say, 'Perhaps if you spent a bit more time with the scrolls and less gazing at arses, you would be able to form a coherent thought.' There were a great many things one did not say. Not if one wanted to remain healthy, hale, and employed. "Have you been practicing your Phoenikian?"

Dardanus, on the other hand, actively groaned. "Is it not the most tediously dull language in the Thalassa?"

"They invented the alphabet."

"You would say that. You're from there, aren't you, metic?"

"Yes." With her deep complexion, she might as easily have passed for an Atlantid—save the golden eyes—but she was well known as a foreigner. It was, she supposed, part of the allure for men seeking to bed her. "But as I also speak Elládosi, Kemetian, Rassenian, Neshian, and a fair bit of Nusantaran, I daresay I am versed enough in linguistics from around the Thalassa to offer the opinion that no language is dull or useless." Unlike some men.

And her affinity for languages was one of her strongest gifts, though one she'd mostly had to develop without any formal instruction.

Dardanus had the decency to look shamefaced and recognise he'd been castigated without her *actually* crossing any lines. He fell into recitation of Sikarbaal with admirable effort, though Pandora imagined he had not the first clue what the philosopher meant in his writings.

It was just as well, in fact, for it meant she needed to listen only to the shape of the words, not their substance. Well, because her mind kept drifting back to the symposium and Kelaino's damn uncle, the Titan who had looked at her as though he knew all her secrets.

If there was one truth that ever guided her life it was this: the very existence of mysteries demanded someone solve them.

WHEN SHE HAD FINISHED with Dardanus, Pandora made her way back into Atlantis's middle ring. The royal island, Atlantis's acropolis, lay at the city's heart, formed by the inner of two concentric canals that ran down from the mountains. Smaller canals bisected the great ones, creating districts within the middle ring.

It was in this central band where Pandora had purchased her modest home by the outer canal. She stopped there only long enough to freshen up, though. A peacock had alighted in her tiny yard, so she scattered some breadcrumbs for the beautiful bird. Feeding them meant they returned oft and gave her something wondrous to study. The grace of their forms was its own fascination, but she had also been working to paint a fresco in the perfect likeness of a peacock and could not pass any opportunity to examine the tail patterns.

She had heard that the Olympian, Hera, bred a flock of peacocks and kept them within the palace walls of Olympus. Loathe as Pandora would be to ever be within a league of Zeus, she would love to see that.

After a few moments watching the bird, she departed and crossed one of the soaring stone bridges that connected to the outer city.

So far as she'd gathered, Prometheus had not taken residence in the royal palace, as she might have expected, nor in any of the other estates in the acropolis. Most visiting aristoi, Man or Titan, would have called upon friends in the city for a place to stay. If he had not done so—and yet remained in the polis—she could only imagine he must have kept a room in one of the few guesthouses in Atlantis.

All those she knew of lay in the harbour district, southeast of the city. Perhaps the Titan had fled Atlantis already, and if so, her whole walk would prove fruitless. But she had the afternoon free and, if there was any chance of understanding the enigma he'd presented, she had to take it. It had been too long since something truly unknown had crossed her path. Pandora could never turn down a puzzle, a chance to unravel a mystery, to answer the siren call of the *new* and break the tedium of the prosaic.

Maybe he'd not speak to her. Maybe he'd even grow irate. Vexed Titans were a terrifying sight, yes, and the thought had a slight sweat trickling down her lower back. But she'd learn naught if she didn't try.

Out in the harbour district, overlooking the ships, stood a massive statue of Atlas himself, namesake and founder of Atlantis. The story went that Zeus had bound him in Tartarus, condemning him to support the weight of the heavens upon his shoulders. To honour their father, the Pleiades had erected a fifty-feet tall statue of Atlas, hefting the world proudly. Sometimes, Pandora had wondered whether Zeus saw this monument as petty defiance. If so, he'd never forced them to take it down.

She strolled the harbour, watching the biremes and triremes sailing in. Some were Phoenikian, of course, and maybe she could have paid for passage back to Tyros. But it wasn't her home anymore, and she couldn't imagine any special welcome awaited her in Agenor's court. Twenty years she'd been gone, and Atlantis was her home.

With a last glance at the ships, Pandora turned about. She had to imagine that, were a Titan to stay in a guesthouse, only the posh *Bay of Dreams* would do, so she headed there first. The place offered several rooms—she'd seen one with a client, actually—and a covered portico for dining, one floor up. The portico extended out over the bay, supported by marmoreal columns cut from local stone. A curved staircase allowed access to the dining segment without heading inside, so she made her way upstairs.

The Titan, Prometheus, did indeed sit at a table there, sipping wine from a bowl and staring not at the bay, as most guests would have, but at a smouldering brazier between the tables. He had shoulder-length auburn hair, skin perhaps a shade lighter than her own, and, like so many Titans, a chiseled build most sculptors would have drooled over.

Well, she had not come all this way to feign demureness, had she? Nor did Prometheus strike her as the type to require such. Instead, she brazenly slipped into the seat across from him.

The Titan startled from whatever he saw in the flames—if he taught Man pyromancy, surely he must practice it himself—and fitted her with his soul-scouring gaze once more. As if he looked into the depths of her heart, of her innermost secret self, and read it like a papyrus roll. The moment was dread and shuddering, masochistic delight all rolled up into one.

"You were staring at me the other night," Pandora said, trying her best to keep her voice level, indifferent even.

The Titan's gaze relaxed a hair, and a hint of a smile tugged at the edge of his mouth. "You were spying upon me and Kelaino for rather longer than the time I afforded to inspect you. It would seem to me, yours is the greater invasion of privacy."

Pandora flushed, though she willed it away immediately. "Does my regard so unnerve you, Titan?"

"It refreshes."

She leaned back in her chair. What did one say to that? Or was it merely another man's vanity, always eager to try to win her affections? As if they weren't for sale. As if they weren't priceless and unattainable. "I'm Pandora."

"So I've heard."

Well, that was news. Her reputation—or infamy among female citizenry—had spread throughout the polis, for certain, but to learn it had reached one who so rarely visited ... Come far and wide, one and all, to see the Phoenikian hetaira. Come wonder at her gifts and the precious treasure between her thighs. Pandora found herself fighting not to grind her teeth. That he should have heard of her was not a fault in him, but still ...

"You seem torn," he said, then motioned for a serving girl to bring another bowl of wine. "You are forever at war with yourself, are you not? There is the part of you that chafes at the sheer inequity of life and the workings of Ananke, and the part of you that strives ever to bury the other. To convince the World and, most of all, yourself that you cannot be broken. That hope must forever endure."

Pandora gaped at him, felt scraped raw at having someone read her so thoroughly, naked despite her clothes. At having hidden parts of herself exposed to light. She couldn't think of what to say and was saved from having to when the servant brought the bowl of wine and offered it to her. Snatching it up, she chugged the better part of the bowl in one swig, then let it clatter upon the table.

"Ananke." She swallowed. "So you lay the blame for all wrongs in the World upon Fate?"

Prometheus steepled his fingers. "Every moment of time is predicated upon that which has come before. Even your own thoughts are born from your history and nature. That nature results from your parents. Endless causal chains stretching into infinity."

"So everything is determined." She'd read such arguments before, not least in Polyhymnia.

"Reasons. Causality. But even if that's true, that does not abrogate one from responsibility for one's choices. Of course they have reasons, all choices have reasons. But unless the reason is madness, a person still made his—or her—choice."

She knew how this went. "But if you cannot change your choices?"

"You cannot change the choices in your past, can you? Does that mean you did not make them? So why should future choice be so very different?"

Pandora felt the smile creeping upon her face. How rare to converse with one who could keep up, even challenge her. How precious to debate when she didn't have to explain *both sides* to the other person. "It all seems rather convenient. You get to maintain Ananke governs everything in the World, and yet can still hold people responsible for their actions, though they could not have taken other ones."

His brow drew up in barely perceptible tension. "If you think Fate convenient, you have not yet felt the true weight of its grasp upon your neck."

Spoken like a man—a Titan, rather—who had felt it. Had been crushed by it. Still, Pandora found that hard to credit. The Titans ruled the whole of this world as godlike immortals. Through Ambrosia, who even knew how long they lived. The Titanomachy was nigh sixteen centuries ago, and Prometheus seemed to have lived long before that. Some tales claimed he'd fought alongside Kronos to help end the Time of Nyx. "Before you go bemoaning Fate, perhaps you ought to try living as a woman for a while. A *mortal* woman."

"A person can offer empathy even to those whose lives they cannot truly understand."

"Do you?" she demanded.

"Understand? Or offer empathy?"

Pandora sipped the last of the wine, swishing it around her mouth, uncertain how to answer. Would either his understanding or empathy make the least difference? Maybe it would. Somehow, though, she felt disinclined to talk over it further. It was like poking at a scab before it was ready to peel off. She chose her next words with care.

"Will Zeus really come here? Will he act against the Pleiades?"

He shut his eyes just longer than a blink. "You do not hide your loathing well."

Rather than let herself wince, Pandora fell stock still. Did he know something about her past? Or did he merely read her disdain for the Olympian King from her features? Either way, he'd turned this around, made it about her, and thus, trod into waters she wasn't willing to sail.

"Perhaps I should leave."

"Wait," he said, laying his hand upon hers, sending a thrill of warmth running up her arm. "There's a drama at the Atlantis Amphitheater starting soon. I was about to go. Let me buy you a ticket."

"Why?" Not that she would refuse. She so rarely indulged, much as she enjoyed the theatre. She always had to try to save as many drachmae as she could. But a chance to see it without paying ... and wasn't it Kalliope's *Fall of Khione*?

"Because I enjoyed our conversation, and pleasant company should be savoured."

She felt heat rising to her cheeks once more and pulled her hand free. How could she refuse, indeed?

THE AMPHITHEATER LAY in the Leukippe District, beneath the mountains. Carved stone seats could sit thousands upon thousands of spectators for these festival dramas, though good seats, like the ones Prometheus bought by the stage, were quite expensive. Oh, the acoustics meant spectators could hear from anywhere in the theatre. The architects had carved it so perfectly those sitting in the highest rows could—if the crowd was silent—pick up the clatter of a drachma falling centre stage.

But from up there, the view was just not the same.

Prometheus chatted with her amiably while they awaited the start of the show, speaking of events around the Thalassa, even into far

Phoenikia. He traveled all over and shared knowledge from his journeys freely. More, he spoke to her as though she were his equal, not some lesser species. Or lesser gender. When was the last time a man had looked at her as better than a commodity? Was it her uncles, torn from her when she was but five years old? Had she held the least respect since then?

Then the actors took the stage, and all fell silent. Pandora listened to the chorus intone about how Atlas had begun the Ambrosial War by trying to seize control of all Ambrosia, which flowed from this very island. The main actors then began—only three of them—with men playing even the female Titans Artemis and Khione, as well the Titan Helios.

Kalliope had apparently dramatised a story Pandora knew only in song, of Khione's assault upon the polis of Helion. She had somehow blanketed the city in snow, for which the crew showered what looked more like sand upon the stage. Then Artemis, Helios's daughter, had hunted Khione and slain her, saving the city from winter and death.

It was, more like than not, based upon some kernel of truth. "Do you think it really happened?" she found herself asking as they rose from their seats.

"Not exactly like that," Prometheus answered.

The way he said that had Pandora faltering, looking over her shoulder at him. "You were there."

"Hmm."

Thousands of years ago. Gods, she didn't even know how many thousands of years. Was it four thousand? She had seen that, once. The Ambrosial War was mostly considered legend. Yes, many historians agreed it had happened, but details were scant, and those who experienced it said little of the lost Golden Age. It was before the time of the Muses, and thus even their writings offered but speculation.

When the drama had finished, they paused atop the steps, Pandora watching Prometheus, who seemed focused on the departing audience.

"Thank you," she said.

He turned, offering her a smile in return. "May I give you some advice, Pandora? When Zeus comes here, if you see him, guard your feelings. If a man like that sees your antipathy, he will play on it for the perverse joy of enhancing it. You do not want his attention."

Oh, that was one thing Pandora knew better than most any other. She had seen the cataclysm of Zeus's wandering eye.

4

ATHENE

1570 Silver Age

A warm, southern wind swept over Ogygia as Athene stepped onto the pier. Across the strait, Atlantis loomed, with Brizo's temple rising from the promontory. From nigh there Athene had sailed the narrow waters.

She tossed a rope to the first dockhand she spotted. "Tie it up," she snapped. While she lacked the icy blue eyes of her father's genos —indeed, no genos favoured grey eyes like her own and it made her stand out—she trusted her bearing to inform these people she was a Titan. Not giving them a second look, she strode from the harbour, following a pitiful dirt path that led to the town of Marsa, nestled beneath the mountain's shadow.

On her way, she passed a handful of travellers bound for the port, most with donkey-drawn, overburdened wagons. Athene couldn't imagine what these islanders possibly exported that anyone would want. But then again, until she'd gone looking for Kirke and learnt she had been lodging here with Kelaino's daughter, Athene had never given Ogygia a second thought. The little island meant less than naught in the scheme of Elládosi politics.

When she reached the village—mostly a collection of small homes and shops surrounded by miles of outlying farms—she saw a great many more people bustling about. She knew, of course, they had their own lives and had not even noticed her, but still, her skin crawled with the sensation that every single one of them stared at her and knew her shame. As when she had come to Atlantis, the urge to seize one by the shoulders, heft him off the ground and shake him, came upon her so powerfully she had to clench her fists to suppress it.

Standing apart from the village, she turned, slowly surveying it. An estate lay upon a hill between here and the mountain, the only home remotely worthy of aristoi, and Kalypso was the daughter of one of the Pleiades. Banished here or not, no Titan, not even a Nymph, would live in squalor. Nymphs lacked the significant Pneumatikoi of greater Titans like Athene, but still, traces of divine blood ran through their veins, and older ones like Kirke and Kalypso probably even had ichor instead of blood. It would be the estate.

Resolved, Athene made her way purposefully up the hill. Beyond, upon the mountain slope, she could just make out the outline of what she assumed was Prometheus's famed Aviary. Under other circumstances, she might have even called upon him, but at the moment, she had no desire to see anyone save Kirke.

She reached the house in the waning afternoon. The main gate stood slightly ajar, and Athene slipped inside without announcing herself. Even calling out to let Kalypso know of her presence seemed too painful at the moment, the effort to form words feeling monumental. Everything felt that way these days, especially if she let slip her anger. That heat was all that kept her walking.

She approached the house proper and caught wind of voices within, laughter, from two women. She knew she should knock, but instead Athene found herself easing the door open, telling herself it was no voyeuristic urge prompting her. No, that might almost have been better, if this was something other than crippling ennui making speech seem impossible.

The estate was modest for a Titan, suitable more for low ranking mortal aristoi than a Nymph of Kalypso's stature. Still, painted frescoes and intricately woven tapestries decorated the walls, giving it a warm touch.

Years of practice had made moving in silence second nature, so when she came upon the two Nymphs reclining by the hearth, neither seemed to have noticed her. Both had their khitons disheveled, and the empty bowl between them glistened with the amber residue of Ambrosia. Kalypso's hand rested upon Kirke's knee as they continued laughing about whatever private joke they'd shared.

Lovers?

A twinge of regret at interrupting such an intimate moment struck Athene. But she had come a long way to find Kirke.

Athene cleared her throat.

Kalypso choked down a yelp and both Nymphs abruptly lurched into sitting positions, gaping at her.

Kirke's wide-eyed expression calmed first, and she shook her head as if to physically dislodge the shock. "Damn it, Athene ..."

Athene wanted to say something, but forming words still felt like pushing boulders up a mountain, and all she managed was a dour shake of her own head.

Perhaps Kirke saw more than enough writ plain upon her visage, for she cast a glance at Kalypso, then rose, grabbing her sandals and straightening her khiton. With one hand upon Athene's arm, she guided her out to gardens in the back of the house. It seemed Kalypso tried her hand at growing a variety of herbs and spices. It boggled the mind that any Titan, even a Nymph, could spend her time on such mundane pursuits.

After strapping her footwear on, Kirke led Athene among the plants that danced in the wind, their fragrant, acrid scents unperturbed by the weight that fell upon people. Athene expected Kirke to pause there, but the woman opened a back gate in the wall and led her up the path onto the mountain.

From here, she caught a better view of Prometheus's Aviary rising from the peak. What a splendid view it must offer. Perhaps, from up there, one could see clear back to Brizo's temple upon Atlantis.

"Prometheus is not here," Kirke said, as if Athene had asked. "He's gone to Atlantis on business to see Kalypso's mother. He won't mind if we sit in the tower."

The long walk offered a fair excuse to delay having to explain her presence, so Athene held her peace and let Kirke guide her to the tower. It too, was unlocked, as if Prometheus could not have conceived of anyone trespassing here. Inside, they found a fountain nigh overflowing with flamingos, while a host of other rainbow-coloured birds rested upon a network of poles over their heads.

Kirke sat upon the fountain's lip and pulled Athene down to join her. "What so vexes you, Athene?"

She didn't call her *sister*, Athene noted. Kirke never did. Perhaps she would have thought it presumptuous. Perhaps she didn't even think of Athene as a sister. Though both daughters of Hekate, Athene was the child of mighty Zeus himself, and an Olympian. Kirke was a mere Nymph, sired by Helios.

For a time, Athene watched a peacock strut about the tower, haughty and proud of his vibrant beauty.

"I ... need ..." The words stuck in her throat.

Taking Athene's hand in her own, Kirke offered a reassuring squeeze. "What do you need? You didn't leave Kronion and come to this little island for no reason."

"I ..."

Kirke sighed. "Hmm. You're one of a handful of Titan women in the whole of the World who doesn't get called a Nymph, Athene. One of the most powerful people in the breadth of Elládos, and Men worship you as a living god." Her half-sister shrugged, as if to soften the rebuke. "Can any of this really prove so dire?"

Athene pulled her hand away and fixed Kirke with a hard look. "One of my fellow Olympians sent for me not so long ago." Pain caused her to speak. "Hephaistos called me to Korinth, claiming he wished to discuss the spread of Nectar in his polis." Kirke frowned, but said naught, so Athene continued. Now she had begun, the words felt ripped from her. "I thought he sought my counsel in handling that blight. It was, however, a ruse, for his clumsy attempts at ... wooing the daughter of Zeus. Perhaps he thought marriage to me would enhance his position on Olympus."

Now the Nymph's gaze turned darker. "Not something you wanted, I assume."

Athene favoured her with a disgusted look. As if she sought *any* husband, much less one like him. "Of course not. I told him I'd sooner march into Tartarus and marry some horror from the black depths."

Kirke chortled. "I wish I'd seen the look upon his face."

Athene grimaced. "He let it be." A shudder built inside her chest. "At least until I slept ... and woke to find myself ..." Her grip upon the fountain's edge tightened. "I found myself bound in orichalcum. It seems my body was more his desire than any union in marriage."

For a brief moment, her half-sister stared at her, tears beginning to glisten in her eyes, though Athene had never been able to shed them for herself. Then Kirke drew her into an embrace. "Go to Zeus. Your father will castrate the fucking bastard. He'd have him flayed and spread his entrails from Kronion to Korinth. Oh, the bards will sing of the fall of Hephaistos in the same breath as the damnation of Kronos!"

Athene scoffed, squirming free. "Shall I turn to my father to avenge myself? That, too, and announce my shame to Titans and Men alike? Behold wise, mighty Athene, used by Hephaistos like just another ..." Athene suddenly realised who she was talking to.

"Another Nymph?" Kirke finished for her, voice like a whip.

"A mortal," Athene said, though they both knew it wasn't what she'd been about to say. There was no denying the stiffness that had jutted up between them.

Kirke sniffed, drying her eyes on the edge of her himation. "Hmm. Ah, well then, what *do* you want to do? You said avenge yourself,

Athene, and I do understand that, and I'd do the same, I'm sure, but you have to know ... Right? If you go down that path, it won't be clean. Yeah, these things are never, ever clean, and people may learn of what he did to you anyway, not that I actually think the shame is yours, of course." The woman frowned and wrung her hands. "Ah, sorry. I know I talk too much, sometimes. I spent a lot of my life alone, and sometimes it's hard to keep it all in."

Funny, Athene found it hard to let the words out at all. "His spawn grows in my belly, Kirke." And those words, too, felt like they had ripped out of her gut. "I need a poison to kill it."

Nodding grimly, Kirke patted her knee. "So you came to the witch. Yeah, well, easy enough. I just need some herbs from my garden."

It was dark by the time they returned to Kalypso's estate, and Kirke said she would get what they needed at dawn. Though Athene did not much fancy going in there with the pair of them, she didn't really want to sleep outside either.

"You can bed down by the hearth," Kalypso said. Perhaps the Nymph sensed Athene's mood, for she kept her distance, save to offer a bowl of carrot and cabbage soup. After Athene took it, Kalypso drifted off into the other room, speaking to Kirke in hushed whispers. Would her half-sister divulge what Athene had told her? The thought of anyone knowing about it twisted in her gut. As if her shame would redouble for every person who learnt of it.

The hearth space had been cleaned of the bowl of Ambrosia and the vestiges of the two Nymphs' time there, and now all that decorated it was a lion-skin rug. She sat on it, sipping at the soup without tasting it. When it was finished, she set the bowl down, unlaced her sandals, and warmed her feet in front of the hearth. It was a pleasant feeling, reminding her of evenings she had spent like this with Hestia.

Hephaistos's aunt, Nyx damn it all.

She could not ever imagine reclining at ease with the Olympian again. Hephaistos had taken that from her, too. Had taken ... so much. Every moment that passed, Athene found some further aspect of her past or future infected with the taint of him.

Maybe Kirke was right. Maybe she should have asked Father to wreak vengeance upon him. Or Mother, even, who could have done so with more subtlety and perhaps even greater agony than Father. But vengeance was Athene's to claim for herself. If she did not do so, could not do so, how could she even claim to be an Olympian? How could she ever again be herself, if she could not own her own memories?

SUNLIGHT FILTERING in through cracks in the shutters woke her, and Athene rose with a groan. The hearth fire had dwindled to just embers. Did the Nymphs still sleep?

No, from the next room, the sounds of someone grinding stone upon stone sounded. Soft, not enough to have woken her, but now she heard it, it was definitely there. Athene stalked across the room and peered into the kitchen.

Working upon a counter, Kirke stood, pulverising something with a mortar and pestle. In a pot, some bile-coloured liquid rested, and the Nymph poured the powder she'd just made inside. Doing so, she must have caught sight of Athene, for she started.

"Nyx, Athene! Stop doing that. I don't even know how you move thus, never drawing anyone's notice."

Training with Artemis, back when Athene was young. All the other Olympians were by far her elders. They had fought with Father in his war against the Ouranid League, had helped him win that Titanomachy, and thus earned their place on Olympus. Athene had been a babe then, and Father had named her to their number out of sheer adoration for her.

Athene drummed her fingers upon the counter. "I ... I find myself wondering how Father would see me if he knew ... what I had let Hephaistos do to me."

Kirke abruptly dropped the pestle. "What you *let* him do?" She fixed Athene with a hard stare. "I don't know what your father would say, Athene, but I know what our mother would say. She'd say you're an imbecile."

Athene flinched. Kirke thought *Mother* would be ashamed of her, too?

"An imbecile for thinking any woman ever allows herself to be raped. That you *let* it happen."

"He ... overcame me."

"He chained you when you were asleep! He didn't best you in combat!"

Athene winced at Kirke's tone, not knowing what to say. She could neither deny Kirke's words nor shake the sense of her own shame. How was she to reconcile logic and the gut-churning truth of her heart? "Is that it?" she asked, trying to change the subject.

"Yeah." Kirke snatched the pestle and ground it a few more times, looking at Athene as if she were mashing her head. Then she stirred the pan, then poured the liquid from it into a clay cup. "I won't lie. It probably will taste like chimera piss, and you'll have stomach cramps something awful, but this will do the task without risk to your health."

Do the task. A prosaic way of saying it would murder the babe.

Athene snatched up the cup, sloshing the liquid over her hand. It reeked of putrescence and Gaia-alone-knew what else. She felt Kirke's stare upon her but didn't turn. Damn it all. "If I don't?"

"If you keep the child?" Kirke asked. "Well, no one needs to know where it came from. There will be whispers, but the Olympians have their share of bastard offspring, don't they? Yeah, I don't think anyone will guess the truth, maybe not even Hephaistos. Oh, but if he did, he wouldn't be fool enough to say aught and risk word of his crime getting back to Zeus." The Nymph cleared her throat. "Could be, in fact, now that I think of it, he never imagined a child would take on the first time like that."

Perhaps not. Something about fortifying the flesh with Ambrosia seemed to reduce fertility, even as it eventually turned the blood to ichor. The more Ambrosia one consumed, the harder it became to have children, or so Demeter had told her ages back.

"Yeah," Kirke said, "well, either way, slow vengeance is the most satisfying. You take your time, you plan your moment, and he can lose as much as you have without you having to call on the king."

Athene clanged the cup down upon the counter with a ring of finality. "It isn't the child's fault."

"No," Kirke agreed.

"No, but before I am done, I will take everything Hephaistos holds dear." Slow vengeance indeed.

5

PANDORA

1570 Silver Age

$\mathcal{I}$n the courtyard of her small house, Pandora sat beneath the eaves, hands idly working at her puzzle box while her tongue worried the pit out of an olive. Her uncle Phoenix had taught her the trick of it as a child. Once the pit was loose, she spit it into a growing pile beside her.

Actually, her other uncle, Kadmus, had given her the puzzle box. It was one of her clearest memories of him. And one of her last.

Phoenix would have liked her little home, though, she thought. Prince or not, he had an appreciation for the little things. She remembered a garden he'd loved, in Tyros.

When she'd bought this place—used almost every last drachma she had on it—she'd imagined that one day she'd turn this courtyard into a garden, maybe fill it with lavender and daphne, perhaps plant a small fig tree. Somehow, saving her drachmae had always seemed more pressing since then, and her garden remained empty stone and a pool she'd never finished digging.

Well, saving drachmae, and the fact she had no one to show the place to, meant upgrading it felt empty. For certain she could have brought clients here, but that would have profaned the space, polluted it with their false friendship and their self-indulgent lies. So instead, the courtyard remained sacred and empty. A hollow.

She didn't need to look at the puzzle box to solve it. Her fingers knew every groove, every lock and shift by rote. In fact, she hadn't actually been *solving* it in years. But it was all she'd had with her when she was taken. The only piece left of a life that now seemed almost a dream, but one she feared to wake from completely. The last reminder she had once been something else. Once had people who were hers.

Staring at the empty space where she'd wanted to plant flowers, she popped another olive into her mouth. She'd only just begun working at the pit when a rapping came at the door.

Though she never brought clients here, people knew where she lived. They sent for her sometimes, though it was not even midmorn as yet, and early for any summons. She rose, straightened her khiton, and hurried through the house.

She'd begun laying tiles on the floor herself, an unfinished art project meant to complement the colours of the as-yet-unfinished peacock fresco she was painting on the main wall. When the floor was done, it would be a mosaic depicting the fabled undersea kingdom of Pontus, said to lie somewhere in the depths of the Aegean. It kept her busy, and most mornings she spent a few hours expanding the design, or tweaking the peacock, or sometimes painting vases to decorate her home.

The courier at her front door was tapping his foot in impatience by the time she opened it, then shoved a papyrus roll in her hands. Pandora raised a brow, though the man hurried off without offering her a second glance. It must have come from one of the Pleiades, for almost anyone else would have scratched a time and date on an ostrakon rather than waste such a valuable material as papyrus on a simple message. From the feel of this one, it was imported from Kemet, making it more expensive still.

After shutting the door, she unfurled the small roll. Another symposium at the royal palace, the second in a fortnight, and this very evening. Another summons from Kelaino. And this party was in Zeus's honour. No doubt he had arrived on the morn, without warning, and the Pleiades scrambled to accommodate the king. Like every other sovereign in the Elládosi world, they reigned at his mercurial sufferance.

Prometheus had been right about his coming. She hadn't seen the Titan since leaving the Amphitheater, but his words had weighed heavy upon her soul. The Olympian King was coming to Atlantis. And Kelaino wanted Pandora at the party in his honour. Probably, she called every famed hetaira in the city, hoping one or the other would sate the king's prodigious lusts.

Perhaps Pandora should decline the invitation. It would vex Kelaino, but Prometheus had warned her not to draw Zeus's eye. And if she saw him, she wasn't entirely convinced she could avoid the temptation to stick a searing poker in that eye. Carefully, she re-rolled the papyrus, then stuck it on a shelf.

She *should* decline.

But she knew she wouldn't. She was in no position to decline much of aught. He was coming, probably intending to castigate the Pleiades for failing to abate the Nectar blight. But a part of her simply could not resist the call. She had to *know* what was going to happen.

And ... another thought. Would Prometheus be there again? Would she have another chance to converse with him and unravel his mysteries? It was too much to pass up.

THE MIDDLE RING featured numerous bath houses. Some were exclusive to the aristoi, some were for commoners. Given her status, Pandora was able to access certain of the elite baths, and thus she made her way through the western water gardens to one such facility exclusive to women, the Nike Springs. Outside the bathhouse—a two-story marble edifice surrounded by a peristyle—stood a larger-than-life statue of Nike, the winged goddess of victory.

In legend, she had sided with Zeus against Kronos and helped him win the Titanomachy. Which probably made her just another Titan cunt who contributed to the oppression of Man.

She frowned, staring at the goddess. But then, Prometheus was a Titan, too, and had proved both tolerable and intriguing. Was it possible she judged all Titans too harshly, based on their king?

The fragrant scents of massage oils bombarded her the moment she stepped inside. Offering two obols to the guard, who gave her a nod of recognition, she made her way down the main corridor. The tiles here—a mosaic of tropical plants—carried heat from the spring that fed the bath, far before she reached the main bath. Which was, itself, a pool some fifteen feet across and perhaps thirty feet long, bounded by an alabaster rim. An open roof allowed in sunlight, though the eaves of the second balcony, supported by fluted columns, overshadowed the edges of the bath.

The back wall bore a fresco of the legendary phoenix, a firebird associated with Nike. Engulfed in flames, and bearing plumage like a peacock, the icon dominated all else here, and no matter how oft Pandora came, she had to admire the painter's skill. She'd long studied the technique herself, when preparing the fresco for her house, though the painting here was so old no one could tell her the artist's name.

"Whore," someone snapped as she approached the spring, attention on the phoenix fresco.

Pandora's gaze locked on Bateia emerging from the baths, water streaming from her. A pair of adolescent slave girls rushed to the princess's side, one bearing a towel, the other the woman's clothes.

Others in the bath house were staring, and even if Pandora could have simply ignored an aristos, she couldn't well do so while they looked on. Instead, she plastered on her most accommodating smile. "If you need some tips on technique, I'd be happy to help. There are ways to ensure husbands never need stray."

The Ilian princess's mouth fell open, clearly never having expected a retort.

"Commoner filth," she mumbled.

Actually, given her golden eyes, Pandora quite possibly had some Heliad blood from way back. Certainly not a direct bastard of Helios, as she'd have been a Nymph with some of the power that went with it. Regardless, as a metic unable to trace or prove her descent, Pandora might as well have been a commoner. "Well, all the more reason I must bathe. If you'll excuse me, Princess." Pandora doffed her khiton and tossed it upon a wooden bench. "Oh, but do let me know if you decide to practice your technique."

Without looking, she could feel Bateia stiffen. Yes, she had quite possibly just lost her commission to tutor the woman's husband. And *still* she was smiling. Sometimes, it was worth it.

She mounted the spring's lip and eased herself onto the shelf that rimmed the edge, toes first, allowing herself to adjust to the pleasant warmth of the water. The shelf gave a place for women to sit and lounge. On the floor beyond, the waters would go up to Pandora's chin, and in the centre, even that floor dropped away into the source of the spring that went Poseidon-knew how deep.

With a relaxed groan, she lowered herself onto the shelf. Sitting, the water reached her ribs, and Pandora liked to luxuriate here a bit before a swim. She had only just settled, though, when she noticed another woman swimming across the pool toward her.

Aegle, another hetaira. The woman pushed herself up onto the shelf beside Pandora. "Bateia likes to bark."

"Bitches do." Pandora squeezed the other woman's hand in greeting.

Like most hetairai, Aegle had enough education to carry on a conversation with aristoi men. Better than many, in fact, including those like Dardanus. In theory, she was Pandora's competition, yes. But she was one of the few women in the whole polis who wouldn't disdain Pandora for her career and freedom. Besides, Pandora had little interest in attaining a permanent patron, and that was *all* Aegle sought. She was a year younger than Pandora and already fretting terribly over growing too old.

Much as she was loathe to admit it, Aegle's worries had no doubt exacerbated Pandora's own.

"You were invited to the palace tonight?" Aegle asked.

"Hmm. You too?"

Aegle nodded with somewhat less than her usual enthusiasm for such things. The woman loved symposiums, with their abundance of wine—not that Pandora minded that, either—and free food. And myriad chances to draw the wealthiest of patrons. But now, her smile was forced, a subtle tension holding her posture.

"What is it?" Pandora asked.

"You heard Zeus will be there, right? I mean the stories say he can be ... rough. Too rough with the women. Io and Europa were pretty much never seen again, right? And Maia and Elektra and all. Do you ... do you think he *does* something they just can't get past?"

Pandora glowered, looking at the phoenix instead of Aegle. Her uncle's namesake rose from the ashes no matter how hard one tried to destroy it.

Zeus had done a great many things Pandora could not get past.

Europa.

Her throat had gone dry and the thought of trying to speak, to give even the modicum of reassurance Aegle clearly craved, felt like trying to scale a mountain with her hands bound. To support the other woman now was to become like Atlas, bearing the weight of the firmament upon her shoulders.

Without thinking of it, she realised she had begun to claw at the shelf's edge with her fingertips. She longed to be somewhere else. To be anywhere else. "I need to swim," she managed to rasp, for Aegle deserved some answer.

Abruptly, she shoved off the edge and took to swimming across the pool. Not just the gentle gliding most of the women practiced here, but to push herself. Back and forth, and again, until her chest heaved. Until her arms began to burn as if the pain in them might drown out the ache in her soul.

Europa.

May Hades drag Zeus screaming down into the Underworld.

Europa.

As if the World convulsed upon a name. As if its echo left a hollow deep into the cosmos.

Panting, she at last splashed up on the far side of the shelf. Nearby, another woman jolted awake. Pandora had thought she merely lazed, but from the way the woman thrashed and flailed about in wild panic, she must have actually been in the throes of some nightmare. The woman's wild movements spilled her into the deeper waters.

Pandora dropped back down, standing on her toes, and caught the woman, easing her back onto the shelf. The woman cast about with wild, unfocused eyes, hardly seeming to see Pandora at all, though her hands grabbed Pandora's biceps and tightened painfully.

When she stood, her height revealed her as a Titan.

"I know you," Pandora said, recognition setting in. Brizo, the Nymph Oracle from the western temple. She did not oft come to the city, but Pandora had certainly seen her on occasion. Perhaps she came when summoned by the Pleiades. Perhaps, desperate for answers, they had called for her after Prometheus foretold the coming of Zeus.

Brizo's grip tightened even further, though her gaze finally settled upon Pandora's face. "It falls!" She swallowed hard, still clearly trying to orient herself. "It all comes crashing down. Great sweeping waves rising like shadowy hands come to close in upon us. The land tossed about like a ship in a storm. Rent *asunder*! Everything breaking and screaming and death and the swallowing deep."

What? What the fuck? Pandora tried to struggle free, but even Nymph strength was greater than that of a mortal. "What falls? This city?"

Brizo abruptly released her. "The whole of the island." Another rough swallow, and now she seemed to be talking to herself more than Pandora. "I saw Atlantis torn to pieces. I saw the end of *everything*." The Nymph trembled, hugging herself. The she vaulted onto the shelf, and again, up out of the pool. She took off, half running, seeming to forget even her clothes, and a slave girl went chasing after her, khiton in hand.

Pandora glanced about, though no one else seemed to have heard the Oracle's words. Was this ... was it even possible? Plenty of tomes and historical records made mention of Oracular prophecy, and these things were not always literal. Maybe the fall of Atlantis was her mind's eye processing a conquest. Or maybe, being a Nymph, whatever she had seen would be centuries or millennia in the future.

But if it was conquest or some other political upheaval, Pandora had to imagine it would relate to Zeus's arrival. Prometheus claimed the king no longer trusted the Pleiades. Which meant, unless his anger could be redirected, he might act against them. Maybe even kill them. Or throw them into Tartarus, as she'd heard he did with those who truly angered him.

Kelaino may have irked Pandora, but she didn't want her dead and certainly not condemned to some eternal torment in the Underworld. Was there aught Pandora could do about any of this? Certainly not from inside the damn bath house.

She needed to get to that symposium. She needed to be there, to see what would happen. Maybe she could stop Zeus from exploding into his infamous wrath, though she shuddered at the thought of standing in the same room as the king. She had to try. Had to do something.

6

KIRKE

1570 Silver Age

A few hours past dawn, Athene departed, ignoring Kirke's half-hearted attempts to get her sister to linger. Much as she sympathised with the woman's plight, her presence on Ogygia endangered Kirke's own plans, and it was better Athene was off.

Thus, when the Olympian had traveled well out of earshot, Kirke returned to the garden where Kalypso was fussing over the moly. It was always so testy a plant to raise. The other Nymph looked up at her approach. "Well?"

"Yeah, she plans to raise the child, which is good and all. Well, that, and to exact vengeance on Hephaistos, which is maybe less good for all concerned. Uh, except us, of course." Kirke shrugged. "Yeah, there's gonna be blood."

Kalypso nodded. "Will she kill him?"

"Oh, eventually, I should think so." Subtly and slowly. From what Kirke had heard, few Titans could have stood against Athene in a fair fight. But then, Athene didn't intend to challenge

Hephaistos to a battle of arms, but to sweep away his control of Korinth.

"One less Olympian then," Kalypso said, returning to dig at the moly. "And she won't go to Zeus?"

"No."

Finally, Kalypso rose, folding her arms over her chest. "Isn't that a good sign? Could she be swayed against him?"

Kirke almost rolled her eyes, stopped only because it would have hurt her friend's feelings. Zeus's favoured child turn on him? "Maybe when the sun rises at night and the seas drink the land. No, she'll never move against her precious father."

Which was why Athene could never be a true sister to Kirke. As an Olympian, she would never understand the plight faced by Nymphs, and she wilfully blinded herself to the vile wretch that was her father.

Kalypso was frowning now. "And has your resolve weakened? She is your kin."

"Psh. Just because Helios wasn't bound in Tartarus like Atlas doesn't mean my family has not suffered because of Zeus," Kirke snapped. "Besides, you know damn well Io was a close friend. And how many more have been crushed under his heel? Zeus stomps around like a Gígas! Bam! You're crushed, *bam*, you're maimed! And what, you think one day I'll say, 'Oh, maybe a little maiming is all right. All for a good cause.'"

Kalypso raised her hands in mock surrender. "Sorry, I just ... You know."

Yeah, Kirke knew. They took terrible chances, and sooner or later, the Olympians might learn of the plot against them. But the World was broken, and maybe Kirke could fix it. If not, at least then she could enjoy her own slow, satisfying vengeance against Zeus and his ilk.

Kalypso stepped into her embrace, planting a kiss upon her lips. Her fingers traced the line of Kirke's hip, sending shivers of pleasure shooting through her.

Well then.

A few cups of wine and languorous lovemaking couldn't help but start the morning off well.

A DARK EXPANSE *unfolded before her, the streets of some polis she could not recognise amid the gloom. There was no moon and no lamps lighting the path, just the sense of edifices enclosing her on either side as her bare feet slapped over the flagstones.*

She was running, fleeing someone.

A hunter in the dark.

He was after her again, always after her, and all she could do was run through, though the landscape before her refused to change.

Run.

KIRKE WOKE from her nap to find Kalypso gone, the trapdoor in their bed chamber thrown wide. Pausing to snatch up a half-full decanter of wine, Kirke made her way down to the basement.

Working her alchemy in the kitchens had been less than ideal, but Kirke couldn't have risked Athene seeing what they did in the real lab hidden under the house.

The lab was a windowless room lit by a dozen candles and a stove that fed into the chimney in her chambers. Within, Kalypso stood bent over a table, easing a drop of moly extract into a mixture. Upon the stove roiled a cauldron filled with their latest attempt at perfecting an artificial Ambrosia. Nectar, the populace had begun calling their brews, and Kirke liked the name well enough.

She took a hearty swig from the decanter. Should she burden Kalypso with another of her nightmares? As an oneiromancer, her dreams might hold some import. Might indicate another of her kind hunted the dreamscape for her—or perhaps for sign of Nectar and thus trailed her without knowing her. Then again, her dreams could also be the result of too much wine before sleep and the anxiety sparked by Athene's plight.

No, she would not worry Kalypso over this, least of all while the Nymph worked to perfect the Nectar. They needed that. Everyone needed it.

If they could get the tonic just right, Nymphs or Men who imbibed it over a prolonged period might fortify their Pneuma and develop Pneumatikoi strong enough to challenge the Olympians. She'd seen Titans run straight up forty-foot-tall walls, punch through marble, and harden their skin to the point spears bounced off. They needed something to allow Men to compete with that if they were to break Zeus's hold upon the Thalassa.

After sipping from the decanter, Kirke moved in behind Kalypso, peering over her shoulder without touching her during the painstaking creation process.

Oh, how they had dreamed of a World free from Zeus's insane autocracy. How many nights had they mused on the possibilities of elevating Mankind to power with which they could challenge the so-called gods? And they were getting closer, with almost every passing iteration.

Yes, sometimes unexpected side-effects cropped up. Mania and psychosis happened even faster than with real Ambrosia, and some-times even worse results.

The moly was unpredictable ... but it was also the only substance flexible enough to mimic Ambrosia. Its mercurial nature was both its greatest strength and its greatest danger. Yes, there had been madness and murder in the wake of their experiments. But what if it finally worked?

Besides, Ambrosia could heal most any wound. Which meant, if they duplicated it without need for the golden apples of the Hesperides, they would have a tonic that could allow Man to survive the injuries and illnesses that now plagued mortal existence.

That they had to sell the other product to keep their coffers full— and to ensure sufficient testing of it—was a small price to pay, consid-ering what they hoped to achieve.

Kirke took another swig of Illyrian wine as Kalypso worked, keeping silent until the other woman rose from the table, stretching. With a wink, Kalypso poured the new concoction into the cauldron, then set about stirring it with a ladle.

"What do you think? Do we have it now? I really don't want another batch that turns piss into acid. That was ... pretty bad. Especially with the farmers who tried to cut down each other's fences with the streams and all." Kirke shivered at the memory.

Kalypso shrugged. "I'm mostly just doing what you taught me."

Waving away the other woman's false modesty, Kirke moved to sniff the cauldron, setting the decanter down on a table nearby. A sweet, heady scent wafted up, seeming *almost* a match for real Ambrosia. "Smells ever so slightly off."

"I know, but that doesn't mean it won't get the same result. We're never going to have an exact duplicate of it without those apples and we'd never get anywhere nigh to those." There was a bitterness in Kalypso's voice she couldn't quite hide. The other woman had prodded her mother for access to the golden apples, and Kelaino had unequivocally refused, claiming the risk of Zeus's displeasure far outweighed any possible gain.

The ancient drakon Ladon guarded the great Tree, and no one got past him save with leave from the Pleiades. Back in the Golden Age, Kirke had heard other sorcerers speculate Ladon was an Old One, a being birthed in the same time before time as the Primordials themselves, perhaps even spawned by them.

And, of course, Kalypso dare not tell even her mother that half the point was in trying to destroy Zeus and the other Olympians. They had imprisoned Kalypso's grandfather Atlas in Tartarus and reduced mighty Helios, Kirke's father, to a shadow of his own lucent self. A puppet. Worse still, Zeus subjugated Men and Nymphs for his own aggrandisement, treating both like his property. Nigh sixteen centuries of rape, tyranny, and petty cruelties.

No, Kirke remembered the Golden Age, and the long centuries under the Ouranid League. Men were dominated even then, yes, and Nymphs remained marriage trophies or mere objects upon which

Titans could sate themselves, true. But not like this ... Not as it was now. Kronos and his generation at least sought marriage from Nymphs to satiate themselves. They moderated their Ambrosial intake. Zeus and the Olympians were incarnations of unbridled debauchery.

Besides, if everyone had Ambrosia, maybe there would be no more gods. Maybe men and women could just live. Or so she and Kalypso allowed themselves to dream sometimes. They had both been to study at the Muses College in Themiskyra, had heard the words of Thalia—and of Themis herself—and had chanced that dream.

In fact, she and Kalypso had argued about whether to try their experiments in Themiskyra. But Kelaino had made Kalypso governor of this little island for challenging the existing order of things, and Kirke's friend could not leave without major incident.

Sometimes, Kirke missed the simpler days, listening to the Muses lecture, watching Amazons train, and drinking Kimmerian wine beneath the stars.

"It's dangerous," she said, knowing the words needless but she had to say them anyway. "Yeah, an improper brew could have more insidious results than we've seen thus far. And we've already seen some shit that would have Cyclopes averting their eyes."

Kalypso snorted. "We're lucky Apollon's Oracular Sight has not already revealed us to him. Sooner or later, the Olympians will discover us, Kirke. If we are not far enough along to have a workable defence when that happens, we're like to find ourselves joining Grandfather in Tartarus."

Another tired argument, and Kirke didn't disagree. She didn't know for certain why the Olympian hadn't been able to find them thus far. Perhaps even her limited gift with the Sight concealed her. Either way, she had to imagine their obscurity would not last forever.

"Maybe ..." Kirke winced at the pain of what she needed to say. These languid days had been a joyous relief from the long centuries of loneliness. "Maybe we need to keep our operation moving, make it harder for them to catch on."

"I can't."

"I know, my friend. I know you have to stay here." Which was why it had always been Kirke to move their product, mostly through pirates or smugglers, into the poleis. She would travel away for a few months, make several stops to avoid arousing any suspicion, and eventually find her way back here. It had worked thus far ... "There are other places I could grow moly. If we work from multiple fronts, it becomes harder still to track us."

The other woman slumped back against the wall. "You don't know what it's like to be trapped on a small island, all but forbidden from leaving, and having no one to talk to."

Well, the first part was true enough, but Kirke had certainly had her share of isolation over the years.

"Oh!" Kalypso said. "Wait, you're not thinking of going back to Themiskyra without me?"

"I don't know," Kirke admitted, hating to see the pain limning Kalypso's face. "Yeah, I'm not sure what I'll do."

"Then stay here! Nyx, Kirke!"

Slowly, Kirke nodded. What else was she to do? She would linger on Ogygia and desperately hope they could perfect their draughts before the Olympians found them.

7

PYRRHA

213 Golden Age

Two years since Sharvara had died—murdered by Hera—and here Pyrrha was, killing a dog herself. She cast the body into the sea in silent offering to whatever power lurked nearby, just beyond the Veil.

Sharvara's murder had helped her first fully pierce the Veil, and now, once more, the death allowed the world to shift for her. colour and warmth bled out, replaced by a land of shifting shadows and chill nether winds. The very edge of the Underworld. The Penumbra.

And it was so much closer than anyone ever wanted to believe. It was always right there, invisible, just a breath away.

Blinking, she rose, stalking through the night. In the distance, closer to the harbour, she beheld a crunch of warriors. Phalanxes of spearmen lurched into existence, raising up their great round shields, clashing with one another before dissipating on the wind. Phantoms that might help her piece together what had happened here, but otherwise availed her naught, for they were not really here. Just echoes of emotion.

No, she needed to find true shades, and once found, discover a means to communicate with them.

Oh, even if she did not sacrifice animals, apparitions haunted her. They whispered to her whenever the sun set, intruding upon her walks and denying her solace. Even had she wanted to take Papa's advice and deny the Sight, she could not stop the parade of ghosts always in her periphery. They walked the harbour and the surrounding lands. They stalked the markets, seeking ... whatever it was the dead thought they needed.

Even, they plagued her dreams. She had woken with a start in the middle of last night, seized with absolute certainty *something* was in the room with her, looming over her shoulder. And the voice, a too throaty growl of something deep and momentous.

... *I TURN WITH YOU* ...

For heartbeats more she had lain there, eyes clenched closed, afraid to even whimper while willing whatever it was to leave her. In dread then, she had turned and found naught save the suddenly oppressive gloom of her room.

The dark horrified, even as it forever beckoned to her.

Most of those she witnessed on this beach appeared wounded, ravaged by pains of both body and soul. Always, they wanted something. But without breaching the Veil with murder, she couldn't maintain the Sight for more than a few breaths. Certainly not long enough to determine what any of these entities actually sought.

Now, though, looking out over the shades of wandering soldiers, she could guess. Twelve years ago, the Ambrosial War had come to Thebes. No one in the palace dared mention it, at least not where Tethys might overhear. But her tutors said the war had raged for some seven years, which meant the assault on Thebes had been early on. And Tethys had lost her husband, like so many wives that day.

Even as no few husbands and daughters had lost wives and mothers.

Perhaps these hapless shades may have sought some return to

their loved ones. Pyrrha had been but a babe then, but Papa had later told her they had lost Mama that day, too, so maybe her soul was among these shades. Most of those Pyrrha saw were men, but not all.

No, when soldiers came to sack a city, men were *far* from the only victims. Once, she saw a woman wandering in an alley, her throat crushed. Later, when she'd caught a phantom echo of four men dragging the woman into that same alley, Pyrrha had known what had happened to her.

According to her tutors, the fighting had reached the walls but never breached them, in part because the Telkhines, Tethys's mer allies, had attacked Kronos's ships. The harbour, though, had been drowned in blood. There was also the whispered rumour that, upon Okeanus's death, Tethys had unleashed a drakon upon Kronos's ships. That its saurian bulk had slithered beneath the waves before scuttling hulls and dragging men into the deep.

In the darkness, she could not help but feel the vague sense of something watching her, out in the far distance. Not a ghost like those in the harbour, but something ... timeless and momentous. A presence that filled up the whole of the night with its enormity. Papa had warned things older than shades and far more dangerous could move through this Penumbra, using it as a transitory space to access the Mortal Realm. It seemed to her, the Veil protecting her world was a very good, if fragile thing.

Pushing her fears aside, she took in her more immediate area. This late, few men were still up in the world of the living. Those she spied around the harbour were indistinct to her, blurred and dreamlike while she looked through the Veil.

On the pier, she paused, watching a flickering phantom ship. Kronos's warriors poured from it in silent waves, though she could imagine their screams as they hefted their weapons, their blood up. They came, brandishing spears and javelins, the wealthy among them clad in panoplies. Some of the phantoms vanished the moment their sandals touched ashore, but others persisted, engaging Tethid warriors, both sides diaphanous.

Frozen moments of rage and terror and pain.

Then, across from them, the same dolphin-plated Titan she'd seen before rose up, leading the Tethid forces in a counter charge. Unlike the phantoms, he had more substance, only the very fringes of his garb breaking away into translucent tatters. Were she not looking closely, she might have mistaken him for a living man, and some of those he led, as well.

The ghost engaged the phantoms for a moment before his gaze fixed upon Pyrrha, and his eyes widened. Once more, he opened his mouth, and now she saw clearly the empty space behind his palate, flickers of starlight shining through it. Whatever he wanted to say was lost in a chorus of moans.

"I don't understand," Pyrrha said, raising her hands.

The ghost's face darkened, and he took a threatening step toward her, brandishing a xiphos.

Pyrrha fell back, keeping her hands up between them. "I want to help you, but I don't know how. Can you show me what you need?"

The inhuman hate that washed over his face stole her breath. Her hand went to her mouth. His form flickered, reappearing mere feet from her. His massive hand snared her hair and yanked her forward, his sword point hovering a hair from her eye. Pyrrha whimpered, heart hammering, unable to move. The palpable rage that wafted off this entity choked her, unlike aught she had ever felt in her life. It threatened to swallow her whole.

Then, without warning, something *else* seized her and hefted her bodily away, to crash upon the ground. For a moment, she lay there, groaning, trying to focus. She blinked through the pain and realised she'd lost her grip upon the Sight. The real world had returned, the cool autumn evening still warmer than the nether cold she'd left behind. The buildings had shifted back into sensible shapes, and the light had a full spectrum once more.

When she looked up, Hera towered above her, face a mask of utter disdain. "What kind of deranged freak goes around killing dogs?" The Titan woman stood, hands on her hips, looking for all the World like a marble statue.

Pyrrha rubbed her head as she rose. "You murdered *my* dog." Bitch.

Hera's scorn slipped into actual loathing, and she took a threatening step toward Pyrrha, forcing her to fall back. "That animal assaulted my sister and I defended her. Only a warped soul would compare that to grabbing someone's house pet that hadn't hurt anyone."

Technically, it was a stray. Still, Pyrrha fell silent in acknowledgment of the point. Yes, she had indeed murdered a hapless animal who had done her no wrong. It had seemed, at the time, the only means of pursuing the truth of what haunted her and of finding Mama's soul.

Apparently deciding her not worth the trouble, Hera offered up a final sneer before turning to leave Pyrrha alone. For a time after the Titan left, Pyrrha stared after her, willing Hera to burst into flame. Her and Tethys's whole royal brood, and their sparkling halls and entitled attitudes. Let the Underworld rise up and claim them all.

The woman would have shit herself if she'd seen half the things Pyrrha had. Not one of them probably began to imagine the truth: that the dead were here, tormented, wandering around outside their precious city. How many of the fallen had died just to protect the royal brats?

Muttering under her breath, Pyrrha made her way down by the water, stopping to claim an oil lamp. Even with the moon almost full this night, wandering without light wasn't a mistake she would repeat. Out there, in the waters beyond the pier, something splashed around.

Telkhines? They preferred the night, true, which made it harder to spot them when they came to trade or report to Tethys. For a time, she stood and squinted out into the waves, hoping to catch a glimpse of a mermaid or merman. When they came, a messenger would fetch the Titan Queen, and she'd come down here and speak to them alone. Oh, to have had the chance to stand in on one such meeting, even if she was forbidden to ask questions.

What was their kingdom of Pontus like? Did they truly reach

Realms beyond this one? Did they speak to fish? Did fish speak *back*? Pyrrha allowed herself a smile as her mind flitted over the innumerable things she could learn from those who dwelt beneath the Aegean.

Ah, but they liked their mysteries, and so far as Pyrrha knew, Tethys alone understood much about their society or nature. Still, she kept casting glances out over the waters as she plodded along the beach.

That, and searching the shore for sign of ghosts. "Where are you?" she dared to call out, some distance from the harbour.

She didn't really expect an answer and didn't get one. Just the whistling wind and the rhythmic lap of the sea, and the fall of her sandals upon wet sand.

Gods, she *knew* there were entities out there, beside her, just beyond her perception. But she couldn't make her vision shift into that Realm just for wishing it. Death brought it on. Would catching a crab or something be enough to trigger the visions?

Probably not.

Sighing, she made her way to a seaside cave she sometimes visited. It rose but a little ways above the water, and the tide had probably cut away the stone in some distant past. Now, it acted as an overhang just deep enough to provide shelter and privacy.

With a frustrated moan, she wrapt her arms around her knees. The answers were right here, but she couldn't reach them. Papa certainly knew more than he'd said, but all he would ever tell her was that she was fine. That she was precious and should enjoy her childhood. Play in the sea, eat the sweet breads, and run for the joy of it.

Not that any of that sounded so awful, just that, how was she supposed to appreciate little things when great mysteries lay close enough to feel them breathe upon the back of her neck? She was special ... she had to use that ...

SHE WAS CRAWLING THROUGH A TUNNEL, *torch out ahead of her. Prodigious, squirming shadows encircled her, almost seeming to tug at her wrists and ankles, making it feel she waded through a mire. Grunting with the effort, she pushed ever forward.*

Ahead, the passage grew narrower, and she had to turn sideways to fit. Pyrrha shoved the torch in first, then twisted, wedging herself inward. Why was she pressing on? Should she turn back?

The thought came to her, and yet her body kept moving, summoned by some ... presence ... deep within the mountain. She could not say how far underground she had delved, but deep.

Was this ... a dream?

Rough stone scraped her cheek. Warmth dribbled down her chin and neck. The passage forced her to worm through it, seeming to close in around her with each foot forward. What if it grew too tight? What if she couldn't turn back and got stuck in here, alone? Would she die of thirst, screaming herself raw for help that could never find her?

The vision of such hit her, and its terror actually made tears rise up at the fringes of her eyes.

And still *she could not make herself turn back. Deeper and deeper, until the passage opened up into a wide cave, the base of which lay several feet below the opening she was in. Despite her attempts at grace, Pyrrha tumbled from her point of ingress, pitching down onto the chilled floor of the greater cavern with a pained grunt. Her torch clattered down beside her and lay there, flames dancing in front of her face.*

She was lucky she hadn't singed herself.

With a huff, she rose to her knees, snatching up the torch to look around. She was in a wide tunnel, but her torchlight failed to reach both sides of the space at once. The cave was smoother than she'd have thought, with no stalagmites and few stalactites. Was this a lava tube?

Forcing herself to rise, she turned about. She couldn't say which way she was meant to go since the tube seemed to vanish into darkness in both directions. Maybe it didn't matter.

Picking a direction, she plodded onward. Her sandals echoed faintly upon the stone beneath her, her steps drawn forward though she could not have said why. Her flesh had grown clammy with chill sweat, and she cast a single furtive glance behind herself. The expanse in both directions seemed a fathomless darkness.

A sick sensation began to grow inside her gut, the feeling she was not alone down here. Some monstrous, alien intellect lurked in the darkness. Was it ahead? Behind? It seemed almost omnipresent in the tenebrous tract she had intruded into, as though she had delved so deep beneath the Earth as to reach somewhere else. Somewhere inhabited by a timeless mind so momentous it spread through the whole of the mountain.

With each step she took, the sensation of wrongness increased, but still her feet refused to turn back. Then came the scraping of something rough over the stone, reverberating through the tunnel, and the sensation that whatever lurked out there, she not only felt it, but it felt her.

... COME FORTH ...

PYRRHA BLINKED AWAKE in the darkened sea cave, heart hammering so hard as to become an actual pain in her chest. She lay drenched in sweat, shivering and sick from the nightmare she'd seen. Nightmares had long haunted her, but this went to a new level of verisimilitude.

And that voice ... Had she heard it before?

Daring not sleep more, she lay in the cave, staring out at the ocean, afraid to close her eyes until pink dawn painted the sky. No, she was afraid even then.

In the early morn, she returned to the harbour, then climbed the stairs cut into the cliff, making her slow way back to Thebes. The city lay far, far above the harbour, and the climb always winded her a bit. Which was fine, she took the time to pause halfway to the landing and take in the view of the waterfall beyond the city and the brilliant cobalt of the Aegean. Today, though, not even that cut through the panic of what she'd dreamt or the horror in the night that had precipitated the dreams.

After passing through the main gate, she made her way back to the acropolis. At its heart lay the somewhat neglected Temple of

Gaia, and beyond that, upon the mountain, the palace of Tethys, reached by a long expanse of marble stairs.

Atop the stairs, she found Hera, along with the twins, Styx and Perse, sitting upon the lip of the main fountain. The moment Hera spotted her, she leaned in to whisper in Perse's ear. The three sisters all stared at Pyrrha as though she carried the plague.

"I bet she kept the balls as a trophy," Perse whispered, none too quietly.

"Maybe she ate them hoping to grow her own," Styx said, snickering.

Hera said naught that Pyrrha could hear, but her smirk was so vile it made her skin crawl. She had beheld the awful malevolence of staring into the eyes of shades damned to wander the world in eternal torment. But sometimes, Pyrrha imagined people like Hera could teach even the damned a new meaning to the word cruelty.

Why was her life always like this? What in the actual Underworld had she done to deserve this fetid pile of shit?

Unable to bear their stares, Pyrrha fled from the front gardens. Hardly watching where she was going, she plowed directly into another Titan in the atrium. Their brother, Poseidon, who caught her and managed to keep the two of them from tumbling into a heap. Poseidon was a bit younger than Hera but still older than the twins, with a knowing smile and an irritatingly handsome face. He peered around her shoulder, spotted his sisters, and seemed to know what had happened in an instant.

The Titan guided her through the atrium and into the courtyard, toward benches set beside the fishpond. "Out all night?" he asked. Without waiting for her answer, he clapped his hands to summon a servant who brought a tray of olives and eggs to break her fast.

Her stomach growled. Until now, Pyrrha hadn't even realised she was hungry. After helping herself to several olives, she managed to meet his gaze. "Thank you," she said, wary of him. He had hardly paid her much mind—even less than his sisters had. One never knew what to make of even a moment of kindness from these royals.

Poseidon nodded, then turned to stare down at the fish so deeply she imagined him naming each of them. "There's a truth you figure out when you get to a certain age. Some people sooner than others. The young are not always pure. People always think, oh children start out innocent. And that's true up to a point, and then life starts to twist them up and they just want be something else. So they hurt those they can and tease and torment." He shrugged. "Sometimes they know they're being brutes, sometimes they don't figure that out until later. When they think about how others hurt them." He huffed. "Maybe I'm no good with words."

"N-no." Oh, wait. That sounded like she was agreeing that he wasn't. "I mean, I get it. And thank you." She grabbed a boiled egg and left him to stare at his fish.

Maybe he was right. Maybe the girls would grow out of their virulent cruelty. But Hera was almost two years older than Poseidon and hadn't even started the process, so Pyrrha wouldn't hold her breath.

Either way, she still needed a way to find her answers. She would not give up without those. Not even if she had to become the freak Hera accused her of being.

8

PANDORA

1570 Silver Age

*P*andora took Taygete's Bridge over the inner canal, toward the acropolis island. The bridge rose up in a high enough arc that smaller boats could sail beneath it and was, in Pandora's estimation, a pinnacle of engineering on Atlantis. Not least for the aesthetic touches—herds of mingling deer worked into relief along the sides.

The bridge led to a gate in the earthen wall that encompassed the acropolis island. Though guarded, none of the guards paid much mind to the stream of traffic passing over the bridge and onto the island, and Pandora paid them no mind in turn. The lower banks of the island held barracks for soldiers in the Pleiades' employ, as well as houses for aristoi graced to live upon the island, like Dardanus. Beyond, marble stairs led up a steep slope to a second wall, this one of silvery tin, and here a pair of Titan men watched entry with far more care.

She didn't know their names, but they'd seen her many times and waved in invitation. She felt their gazes linger upon her, perhaps drawn by the clink of her silver anklets or the glint of her jewellery. She had donned her finest for this evening.

The acropolis proper lay beyond the tin wall, complete with temples for worship and homes for the most vaunted of aristoi, outside the Pleiades themselves. *Their* home was the royal palace, a citadel encased in a third and final wall. A wall of rosy-gold orichalcum, the most precious metal in the world, found only in Atlantis. In value, it was second only to Ambrosia, and Atlas had built his palace from the stuff.

Wrought with the Art long ago, the orichalcum wall was said to be indestructible.

Slave doormen escorted her around the fish pool courtyard, through the colonnade, and into the palace proper, which already overflowed with the scents of salt pork, figs, and other delicacies. The drinking would not begin until after the guests had gorged themselves and could thus imbibe copious amounts of wine. Pandora spotted trays of apricots and walnuts, of olives and sweet breads, and of oysters and clams probably traded for with the mer down by the Cove of Poseidon.

She helped herself to an apricot and strolled among the myriad lounges abutting the main courtyard—a garden filled with more colourful flora than she could ever hope to imitate in her humble home. Most of the lounges were thrown open, with guests reclining on wooden couches or upon cushions on the floor. Already, some few flute girls had begun to play. Clad flutists, this time, so perhaps the Pleiades aimed for a hint of subtlety with Zeus.

Aegle leaned against a column in one of the lounges, chatting with a small group of men, working her charms. Pandora caught her eye, trusting the other hetaira to come to her when a lull in conversation allowed. Kelaino would no doubt expect Pandora to sing and play the lyre or harp when the feasting ended and the symposiarch declared a start to the drinking.

The man, chosen by roll of the dice, would say just when and how much the guests must drink. If Kelaino had any control over him,

Pandora imagined the man would strike a delicate balance between calling for enough wine to get Zeus relaxed, without allowing enough to leave the king rowdy. Not a job Pandora would envy.

She passed by another lounge and, despite looking for him, still almost tripped over her own sandals on seeing Zeus there, being fed grapes by a young girl. The King looked no different than ever, with long platinum hair and beard, and eyes like blue ice, hallmark of Kroniads. Beside him stood a woman Pandora had not seen in years but would never forget: Zeus's vicious attack dog, Hekate. Men called her a witch. A monster, even.

Of the latter, Pandora could attest. The Heliad had been the one to drag Pandora screaming from her home as a child.

Pandora's fingers had clenched into fists, gripping her peplos as she passed. It took a momentous effort of will to keep walking, to keep from staring at the two most monstrous Titans she had ever heard tale of.

Rather than wait for Aegle, she pushed on, putting distance between herself and the Olympian King. She doubled back to the main feast tables, grabbed some walnuts, and slipped away from the bustling lounges. She passed one where Zeus's son Ares—and the younger Titan's lover, Enyo—were shouting in the midst of some discussion, as if inclined to turn debate to blows. Given their reputation for inciting bloodsport, perhaps that was exactly their intent. What else should she expect from Zeus's get?

The lot of them fed on suffering, happy to provide themselves a feast wherever they trod. They made playthings of the lives of Mankind.

Back in the gardens, she found Prometheus sitting upon a stool, playing draughts with another Titan. Their board rested upon a short wooden table between them, and the other Titan leaned over it as if in deep thought, though his gaze kept darting up at Prometheus.

Pandora lingered beneath the shade of a plane tree, watching the game. From the look of it, Prometheus had it well in hand. After a few moments, the other Titan rose and offered Prometheus a nod of concession. As he departed, his gaze fell upon Pandora and lingered, not with lust like so many others, but with something akin to the piercing insight Prometheus himself seemed to possess. It was all Pandora could do to remain still and not squirm inside her own skin.

Nearby, a flutist took up a song Pandora knew. A classic party tune, one that always lightened moods, even if the playing of it took only modest skill. The flighty song *also* probably meant the wine was being served, and Pandora teetered between approaching Prometheus and heading back to grab a bowl to steady her nerves.

In the end, he made her choice for her, waving her over to take the vacated seat.

"Who was that?" she asked, settling down before him. Though she'd met Prometheus only twice before, and not in the past fortnight, there was a strange calmness to resting upon the stool, as if she'd sat across from him like this innumerable times before. As if she had but reclaimed a place prepared for her.

"Morpheus."

Another famed name. One of Zeus's sorcerers, one specialising in dreams. Legends claimed he passed messages between the king and his allies by intruding into one's mind when one slept. The very idea had her stomach fluttering. A violation of one's own mind.

"You know of him," Prometheus said, reading her reaction even as she tried to hide it. He began resetting the board.

"I know him as someone to fear and avoid."

"Such is probably true of all sorcerers and most Titans in general."

Pandora quirked a smile. "And you?"

"Do you inquire if I am dangerous?"

"Are you?"

Now it was his turn to smile. "Probably." He spun the board so she could make the first move.

She did. "I've heard claim they have far deeper versions of the game in the lands beyond Nusantara."

"Oh, yes. In Yindai, they play on another level entirely."

Spoken like someone who had actually visited the fabled land.

Pandora studied his face, only half watching the Titan's cautious moves.

"Yes," he said, in answer to her unspoken question.

Pandora started, shifting on her stool in what was no doubt a vain attempt to cover her surprise. Yes, he had visited Yindai. Was she so easy to read?

For a few moves, she concentrated only on the game, giving herself time to catch up, to steady herself.

"I'm envious," she finally said, choosing honesty over prying. "I cannot imagine having been quite so free to travel."

"There are few ways to so expand understanding." Another cautious move. Too cautious, as if toying with her.

Pandora claimed several of his pieces, and his smile only deepened.

"Perhaps one day you will travel freely."

Now she frowned, sitting up straight. "I'm a woman." To say naught of the insurmountable cost of wide travel for someone in her position.

"I rather think, Pandora, that you can accomplish aught you truly desire."

When she next looked back at the board, she realised her aggressive claiming of his pieces had played into a trap. That she had won almost every move but was set up to lose the game, regardless.

Prometheus leaned back, clearly recognising she had seen her doom.

"Well played," she offered. Never had she so badly underestimated an opponent. By Hades, she couldn't even remember losing at all since she'd been a small child.

"*Pandora.*" Kelaino's voice scraped over her nerves before she had time to say aught more to Prometheus.

She rose, turning to see the queen beckoning her over with one finger. Offering a nod of farewell to the other Titan, Pandora came as bidden, though she'd much rather have challenged him to a rematch, one where she could direct her undivided attention to the board.

Like a marble statue, Kelaino stood, hand upon her hip, eyes hard. "I did not summon you to this event merely to entertain my uncle, and I'll certainly not pay you for it." Because he was the one Titan here from which she had no fear?

"I'll find a harp, then," Pandora said dryly.

"Find Zeus and work your charms," Kelaino said. "I want him in the best mood of his long, misanthropic life when he comes to call upon me."

Pandora glowered, not even bothering to hide her ire. Should she greet the king on her back? After all, he seemed to get every other woman he ever saw in that position. It was what he'd done to Europa all those years ago, in front of Pandora, even as Hekate buried Pandora's face in her robes. Five years old, and she'd seen—or at least heard —her adopted mother raped, though she had not understood what was happening until some years later.

She opened her mouth, intent to suggest that maybe *Kelaino* ought to be the one to alleviate Zeus's tensions. His vexation was with her and her sisters, after all, and he clearly had a taste for Pleiades. How many of them had born his bastards now?

Kelaino grabbed Pandora's chin, actually hefting her slightly off the ground by it, forcing Pandora to stand upon her toes as lances of pain shot through her neck. "Do not challenge me on this, hetaira. If the king leaves here angry, I'll make certain we are not the only ones to suffer for it." Abruptly the Nymph released Pandora who stumbled away.

She stretched her neck as much as an excuse to cover the shame and horror—and knew Prometheus had risen and moved to her at this—as to work out the kinks Kelaino had introduced. She couldn't face him.

Glowering, Pandora spun off on her heel and fled.

Oh, did Kelaino want an impression made upon Zeus? How much impression would a knife in his jugular make? Would that get his attention, as his golden ichor sprayed over the Pleiades' mosaics? The image danced through her mind, round and round, made almost real by will alone. If she actually managed to kill him, would Kelaino thank her?

Perhaps not, for the remaining Olympians would no doubt make an example of all Atlantis.

I saw Atlantis torn to pieces. I saw the end of everything.

Pandora shuddered. Gods, she wanted to retch. To spit. To flee from all this. Maybe not merely from this symposium, but, as Prometheus had suggested, from Atlantis itself. From the life she had built here out of the ashes of her ruined childhood.

She felt cast adrift, as if she had lost her grip on the hope and tenacity that had so long guided her. She was not the giving-up type, but this had become unbearable. Was the Titan right? Could she do whatever she desired? Perhaps, if she could bear the price of it.

Listless, she came into an empty lounge, slipped on spilled liquid, and pitched hard onto the tiles. Her cheek smacked the ground and white haze filled her vision. It took her a moment to even notice the warm wetness upon her face. To push herself up onto her elbows.

Only then did she see the body. Only then did the scream rip through her of its own accord. It tore out of her belly, a primal shriek of horror.

She lay in a pool of golden blood from a Titan. From Enyo. Burns marred the Titan's face and neck, and her throat was crushed so severely her spine had broken out the back of her neck.

When at last the scream died in her, Pandora stared at the corpse in rapt disbelief. Had Zeus done this? But no, she'd have heard his lightning, and anyway, he'd never have vented his wrath privately. He *bathed* in spectacle. Which meant someone had done this to his staunch ally. Zeus had other enemies besides just Pandora. And if those enemies could do this to a body—to a Titan!—her idea of attacking Zeus with a knife was laughable.

An iron grip seized her by the back of the neck and hefted her up off the floor before thrusting her against a pillar, her sandals dangling as Hekate held her aloft. The witch Titan's golden eyes darted back and forth between Pandora and the mauled corpse, expression caught somewhere between shock and, perhaps, frustration.

It was Taygete who came in next, Kelaino's sister, with her hand to her mouth. The Pleiad didn't even get the chance to speak before Zeus shoved her to the ground beside Enyo's corpse.

"Treachery!" The king roared. "Treason!"

Hekate tossed Pandora aside and fell back out of the room, perhaps searching for other conspirators. Pandora landed on her knees, the impact sending daggers of agony up her legs. For the pain, she couldn't move, only gape as Zeus's fist descended upon Taygete's face. The Nymph's skull deformed under the blow, crunching inward like a broken vase.

Still, she did not die, but rather lay there, gurgling wetly as Zeus snared a hand in her hair, hefting her upward.

They'd kill Pandora just for being here. No Man could have committed this murder, but they wouldn't care. Whimpering, she crawled away, trying not to retch. Then she was on her feet, a stumbling, shambling run as she made back for the courtyard.

Alkoune stood before her, and from the look on her face, she seemed about to apprehend Pandora. Before the Nymph could do so, dark clouds covered the moon. A single rumble of thunder was the only warning. The bolt that streaked down from the heavens lit the night sky blue for an instant before the radiance sent spots dancing upon the edges of her vision.

The lightning bolt slammed into Alkoune, and the Nymph convulsed for a heartbeat before her charred flesh ruptured. The sickly-sweet scent of it drove Pandora's stomach to heaving, and she retched even as Alkoune's corpse collapsed in a smouldering heap.

Another hand yanked Pandora upward while she retched, Prometheus heaving her forward.

Chaos erupted like a volcano, the spilling of blood. There, to one side, Ares had begun hacking into Pleiad guards with abandon, his strength and speed unmatchable. The Olympian kicked off pillars with such grace as to seem to actually fly about the courtyard, cutting down screaming prey whether they fought back or no. More bolts of lightning crashed around the citadel, and Pandora didn't want to even imagine their victims.

Men and Titans dashed one way and another, and the stench of blood was almost overpowering. Fires leapt about the courtyard, catching bushes and trees, igniting tapestries, and immolating the corpses of the fallen.

Prometheus grabbed Pandora's hand and ducked into a lounge, pulling her behind him to take a back door out into the fish pool courtyard.

Releasing Pandora, the Titan raced to intercept Kelaino, who was actually running toward the chaos. Flames engulfed her hands, swirling about them like writhing serpents.

Stepping out of the shadows, Zeus's witch Hekate interposed herself between Prometheus and his niece, and Kelaino drew up short. "I do not want to hurt you ... but I will if I must," Hekate warned Prometheus. "I have orders to bring every last one of them to the king."

Even from where she stood, quivering, Pandora could see the tension tightening Prometheus's shoulders, and beyond Hekate, Kelaino raising her hands in what might have been a fighting posture.

"You do not want to fight me," Hekate warned Prometheus.

"You do not want to become *this*," Prometheus snapped back, waving his hand at the chaos engulfing the palace.

Ignoring him, Hekate spun. A coiling tendril of mist lanced from her outstretched fingers and caught up Kelaino, driving the Nymph to her knees.

Kelaino growled and thrust her arms forward. A half dozen arcing parabolas of flame raced across the courtyard, incinerating aught they passed as they converged upon Hekate. The witch raised her arms in front of herself and a shroud of icy mist sent the flaming tendrils hissing into vapour, even as they scorched away Hekate's veil.

"Stop this!" Prometheus bellowed.

But the Nymph and the Titan paid him no heed. Kelaino reached toward the blaze raging nearby, and more fire leapt toward her hand in sheets of flame that began to twist about her in a vortex. An ever-expanding maelstrom.

"You come into my home and bring death and chaos!" Kelaino spat.

To Pandora's utter shock, Hekate fell back, hands calling up wafts of mist and barriers of ice over and over in a seemingly vain attempt to forestall the Pleiad's wrath. A *Nymph* was overpowering a full-fledged Titan. What was she even seeing? She had heard each of the Pleiades had a gift, but this was, this was ... beyond belief. The conflagration overcoming the palace bent to her will, an inferno closing in upon Hekate, and the goddess seemed poised to fall as flames licked at her from all sides.

And then another blinding flash coursed through the sky, a bolt of lightning crashing down into Kelaino.

"No!" Prometheus shrieked.

Kelaino convulsed, all her flames abruptly sputtering out, washed away in Hekate's freezing vapours. The Pleiad dropped, flesh charred, steam rising from her corpse.

Growling, Prometheus roughly snatched up Pandora's wrist again and dragged her away, dashing through the courtyard.

PROMETHEUS GUIDED her quickly out through the gates—it seemed none of Zeus's people had had time to seal them yet—across the bridges, rushing through the moonlit city and down toward the harbour district. They skipped around it, however, toward the south of the city.

While his grip on her wrist had become gentle with the immediate danger having passed, Prometheus had still said naught the whole way, lost in his thoughts—and grief no doubt—and Pandora had not dared intrude into either. But now ...

"Where are we going?" she ventured.

Finally, he paused, looking at her with those sapphire eyes. "The Cove of Poseidon."

"The mer embassy?" Poseidon's son, Triton, served as emissary to

Atlantis, and a small segment of his palace lay above water for human visitors. "Why? What could they possibly offer us?"

Prometheus glanced behind them—checking for pursuit?—then resumed ushering her forward. They passed south of the city, to the Cove. A paved path led the way to a beach encircled by jagged black rocks. Tied to a short stone pier, they found three small boats. The Titan took one and guided it out with practiced ease, toward a stone platform rising from the waves.

Upon the platform rose up a peristyle-ringed palace that resembled a temple, complete with oceanic-themed pediments depicting sea horses and fish, and crowning sculptures of mermaids and mermen.

As their boat drew up along the platform, a mermaid abruptly splashed up beside them. Pandora yelped, covering her mouth with her hand. The creature had Atlantid dark hair and complexion, though gills flexed beneath the strands of her wet hair, and scales poked out from beneath the skin of her neck and face.

The mermaid snared a line from the boat and tied it to the platform.

"Thetis," Prometheus said.

"The ship's ready," the mermaid answered.

Pandora's mind whirred, not least because she'd never seen a mer this close before. Close enough to reach out and touch, had she been so bold. Given that these creatures were essentially undersea gods, she thought better of it. So, Prometheus had arranged with these mer to have a ship waiting for him. He'd paid or bribed or traded with them, or at least with Thetis, to have an escape prepared. He'd known or suspected Zeus would turn to violence here.

What did that mean? Had he done enough to forestall that violence? Certainly she'd heard him try to warn Kelaino, but the worst had happened anyway.

Prometheus leapt ashore, then extended a hand to her. When Pandora took it, he hefted her onto the platform. Thetis swam alongside them, guiding them to a small sailboat just a bit larger than the boat they'd left. Small enough for one person to sail it, though she doubted it would do well if he tried to make a crossing over the full Thalassa.

Which meant he must have somewhere else on this island in mind. Prometheus climbed aboard.

Pandora cast a last glance back at the polis that had been her home. The Pleiades were dead, and *maybe* Zeus and his minions would have tracked her down if she stayed. Maybe not, though. She was just a mortal. There was a chance she could have slipped back into her life.

But then, if she refused Prometheus, she'd never have access to the mysteries he presented. Never solve this puzzle. And was her life in Atlantis truly so blessed she could not stand to leave it?

So, she took his hand and hopped onboard.

INTERLUDE: KADMUS

1550 Silver Age

*T*he delicate touch of a finger along his jaw, tangling in his beard, giving life to flesh that ought to have surrendered long since. It tore him from the well of himself, forced light into his eyes. Such sensations left Kadmus wondering if this fresh torment was born of his deteriorating mind or actually conjured by the Kabeiri themselves. But it was not his captors he beheld upon opening his eyes, but the Nymph Harmonia, now holding his hand, eyes moist with unshed tears.

On his behalf? Even now, after all he had done to her?

Stone mounds yet held fast his ankles and he could not even guess how long it had been since he'd been allowed to even sit. His knees ached with the unbending stiffness, but even that paled before the grinding mess of knots that had become his lower back. All he could do, trapped in this cavern, was peer down into the ravine beside his unwalled prison and imagine jumping. Dried blood now cracked on his hands and thighs and he tried to push away the memory of what all these creatures had done to him. Besides the candle Harmonia bore, the cavern was lit by but a single torch in the distance, one that failed to do more than adumbrate the vastness of his prison.

"I did not want this for you," she said, heartache not *quite* suppressing the lyrical pitch of her voice, as if every word was an aria.

He believed her, of course, that she had not wanted it. Ah, but she had known it would come to pass. Of that, Kadmus no longer had any doubt. Had known it as an Oracle and tried to warn him—even knowing he would not listen, and this must invariably prove his end. The Fates had their threads wrapt around his neck like a noose, and he, the fool, kept pulling it tighter and tighter of his own accord.

The Kabeiri themselves offered the Nymph no impediment. Instead, they merely lingered in shadows like tenebrous monstrosities, waiting for their chance to feed upon yet more suffering. He wanted to believe Men incapable of the egregious cruelty they had visited upon him. Wanted to, but knew better, for he'd been a part of it. Willing to hurt because he'd been hurt, to take any steps to assuage his own pain and need, even if it meant perpetuating the cycle.

"You must understand," Harmonia said and looked over her shoulder at the misshapen spirits haunting the cavern. "He must bear witness to the cavalcade of time."

A snicker answered her, then the stone around his ankles melted into mud. Harmonia caught Kadmus as he pitched forward, and he managed to free his feet with a succession of wet *plops*. The agony of liberation seized him, drew forth the gasp of an aborted scream, his muscles protesting their sudden freedom. The Nymph eased him to the ground, and Kadmus moaned, giving in to his discomfort. How long he had been forced to remain standing, he could not even say, but it felt like days.

In the darkness, surrounded by these spirits, he had wept over the tortures they wracked him with, but now, before this woman, he could not indulge in such weakness. Could not let her see him thus.

So ... if he was not to die now, and not to be taken by one of these Kabeiri just yet, the only other course was forward. Much as it pained him, Kadmus pushed himself up to look into Harmonia's ochre eyes. There was pity there, so deep he could have drowned in it. In truth, he had to suppress the urge to beg her to help him, to save him.

But then, maybe she couldn't. Could never have done other than whatever her Oracular sight had revealed. He could go forward, where before there was naught save the endless bitter *here*. Was that not an improvement? In such straits, hope seemed almost a self-inflicted torture.

The Nymph draped his arm around her slight shoulders and helped him rise. She aided him easily enough. Had he misjudged when he thought her not gifted at all with Titan strength? Perhaps she had simply chosen not to resist when he dragged her from her home with such undue violence.

Oh, Kadmus had earned the torments that had befallen him, hadn't he? The wheel turned and turned, victims begetting yet more victims. And, oh Dagon, she had deserved so much better than he'd given her.

"I need him to see it," Harmonia said, apparently to the Kabeiri.

None of the spirits spoke, though they formed up into flanking columns, as if showing her the way to wherever the Nymph guided him. Supporting more of his weight than she ought to have had to— he'd grown even weaker than he realised, Ba'al take him—Harmonia led him beyond to stairs cut into the side of the ravine that bifurcated this cavern.

Kadmus almost groaned at the thought of climbing stairs in his condition, but then, aught was better than returning to where he'd just been.

They descended slowly, both due to his weakness, and because the stairs were steep and warded by no rail or barrier on one side. Harmonia's candle did very little to push back the expansive gloom below them. The wall twisted round the cavern, and the stairs actually doubled back beneath themselves at one point, creating quite a circuitous path to the base.

At last, they reached the bottom and found it uneven, lumpy and unworked, broken by stalagmites, and slick with water. Harmonia guided him further, until they came to a pool some four feet across, almost perfectly round, and bounded by a seamless stone lip.

Kadmus was parched and leaned forward for a drink but hesitated. The liquid didn't quite look like water and glinted silver in the light of Harmonia's candle.

"Quicksilver," the Nymph said as if he had asked his question aloud. "A Seeing Pool."

"What are we doing here?" Much as he hated to hear the edge in his voice—she did not deserve his resentment—he'd have killed for water. What use for this quicksilver if not to slake his thirst?

"You wanted to know about the whispers of Gaia? This quicksilver is the very same substance the Olympians use for their Seeing Pools within the Throne of Zeus. It shows them the World and, sometimes, a little more."

The Olympians spied on Men. It should not surprise him, one more violation from Zeus. Should not, yet ... "More what?"

"More of themselves," she said. "If you would look, perhaps you'll see the truth. You may even see her. You will not, however, *find* her, Kadmus."

He didn't want to cave in to Fate, but after all he had witnessed, it had become harder to deny its implacable grasp upon his life. Still, he pushed himself up onto the stone lip and looked, peering down into the shimmering pool. At first, he saw but a hint of his reflection.

Then something deeper, moving within the fluid, or perhaps within himself. As if the mirror spoke to him.

Life is moments.

And so very many had led him here.

THEY MADE SAIL FOR THEBES, Kadmus trusting his crew to navigate by starlight and knowing they'd mostlike arrive shortly after dawn. For his part, he stood at the bow, watching the waves break before the ship, imagining colonies of mer down there, gods of the deep. Ah, but then, even if such existed, his god Dagon must dwell in the waters around Phoenikia, and the Aegean belonged to Poseidon the Olympian mer.

When she had taken food and rest, Harmonia joined him up front, hefting herself to sit upon the gunwale with surprising grace. Or perhaps it ought not to have surprised him in the least, her being of Titan blood. In truth, all the genē—the aristoi bloodlines—claimed descent from Titans, but their blood was mostly so diluted with mortal lineage that only hints of the divine remained to Men like himself.

"Tell me, Titan," he said without looking at her—for her face held almost the same hypnotic quality as her voice. "How can it be that Poseidon is both a mer and a Titan?"

"Hmm. An astute question, *mortal.*"

Ah, yes, and she would have him use her name, as though they were allies or even friends? Still, her jab was a good one.

She murmured something under her breath, then he felt her gaze upon his back, drawing an inexplicable flush from him. "I cannot say with any certainty, to be honest, for such events were long before my time. Before even the Titanomachy that created this age. Just that he was a son of Tethys and came to be taken by a mer spirit."

"A *what* now? People can become mer?"

Harmonia drummed her fingers on the gunwale, the tips precariously close to his elbow as if in tease of some accidental caress. As if he might deserve such. "Beyond our world, some say beyond even the Underworld, lies a Realm of other beings. Spirits. To enter our world, they must share our bodies. More than that, I cannot really say. Certainly, though, Poseidon must have suffered such a fate."

"You speak of Fate quite often."

"Hmm. Did you know that Tethys had a husband, Okeanus, for whom the ocean is named?" He had not known. Another detail Europa would have loved, assuming she didn't already know. "He died in the Ambrosial War long, long years before the Titanomachy. Then some of Tethys's own children turned on her during that final war, and I guess she could bear it no more, for she fled, abandoning Kronos and the others to Zeus's wrath.

"Hera was the last, greatest of remaining Tethids and perhaps should have inherited the polis. But she rejected Thebes to found Argos, and Zeus granted Thebes to Demeter, whom he had wooed some time before." Now her fingers did brush his elbow, sending tingles up his arm. Kadmus pulled away. He would not give in to such manipulations. "I tell you this, Kadmus, because Thebes has a storied history, one so thick the polis nigh crumbles under the weight of it. Once, this place was Demeter's prize, but now she withers in despair over the loss of her daughter, whom she can never find again."

"I heard Hades must send her back every spring."

Harmonia laughed bitterly. "And you do imagine real life is so very pleasant as the fables we tell children? Demeter had her moments with her daughter and, when they passed, there was no reclaiming them." She grabbed his chin and pulled his head around to look at her so roughly he had to fight the urge to pull away. "Do you grasp my meaning, Phoenikian?"

Far more than he cared to. That his moments with Europa—with *any* of his loved ones—were, by definition, momentary, *transitory*, and transitioned, now, into mere memory. That any attempt to relive memory was doomed to failure.

And that knowledge cut him to the pith, leaving him raw beneath the paralysing intensity of her ochre gaze.

"I am not surrendering to Fate just yet," he snapped.

Harmonia released him. "Then brave the Underworld, find a way to reach it alive, claim *your* Persephone, even though by now she must too be a shade unable to bear the light. Still, drag her screaming beneath the sun and demand she return to what she was, though she will ever pale beside the memory of that time."

Kadmus balked at the image she conjured. "Save your metaphors. Europa yet lives and is neither Persephone nor Io nor any of the others."

Her smile seemed so sad he felt he could weep for seeing it.

🐌

SOME CLAIMED Oracles received their visions from the Fates themselves, though Kadmus had heard others claim the Olympians granted such insights. He couldn't say truly what he believed. To hear Harmonia speak of Fate and moments was to become entranced, not by the mere lyrical cadence of her voice, but by the impression that one sat before a campfire, hearing a tale from a bard who knew it backward and forward and might weave the telling in any order she wished.

Only a fool doubted the existence of Oracles, for surely some men and women predicted the future with alarming acuity, if rarely efficacious outcomes. But to sail beside one, to talk to an Oracle—if Oracle Harmonia was—not in the shadowed recesses of a temple, but beneath the open moonlight, seeing the wind whip her hair as though she were also but a mere woman ... such an experience sent the worlds of the sacred and vulgar crashing together in ways for which one could never prepare.

As they made port in Thebes and he followed Harmonia off the gangplank, Kadmus could not help but stare at the transcendent Nymph beside him. Were what she called whispers of Gaia merely a name for Oracular insight? If so, then the real question became, just how much of the future did she really foresee?

Here, by his side, walked an Oracle that intimated he would fail to find Europa, would, in fact, suffer because of his quest against her father. Or, if not an Oracle, perhaps she was a more loyal daughter than she appeared, leading him astray. But Kadmus felt elsewise, deep in his very bones.

Seemingly unaware of the awe that had settled upon him, Harmonia led him into Thebes's harbour. The city itself lay some seven hundred feet above them, upon a cliff, and Kadmus could scarcely imagine climbing it, though a simple marble staircase cut into the cliffside offered the only means of reaching the city.

"Shall I comment on the irony that Tethys, famed for her love of the sea, would build her city so far above the ocean?" he asked.

"Before the peace that followed the Ambrosial War, skirmishes were the norm between Titans. Any defensive advantage might mean the difference between life and death for the citizens of a polis. So she fortified a defensible position and relied, through pacts with mer, on dragons and sea monsters spawned by Echidna to defend her waters. Maybe that's how Tethys actually wound up one of the winners of that war."

Ambrosial War? The Titans strictly controlled the Ambrosia, this much he knew. Was the war how they formed those laws? Whatever Harmonia spoke of seemed so long ago, he could not harbour a guess at its import.

They reached the steps, and he had to crane his neck to even see the cliff peak. Further up the cliff, the sound of rushing water emanated from a severe cataract pitching over the cliffside and down to the sea.

"I hope your ribs have finished healing," Harmonia teased as Kadmus looked back to the stairs.

"I'm fine."

Still, they paused at a landing halfway up, and Kadmus came to the balustrade with a show of taking in the view of the sparkling sea. An affectation that allowed him to catch his breath. Others passed them while he rested, including a group of porters carrying crates so unwieldy it put him to shame for claiming this respite.

"I try to imagine what life was like in the last Age," Harmonia said. "The Ouranid League ruled all these lands between them, and Titans around the world obeyed their laws if they wanted the Ambrosia to flow into their goblets."

Ambrosia ... the very lifeblood of Titans, so it was said, utterly forbidden for mortals.

Kadmus sneered. "How is that the least different from how your father runs things, save now one Titan controls it all and thinks aught he beholds his due?"

Harmonia snorted lightly. "I suppose that means you're ready to continue the trek upward."

It was hard to argue with that, given the jibe he'd just made, so he followed her the rest of the way to the clifftop. From here, he could get a better view of the fall north of the city. Despite his fatigue, pain, and desperation, he felt the edge of his mouth curve in a smile at the stunning sight of so much rushing water.

"There is beauty here," Harmonia said, following his gaze.

They had to pause before the great wall encircling the polis, joining a queue of visiting aristoi waiting to enter the gate, though Harmonia cut ahead of the merchants and other commoners. Perhaps the guards knew her, or perhaps they simply recognised her as a Titan by her aspect, but all waved her right through, and Kadmus followed in her wake.

Beyond the wall, a main street led to an agora, and beyond that, to a hill—perhaps even a mountain, if one were generous—upon which sat the acropolis.

"Fuck," he mumbled, unable to help himself.

"We can rest first." She pointed to a street vendor selling apples.

Yes, a bit of rest. Then more climbing. Then, maybe, answers.

Moments scattered and ran from him. They bled one into the next, flowing round and round without need or desire for mortal conceits of order. Moments were memories, and memory was like water. Once a drop joined an ocean, it became inseparable from the whole.

Life is moments, *she had said.*

And he was those moments.

Little as it surprised Kadmus, Helion proved fruitless in their search for Europa and Pandora. Despite his misgivings—for Helios was the last of the Ouranid League who had once stood against Zeus and thus not a likely ally to the Olympian—he'd given in when Kilix insisted on searching the isle. The island of Helion served as the gateway to the greater Elládosi world. Helion might have—had the Fates been on their side—offered some clue.

Thus, they had come here, walked the streets, gaped—as Kadmus ever did—at the gold-plated palace of the great Titan, asked their fruitless questions, and found themselves bereft of answers. No, Zeus had not stopped on this island, and they had lost another day.

Now, Kadmus wound the line of their small bireme, preparing to head underway with all possible haste. The ringed harbour at Helion polis, while smaller than that of Tyros, dwarfed Kadmus's home port in grandeur. Not least for the towering bronze statue of Helios himself straddling the inlet.

The Colossus, Men called it.

"Think the Titan intended for everyone to have to pass between his legs to reach him?" Kilix asked, apparently following Kadmus's gaze. Some among their scant crew laughed at that.

Kadmus found little amusing in considering the prodigious lusts of Titans. Zeus had raped his way around the Thalassa Sea, taking any woman cursed with beauty that fell under his gaze. Kadmus offered little credence to any claim the Titan King had grown worse in the past few centuries—a man was what he was, and he imagined Zeus had been forcing his way upon women since the dawn of time. People just talked about it more once he declared himself King of the Gods. For that matter, some bards' tales claimed he'd turn into animals or other such foolery just to enable his assaults. Ever more outlandish tales glorifying the king's appetites.

As for Helios, that one did not hear about as many of his victims compared to Zeus did little to alleviate Kadmus's ire. How many golden-eyed Titan-descended Heliads bore his blood? So far as he knew, both Nike and Kirke were Heliads, and they might well have played a part in all this. Bah! Dagon take all Titans, then. Let the mer god drag them all into the deep and leave the Earth a better place.

"Well," Kilix said when Kadmus offered no answer. "I think we can agree Hera would have Zeus's balls for a necklace if he brought a mistress to Olympus."

Now Kadmus turned from the Colossus to favour his brother with a withering stare. "You think his wife controls him? He took Io right out from under her nose in Argos, did he not?"

"Hera wasn't there at the time," Kilix pointed out. "And for that matter, I doubt Zeus would be so bold as to take Europa back to Hera's own city, either."

Kadmus sighed to concede the point. No, Hera might not control Zeus, but if tales told true, neither would the King of Olympus be so brazen as to bring his new pallake to her doorstep. "Perhaps he took them to the Aegean Islands?"

"Seems a fair guess, I'd wager, but perhaps we ought to check Lydia and Phrygia on the way. Hera's influence there has limits."

And Lydia lay just beyond Helion, though they'd have to skirt the coast to reach Phoeba and any hopes of finding leads. It would waste a bit more time if Kilix was wrong, but there was a chance …

The impossibility of his task settled upon his shoulders like a physical weight. Were they to search the entire ambit of the World? To spend years in the vain pursuit of a Titan they'd never find? Or to give up and forever know they had abandoned their own sister?

Kadmus turned away from his brother, once more looking to the Colossus as the ship made sail. No one spoke among the sailors. Indeed, the somber mood had held since they'd left Phoenikia on an errand they all had to know they would mostlike never return from. Given the king's command not to come back without Europa, Kadmus had chosen crewmen without wives or children to miss. Oh, if they lived through challenging Zeus and still failed, he supposed some of these men might make their own way back to Tyros.

Some.

Not most.

Most of the ninety men that had come would not return.

"You're petulant," Kilix said, glancing up at the Colossus as they passed beneath. "The sculptors didn't carve the goods under the tunic, of course."

"What?" Kadmus demanded.

"Helios has no cock up under the—"

"Who the fuck do you think you're calling petulant?" Kadmus had half a mind to hit his older brother, even knowing that given his bruised ribs, he'd like as not have wound up on his own arse for it. "Shall I dance and cavort at the murder of my brother and rape of my sister? Shall I sing shanties and fantasise about mermaids in Dagon's palace?"

"No," Kilix said with a shake of his head. "Grief is fitting. But your sullenness extends beyond it, as if you find no balance between soaring in elation and wallowing in despair. You were always that way, and it becomes so tedious for the rest of us. Worse still, you yet deign to blame *me* as if you think I might have stood up to the most powerful Titan in the World had I been there. Even had he not brought Hekate to assist him with witchcraft." He spread his hands wide in mockery. "So, what is it? Jealousy over me getting my flute wet while you were getting your arse beat? Does that so vex you, brother?"

Fair enough. Sometimes it was worth getting hit back. Kadmus's sudden jab took Kilix right in the mouth. His brother stumbled into the gunwale, flailed, and pitched over backward. Kadmus grabbed his tunic, just barely keeping him from falling into the ocean—tempting as it was.

The man, however, didn't hit him back on regaining his footing, instead, opting to rub his jaw and fix Kadmus with a glare. "Right, then. Feel better for it?"

Kadmus looked away, out at the sea. "You have no idea."

No, that wasn't where it began. Something before.

THE GENTLE SPRING had drawn on, rolling into a lazy summer by the time the trireme made harbour in Tyros once more, laden now with saffron and dozens of amphorae of Elládosi wine. While Kadmus had not sailed for Atlantis for mere trade, one did not visit the great city without bringing home goods aplenty from the farthest reaches of the Thalassa.

Goods, and a few treasures besides. Kadmus offered the bundle wrapt in his satchel a pat, reassuring himself it was still there. Soon enough, his sister's child might have a *new* favourite uncle. Hand on a line, he hopped onto the gunwale and stared at a pier that could not approach too soon.

No, and Tyros harbour was thick to bursting with ships coming and going. There, a Neshian bagala probably heavy with furs and ivory, and beyond, a Nusantaran dhow, no doubt bearing silks and maybe even sapphires out of the mountains of Mu. Mostly, though, other Phoenikian triremes and biremes crawled about in their intricate dance. Kadmus's people had long since dominated the eastern Thalassa, so much so, others called them the Sea People, a name that invariably brought a smile to his face.

As soon as it drew close enough, even before the ship was made fast, Kadmus leapt onto the pier, sandals slapping the docks as he raced along them, almost reeling from the sudden reek of fish, spices, and humanity. A man could forget the stench when amongst it long enough, but after the clean sea air, the odours here seemed redoubled.

The harbour district actually lay on an island just offshore of the mainland, and Kadmus wended his way through narrow, crate-clogged alleys to navigate the isle. The main breezeways were so thick with merchants and porters it would have taken twice as long to reach the causeway that connected the harbour to Tyros proper.

Of course, when he finally did get there, that too—an arching bridge over the strait—was congested with carts and pedestrians flowing in both directions. A defensive wall surrounded the main city, but the gate guards paid only half a mind to those streaming into the city and none at all to those leaving. Still, when he drew nigh, the pair of them snapped to attention.

"My prince," one said with a polite incline of his head.

Kadmus quirked a smile. Yes, he could have reprimanded them for their lackadaisical demeanour, but then he'd have ruined his own mood as well. Besides, the summer had that taste to it, as if something in the air whispered of afternoon naps and long nights watching the stars and sipping spiced wine. Who was he to steal that from anyone when no danger had threatened Tyros since his brother had united their family with the Arabus dynasty of Byblos?

Instead, he slipped past the guards and made his way into Tyros. Here, the exotic aromas of the harbour no longer dominated, allowing the full reek of human waste to come to the forefront, like a slap in the face. "Enough to wake one from fancies ..." he muttered. There was no imagining spiced wine while avoiding stepping in piss-filled gutters.

Here and there, citizens recognised him, especially as he drew closer to his father's palace upon the Hill of Epaphus. They greeted the youngest of their princes with cheery smiles and hearty welcomes, clearly having been inside the walls long enough to become inured to the local fragrances. As would he once more, no doubt.

Kadmus paused very little in his hurry to reach the court. The moment he did so, heralds rushed in to tell his father he had returned. King Agenor indulged his children's whims and fancies, without doubt, but he demanded a certain respect, especially in front of the watching court. They were, after all, mortal heirs of Titans and as such compelled deference, at least publicly.

So Kadmus paraded himself through his father's hall, gaze locked upon the man on his throne, before falling to one knee. "Father." Let the court have their performance. "I return from Atlantis successful."

His father motioned him to rise and Kadmus did so. "Tell me."

"Queen Elektra has agreed all Nusantaran imports fall under our purview. Any ship that attempts to circumvent us may be seized with impunity, even in Atlantean waters."

And thus, the Sea People maintained control of all the Thalassa east of Atlantis. Drachmae would flow like water, and all would name the sister cities of Tyros and Byblos with awe.

Almost imperceptible lines of worry eased from the king's brow. "Well done, my son."

Taking it as a dismissal, Kadmus rose.

"I'll call for a symposium tonight in celebration." A pause. "Your brother is in from Byblos, you know."

No, he had not known or imagined, and he had to stop himself from dashing from the throne room just to find the man. Dagon's deep! He'd not seen his brother in a year and had enough stories to tell to keep them up late for a fortnight!

A quick inquiry with the servants revealed Phoenix had taken to the courtyard gardens, and indeed, the man now lounged amid the cedars with his bride. Who was clearly thick with child, hand resting upon her bulging belly.

Kadmus planted his feet before the pair, hands on his hips. Before he could even open his mouth, Phoenix had lunged to his feet, sweeping him up in an embrace that actually hefted him off the ground.

"Little brother!"

Kadmus wriggled free and, instead of looking straight at Phoenix, turned to his wife. "Kassiopeia didn't seem to think me little ..."

A mock scowl crossed his brother's face, though the princess of Byblos smiled indulgently. "I'm afraid the child is Phoenix's." A wink. "This time."

"Uncle Kadmus!" He'd not been gone long, but he swore Pandora's voice had changed.

Kadmus spun to see the five-year-old girl racing toward him, trailed by her mother. Of course, Europa, his little sister, wasn't *actually* Pandora's mother but had taken the orphan child as her own, though she remained unwed. After all, their father denied Europa naught, and besides, when a Titan asked you to care for a child, you did so. Kadmus had oft wondered whether Pandora was, in fact, Nike's own bastard girl, and if the Titan had given her up to avoid the shame of it. Pandora had Nike's Heliad eyes, though many throughout the Thalassan world did.

"Uncle Kadmus, Aunt Kassiopeia got a babe in her belly," Pandora blurted, throwing her arms around him. "She ate it and if I'm naughty she'll eat me too and then I'll be her daughter instead of momma's or maybe I'll have two mommas and I missed you. And, Uncle Kadmus, I made a trireme out of branches and it really floats! You have to see my trireme that I made today. It floats!"

Kadmus knelt before the girl and withdrew the bundle from his satchel, handing it to her. Pandora tore away the cloth wrapping and tossed it aside, revealing the wooden cube beneath it.

"A puzzle box!" the girl exclaimed, immediately setting to pushing and prodding, trying to figure out how to open it.

Kadmus winked at Phoenix. Who was the favourite uncle *now*?

"Thank you," Europa said on the girl's behalf.

Kadmus embraced his sister too. "Any sign of our last sibling?"

Phoenix snorted. "Kilix is Kilix."

So he was. And that meant Kadmus would most like see the man when the wine began to flow at the symposium and not a moment sooner.

Instead, he walked with his brother and sister towards the garden pool, while Kassiopeia trailed behind with Pandora. This, Kadmus was wise enough to know, was the good life. Oh, by Ba'al's stormy arse, he'd spent enough time as a young man in perpetual disquiet, clamouring for honour or attention through feats of swordplay, seamanship—piracy, oft enough—or general foolery. It had been Europa, in the end, that had reminded him he needed to enjoy his moments.

"Life is moments, so treasure them and share them," she'd said, with the air of repeating something she'd heard or read.

"It seems," Kadmus observed as they reached the pond, "now you shall both have children to dote on, while I remain alone."

"Perhaps you ought not to have rejected the princess of Nineveh."

"Oh, I am not truly bitter." Well, maybe a little. Besides, it was Father who had rejected that suit when the King of Nineveh demanded a bit too generous a maritime concession.

"Solved it!" Pandora blurted, proudly hefting the now open puzzle box over her head. "Uncle Kadmus, I solved it and I liked it and I loved it!"

Kadmus gaped at her. It had taken him the better part of an evening fiddling with the box to open it. Titan-spawned child, indeed. She was too smart for her own good.

Europa shrugged as if reading his mind. "She's started reading Sikarbaal since you left."

Kadmus hadn't known the child could read at all.

Phoenix slunk down on the silt. "Shit. I can barely understand that philosophical drivel."

"Oh, I doubt she grasps the concepts," Europa admitted. "But the sheer possibility she's been learning the *words* astounds."

A prodigy. Kadmus roughed up her hair. "That's my girl." He looked to Europa and smiled.

Moments.

Just moments.

IF ORACLES like Harmonia could see the future, did that mean it existed alongside the present? Was time, then, but a story Men told themselves to feign order in the face of chaos?

THE HEART of Thebes's acropolis was the Temple of Demeter, a blocky and relatively unadorned edifice without pediments or any real indication of which Olympian drew worship. The columns were unfluted, the stonework simple, almost seamless.

Harmonia led Kadmus not to the temple, but around it, to a palace that seemed pretentious next to the unassuming place of worship. Great marble stairs ran up the mountain to a fresco-painted hall covered in greenery and surrounded by flower gardens boasting anemones and hellebores and more plants Kadmus didn't even recognise. Laurel shrubs and plane trees enclosed the whole of the place.

Walking up these stairs had the hairs on the back of his neck rising, as if he strode into another world, a place mortal Men had no business treading. Here, his breath alone violated some unspoken tenet of the World. Though he knew Demeter must surely receive

Men as petitioners and slaves, he could not push down the lump in his throat nor still his dancing stomach.

At the summit, a barely clad woman—another Nymph, perhaps, given her radiant beauty and above-average height—received them and exchanged a few whispered words with Harmonia. The woman then waved them onward, into the palace proper.

Inside, the only light came from the atrium, with the braziers unlit. A woman he could only take for Demeter herself sat on the grass, within a beam of sunlight as if the rays had carried her down from the firmament to grace the Earth with her presence. Or perhaps that was the effect the Titan cultivated deliberately. She had the dark, almost ebony skin of the people of Inumiden, a race Kadmus had met but a few times on his sea voyages, and jet-black, disheveled hair badly in need of attendance.

The Titan glanced at them with glassy, empty eyes. A visage that offered the impression of a shade wandering the Underworld, hollow and listless. Here, an Olympian, a self-styled goddess who ruled the Elládosi ... Broken and hollow, like so much cracked ostraka scattered across the floor.

Hand on his back, Harmonia gave him a gentle shove toward the Titan, and Kadmus fell to his knees before her. Though Demeter met his gaze, Kadmus could not shake the impression those lifeless eyes failed to see him.

"I ..." He cleared his throat. "I am Prince Kadmus of Tyros, and I come to you in the most dire of need, Lady Demeter." The urge seized him to glance back at Harmonia, as if she might help him plead his case, though he knew he must do this himself. "Just under a month ago, Mighty Zeus came to our fair city and called upon my father's palace. Without preamble he demanded my sister, Europa, as his pallake." He hesitated. "It is not the first time the King has ..." Why was he even saying such? Everyone knew about Zeus. His tongue felt heavy, his words uncooperative.

With a grunt, Demeter climbed to her feet, revealing a height much greater than he'd realised. A full foot taller than himself, at least. "So, the King once more continues the trend of *men* who think us here but for their benefit. And you respond in kind, yes?" Her gaze flicked to Harmonia.

"What? No, I never—"

The Titan grabbed him by the back of the neck and hefted him up, leaving his feet dangling, the edge of his sandals just brushing the grass. "Did you or did you not abduct this Nymph? Threaten her? Force yourself upon her?"

"No!" Not that last one, at least.

Again, a brief look at Harmonia, then back at him. "Either way, you think yourself so much better than Zeus while you abduct a woman as well!"

How did she even know that? "But I—"

"You come here, whining over the disrespect shown to your womenfolk, while perpetuating the same yourself. Does your greater physical strength justify you to give no consideration to the dignity and will of women? Is that the World as you see it?" Demeter bared her teeth at him. "All right, then. Let strength rule."

A flick of her wrist flung him out of the atrium and onto the marble floor. The impact dazed him, and before he could rise, guards he hadn't known were there had seized his arms and yanked him upward.

"Take the abductor to the Children of Gaia," Demeter ordered.

"Wait," Harmonia protested, though not with the fervour Kadmus might have hoped for.

"No," Demeter snapped. "No, he walked his path willingly, and I imagine you warned him it would lead him to a bitter end. Let him see the fruits of his life."

Without further prompting, the guards dragged him from the palace, and Kadmus did not bother trying to resist. They carried him back into the sunlight, planted him on the ground, then forced him to walk down the stairs and, finally, into the Temple of Demeter. What were they about? Did these Children of Gaia live in the temple itself?

He could not imagine these men would answer his questions, so he posed none. Inside the temple, they shoved him forward, past a sacrificial altar, and into dark recesses normally reserved for priestesses. Within these shadows, they guided him to a staircase leading down into the floor itself, into some basement.

"Go," one of them snapped, and Kadmus could have sworn a slight tremor shook the guard's voice.

Perhaps he could have fought them, fatigued and bruised as he was. But what would it avail him? Besides, Harmonia had claimed these same Children of Gaia knew secrets of the future and might have the answers he sought. Maybe, then, Demeter's sentence upon him could still serve his ends.

Thus, he descended into darkness.

§

QUICKSILVER STRANDS TUGGED UPON KADMUS, *leaving him caught as if in a maelstrom, mind roiling upon the threads of his life, even as he sought after Europa's. And behind that maelstrom lay a dread, as of Fate circling him like some squamous, saurian predator ready to trap him in inescapable coils, ensnaring him in an incandescent gaze.*

Time, twisted in maddening whorls.

§

IF ZEUS PASSED THROUGH LYDIA, he would most like have come through Phoeba, the capital city and major port. Founded by Phoebe, the polis was now ruled by her granddaughter, the Olympian Artemis. Since all the Olympians were—so far as Kadmus knew— loyal to their king, it seemed fair to imagine he'd have trusted her.

Whether or not that meant they walked into danger in coming to Phoeba, Kadmus could not wager a guess. Would Artemis even note their presence, and if the goddess did so, would she give one whit about the hopeless quest of a pair of mortals to save their sister?

Either way, they sailed into the port a day after leaving Helion, made fast the ship, and took stock of the city. Kilix had come here before, but this was a first voyage for Kadmus and, despite it all, he found himself revelling in the sights. Was that a betrayal of Europa? Was it wrong for him to take even momentary joy in these travails?

How could it *not* be wrong?

Kilix pointed to an island just barely visible upon the horizon beyond the harbour. "That's Lesvos. It's one of the largest of the Aegean islands, so probably worth a look if we find naught here." Then, he indicated the main city, out on the plain. "I'll head up to the acropolis and check to see if he called in upon Artemis herself."

"You plan to ask her?"

"Of course not, don't be daft. But servants will know if he came to her palace, and she has a grand temple up there. Lots of people around. Other aristoi may talk to me." Kilix pointed to the lower city. "You talk to the merchants and commoners below. If his ship came through at all, they may know about it."

Kadmus squinted at the city. Far beyond it, in the hazy distance, lay the great Arad Mountains he'd long heard about but never seen. Not so impressive compared to the mountains of Phoenikia, so far as he could tell. Which meant Kilix was the one getting to see the only aspects of the polis worth seeing.

But then, Kadmus had not come here for pleasure. Europa was everything. "Fine. I'll lay down a few drachmae and see where it leads. Meet back here at sunset."

❧

AS IT TURNED OUT, the lower city actually featured a rather impressive amphitheater dedicated to Artemis's mother, Leto. Under other circumstances, Kadmus might have enjoyed spending time there, chatting with the locals, but instead, he'd managed to bleed through drachmae and find no leads amid sailors, merchants, or even a herald. He'd left Tyros with a full purse, but at this rate, he'd be a pauper in a fortnight.

If Zeus had come here, he'd done so in a disguise so convincing no one recognised him. Or he'd simply avoided Lydia altogether.

Either way, time was of the essence. The longer they spent searching, the slimmer their chances of ever finding their sister became.

And the only word anyone offered was a rumour that the King of Olympus had a hidden refuge on Lesvos. A slim chance indeed, one perhaps invented by him freely throwing around coins. Flash money about, and someone would offer answers, even if that someone had to retrieve said answers from his own arsehole.

As he walked, Kadmus had to keep forcing an image of Europa from his mind. A vision of her victimised by that monstrous Titan. Sobbing, hoping for her brothers to save her. They could not even *find* her. Self-loathing had his gut roiling, as if a pale fire burned in his chest. He could not even recognise the man he had become.

It was, in fact, before sunset when Kadmus boarded their bireme once more and leaned against the gunwale. This entire polis had proved a waste of time, and now they had lost another day. He banged his palms upon the wood and, finding it offered no solace, did so harder and harder, ignoring his growing pain. Ignoring the stares of nearby sailors.

Did they wish to look upon his display? Dagon's deep, how he wanted to scream at them! To rage and roar at how they had no idea what he endured. What his sister endured. No one could imagine the weight of such circumstances. How *dare* anyone judge him for his temper in such straits? How dare the very Fates saddle them with such times?

"Brother?" Kilix asked from the gangplank.

Kadmus spun on him, glowering. Maybe Kilix had been right before. Maybe he couldn't have done a godsdamned thing had he been in the throne room, save perhaps join Phoenix in death. Yes, Kadmus threw blame at him ... for he could not shoulder the burden of it all himself. He had tried and failed. He'd had Zeus in his very grasp and been tossed aside like a child, his blows of little more effect than ... if five-year-old Pandora had attempted to physically overpower him.

Even knowing this, feeling the truth of it, he still could not forgive Kilix. He had to blame *someone* else.

"What?" Kadmus demanded.

"There is naught here."

"Then get onboard. We can still make Lesvos tonight before sunset."

Kilix didn't move. "No."

"What?"

"No, I'll search all of Lydia and Phrygia even if I must call upon Artemis and Apollon themselves. If Zeus came here, I will find him. And if I do not, brother, I shall accept Fate and go no further than these lands." Kilix's visage seemed to waver between a sad smile and utter despair.

Fate? Fucking *Fate*? Kadmus faltered, the pain in his ribs suddenly grown worse. "What are you saying?"

"We always knew Father sent us on a fool's errand. Perhaps, apart, we increase the chance one of us finds her and might return home a hero. Or stay together and most like both see in the other a reminder of our failures."

"If this is because I hit you—" Kadmus began.

Kilix raised a hand. "Do you really think we shall work this out, brother? Do you truly believe we can succeed at all, much less while at each other's throats? Go to Lesvos, go to Naxos, go to godsdamned Kronion if it pleases you." He hesitated, then sighed. "Should I find her, I'll send word. But we cannot do this together, and you know the truth of that. We are not boons to one another. Not after this, and maybe we never were."

No, perhaps not. It should have been Phoenix who lived.

The thought slipped into his mind like a loathsome thief, unbidden and unwelcome. A burglar who stole from him his very self-respect. For what sort of man thinks thus of his brother? The very thought disgusted Kadmus, even as he could not shake it. Yes, Phoenix would have fought harder, braver, more loyally.

And Kadmus deserved to be blasted from this Earth by Ba'al's bolts for such ruminations.

Perhaps Kilix saw it upon his face. Perhaps his brother merely had given over any further interest in conversation. Either way, the man turned and strode back into the city.

And Kadmus knew, almost of a certainty, that he had lost another sibling.

❧

THE LAST RAYS of the sun glinted off the sea like a radiant field as the bireme drew up along Lesvos. No doubt, had Kadmus had a mind to search for it and perhaps wait for morn, he might have found a town to make port in. Instead, saying naught to the crew, he vaulted the gunwale and dove into the waters.

The sudden cool rushed over him, a shock back into the present, forcing him to acknowledge he yet lived. Swimming ashore, though a short distance, *also* reminded him of his bruised ribs.

By the time he reached the land, his sides felt apt to burst at the seams. Kadmus pitched onto his knees, panting. What in Dagon's deep had he been thinking?

He wiped seawater from his eyes with the back of his hand. Oh, of course he knew what he'd been thinking. He'd thought he'd now lost all his siblings. He was thinking his life amounted to naught if he could not find Europa, and soon.

He'd allow himself a night and day to search this island, then on to the next.

There was a possibility the stories in Phoeba would prove true, and Zeus, perhaps, really did have some hidden refuge on this island. If so, it would not be in any town, but out among the hills in the island's heart. A slim chance, he knew, for men would tell most any tale one wished to hear when drachmae were involved, and Kadmus had thrown around plenty to be sure.

Groaning, he pushed himself. With the sun now dipping behind the horizon, he'd not easily find hidden shelters, but he could at least make his way up to the hills themselves, so he'd have less ground to cover in the morning.

His sandals made wet smacking sounds on the sand as he

tromped away from the ocean. Taking another night meant Europa would probably suffer ... No. Such thoughts would not avail him. Zeus had made no secret he'd taken Kadmus's sister out of lust and he'd no doubt made good on his desires many times by now. Kadmus could not spare her that. He could, however, still find her and bring her home. He'd lost Phoenix and Kilix now, and he would not lose Europa.

He had to hold on to the memory of her face.

Away from the shore, the landscape began to rise into open plains and gentle hillocks. Ahead, by moonlight, he could make out steeper slopes and valleys, any of which might have offered secluded places for a Titan's bastion.

Of a sudden, his sandal caught on a rock and sent him sprawling into the grass. The fall drove a fresh jolt of pain into his ribs, and Kadmus lay there groaning. Unbidden came the memory of that night.

The blinding light, the ringing in his ears. The explosion, the wine aflame. The calamity of ...

Of Zeus and his witch, Hekate, taking *everything* from his family without a second thought. Capricious, callous Titans who thought Men were animals to be used and discarded as it suited them.

With a moan, Kadmus rolled over. He'd barely slept since that night. As he had no camp to pitch—had brought naught save his leather cuirass and his xiphos—he just lay there, unsure whether he longed for sleep or dreaded it. If he closed his eyes, would the lightning be there once more? The terror and pain and, worst of all, the horror of waking to find it had all really happened?

Despite his efforts, sleep claimed him anyway.

Life is moments.

Memories and moments.

But she hadn't meant that. Not such moments.

ॐ

Dawn awakened him and he found a stork watching him, as if shocked to see a Man out here, so far from his fellows. Kadmus regarded the bird for a few breaths before pushing himself up.

Europa had no time for any such petty indulgences as watching birds. Maybe not even time for him to kill and eat the thing.

No, he paused just long enough for a piss and then took off for those hills once more, barely suppressing the urge to call her name over and over, to shout for her.

Europa! Europa!

Could he have done more that night? Could he have stopped Zeus somehow and averted all this madness? Averted the loss of a sister and two brothers, as well, to say naught of little Pandora.

Hour after hour, hill after hill, on and on, until despair slithered around his heart like a constricting serpent. Until he thought of giving over his search, oh so many times. Until the pain in his ribs redoubled from climbing so many slopes.

Then, there, in a valley nestled between two hills, he caught sight of a tiny plume of smoke. Following this, he found a tiny house near a stream. Tiny, but hardly humble, for a peristyle of caryatid columns surrounded the abode, making it seem more a rural temple to Artemis or Demeter than a home.

A palace for Zeus to bring his conquests? Slipping loose his sword, Kadmus plodded slowly down into the valley. He fell into a crouch as he slunk closer. His only chance against a Titan, especially one like Zeus, was to catch him by surprise and put a blade through his neck before the god could react.

As he drew nigh to the bastion, a gentle song reached him, a woman singing of the founding of Thebes, so long ago by the Titan Tethys, now fled the world. Ironic, given Tethys was ancestress to the Tethid line, and thus to Kadmus, through Io.

Europa? Could that be her voice? It became harder to tell when she sang.

The strumming of a lyre soon joined the words, light and Etheric.

Kadmus rose to his full height but continued to move with caution, trying to silence the slap of his sandals upon the marble floor. Beyond the peristyle lay a fresco-painted great chamber, with an open-roofed courtyard in the centre, where sat a woman playing the lyre with her back to him.

For a moment, he took her onyx hair and deep complexion for Europa, but no, it was not her.

Continuing to creep, Kadmus made his way to her side and rested his xiphos upon her shoulder, the sword's blade just shy of her cheek. The song stopped abruptly, and the woman stiffened.

"Who are you?" he demanded.

"Harmonia." As her name implied, her voice held a musical quality, one he *so* longed to hate her for, as if such perfection was an affront to the rest of humanity. Slowly, the woman turned, pushing his blade away with two fingers. Her dark eyes meant she was probably of the Atlantid genē rather than the Tethid one, like Kadmus and his blue-eyed kin.

"Is this not the bastion of Zeus?"

"It is," she admitted.

"And are you one of his pallakae, Harmonia?"

Now she snickered and offered a single shake of her head. "His daughter, by Elektra."

Oh. The Titan's own daughter, by one of the Queens of Atlantis no less, hidden here to secure her from Hera. That she was in hiding probably meant she was a Nymph, a Titan of lesser power, for Zeus did not hide his stronger bastard children.

"You see the truth of it," Harmonia said, staring into his eyes as if she could read the very pith of his soul in them.

Her gaze left him squirming and, despite himself, falling back a step. "Where is Europa?" he spat at her, knowing he ought to have explained himself but too irate to care.

Harmonia folded her hands in her lap. "I know who you are." As if she had any *right* to know things no one could have told her so quickly. "I know it well, Son of Agenor. So, believe me when I tell you, it behooves you to abandon this quest. It does not end with you bringing your sister back to Phoenikia. It cannot end how you wish, for the Fates have decreed otherwise."

No. He refused to accept that Fate had demanded he fail. Instead, he pointed his xiphos at the Nymph once again. "Where would your father have taken my sister? Tell me, woman, or Zeus shall also know the pain of losing those he loves!"

Harmonia rose, striding toward him as if utterly unafraid of his sword. The brazenness—so like her father—left his knees weak. What if he had misstepped in threatening her? What if he had misjudged her as Nymph, when she actually held the greater powers of a full Titan? Surely not to match an Olympian like Athene or Artemis, but enough to smite him despite him bearing the blade.

"I enjoin you once more—turn away from a quest that will bring you only pain, Kadmus."

Well, Ba'al's stormy arse. If she smote him now, it was hardly unexpected. He had known that to pursue a Titan, to strive with him and his kin, was to court death. And if so, he would at least look death in the eye before it sent him to the Underworld. "Abandon my sister, you mean? Live in ignominy and failure?"

"It is not failure to accept Fate."

Kadmus lunged, caught her wrist, and yanked her toward the doorway. His gamble paid off, for she stumbled, offering no more resistance than a mortal woman. Once more, he pointed the sword at her. "Move. If Zeus has taken a woman dear to me, I shall return the favour."

PART II

***

With Ambrosia forbidden to Man, it was, perhaps inevitable that someone would attempt to concoct a facsimile. Thus were the Silver and Bronze Ages plagued by the blight of Nectar. The nature of its underground distribution muddles any attempt to accurately uncover exactly where it began, but records indicate there were multiple variants of the brew. One thing seems certain, however. While Nectar did offer some facsimile of the benefits of Ambrosia, it also caused a rapid onset of madness, violence, and, on occasion, complete metamorphosis.

— Kleio, Analects of the Muses

9

PYRRHA

216 Golden Age

*A*t fifteen, Pyrrha found she could shift her focus to embrace the Sight without the aid of death. At will, she could look across the Veil and perceive the cavalcade of shades who flitted through Thebes and its harbour. Outside the city, the ghosts grew fewer in number while the sense of other, *older* presences watching intensified.

As on this misty evening, while she wandered the woods beyond the polis, ever searching for sign of spirits. Men told tales of dryads or other sylvan denizens lurking just beyond the bounds of civilisation, and though she felt the presence of something she could not name, she rarely saw sign of aught besides ghosts in the twisted shadows of the Penumbra.

She found no dryads, though she saw trees here bent back in unnatural angles such that one could imagine they writhed with some alien presence inside. In the deepest dark of midnight, she sought for keres, but found none. In the midst of raging storms, she had stared defiance into the lightning, scouring the clouds for the signs of harpies. No, the only spirits she ever saw were the Telkhines, those sirens of Pontus pledged to Tethys.

It had grown so dark that, even with the lamp in hand, it had become a challenge to see the roots before her, so Pyrrha began to wend her way back to the harbour. Once again, she looked into the shadows of the Underworld and saw no sign of the greater powers she knew lurked out there. But that night, three years back, she had felt the presence of a colossal will, and it would not hide from her forever.

As she drew closer to the polis, the numbers of shades increased. More men and women lived in Thebes, so naturally, more died there. The wandering shades seemed most oft those who met violent or perfidious ends. Pyrrha could only guess such deaths left them feeling trapped here, wanting retribution for slights perceived or real. Sometimes, even, she had been able to exchange words with a ghost. Their voices seemed wispy and tattered, their speech more susurrations than fully formed words. When she understood them at all, she heard only lamentation.

The procession of the dead seemed endless, shades bemoaning their pain—death did not seem to abate it, at least not for those trapped upon the edge of the Underworld—and demanding she act against whoever had wronged them. Once, she met the ghost of a man who accused his brother of murdering him and claiming his wife. In an attempt to assuage the shade's pain, Pyrrha had sought after the murderer, only to find he had died himself in the Ambrosial War fifteen years ago. When she had told the ghost, his wails had only redoubled, and he cursed the Fates that his brother would never face retribution.

The hatred in his eyes had scourged her soul and left Pyrrha trembling, afraid to shut her eyes, much less venture out at night. The terror had persisted for days. In the end, she had been left to wonder, even had she found the murderer and somehow gotten the magistrate to prosecute him, would the ghost have still found another reason to lament his Fate? Was the murder itself a mere focal point for directing misery? Was peace an illusion the dead strove for but could never actually find?

Out in the brume, a female figure drifted, her hair and dress wispy, her skin pale as moonlight. At first, Pyrrha took her for another shade, but her weeping, while Ethereal, sounded more real than that of most shades. For that matter, why was the mist so thick in the Penumbra? "Wait!" Pyrrha called, chasing after the woman. But the figure vanished out into the vapours as though she had never been.

Had that been a lampad? A spirit of Mist? She'd heard Nymphs speak of them before, some even claimed that great numbers of them had come to foretell death before Kronos's assault on Thebes.

Dashing through the mist, Pyrrha chased after the spirit. Ahead, she heard the muted roar of the waterfall north of Thebes. Within the Penumbra, the water lost substance, and thus the falls became more a whisper. In her hurry, her foot caught on something and Pyrrha pitched face forward onto the shadowy ground. The impact jarred her.

By the time she had her senses, it felt as though the land had begun to cling to her, pulling her down like tar. Grunting, Pyrrha lurched upward. Shadows tugged upon her flesh ever so slightly. An image flashed through her mind of herself sinking into the ground before the river as though it were a mire. What dark depths of the Underworld might that carry her to?

Struggling to her feet, she felt rather than saw a presence above her. She looked up to behold a towering ghost staring down at her with rage-filled eyes. He still bore the dolphin-encrusted breastplate, splattered with blood and ichor. A scream died on her lips, escaping only as a whimper.

The dead Titan tried to speak, revealing the wretched hole in the back of his mouth. Had a spear done that?

Pyrrha forced herself into composure. Showing terror to the dead oft seemed to increase both their power over her and their fury at her. Strength was needed here, whatever ran through her heart. "Y-you're Okeanus, yes?" Tethys's dead husband, slain during Kronos's assault upon Thebes fifteen years ago, when Pyrrha was but an infant.

The Titan's visage calmed a hair. Perhaps she imagined it. But now, his gaze settled intently upon her face.

"Did Kronos do that to you?" she asked.

The Titan rasped something incoherent and Pyrrha could only grimace.

"I want to help you, but I don't know how. If you help me, though, I'll try. I want to find out what happened to my mother that day. Can you tell me if you saw—"

A scream that pierced into the Penumbra rang out from across the river, and Okeanus—if it was he—looked sharply in that direction, as did Pyrrha. She couldn't make out aught through the shadows and the mist, but that had been very distinct? Some connection to the lampad? Next, she heard more screams, grunts, and the sounds of crashing. There were woods on that side of the river, too, and somewhere in there someone was fighting.

Fighting with such fury it punctuated the Penumbra with echoes of the passion.

Sudden rage seized Okeanus and he grabbed Pyrrha, heaving her off the ground with a rasping snarl.

"Wait!" she shrieked, her legs kicking in the empty air beneath her. Even in death, the Titan had strength far greater than hers, and she was powerless in his grasp. She tried to blink away the Sight, but it wouldn't fade. In contact with the ghost, her soul remained trapped on the edge of the Underworld.

The Titan leaned in, opening that hideous mouth too wide just in front of her face almost like he intended to bite off her nose. Had the sounds of another battle like the one that had slain him triggered his rage? Pyrrha barely had time to form the thought before the ghost slammed her down into the umbral sands. The impact knocked all coherence from her.

Next she knew, she was flailing around beneath dark currents, water shooting up her nose. Twisting, Pyrrha managed the surface, sputtering and gagging. She cast herself upon the riverbank and coughed up a torrent of choking fluid. Spasms seized her and she fell upon her elbows.

"Pyrrha!" someone was calling. "Pyrrha!"

A rowboat scraped in the sand, and someone hopped out to stand beside her. Strong arms hefted her upward and patted her back.

Blinking through her tears, she saw Poseidon. As though she were a child, he hefted her up then set her into the bottom of the boat. Pyrrha contented herself to close her eyes a moment to catch her breath.

Papa had warned her, she remembered. He had warned her long ago the dead were angry and dangerous, unpredictable.

"Leave the dead be and remain tethered in this world."

Ha. But so little tied her to the world of the living ... Still, inexplicable rage had seized Okeanus, and he might well have forced her to join him permanently. Had he tried to drown her? Had the presence of his son across the Veil stayed his hand? She had too few answers about the dead and what drove them. Or maybe it was madness that compelled Okeanus, even as madness had driven the ghost she had once told about his brother. Trying to ascribe logic to their actions was a path fraught with futility.

"What in the depths of the Underworld happened to you?" Poseidon demanded. The Titan had begun to row them out, away from the falls and into the sea, where the roaring falls would not swallow his words.

Ah. 'Depths of the Underworld' was far more apt than she was inclined to admit to him, wasn't it? She had plumbed deep recesses beyond the Mortal Realm and almost died for it. And she was no closer to answers about either the Underworld or her mother. Would that lampad have aided her, had she managed to find the spirit?

"I, uh ..." She blinked and groaned.

Poseidon brushed her sodden hair from her face. "Are you all right?"

"What were you even doing here?" she asked.

He frowned, looking somewhat abashed. "Well ... Sometimes I come here at night. This is where I feel close to my father."

Gaia's breath! Pyrrha almost laughed at that. If only he knew how close his father had been this night. Closer than he would have liked, she suspected. The living oft thought they wanted to reconnect with the dead. So few of them would actually have liked to hear the dead were wandering around in their midst.

With his thumb, he traced the line of her jaw.

"What are you doing?" she asked, as he leaned in uncomfortably close.

"You've grown quite beautiful, you know that."

Had she?

"Hair like fire ..."

Pyrrha caught his hand and pushed it away. "Thank you." He was really too close now.

His other hand tangled in the folds of her peplos. "Well, I know what would make you feel better and take your mind off all your troubles."

Scoffing, she pushed him back. "What, you help me catch my breath so I open my legs to you? A real comfort to me, huh? Get off me!"

The sudden fury that overtook his face looked so much like the rage she had just beheld on his dead father's visage that it stole her breath. "You could really use a friend, Nymph. Someone on your side."

She gaped at him, not quite certain whether he was offering a bribe or a threat. Either way, he was just another Titan who thought he could have whatever the fuck he wanted. Whomever he wanted. Had he imbibed Ambrosia? She'd heard it made people like that.

"You want to be close to your father?" she snapped. "Well, he's here, watching you even now. You really want to put on a show for him?"

For a moment Poseidon looked at her, the wrath in his face giving way to confusion, before his eyes narrowed once more. He grabbed her by the hair and hefted her upwards. "Want to be alone, you sick bitch? Then be alone."

With a shove, he sent her tumbling over the side of the boat. She pitched back into the chilly waters. This time, she had the chance to suck in a breath before she hit. Before black engulfed her. Beneath the sea, she swam away, coming up out of reach of his oars.

While she struggled for some witty retort, he had already begun to row away. Pyrrha spit in his general direction, then swam for shore, fuming. Who did that pompous prick think he was? Was he truly so used to any woman he wanted submitting? Did Tethys know about it?

When Pyrrha finally reached the shore, another woman was there, wrapt in an embroidered cloak, with only a few strands of hair dangling down from her hood. The woman offered her a hand up and pulled Pyrrha to her feet. "I saw that," the woman said.

Pyrrha took a moment to wring out her hair, then wrapt her arms about her shivering chest. The second time tonight she'd wound up going for a swim in waters too cold for it. "He mistakes his simply being present for wooing and a lack of revulsion for interest."

The woman shrugged. "The powerful cannot conceive of their so-called lessers not worshipping them."

Damn if that wasn't the truth. "I'm Pyrrha."

Now, the woman nodded. "And I am Enodia, a sorceress formerly of the Circle of Goetic Mysteries. I have felt you, Pyrrha, and sensed your potential from long back. I can help you open your mind and reach that potential if you so desire."

All Pyrrha could do was stand there, mouth agape, peering at the hooded woman. What exactly the Circle-of-whatever was, she had no idea ... But a sorceress! Oh, there were always rumours about that sort of thing. Women on the fringes who balked at the hierarchy of the World, who took to forbidden studies for the chance, for *any* chance to not have to bend their wills and bodies to the whims of men. "You're offering to teach me sorcery? It's real?"

Enodia snorted, then clucked her tongue. "Mmm. It is real, but your bumbling around in the Penumbra will not give you such power. If you ever managed to confront a spirit thus, it would mostlike slip inside your body and ride you like a horse, sating its perverse desires using your flesh. It would feast upon your soul and leave you an empty husk, perhaps after enduring centuries of slavery."

The sorceress's words only intensified the chill that had seized Pyrrha. "Why?"

"Why then would people like me dare hold concert with the denizens of the Ether? Why would any save madmen touch the Otherworld?" Enodia took a step forward and seized Pyrrha by the arms. "I offer you more power and knowledge than you could ever have imagined. Is that not what you have sought after, combing through the dark? Did you imagine such would come with neither risk nor price?"

And there was only one thing to say to that. One answer appropriate for a woman who might be like Pyrrha, who could understand her. Who could see the umbral horrors that had forever haunted her. "Teach me."

When night fell, Pyrrha would wander down to the seaside cave she had once taken comfort in as a small child, and there meet Enodia. The sorceress would speak in cryptic riddles about the Realms beyond this fragile Mortal one, where Etheric beings dwelt. Ghosts inhabited the Penumbra and the Underworld, Enodia told her.

"Beyond there lies the Spirit Realm, where the greater powers dwell. Do not think, however, the Penumbra is free from dangers. Ghosts, especially wraiths, offer terrible threats, and spirits can enter there if they wish to do so."

"Why would they?"

"Perhaps to influence our world. Perhaps about business we cannot fathom. Either way, sorcery evokes eidolons—ghosts and spirits—and compels them to do our bidding."

Pyrrha fidgeted on the cold sand, digging rivets with her fingers. "You mean you enslave these beings."

"Yes. Just as they would happily enslave your body given half the chance. They are parasites, never forget. A moment of doubt, a faltering of the will, and they will have you. They can sustain a mortal form long beyond its natural lifespan, and you do not wish to even imagine the ravages they shall visit upon you."

Pyrrha felt ill at the thought of it. But this was the source of power beyond even the dreams of Titans. "What of mer?"

Enodia shrugged. "Mer are just another kind of spirit, possessing mortal hosts. The strongest hosts sometimes arrange a kind of symbiosis with the spirit, but most remain enslaved."

And the more they talked, the more she learnt, the stranger her dreams became. Like a voice echoing down through the centuries, whispers came unbidden into her mind and teased and taunted, promising all the power of the cosmos if she but stepped into shadow.

Ꝯ

... COME FORTH ...

The voice bombarded her, even as it had come to her in dreams down through her years. It had known. It reverberated inside her skull with all the discordant force of Supernal invocations, as if able to bend reality to its whims.

Was that Python speaking in her mind? She had not dared to believe the drakon could hold such power. Ahead, she once more heard mammoth grating of scales over stone. The slithering was intermittent, as if the massive serpent only sought to reposition itself on occasion. Nevertheless, Pyrrha winced with each grinding echo.

Her fist trembled at her side. Every instinct bellowed at her to flee this place, crawl back into the tiny tunnel from which she had emerged, and never look back.

COME FORTH ... BRIGHT ONE ... YOUR MIND SCRAPES THE ABYSS ... SO VIBRANT ...

An Old One, Tethys had called Python. A creature from before time itself, spawned by the fathomless Primordials.

It beckoned, and she approached. She plodded further down the tunnel, until her torchlight glinted off a jagged wall ahead. An abrupt sense of cyclopean immensity settled upon her, as if the Earth itself reared before her, alive and aberrant, utterly beyond the scope of comprehension.

YES ...

An incandescent eye opened in the wall before her, its faint radiance adumbrating the shape of a saurian head rimmed with a thicket of broken horns and spines.

SHE WOULD WAKE EACH MORN, drenched in chill sweat, aware of the essence of the dreams, while the substance had faded.

There was no turning back.

10

PANDORA

1570 Silver Age

*A*s it turned out, Prometheus used their small ship to skirt the coast of Atlantis, offering her a view of the magnificent landscape she'd never really experienced. Even from far off, the great Evenor Mountain seemed to scrape the stars. For a time she watched the coastline, then huddled down amidst some blankets, arms wrapt around herself.

Exhaustion had snared her of a sudden, the night's wild flight catching up all at once. Prometheus nodded as if to tell her to rest, and she did.

When next she opened her eyes, the sun had risen, glinting brilliantly off cobalt waters, almost blinding in its radiance. Away from the polis, natural beauty dominated Atlantis, with woodland covering most of the southern peninsula. She judged they must be cresting around that now. Prometheus stood at the tiller still, apparently having moved little while she slept.

"I'm sorry about your nieces," she said, then regretted it. Such sympathies fell so far short of being enough to salve wounds so deep. 'Sorry that the king murdered seven members of your family in one night.' Or six, perhaps, as Merope had left for Korinth and … Oh, damn. After Enyo's death, Zeus must surely send someone after her as well.

"Thank you." His voice was dry, scratchy. He didn't seem to have wept in the night, though he certainly looked as though he could have used it. "Rest a bit more. It'll be hours still until we make Marsa."

"Where's Marsa?"

"The port on Ogygia."

A small island off the coast of Atlantis. It explained why he'd only needed this tiny ship. Ogygia was ruled by Kelaino's daughter, wasn't it? Would they be safe even there?

Not knowing what to say, Pandora lay back and watched the clouds passing overhead.

Upon a precipice on the western shore of Atlantis stood a modest temple, jutting up like a boulder topping the cliff. Based on the location, it had to be Brizo's temple. Seeing it refreshed the Oracle's warning from yesterday. As Brizo had promised, Atlantis had fallen. The dynasty that had ruled for sixteen centuries was wiped out in a single night. Half the royal palace had probably burned down, and Pandora didn't even want to guess at the number of souls sent screaming down to Hades in the Underworld.

Beyond that precipice, they broke away, for the smaller island of Ogygia. It was dominated by a single mountain that covered most of the land, with light woods poking out from the rocky coastline around it. They made port at a harbour on the southern shore that, after the grandeur of Atlantis, seemed quaint. The town of Marsa proper lay up a dirt path a bit, in the foothills beneath the mountain.

Prometheus pointed. "I have a home here, upon the mountain slope. My Aviary, the locals call it." Aviary? For birds? Pandora loved birds. "We'll be safe there. They cannot find you here, while you are with me."

"Because you're an Oracle." Was that, after all, not what pyromancy meant? Divining hidden truths from the fire.

He glanced her way, brow raised.

"And even if they had another Oracle, they couldn't see you. Your visions interfere with each other, yes?"

A hint of a smile was her only answer, but she was almost certain she was right. Certainly, Zeus had Oracles working for him, divining the future, spying on his foes. So the only reason she could imagine Prometheus could be certain they'd be hidden was if he knew none of Zeus's Oracles could see *him*.

"I need to make a stop," he said when they reached the town. They'd passed a few spice farms before reaching the centre of Marsa. Here they saw a modest market, fragrant with the scents of cloves and marjoram and a dozen other spices. Workers bustled about, packing these goods into barrels, oblivious to how their world had just changed. "Kalypso needs to hear about her mother."

It was another punch to Pandora's gut. A task dreaded, though inevitable. Necessity—Ananke—demanded Prometheus carry it forth before she could hear the news from someone else. The bolt that had slain Kelaino had surely come from Zeus himself, even as he had murdered Alkoune.

Rumour traveled with the swiftness of Aiolos's winds. Word would come of the massacre soon, and then there would be the panic, the chaos of not knowing who their new overlord would be.

Another thought struck her. With the Pleiades dead, Zeus could appoint whomever he wished to oversee Atlantis. Which meant overseeing the Ambrosial distribution. Was all of it, even the Nectar propagation, a veneer for his political manoeuvre? Did the king think it unwise to simply execute Atlas's daughters without charge and thus *find* something to accuse them of? Did it rankle him that Nymphs not directly loyal to him held ostensible control of the most valuable commodity in the World?

The stiffness in Prometheus's steps, the tension in his shoulders, told her he could not bear to speak of such things as yet. Not with the agonising news he must now deliver. So she followed him in silence, unable to stop herself from casting pensive glances his way, though she suppressed the urge to ask him if he was all right. Because, of course, he was not.

In the end, she slipped her hand into his and squeezed his calloused fingers, drawing from him a look of such profound gratitude Pandora felt herself flush. Maybe, sometimes, all one really had to do was be there through a tragedy. Certainly, it would have helped had someone been there for her, all those years ago.

It would have meant the World.

They came to a walled estate atop a hill. Though it had a gate, it was unguarded, and Prometheus simply eased it open and slipped inside, beckoning Pandora to follow. They entered the house beyond, one decorated with colourful frescoes and tapestries depicting pegasi and mermaids and a multi-headed chimera. The estate was certainly modest compared to the splendour of homes in acropolis island on Atlantis, but compared to Pandora's house, it seemed a palace, and she found herself turning about, admiring the artwork. She paused in front of one depicting a griffin soaring over snowy mountains, its eagle head and plumage brilliant. The painter had clearly seen eagles up close—or perhaps even borne witness to the legendary griffins said to live out beyond wild Phlegra.

"Kalypso?" Prometheus called out but received no answer.

After a moment of looking around, they pressed through the kitchens and out a back door, Prometheus leading the way into a garden resplendent with herbs and spices and layers of rich and fruity scents, not all of which she could identify.

Their steps into that garden were the foreshocks of a tremor that would shatter a daughter's world.

Two women knelt in the dirt, tending the herbs. Titan women, Pandora realised as both stood and looked at her. One had the golden eyes of a Heliad, while the other—Kalypso presumably—had Atlantid features.

The Heliad tilted her head to the side as she took them in, then her mouth turned up in a sneer and she abruptly shoved past them, back toward the house. Her shoulder caught Pandora as she did so and actually sent her tumbling down into the dirt herself. The Titan's strength made Pandora feel a child, and she stood slowly, brushing off her peplos—suddenly aware it was still stained with blood and golden ichor.

"Kirke!" Kalypso shouted after the other woman.

"Let her go for now," Prometheus said.

Concern blanketed Kalypso's face. "What happened, Uncle?"

The elder Titan took her hand in his own. Pandora braced for the quake.

AT HER REQUEST, they had left the ravaged, weeping Kalypso alone in her garden. Pandora imagined her drowning in an ocean of pain and tears, tearing her khiton, ripping plants out by their roots. Wailing. All the things she herself would have done.

The image—half memory of her own early years—left a hollow in her chest as she and Prometheus made their way up the mountain. There was a path, not terribly well-worn and steep, littered with jagged rocks and narrow ledges that threatened to pitch her down into a gulley below. It took most of her concentration, at least at times, and the peplos she wore, while suited for formal symposiums at the royal palace, did not lend itself to mountain climbing.

They paused on a small plateau and Pandora eased herself onto a rock outcropping to rest. A great spire rose up from the peak, as if embracing the sun itself. Prometheus's Aviary.

After catching her breath, she looked at the Titan. "Why did the other Nymph react thus *before* we gave the news of the Pleiades?"

Prometheus folded his arms, seeming not the least winded. The breeze blew his auburn hair about his face. Though stubble had begun to grow in, he was beardless. Yet another way this Titan seemed to eschew the traditions that so bound all others. "Kirke has the Sight."

"She's an Oracle?" And had known the dire news they brought before they spoke? Blaming Pandora for the message, however painful, just made her one more Titan bitch.

"Yes, but the Sight is more than that. Mostly, we call Oracles those who can use the Sight for prescience. But there are other aspects to it. Whether prescience or some other intuition, perhaps she saw something in you that disquieted her."

"In me?" As if Pandora might have some grand future. She was, at best, merely a herald of tragedy.

Prometheus's brow creased, ever so slightly. "I'll prepare us something to eat."

She opened her mouth to object that she wasn't hungry, then realised she was, in fact, famished, having not eaten since the symposium almost a full day ago. The events that had swept her up had hardly allowed her to stop and breathe, much less realise her needs. Her stomach growled, as if the mental acknowledgment was the only permission she needed.

"There are guest rooms in the Aviary, and you may claim any that suits you."

Another question she'd had only the barest chance to ponder on the ship. "Just how long are you inviting me to dwell with you for?"

He cocked his head to the side. "However long you should so desire, Pandora. I will not abandon you or turn you out, if that's your fear."

"Why? Why risk even the chance of antagonising Olympus on behalf of a mere mortal?" And a glorified prostitute at that.

He knelt beside her and took her hand. "You are not *mere*, Pandora. And as I told you, I enjoy your company."

"Most men pay me for my company and conversation."

He dropped her hand, looking, for a bare instant, stung. Shit! Why had she said such a petty thing? Sometimes she could not control her godsdamned tongue.

"S-sorry, I ..."

"You're fatigued and hungry and have been through an ordeal.

Little wonder you should seem overwrought." He said it gently but stood, nevertheless, the tender moment between them spoiled.

All she could do was nod.

۶🙚

AS THEY DREW NIGH, Pandora gasped at the wonder of the tower. Vines grew about the stones of it, sprouting a rainbow of flowers. She spotted poppies and agapanthuses, and the wind carried down the fragrant blooms of daphne. That, and the song of hundreds of birds in resplendent symphony. Thousands of interwoven melodies. Warblers and partridges alighted in great arching windows higher up in the tower. She spied nightjars and cuckoos and petrels and so many more.

A dozen peacocks pranced about outside, displaying their vibrant plumage, even allowing her to draw up close to inspect them. Prometheus offered an encouraging nod, and so Pandora knelt beside one, memorising every subtle variation in its colours. The bird even seemed to revel in her attentions, strutting with yet more pride.

When they entered the open doorway, she saw brilliant pink Kemetian flamingos—the first she'd ever seen—bathing in a fountain. Above them, poles crisscrossed the tower as perches for yet more birds. Even an eagle!

"I guess I'm not the only one who likes birds," she mumbled.

He chuckled. "Some of the locals swear the eagles report back to me whatever they spy while circling out over Atlantis."

"The same people who probably fear the evil eye and the moderately wicked nostril, no doubt."

He cast her an amused glance, then showed her around. The floor was a grate continually washed clean by overflow from the fountain. They followed a winding staircase up to a landing with a plot of sand decorated with strewn rocks. Outward from each rock radiated waves of impact from where each rock had landed.

"You just sit here to study this, I take it?" she asked.

"To meditate, at times."

Pandora snickered. "Wondering what the stones ruminate over."

"You'd be surprised."

Upon the next level, a glass dome protected a library jammed with papyrus scrolls and actual bound tomes. While she'd heard of the latter, the public library in Atlantis offered no such books, and she'd only ever seen a few as a child in Phoenikia.

Prometheus waved a hand at several doors encircling the library. "Any of these rooms are free for you to claim. Refresh yourself while I cook us something to eat. If you want to use the library later, feel free. We can eat outside if you like."

"Thank you," she said, her voice almost breaking. People—least of all Titans—simply did not offer such kindnesses or considerations. Everything had a price. It always did, did it not?

Inside each of the rooms she found a comfortable bed, a wooden bench, and a wash basin. She chose a room from which she could look over the bay where Marsa sat. She dare not lay down for fear she'd sleep through supper, so instead she took to exploring the tower.

Soon the smells of grilled fish filled the tower, though it turned out the Titan actually cooked in a fire pit outside the Aviary itself. He'd placed a sea bream on a spit and was slowly turning it, perhaps oblivious to Pandora watching him. Or she thought so, until he turned.

"It's ready."

They spoke little during the meal, both clearly ravenous, and Pandora seared her fingers tearing at the fish. She hardly cared. After they'd eaten, he ducked inside the tower and re-emerged with an amphora of wine. A Phoenikian vintage, she realised, as he poured it in a bowl and she took a sip. Maybe grown in vineyards around Byblos?

"I feel I must offer you *something* in exchange for all this," she said. And if he wanted her for it, giving her a place to stay, food, and luxury was far more than most men paid her. To say naught of saving her life.

"Do you? Hmm. Then sing for me."

Huh. Pandora swallowed. A song popped into her mind, forbidden by Zeus's decree, for it lamented the fall of the Golden Age, when the Ouranid League had ruled these lands. A time before Men called Titans gods. To sing such a prohibited song courted a beating, or worse, and it was sheer folly to even consider singing it to a fucking Titan.

She started singing it anyway. Why could she not help herself? Why the need to test even him, who had shown her such kindness?

Prometheus lounged back, eyes shut as she sang, smiling lightly, not seeming the least offended by her choice. Not as she sang of the breaking of the Ouranid League, nor the decline in the station of Man.

When the song finished, he opened his eyes and she caught a hint of weariness in them. He hadn't slept on the ship when she had. Even a Titan must tire.

"I should let you rest," she said.

"Not yet. Please."

She hesitated. Swallowed. "Were you there? Did you see it, when Men began to bow to gods?"

"Yes." The word seemed to be drawn from him like poison from a wound. "I was there. I aided Zeus in his war against the Ouranid League."

Why? In what possible circumstance had that seemed a good idea? How she wanted to ask, but he seemed pained enough. And ... and ...

"When I was five years old ..." Pandora swallowed. She did not tell this story. At symposiums and with clients, she spun tale after tale, but not this. Not *her* tale. "I was raised in the court of King Agenor of Tyros, ward of his daughter, Princess Europa. When I was five years old, Zeus and Hekate came to the court and Zeus decided he wanted Europa as his pallake." Concubine, though slave seemed a more accurate name for how Zeus treated his women. "My family resisted, and so they murdered my uncle, Phoenix. He um ... my uncle, he was kind, always had time for me, even though I was small.

"I mean, I had other uncles, too. Kadmus, for one, who knew I loved puzzles and gave me a puzzle box I so loved." Lost now, in her house in Atlantis. "I, uh ... I don't know what happened to him. But Phoenix I saw die. Then Hekate, she took me and Europa out for Zeus, put us on a ship. Zeus, he raped Europa in front of me. Later, they dropped me in Atlantis and sold me to an aristos, Tantalus. Maybe I'd be there still, expect the fool apparently traded in Nectar and it got him killed." She was rambling, she knew, but the words seemed to spill forth in a deluge, unstoppable. "Tantalus made me his whore, so when he was gone, how could I have been aught else?"

Prometheus scooted closer, wrapping his arms around her shoulders. He said naught.

Maybe there was naught to be said.

Just warmth and, finally, for the first time in her life, it was enough for someone to *know*.

⚜

SHE WOKE WHIMPERING, the phantom scent of lightning-charred flesh in her nostrils, the echo of thunder still ringing through her mind. For a moment, she lay there amid sweat-soaked sheets, willing her heart to calm itself.

Slowly, she slapped her head back against the headboard, eyes clenched.

It was like back then, in Tyros. The scorched air. The sickly-sweet reek of cooked human flesh when Phoenix died, just as Alkoune and Kelaino. The jarring wrongness of one who commanded the forces of the sky itself. Too much power for anyone who walked the Earth.

And Zeus was drunk on it.

After a moment more, Pandora threw off the covers and paced about, letting the breeze blow over her bare skin. Letting the wind reassure; it was clean and carried no scent save that of the sea. No sound save the chirping of birds around the Aviary.

But then, there would be no sleeping after such a dream.

She donned her stained peplos—she'd have to see about getting new clothes in the morn—then laced her sandals. A walk maybe, to cool the mind as well as the flesh.

For a while, she paced the tower, looking at the birds. Most slept now, only a few nocturnal ones still sharing their stories with her. It had to be past midnight.

When she came to ground level, intent to step outside, she caught sound of the clink of metal upon metal. That was coming from beneath the floor grate. Pandora glanced about until she found a door. It led to another staircase, this one descending into a basement. The stairs circled around the main grate above, and she could see where the fountain runoff poured into a drain.

Faint light from an adjacent room painted the basement in chiaroscuro while seeming to beckon her ever onward. Her steps felt compelled, as if she never could have taken any other path. As if she yet dreamed and followed the winding course her unwilling mind laid before her.

On the threshold she paused, gazing into a room lit by both a brazier and an oil lamp set upon a table. It was over this table that Prometheus stood bent, clinking away with a tiny artisan's chisel at some metal object. Numerous other tools bedecked the shelves around the room, from metalworking instruments to implements she thought used for gem-cutting, and there, blacksmith's equipment, though she saw no anvil or forge down here.

What did he work on here? Maybe she should have turned away, afforded him his privacy. Probably, she should have. Nevertheless, her feet carried her forward. "What is it?" she asked.

He turned to look at her, mopping at a sheen of sweat upon his brow. Beyond him she could see him making a metal cube set with innumerable tiny gears and the most intricate inner workings she had ever seen. "A puzzle box. A present for you, once it's done."

Pandora took a faltering step forward. At supper, she'd told him about the puzzle box she'd had from Tyros. And had he now spent *all night* working on a new one to replace it?

"Why show me such solicitude? What did I ever do to deserve

your regard, Titan?" This felt ... too much. It was a trick, a ploy, a manipulation. It had to be.

He set the chisel and hammer down and twisted all the way around to face her. "You have suffered so much in your life, Pandora. The story your told me of your stolen childhood wrenched my heart from my chest. Is it so hard to believe someone might simply want to make your life better?"

Yes. It was almost impossible to fathom, for when had life ever treated her thus? "Can a puzzle box change all that?" Damn it, she was again pushing him back, goading him, chiding him. Was it ... fear? Was that why she rejected his benevolence?

He shrugged. "Maybe it can change everything. Maybe naught at all. Maybe just your perspective, a little." He strode toward her, then took her hand. "If the World is cruel, and Fate is relentless, that is all the *more* reason we must take care of each other. It is only thus we retain any shred of humanity."

He wasn't human. The retort almost leapt from her mouth, but she managed to still it, barely. Tantalus had tried to beat the acerbic tongue out of her. Tried and failed.

Prometheus, though, put forth such extraordinary efforts for her. Could a woman and a Titan have a true friendship? Could they have aught at all?

A reassuring squeeze of his hands seemed to offer his answer. For whatever reason, he remained unflappable.

As if utterly determined to give her another chance at a life. The least she could do was seize that chance. Yes. Standing in his workshop beneath his Aviary, Pandora swore she would claim the occasion he offered. She would be more than she had been, more than anyone had ever thought she could be.

From the ashes of her past, she would build something new.

11

KIRKE

1570 Silver Age

A shriek and a wail, and a hurled amphora that shattered against the wall of their shared laboratory, causing Kirke to cringe.

Then Kalypso was doubled over, clutching her knees, moaning, and Kirke raced to her side, grabbing her shoulders. She eased the other Nymph to the ground and wrapt her arms around her.

"My mother ..." Kalypso moaned for the hundredth time. "My mother ..." Then, almost inaudible, the whisper. "Mama ..."

Kirke said naught, for there was naught to be said. Sometimes, life so ravaged a person that all you could do was hold them in place and keep the pieces from blowing away in the wind.

❧

"PROMETHEUS and his new girl didn't do a damn thing about all of this," Kirke grumbled the next morning, while the two of them sat beneath a cypress tree on the estate's edge, sipping from a bowl of wine. Well, Kirke might have done more than sip, having no interest in the figs Kalypso ate. "Maybe even made it worse."

"Oh, leave over," Kalypso snapped. "They didn't have aught to do with it."

"She's trying to seduce your great-uncle," Kirke complained. Girl seemed damn familiar, too. Another of her father's bastards, perhaps removed by a few generations, not even worthy of being called a Nymph.

Kalypso favoured her with a withering look. "As if that's our great concern at the moment. Zeus just murdered my mother—and the rest of the Pleiades. For sixteen centuries he trusted them to govern Atlantis and manage the flow of Ambrosia to Olympus. And now ... Now ... What if he comes for us as well?" The woman paled. "He might not know about you, but if he turned on my mother, how long before he decides I'm a threat?"

It was ... a possibility. Zeus was unpredictable, as always. He'd banished Atlas to Tartarus but allowed the great Titan's daughters to rule Atlantis until now. Still, he might not act without some provocation. She took a long drink from the bowl before setting it aside, drained. "Yeah, I think him more like to observe you first. Wholesale slaughter of the Atlantid genos would weaken his support, even among the other Olympians. People tend to get worked up about that sort of thing."

"Observe?"

"Yeah, well, he's been known to use Morpheus to hunt through the dreams of those whom he has begun to doubt." Was that what had been sparking Kirke's nightmares of late? Did Morpheus hunt her specifically, or merely comb through the dreams of all Titans in this region? "Morpheus is one of those men who values privacy. He likes to take your privacy and keep it all for himself. He's like ... like a secret-hoarding magpie, you know?"

Kalypso grew paler and clutched Kirke's hand. "Can you keep him out?"

"Ah ... I wish I could, but I'm not that powerful of a sorceress. He's the strongest oneiromancer I've ever heard of. No, my friend, you have to guard your own mind. Control your thoughts and your fear. Forget what we've been up to for a time."

"W-will I know he's inside my head?"

Kirke squeezed her hand, wishing she had more reassurance to offer. "Maybe. Such things have no easy answers. It depends on you and your mind and how aware you are of it." And on how deep Morpheus chose to push into her dreams, if he came for her. "Believe me when I tell you, staying calm is our best defence." If Morpheus pulled incriminating thoughts from Kalypso's sleeping mind, she and Kirke could well both be damned.

"Why would Zeus do this?" Kalypso abruptly moaned. "Why now?"

Kirke sighed. "Why does a megalomaniac do aught he does? Maybe he snapped from too much Ambrosia. Maybe he sampled a bad batch of Nectar."

For a moment Kalypso's eyes widened, appearing to try to judge if Kirke was jesting. Not even Kirke was sure about that. Either way, Kalypso's face darkened, and she snatched her hand back and rose, storming away.

Not knowing what else to do, Kirke rubbed her forehead and remained sitting beneath the tree. What in the very gates of Tartarus had happened on Atlantis to prompt Zeus to such madness?

And now, even Kirke's very presence on this island might make her and Kalypso look more suspicious. So what was she to do? How was she to comfort her friend and still protect them both? Kirke banged an impotent fist against the unforgiving ground. All their dreams were flitting away, broken before they had truly begun.

Was it possible Zeus had *known* the Nectar came from Ogygia? Had he acted against Kelaino to punish Kalypso? It seemed too subtle for him, but who knew what wild gyrations went through the king's mind?

One thing seemed abundantly clear though. They needed help before Zeus came for them.

≈

THE CALIGINOUS CITY streets had fallen away, revealing rugged hills and an even more shadow-drenched forest. Kirke could make out so little, but still she stumbled forward, half running, dead certain someone followed her.

The one thing she knew: someone stalked her dreams, and she could not allow him—or it—to see her. So she ran in the darkness, darting between trees and—

Her foot snared on a root sending her crashing down amid fallen leaves. The impact jarred her shoulder, and she lay there moaning. Before she could right herself, a snake slithered in front of her face. Kirke froze, not daring to breathe. In the darkness, she had no idea what kind of serpent it was or if it was venomous.

A moment later it was gone, disappeared into the fallen leaves.

Somewhere, in the direction she'd come from, footfalls crunched more leaves.

Ah, shit.

She hurled herself to her feet and raced onward, certain that whatever followed her would be worse than stepping on a snake in her blind rush. Her elbow scraped rough tree bark as she fled, and underbrush tore at her khiton.

Her pulse had begun to pound in her ears.

Her mad flight brought her atop an outcropping over the hills, where the land pitched away into the utter darkness of an unseen valley, and she lurched to a stop, arms flailing to keep from tumbling into the abyss.

The sound of running behind her intensified. Whoever chased her was growing closer.

This was a dream.

It was only a dream.

But if her pursuer caught her, it would become something more.

Kirke leapt into the void.

≈

NEITHER WOMAN SPOKE much as they climbed the mountain. While mostly keeping her gaze upon Prometheus's Aviary, Kirke could not help but steal glances at Kalypso when she wasn't looking. All oneiromancers suffered nightmares full of portent and metaphor and, as now, the persistent fear of other oneiromancers stalking them. Oh, such uses of the Art were potent and could be used to pass messages without regard for distance.

But as with every other branch of the Art, there was terrible risk.

A fortnight since learning of the Pleiades' fate, and her nightmares grew worse, and with them, the sense of everything coming to a head.

And maybe Kalypso would be better off if Kirke was as far from her as possible, both physically and emotionally. If it was Morpheus stalking her, sooner or later, he would catch her, and her mind would unfold before him like a papyrus roll.

Was she betraying Kalypso by even thinking of leaving her in such circumstances? Or did she betray her more severely if she let her affections for the woman stop her from taking steps to protect the both of them?

While she did not relish the thought of being alone, she had spent ages traveling the seas with little or no company, and she could manage if she must. As a child she'd grown up in Helion, in her father's court, though she had spent her earliest years in Byblos before that, in times she barely recalled. But both had been ages back, and so much had happened since then.

Then the Titanomachy had come and, in the last days of the war, her mighty father had abandoned Kronos and bent his knee to Zeus. Mostly, she blamed Artemis for that, but the bitch had help, and Kirke could not forgive that. For thousands of years Helios had been one of the greatest forces in the Thalassa, and Kirke, while still a Nymph, was a princess worthy of respect. Now what? Now she was *just* another Nymph daughter of a fallen Titan, a shadow of his old self, who held his puppet throne only by sucking at Zeus's teat.

Such things dashed about her mind more and more these days.

Memories of the Golden Age. And the World grew harsher for anyone not reigning from Olympus.

Atop the mountain, Prometheus met them, not inside his Aviary, but past it, beckoning them over to where he sat in sunshine upon the cliff's edge, watching the sea. Kalypso paused a moment by the tower, sniffing the daphne and lingering, perhaps now dreading the conversation they must have with a Titan more ancient than even Kirke. Maybe more ancient than Kirke's father. Prometheus had been there, in the dawn of time, when Ouranos drove back Nyx, or so some legends told it. And he, too, had helped Zeus overthrow Kronos, though Kirke could not fathom his reasons.

He gave Man the Art of Fire and pyromancy, taught them trades and arts and so many things, and they called him benefactor. Yet he helped enthrone the greatest tyrant in the ambit of history. Whether in weakness and fear, like her father, or out of mere poor judgment, his mistake was not something Kirke could forgive.

Not waiting for Kalypso, Kirke strode over to where the Titan sat and slumped down beside him. "Word has already spread about the fate of the Pleiades, you know. And by now I'd have to imagine it's the talk of fishwives in the harbours of Korinth and philosophers in the streets of Kronion." Kirke spread her hands for effect. "Maybe it was inevitable, too, right, Prometheus? I mean, if you let a madman take control of the land, let him think himself a god ... if you let him reinforce that belief by allowing him to force others to call himself a god, well then you've set the stage for your own execution, haven't you? Yeah, maybe we ought to start selling tickets to this show, too, because something tells me we haven't reached the climax yet. Have you got a comfortable seat for it, Firebringer?"

As Kalypso approached, Kirke could almost *hear* her wince at Kirke's tone. No, this hadn't been how she'd planned for this conversation to go. Browbeating a Titan wasn't like to produce results, but the words had rushed out of Kirke without her having much say in the matter.

The Titan, however, favoured her with a sad smile, sympathy touching his crystal blue eyes. "You hope that, perhaps, I will somehow join you in a second Titanomachy? You imagine that, if you could gather enough supporters, you might wage some grand war to overthrow tyranny and establish a new order, better than what we have."

"Yes!" Kirke snapped. "Yeah, I want you to fucking *do* something, Firebringer. I mean, something more useful than sitting on a mountain collecting birds and naming the clouds."

Prometheus frowned, ever so slightly, though whether at her outburst, profanity, or some war within himself, Kirke didn't know. "I am, always, doing a great many things. And naught lasts forever, Kirke, not even Zeus's reign. But I will not join in a war against the Olympians."

"They slaughtered the Pleiades," she said, barely able to stop from screaming at him again. "They murdered them all, and no one will do aught about it."

"Indeed, I was there," he reminded her. "And Zeus and his ilk will do worse still before things are done. But I cannot do as you wish."

Kirke hesitated. "I think he sent Morpheus after us."

She felt Kalypso stiffen even as Prometheus's frown deepened. "I will see if I can direct his eyes away from you," the Titan said softly.

"Uncle ..." Kalypso moaned. "What he did to Mother ..."

Prometheus inclined his head to his great-niece. "Kirke had the right of it, Kalypso. We do set the stage for our own end, Zeus included. His actions may yet prove his undoing, but a war against Olympus now would be doomed to failure."

"Oracular insight?" Kalypso asked.

"Call it that."

Oh, but if he had seen a war, it meant that one must impend. Or perhaps, rather, he had seen himself warn them of this very moment, and thus relied upon his statement that a war would fail to know it would. Prescience was always so twisted, bent back upon itself.

Either way, there was no aid for them here.

DESPITE NOT HAVING SPOKEN in the climb up the mountain, somehow the silence seemed even deeper as they returned to Kalypso's estate. Kirke had to wonder, over and over, what Prometheus thought he would do against Morpheus. A weaker Oracle could not see a stronger, but oneiromancer dream stalking was different, and, so far as she knew, Prometheus had no such abilities.

By tacit accord, she and Kalypso wandered the grounds aimlessly, neither quite able to meet the gaze of the other.

Was this what it had come to? All their plans to right the World, all their experiments, the long summer nights of making love, the dreams of time when Nymphs could choose their own Fates ... Dwindled-down embers before they had the chance to even catch flame.

Like unspent tinder, they would blow away in a strong gust, and all they had sought would be forgotten. Maybe they had never had a chance. Or maybe ... maybe she still could, but she needed to perfect the Nectar, no matter how long that took. And clearly, Kirke could no longer do that here, with Kalypso.

They drifted into the garden, where Kalypso knelt and poked at the moly crop. The little white bulbs just eased out now, ready to bloom. After a few moments, Kalypso rose with a sigh. "What about your father? He has forgotten, hidden his strength, but surely it remains there, quiescent."

Kirke could barely stop herself from scoffing. Once the most radiant of the Lords of the Ouranid League, her father's fall had been tragic. Watching it had torn her to pieces, even as his most precious children, Artemis and Apollon, had sided with his enemy. "He won't act against Zeus."

"He lost his status in the Ouranid League," Kalypso objected, as if Kirke could ever forget.

Kirke huffed. "After he betrayed them for Zeus, yeah. He won't take any step that might risk him losing what remains of his empire. My father yet controls Helion, Thrinakia, and numerous smaller islands, you know? He is the most powerful Titan outside of Olympus. You think he'd jeopardise that?"

"Not even if it meant the chance to rule instead of licking Zeus's sandals?"

Kirke folded her arms. "We don't have any moves left right now. The best we can do is lay low and hope Zeus and his minions won't associate us with the Nectar."

"They just murdered my mother!" Kalypso blurted. "You want me to lay low? Shall I perhaps fetch a rod for them to beat me with while I'm at it?"

It was always going to come to this, and Kirke couldn't help but glare at Kalypso. "You think I've no quarrel with them? But if you don't want to join the Pleiades in the Underworld, you have to bide your time. Sell what's left of the stock. We cannot afford any chance of discovery right now. I can always make more when things have quieted a little."

"You're leaving." Kalypso fair spat the words in accusation.

"For now. Laying low, remember."

The look of betrayal upon Kalypso's face ripped straight into Kirke's heart. But before she could say aught more, the other Nymph stomped into the house.

With a resigned sigh, Kirke paused long enough to pull up two of the moly herbs. She'd need the seeds to plant more crops wherever she ended up.

And she needed some damn wine. A lot of wine.

One thing was clear: she needed to get off Ogygia as soon as she could figure out a destination.

12

PANDORA

1570 Silver Age

*A*fter a fortnight of living in the Aviary, Prometheus still had not made any effort to touch Pandora. Though, in moments of self-reflection, she had begun to wish he would. Nor did she think it from lack of desire on his part, for he seemed interested in her, almost affectionate at times. Mulling it over, all she had come up with was that, perhaps, he thought her so wounded by the past as to need convalescence from it before she could claim aught substantial in the present.

The thought, once it had occurred, had haunted her like the screeching voice of a Fury, nagging and needling in every private moment. As now, when she walked in the spice fields outside Marsa, trying to slow her mind by speeding her heart, if only a bit.

A farmer waved to her as she passed and Pandora returned the gesture.

When word had come of the events in Atlantis, a kind of hysteria had blazed through the town. People hid in their homes. Others drowned their growing consternation in wine houses. She'd heard one fisherman had loaded up his family and made to sail for Neshia, though she couldn't imagine a fishing boat could make the voyage across the Thalassa.

And then, almost as fast, when naught came of it all, the madness had burned out, the fever of it broken overnight. The Pleiades were murdered. Zeus was a despot. And life continued much as it ever had, the atmosphere of dread unsustainable even in the wake of such turmoil. Aught could be passed over, so long as it did not come *here*.

Perhaps that was one reason Zeus forever retained power. Those not directly affected by his depravities could only maintain umbrage for such a short time. *Oh, wasn't it awful what happened to Europa? Oh, poor Kelaino! I hope it won't disrupt the salt shipments, dear.*

But for Pandora, her nights remained restless. Her dreams had become turbulent maelstroms of violence from both then and now, haunted by the vague sensation that something *saw* her, stalking the shadows of her sleep. Could Morpheus be hunting her, even now? Or was all that merely the product of her own tormented mind? She had spoken to Prometheus of it, and he'd suggested more exercise in the day and meditation in the evening.

Thus, walking now, and staring at sand and rocks later. A few times, he'd invited her join him atop the tower, to stare into the braziers there. She suspected he saw something in those dancing flames, but to her, it was just pretty patterns and soothing quiet.

As she passed beyond the spice field, a scream echoed out from the farmer's dwelling. He must have heard it too, for he took off at a mad dash back to his house. Pandora hesitated only a moment. Someone might need help. If it turned out to be a private family affair, she could leave. She broke into a run.

Inside, she found the farmer holding his wife in his arms. The woman shrieked like an animal, flailing about, clawing at the air and her husband both.

"Zoe!"

What in Hades's infernal court? Pandora dropped to her knees and grabbed the woman's wrists. Her fingernails were torn bloody.

After a frantic glance around, Pandora spied why. The farmwife had seemingly tried to dig through the mudbricks of her house and actually broken off several nails.

"What's wrong with her?" Pandora asked. "What happened?"

"Zoe ..." the man moaned, seeming not to even hear Pandora.

Maybe some wine would calm the woman down. Pandora cast about the tiny farmhouse looking for an amphora. Beside the hearth she found one. Alongside a cracked ceramic phial. A hint of glistening, amber liquid wet the floor before the unlit hearth.

After a glance over her shoulder at the still oblivious husband and wife, Pandora sniffed the spill. A sweet fruity aroma tinged with some kind of exotic herbs. Definitely not wine or even Kemetian beer. That scent ... Pandora had smelled that before. In Kalypso's garden, that unidentifiable herb she'd noticed.

Her mind raced. Atlantis was plagued by Nectar, an Ambrosial facsimile being peddled to Men. Nectar addicts oft went mad, she'd heard. Maybe just like this farmwife.

Gnawing on her lip, she turned back to the woman. The farmer had managed to ease her into a bed and was dabbing at her brow with a cloth. There wasn't aught Pandora could do for her, but if Nectar had spread into Marsa, then ...

Ah. No, it hadn't spread to here. It had come from here, hadn't it? From the garden of the daughter of one of the Pleiades. Was Zeus *right*? Had the Pleiades been complicit in the distribution and spread of this drug? Pandora's mind spun. Did it even matter? Even if the Nymph queens were guilty, Zeus's response had been madness ... but still it meant part of what happened on Atlantis fell at their feet.

After finding another cloth, Pandora mopped up what remained of the gilded fluid and wrapt up some of the ceramic shards as well. Prometheus needed to know what his grandniece was up to.

If he didn't already.

Outside the farm, she hesitated. Prometheus had offered her a home and considerable generosity. It didn't mean he'd want to hear his kin besmirched without proof.

Which meant Pandora needed more than a hint of a smell that

might have been a mysterious herb. At the very least, she needed the herb itself. She needed to be *certain* of the truth.

THOUGH SHE KNEW it for reckless, Pandora climbed the hill to Kalypso's estate. The gate remained unbarred, so she slipped behind the wall. Keeping low, she crept around the house itself to the garden in the back.

The voices came to her before she reached the corner.

"He won't act against Zeus," a woman said. Daring to peek, Pandora spotted Kalypso and Kirke facing off against one another in the midst of the garden.

"He lost his status in the Ouranid League," Kalypso objected.

Kirke scoffed. "After he betrayed them for Zeus, yeah. He won't take any step that might risk him losing what remains of his empire. My father yet controls Helion, Thrinakia, and numerous smaller islands, you know? He is the most powerful Titan outside of Olympus. You think he'd jeopardise that?"

"Not even if it meant the chance to rule instead of licking Zeus's sandals?"

Kirke folded her arms. "We don't have any moves left right now. The best we can do is lay low and hope Zeus and his minions won't associate us with the Nectar."

"They just murdered my mother!" Kalypso blurted. "You want me to lay low? Shall I perhaps fetch a rod for them to beat me with while I'm at it?"

The Heliad glowered at the other Nymph. "You think I've no quarrel with them? But if you don't want to join the Pleiades in the Underworld, you have to bide your time. Sell what's left of the stock. We cannot afford any chance of discovery right now. I can always make more when things have quieted a little."

"You're leaving." Kalypso fair spat the words in accusation.

"For now. Laying low, remember."

Kalypso groaned and stormed back into the house. Pandora

pressed herself flat against the wall until she was certain Kirke had walked off as well.

Her heart hammered in her chest. Maybe she ought to just leave. Their words had confirmed their guilt—of both of them!

But what if Prometheus wanted more proof? She slipped to her knees, crawling forward into the garden. And if the Titan already knew what his niece was about? Well, then Pandora might in fact be damning herself. Too late to worry on that now, though. She crept up to the unknown herb and dug her fingers into the dirt so as to ease out as much of the roots as possible. It had little white bulbs and looked so innocuous. Could it really be an ingredient in a drug insidious enough to have sparked such slaughter on the acropolis island?

Plant in hand, she crawled up to the estate's wall. She dare not go back out the front while not knowing where the Nymphs were. But the wall was only about seven feet high. Low enough she could jump up, catch the lip, and pull herself over it.

She rolled over the top, fell with a thud, and huffed.

Gods, she hoped that was the hard part.

UNBELIEVABLE THOUGH IT SEEMED, her heart pounded more heavily upon drawing into the Aviary than it had sneaking into Kalypso's estate. She found Prometheus sitting up on the terrace where he oft greeted the dawn. A circle of braziers surrounded him, and he was staring into one, its fires dancing slightly out of accord with the gusts of wind that whipped his hair about.

"You're back," he said, not looking up from the flame.

It was hard to swallow. One misstep here could cost her the home she had just made. Could make her fresh enemies. But if he *didn't* know, then his grandniece placed him in monumental danger. He deserved the truth and she had to know whether he already knew.

Pandora knelt at his side and unwrapt the cloth she'd mopped up the Nectar and ceramic shards with. Beside it, she put the strange herb.

Now Prometheus looked to it, then picked it up to examine it. "Moly. Very rare, hard to cultivate."

"Your niece grows it." She swallowed. "She's making Nectar and selling it."

Prometheus's face remained unreadable, save for a creasing of his brow so subtle she might have imagined it. "Hermes came this morn. He summons me to Olympus, and I cannot refuse."

The words knocked the wind from her. Pandora actually fell back on her arse and shook from a chill having naught to do with the wind. Zeus. The madman. He had sent for Prometheus. The king *knew*.

"You have to tell him Kalypso is responsible."

His visage seemed more weary than irate, and he shook his head. "I'd not cast her adrift to flounder alone, Pandora. I will go and placate the king's ego, as I have done oft enough in the past."

"He will *hurt* you," Pandora said, hating the tremor in her voice. "I can't ..." She shook her head.

"You have to come with me. If I leave you here alone, Oracles may find you out. Once I've waylaid Zeus's ire, you'll be safe."

Come with him. To *Olympus*. The very haven of the tyrant who had twice destroyed her life. She would be asked to walk into his sanctum and grovel before his person, hoping to conceal the loathing in her eyes.

Pandora's breath caught. Her chest ached.

THEY SAILED from Ogygia all the way to Delphi, Prometheus saying little—though the voyage took several days—no doubt lost in the roil of his thoughts. As was Pandora. The Titan believed he could sooth over the King of Olympus, but all Pandora had ever seen of Zeus was lust and madness and charred bodies in his wake.

There was a strange surreality to it all. The sense they walked to their own deaths as they crossed the many miles overland to Olympus, following a well-worn dirt road out of Delphi.

"You seemed closer to Kelaino than your other nieces," Pandora ventured as the mountains drew ever closer.

"She was my student, long ago."

"And Kalypso?"

"Her daughter, of course."

Yes ... Well, ask him, then. "But is she *your* daughter, as well?"

A slight snort escaped him. "Only in spirit."

"That's why you won't allow her to fall, even for her own actions." Even if it might save himself.

"We try to value all lives, of course, but some invariably come closer to our own souls. Such is life, binding us to others in intricate webs."

When more miles had passed, they reached the Olympian Mountains. The greatest peak amid them, Olympus pierced the firmament. Swirling storm clouds encircled the summit. Tale claimed they never parted, testament to the implacable will of Zeus.

A paved road led up the lower steps, and as they walked along this, the urge to take Prometheus's hand once more seized her. She pushed it down. Was he leading them both to their deaths? But he had saved her life in Atlantis, more like than not, and been a friend since then. Even if all he had bought her was a reprieve, she would not leave his side now, in this dire hour.

The path ended at a peristyle-encircled temple. Prometheus ignored this, leading her to a marble staircase, this some forty feet wide, then bent around the mountainside. Had Zeus claimed this towering peak and built his palace upon it merely to show he *could*? Was this one more gesture of self-aggrandisement meant to share his glory with the whole of Elládos?

He cast a final look at her, then began to ascend the stairs. Before long, she was huffing from the effort. It took much to keep climbing, though Prometheus set a leisurely pace for her.

"Pyromancy," she panted after climbing more steps than she'd have cared to count. "You see the future in the flames, yes?"

"I see pieces. The future is not always what we think. Just because we see a thread does not mean we can glimpse the whole of the tapestry or guess what it depicts."

"But do you know what lies ahead of us, atop these stairs?"

Prometheus fell silent a moment. "I know some."

The stairs led them past cascading cataracts and beyond, to plateaus that housed palaces for other Titans in service to the Olympians. Eventually, when Pandora's head spun from exhaustion and the thinning air, they came to an agora rimmed by colonnades. Up here, dustings of snow covered the rooftops and painted the stones white.

Prometheus led her to a vendor beneath a colonnade and bought her some spiced wine. Its warmth eased the pain in her chest.

In silence—she wasn't sure she could have spoken much through her heaving, regardless—they sipped. She wanted to take in the opulence of this place, for beyond the agora lay more temples supported by columns stretching forty, fifty feet into the air. The reliefs depicted scenes of import to each of the twelve Olympians. The hearth-fires of Hestia and there, on Apollon's temple, the slaying of the ancient drakon, Python. Legends come to life.

She wanted to gawk at such things, though her gaze drifted ever back to Prometheus and the taut set of his muscles. The way his jaw shifted so oft, as if he wanted to speak but had at last become lost for words.

When they finished the wine, he led her onward, along the same path to yet *more* stairs, these climbing past the agora and into the true acropolis. Another hundred or so steps and they came to the final landing, just below the summit.

Here, the air had grown so thin she felt no amount of gasping truly filled her lungs. She teetered, hands upon her knees, struggling to catch enough breath, shivering in cold winds. Prometheus's warm hand fell upon her back, then eased her upward.

"Do not allow them to see weakness in you."

Pandora gasped, but nodded. Olympians sounded much like wolves.

Alongside the acropolis ran canals of crystal-clear waters without apparent source. They pitched over the slopes, no doubt feeding the falls they had passed earlier. Arching bridges spanned the canals, each leading to a mansion more ostentatious and grandiose than aught she had ever imagined, even in Atlantis itself. From the architectural flourishes, she could guess which of the Olympians each belonged to.

Certainly, the one at the end of the acropolis, the famed Throne of Zeus. The sprawling complex left her gaping. A many tiered palace supported by great buttresses that spanned gaps to rock islands floating in the sky, supported by absolutely naught at all.

"What? How?"

"Skystone," Prometheus said, continuing forward to their ominous destination. "Mined from the World of Sky long ago."

Another world? What did that even mean?

Birds soared about the air amid those floating stones. Or not birds, she realised as they drew nigh, but pegasi. Steeds to the Olympians. Which explained why they didn't mind living up here. Only others had to make this climb, a symbolic obeisance to call upon their gods.

In the distance, on the sky islands, she also caught sight of winged, bird-legged women. Harpies? She'd read of such creatures but thought them fancy rather than fact.

Prometheus noted her gaze but said naught. He guided her up the final stairs to the Throne of Zeus, and her raging pulse was not merely from the throes of physical exhaustion.

The gates here—great doors ten times her height—were thrown wide. Inside bustled numerous Titans, mortal slaves, and more than a few she could not say with utter certainty whether Man or Titan. They passed through a great vestibule into an inner chamber. Beyond this, she spotted a green courtyard that seemed somehow warm despite the height upon the mountain. Within this pranced innumerable peacocks, and Pandora took a step toward the birds, entranced.

Prometheus, though, took her hand to guide her to another set of great double doors, no chance to revel in such a place. It was not for her. Through this secondary gate, she could make out steps leading up to a dais, mounted with a golden throne that must have stretched twelve feet tall. Upon this sat the King of Olympus himself, a mountain of muscles forever in his prime, platinum hair falling about his shoulders, ice-blue eyes fixed upon some petitioner standing before him.

About this inner chamber milled copious other Titans, far more than Pandora had ever seen in one place. Too many, in fact. Despite the chill from the mountainside, sweat drenched her back.

So overwrought was she, she did not at first notice the approach of the Heliad Titan. Not until Hekate stood at their side. Pandora felt every muscle in her body clench, from her fists to her arse. This witch had dragged Pandora screaming from her home.

Now, the Titan didn't even look at her, but only at Prometheus.

With a gentle hand on her shoulder, Prometheus guided Pandora toward Hekate. "Go with her."

W-what? Pandora gaped at him, mind refusing to grasp at what her ears had just heard. Madness. He would not betray her to this abomination.

"She will not harm you," Prometheus promised, easing Pandora forward.

Hekate's grip snared her elbow and pulled Pandora to her side, still looking only at Prometheus. Pandora could feel the iron strength in the Titan's fingers, though she wasn't rough.

For a moment more, Prometheus held her gaze, sadness in his sapphire eyes. Sadness and *fear*.

Was this betrayal? Or was it the only way he could keep her safe?

Pandora's stomach seemed to drop out from under her. What had Prometheus beheld of his own future? What dread did he tread into?

The moment broke, and he entered the throne room.

13

PYRRHA

218 Golden Age

For two years, Pyrrha had striven under the tutelage of the sorceress Enodia, always seeking to conceal her studies from her father and the rest of Tethys's court. Sorcery, as it turned out, was but a single discipline of a greater field of arcana that Enodia termed 'the Art.' According to the sorceress, studies of the arcane dated back to the Time of Nyx, but whatever knowledge the ancients had held was mostly lost. A handful of lodges around the world, including her own former order, the Circle of Goetic Mysteries, sought to recreate that lost knowledge and power.

Other disciplines included alchemy, and Enodia had shown her the brewing of potions and crafting of reagents to imbue the body with greater strength or aid against illness, as well as poisons to enervate even the strongest of Titans. But in sorcery lay both the greatest risk and the greatest potential reward, and thus Pyrrha had always sought after that knowledge above all else.

Enodia, though, held Pyrrha back, demanding she wait. "The

evoking—or even invoking—of ghosts or spirits is not to be taken lightly, child."

Of course, the sorceress only called her *child* when she used condescension as a whip to rebuke her failures. Every time, it had Pyrrha grinding her teeth in frustration. She knew she could do *more*.

She could feel the puissance of the world, thrumming through the night air. Night had become her time more than ever before, and she stalked it like a lion, so aware, so alive. Vibrant as the twinkling stars.

Only once had Enodia allowed her to summon a spirit, one she used for scrying. Slowly, staring into a pool of water, colours had swirled up, shaping into images in a distant mirror. It had allowed her to spy upon the inhabitants of the palace, to watch Poseidon as he drew yet another hapless slave girl into his bed. Oh, the girl didn't dare resist, but from the look upon her face in their coupling, she endured the process rather than enjoyed it.

But for a hair of difference in station and the will to stand up to him, that could have been Pyrrha wincing beneath his unwanted thrusts. And seeing that had been enough to resolve her. Once, she had believed Poseidon kinder and more worthy than his sisters. But while they vented their frustrations with petty cruelties visited upon any they could, at least Pyrrha could empathise with their desire to demonstrate some degree of power in their lives. Indeed, Styx and Perse had been named Nymphs themselves, and were thus destined for eternal mediocrity.

Poseidon, though, had no frustrations worthy of the name. This world was his to claim and abuse, the people in it existed but to service him. If he weren't Tethys's son—if the Titan queen did not, in fact, encourage this behaviour through not speaking against it— Pyrrha might have been inclined to ask her how Tethys, a woman, achieved dominance in such a world.

Tethys and Phoebe alone comprised the females of the Ouranid League, and Pyrrha kept circling back, wondering how they attained it. Ah, but then, the answer was in front of her all along. She had no idea how Phoebe had managed her position, but Tethys had the

Telkhines—mer spirits—working for her. Combined with Okeanus having died in Kronos's assault, Tethys had seized the Aegean through sheer arcane might.

Was that not, then, the perfect model for how Pyrrha could begin to build her own sphere of influence?

Thus, when Enodia had at last given her blessing, Pyrrha had traced spirit glyphs along the beach, forming a wide circle. The glyphs were key, Enodia had taught her. A foolish sorceress could simply call up a spirit by name and it might well answer. Many such sigils represented the soul of one entity, and if you knew the glyph for a spirit, then that one would *definitely* answer, drawn right up to the edge of the Veil, and effectively invited in by the summoner. The circle served to ward against the evoked entity, to invoke other spirits in order to counter its influence. Like the stones of an arch supported one another, the ring of spirits each served to compel and hold back the others, so a sorceress could focus her energy and will upon just the one she needed.

Oft named sirens, mer were spirits of Water. On the seashore, they could be called up close to the Veil. Sitting upon a rock in the midst of the circle, Pyrrha stroked the back of a chicken she had claimed for this purpose, trying to calm herself as much as it. She glanced up at the moon, trying to judge the lateness of the evening. It had to be closing in on midnight now, and she needed to trust Enodia would arrange things as she had promised.

She needed to begin.

Poseidon was a symptom of all wrong in the World, and someone needed to chasten him. He was the perfect person to test her own limits on.

But ... she had never incanted aught without the presence of her mentor. Nor had she counted on just how hard her heart would begin hammering at the idea of casting a spell without Enodia watching over her shoulder. Yes, she had practiced this, as much as one could practice such things without risking the invocation of actual spirits. And true, Enodia had inspected her glyphs before departing for the polis.

Still, one misspoken syllable, one faltering of her will, and Pyrrha would suffer under the thrall of any one of the spirits she now invoked or evoked.

When she spoke, her voice reverberated in her own head, the discordant resonances of Supernal feeling apt to shatter her skull. It was the language of spirits, and the purest language for incantations. It was also supremely alien to the human tongue. Her words sent vibrations thrumming through the air, pulsing like shockwaves through the Penumbra. Perhaps, had any outsiders walked the beach at this hour, they would have felt an unnamable wrongness seeping into the air. Perhaps they would have heard the words she spoke and thought them the ravings of a madwoman.

Perhaps, even, they would have dared brave the malaise that would saturate this shore and watch her, as she drove her knife into the chicken's breast, letting its hot blood wash over her hand before casting the bird into the circle. Blood and death, after all, acted like a clarion to the Otherworldly.

But no one came from the Mortal Realm. Rather, her onlookers drew in through the Penumbra, drifting towards her circle in ones and twos, shadows upon the fringes, drawing nigh slowly, like circling sharks. The dead came and watched, hunger in their eyes, tongues lolling. They were first. Then, from the woodlands, she watched as a tree split, and a naked female writhed from it, lurching free. The entity pitched onto the ground, then scrambled forward almost more lizard-like than human. Her flesh was discoloured, with a texture that appeared bark-like, and her eyes held a faint green luminosity.

She was followed by two lampades, the pale mist spirits wafting in on vaporous currents and moving to circle round the perimeter of Pyrrha's ritual.

It was the approach of the mer, though, that drew her attention. Covered in scales and barnacles, with flapping gills and fins, the creature appeared almost like a humanoid shark. Its too-wide maw leered at her and its opalescent eyes nictitated in a way that made her squirm, though she dare not cease her incantation.

While the other spirits edged around her circle, tracing fingers over its perimeter, the mer pushed against it with webbed palms. As if a membrane separated them that impeded but did not stop it. Slowly, it pushed through, into the circle.

On the Mortal side of the Veil, she caught sight of Poseidon at last, his signature brighter than most mortals for the amount of Pneuma coursing through his flesh. Wanting to see his face, Pyrrha blinked away the Sight, the spirits vanishing from view. Behind him, Enodia stood, clearly having guided him as she had promised, and exactly to a spot he could walk through without disturbing the glyphs or even noticing them. Without noticing much of aught, in fact, though his expression revealed a disquiet in him. He sensed the Otherworld bruising the Veil from here, even if he had no idea what the feeling was or what caused the hairs to rise upon his arms.

Of course, he could not resist the lure of a tryst. Of course, he could not bring himself to imagine that, when Enodia told him Pyrrha wanted to see him on the beach at night, she might have had aught in mind for him save the sating of his desires.

While she could not cease incanting, she lowered her voice to a whisper and allowed her peplos to drop free of one shoulder. She needed him to join her in the centre of the circle. A sudden thought occurred to her, even as she struggled to concentrate on the incantation and hold his attention. If he saw the chicken blood dribbling off her fingers ... Well, damn it. She couldn't explain that. To keep his attention, she further shrugged free of her peplos, exposing one breast.

When he drew nigh, he reached for her flesh. She placed her hand upon his chest, tracing a quick glyph to which he paid no mind.

"What are you saying?" he asked with his usual haughtiness.

"Nereus," she answered, then flicked blood off her hand into his face.

Poseidon staggered backward, blinking. "What the fuck?"

"Nereus, Prince of Pontus!" Pyrrha called and allowed her vision to shift back into the Sight.

Across the Veil, the mer launched itself at the victim marked with its glyph. The shark-thing hurtled into Poseidon, who spasmed.

Pyrrha could not see his face now, but she could imagine the dawning horror commingling with the pain.

Vaguely, she wondered if that was how slave girls felt the first time he intruded inside them. The spirit wrenched open Poseidon's mouth and drove a webbed, clawed arm down his throat.

Pyrrha almost gagged herself as Nereus somehow, impossibly, began to climb into Poseidon. The mer wriggled like an eel, and though it should never have fit, slowly—in time with the Titan's immense convulsions—it dragged itself within his body.

Poseidon pitched over, his convulsions intensifying. His legs snapped together and began to fuse even as scales punched through his flesh. His neck ruptured, gills tearing their way from flaps of skin.

An inarticulate moan drew her gaze outside the circle. Okeanus's ghost hurled itself against the circle's edge, drawing a yelp from Pyrrha. Her wards held, but as the shade slammed into them again and again, she had to wonder ... could a shade break through with sheer force of will?

Her heel brushed against a stone and she realised she'd begun to back away from the fury on display before her. "Nyx's bosom," she cursed.

The ghost's gaze landed upon her, its eyes glinting red with inhuman rage. It flexed its arms and bent its knees as if promising to rush her the moment she left the circle's confines. Then Supernal incantations rent the Ether once more, and Okeanus wilted, driven to its knees. It turned toward the source—Enodia approaching, deep in her cants. The sorceress pressed her palm against Okeanus's forehead.

A heartbeat later, the shade trembled as if the whole of it was liquid and someone had cast a stone into its body. It flailed and writhed, then began to melt into pooling shadows that lashed about it, drawing it into the dark beyond the Penumbra, a space Enodia called the Roil. Hard as it was to believe, Pyrrha could have almost sworn actual fear washed over its face in its last moments. Enodia ... frightened a ghost? How Pyrrha *longed* for such power.

When she looked back to the Mortal Realm, the mer that had

seized Poseidon had formed up legs once more and regained its feet. It cast aside his garments and, utterly naked, stared at her with opalescent eyes, its expression unreadable.

Only then, looking upon the spirit within its human host, did Pyrrha recognise the shrill scream that had been unfolding for Gaia knew how long. Only then did she look and see Styx, hands on her face, wailing at the horror Pyrrha had unleashed upon her brother.

IT WAS LIKE A DREAM, when the Telkhines came for her. Two of the mer, walking on legs, clad only in loose cloths wrapt around their waists. They grabbed her and dragged her up the cliff to Thebes, and on, into the acropolis where Tethys surged up from her throne like a cresting wave in a storm-tossed sea.

"How dare you assault my son!" It was, perhaps, Pyrrha's imagination, but the Titan's wrath shook the throne room. It dominated the whole of the acropolis, filling up the space of the palace with a turbulent force that drowned out all other sound and thought.

Pulse pounding, Pyrrha found all she could do was stare at her sandals and chance fleeting glimpses at the Lady of Thebes. That someone would have seen what she had done, that it would make it back to Tethys, had not *once* crossed her mind, fool that she was. Enodia had warned her that her desire to punish Poseidon would come with a cost, but Pyrrha had been so obsessed with vengeance she had assumed the sorceress meant a cost to her *soul*.

"Every incantation you utter tears at your essence," Enodia had said in *their earliest lessons. "And every spirit you evoke or draw upon feasts upon your life, ever so little. A sorceress is flensed over and over, until naught remains save a walking corpse."*

Tethys flowed about the throne room as if guided on some unseen force, gaze perpetually locked upon Pyrrha. Oh, Pyrrha could feel it, even as the Titan stormed across the space behind her. She could sense it, even while she focused upon her own toes. Naught one said at such times could make things any better.

At last, Tethys came to rest in the space before Pyrrha, close enough her breath fell upon the top of Pyrrha's head. "That you are my guest, Prometheus's daughter—and that my son Poseidon does still live—makes me consider his pleas for mercy on your behalf."

Now, despite her throbbing heart, she dared look up at the Titan.

"Exile," Tethys said, stretching the word to several syllables. "And should I hear of you nigh to my lands again, I will have you *hunted*. Like a pig, before I roast you upon a spit."

"Kill her," Styx implored, quietly, from amongst the columns.

Her mother ignored that. With a wave of her hand, the Telkhines reappeared, and each snared one of Pyrrha's arms. They ushered her from the palace with such force only their grip upon her kept her from tumbling down the acropolis stairs.

Most sentences of exile began at dawn, but the Telkhines ordered the gates thrown wide and shoved her outward, sending her sprawling upon her face.

"Be well away before dawn," Sirsir warned.

With a groan, Pyrrha looked up at the mer. Not bothering to answer, she pushed herself up and plodded away. She could have descended the cliff and returned to the harbour, but she half suspected the Telkhines might have orders to harry or even kill her if she tried, so instead, she headed for the river. If she followed it far enough, she would reach Korinth.

Thus, in the predawn blackness, she trudged along, the riverbank on her right and the plains leading to the cliff on her left. There was naught left for her to fear in the night, especially if she didn't try to look across the Veil. Well, naught save Men, for bandits might prowl the hills to the south, though she doubted any were about so early.

As she walked, though, a shape rose from the edge of the river not far beyond Thebes. It took a moment to recognise her father's silhouette, his crystal blue eyes.

"Papa." He had pleaded with Tethys for her and must have come here before her audience. Knowing which way she would come. He always knew such things.

Without a word, he approached and drew her into an embrace.

The warmth of it broke something inside her, and she shuddered. By Nyx, what a night she'd had. Papa stroked her hair as he had done when she was a child.

At last, he held her at arm's length, staring into her eyes with his own vibrant blue ones. "Pyrrha." Lines of tension marred his face. "You must turn back from the path you have set yourself upon. The Art has broken entire civilisations. It has rendered death on a scale you cannot conceive, blanketing the land in night. I beseech you to give over any further pursuit of this."

His grip was so tight upon her arms she yelped. Immediately, he released her, looking even more distressed that he'd hurt her.

Pyrrha rubbed her arms for a moment. He didn't understand. Oh, she knew he loved her, but he'd never understood what she needed. He had answers about her Sight and almost certainly knew more about her mother's death than he'd ever shared. Always, he held things back from her. A sudden realisation settled in upon her. On seeing him here, her heart had leapt, seizing upon the idea maybe she was not alone.

But if he came with her—and he would unless she denied him— he would only hold her back. Enodia was the one true friend she had ever had, for the sorceress alone had offered her power and answers.

"I'm going, Papa. I must make my own way."

"We can go to Ogygia, I have land there—"

Her raised hand cut him off, and the clapping shut of his mouth, the pain writ upon his visage, it tore through her. Gaia steel her resolve. "I must make my own way," she repeated.

And there was naught left to say.

14

PANDORA

1570 Silver Age

*W*hen Prometheus had made his way into the throne room, Hekate guided Pandora in behind him, then around to the side. They took up a position in the shadow of one of a dozen great fluted columns, watching as Pandora's Titan friend at last came to rest at the foot of the dais.

Numerous other spectators stood around the hall. Zeus's sycophants, no doubt, come to weather or bask in the mercurial whims of their mad king.

Braziers dangled from great chains running to the ceiling, providing additional illumination, though windows far overhead also let in beams of sunlight that crisscrossed the hall.

Zeus leaned forward, elbow upon his knee, hand stroking his beard. "Your nieces are dead, Prometheus."

Though she could not see his face, Pandora imagined her friend staring daggers at the king.

"They burned for their crimes and now I grow more tired still of your recalcitrance. Someone betrayed and murdered my son's loyal lover, and still, you have not told me the identity of the one who will betray me, though I know you have it, Oracle." The king stood abruptly. "Give me the name! Tell me of my perfidious kin, or the Pleiades' fate will seem paltry compared to yours!" The king had broken into screaming, but abruptly fell silent and brushed back his hair. "Tell me, my loyal ally. Tell me what the flames have shown you. Where do the traitors hide?"

"I can tell you that," Prometheus said, "unless your son fights at your side, Olympus itself will one day fall."

"That is not what I asked!" Zeus roared. The room trembled, the braziers dimming. A gust sent everyone's hair and clothing flapping, though it ought not have reached down from windows so far overhead. "Shall I call you Epimetheus now? For clearly you lack the foresight to know what will befall you if you deny me."

Zeus's icy eyes seemed have grown cloudy. Pandora whimpered, and Hekate's grip upon her elbow grew painfully tight.

"A name, a name, a fucking name, you ingrate cunt!" Zeus waved his arms in the air, and galvanic arcs actually leapt between his fingers, coruscating through the air.

Now Pandora wanted to weep. Not this. Not *this* again.

"I have no names for you this day, King," Prometheus said, the defiance—the *disdain*—in his voice so palpable Pandora might have choked on it. Might have cheered for it, had she not known what would follow.

"You would try to serve as the very hand of Ananke," Zeus bellowed, the spittle flying from his lips visible even from so far back. "You think yourself of a level with the Moirai? We shall see, Fatespinner. Your torment shall be the stuff of legend. Bards shall weep as they tell tale of fallen Prometheus, who thought himself wiser than even Zeus. Mothers shall frighten their contumacious offspring with bare hints of what you shall suffer!"

A wave of his hand, and a trio of Titans surged forward—all of them pushing seven feet tall and bulging with muscle—seizing Prometheus. Two females and a male, their postures and gestures lit with zealous malignancy, so clearly delighted were they to execute Zeus's mockery of justice.

"Who are they?" Pandora rasped.

"Kratos, Bia, and Zelus," Hekate said, voice trembling ever so slightly. "Styx's brood."

"Bind him over the black walls of Tartarus itself!" Zeus screamed, half cackling. "Let the ruination of his flesh serve as eternal reminder of the cost of treason!"

The male, Kratos, slammed his fist into Prometheus's gut. Pandora's friend doubled over, even as the two females dragged him backward. He looked up at her, though, his sapphire eyes locked upon her in silent warning and, perhaps, even sympathy. For *her*. As if he knew the pain she'd suffer at having another she cared for ripped away from her.

Pandora opened her mouth to scream and Hekate's grip on her tightened to the point it stole her breath. "He wanted you protected," she grated, dragging Pandora toward an archway behind the column. "I shall honour that."

The Titan witch guided Pandora roughly into a side corridor, not quite hiding the trembling in her free hand.

"Please," Pandora whimpered. "Please don't let this happen."

"Simpering imbecile," the witch snapped. "You speak as though the will of Zeus could be circumvented. One does not stand against him—one weathers his whims as best one is able."

Spoken like someone who had suffered her share beneath him. "They call you his dog," Pandora blurted, no longer even caring about the consequences. "More deserving still because I can see you loathe his paroxysms!"

The passageway they took fed back into the vestibule, and the witch shoved her onto the floor. Pandora landed on her elbow, the cold marble surface sending a knife of white pain shooting through her whole arm, stealing further words.

"He gave you freedom by focusing the whole of the king's wrath upon himself. Use the gift wisely. Do not return to Olympus." The witch stormed back toward the interior hall, giving Pandora not another look.

꙰

THERE WAS ravishing of the flesh that might scour down to the very soul. These wounds Pandora had suffered so oft she could no longer count their hidden scars. Then there was the savaging of the soul itself, direct and unmitigated by corporeal transmission. Such trauma sundered the very self.

The murder of Uncle Phoenix before her eyes.

The abduction and rape of Europa.

The eternal damnation of the one Titan who had ever shown her true empathy or friendship.

Upon the agora landing, Pandora stumbled, seized by her silent screams of defiance. Of rejection of Zeus and Fate and the sum of the World that could lead to this.

Almost, she could see herself tearing her very heart from her chest and casting it down the mountain, if only she could cease to feel these moments of fathomless anguish.

Some few onlookers peered at her, but none moved to help her in the least. Perhaps broken people descending this slope were too common a sight. Perhaps they could not be moved to care regardless.

No, but she would mend this. She would not surrender Prometheus to his fate. Swallowing, panting, she turned to face the repugnant palace on the acropolis. "I swear I'll fix it. I swear."

The temptation arose, of course, on the long climb down, to think her own words futile. Pandora refused to surrender to such thoughts. She refused to surrender any kernel of hope. Her desperation could not be allowed to give way to despair.

Slowly, her mind a roil, she descended the mountain. There would be long miles back to Delphi to brood over all that had transpired. As minds were wont to do, hers would revisit every moment from the time they left Ogygia to the moment Kratos and the others dragged Prometheus away. Would look, pointlessly, for somewhere she might have acted differently, spoken differently, led him to another end. More importantly, she searched for a way forward.

She would find one.

I rather think, Pandora, that you can accomplish aught you truly desire.

Now she had the truest of desires.

In Delphi she found a boatman awaiting her. Or at least he waved her over when she approached the docks.

"You're Pandora?" he asked.

She nodded.

"He thought you might come, might seek passage back to Ogygia."

Pandora shut her eyes. Had the flames told him so very much? Had he known he would ascend the steps of Olympus and not return? And he had gone anyway, even while making arrangements for her return.

"You know him?"

The boatman nodded. "Off and on, as his wanderings and mine cross. The name's Enki, and I can take you back, if you wish."

Ogygia was his place, even if Kalypso officially ruled the island. It was his, and maybe there, closer to him, she could see a way to reach him. To do the impossible and save someone from Tartarus itself.

"Yes. I will go."

The man—or Titan, perhaps, though his height was not quite high enough to say for certain—Enki, dropped her in the town of Marsa. He had held his peace on the voyage, which suited her, given her need to mentally review all that had happened. All that might yet happen.

Again and again, she had weighed the consequences of

confrontation with the ruler of Ogygia. More like than not, no good would come of an altercation, this she knew. And yet, Kalypso deserved to know what had happened to her great-uncle. Besides, times of emotion might shake loose hidden truths. And Kalypso and her Nectar bore at least part of the blame for Zeus's most recent bout of paranoia.

She flung open the door to Kalypso's estate and found not Prometheus's grandniece, but rather the Heliad Kirke, satchel over her shoulder. Pandora had thought she was leaving days ago, but it seemed she had lingered, perhaps waiting for word of Prometheus's fate herself.

"Where is Kalypso?" Pandora demanded.

Another sneer. Pandora had begun to wonder if Kirke's face could manage any other expression. "You presume rather much to come in here with such bravado."

Bravado, was it? Kirke had seen naught of that yet. "Did you know that Prometheus knew of what you and Kalypso brewed up here?"

The Nymph dropped her satchel and took a threatening step toward Pandora.

Pandora plowed on anyway. "He knew, but he refused to let you suffer the consequences of your own actions, so Zeus threw him into Tartarus!" The words had begun to pour forward, and she couldn't have stopped them if she'd tried. "He pays for your crimes! They beat him, they mean to torture him! He suffers Hades-knows-not-what because of—"

Kirke seized her by the throat, cutting off her words. The taller Nymph hefted her aloft, eye level with herself. "Shall I answer to you, now? If Prometheus suffers, he does so for his own reasons, while you chase after all that is unseen." Her grip tightened and Pandora's vision dimmed. "Trust me when I say you do not wish me as an enemy. Yeah, I can see how few friends yet remain to you, and still you keep making enemies."

The Nymph hurled her backward, and Pandora flew three feet through the air before collapsing on the ground, gasping, rubbing her throat. For an instant, she feared Kirke had actually caused real damage. Every breath felt like sucking down volcanic ash. By the time Pandora was certain her windpipe remained intact, Kirke was gone.

Maybe her anger had gotten away from her, just a little.

Maybe it was fucking rage.

❦

IN THE AVIARY, at sunset, Pandora stood over a table in the library. Two dozen scrolls were spread before her, with more scattered about the floor. First, she had looked over every recent missive Prometheus had collected. Maybe, she had imagined, she could find something in his correspondence that might aid her.

He had known Zeus might act against him, for he'd arranged that boatman for Pandora to return. Would it not stand to reason he would have then left some clue here for her as to what she should do next? That was, of course, assuming he'd known Zeus would cast him into Tartarus rather than offer some more mundane imprisonment.

Next, she began scouring his scrolls for reference to Tartarus itself. Of which, she found little. It was a nightmare prison. It lay, despite popular misconception, not in the Underworld, but *beyond* it. Beyond the scope of the entire World, and into some unknown darkness. It abutted but was distinct from some Otherworld called Erebus, the World of Dark.

Some of this came from speculation from some order called the Circle of Goetic Mysteries. Others were passing references from the Muses College in Themiskyra. Polyhymnia, in particular, favoured such subject matter, though she did not dive deep into aught that lay beyond the Mortal Realm, much less beyond the very World.

Growling, wanting to scream if her throat did not hurt so badly, Pandora heaved the scrolls off the desk. They smacked the oil lamp, which teetered. She grabbed it, searing her palm even as she managed to stop it from pitching down onto the papyrus.

"Grraaa!" she shrieked. The burning in her hand made the rawness of her throat dim.

Bubbling over with frustration, she stumbled down two flights of stairs and she plunged her hand in the fountain. A pair of disturbed flamingos squawked angrily at her disruption, so Pandora settled a withering gaze upon one.

"I've never eaten flamingo, you know. What do you think you taste like?"

Predictably, the flamingo did not answer.

Rising, Pandora flexed her palm. It still hurt. Everything hurt. Her soul ached.

Much as she'd told herself she'd shed every possible tear as a child and had none left, she felt the dampness threatening in her eyes as she continued to wander the empty Aviary. His place, and without him, even the birds somehow seemed more foreign than beautiful. The life here was gone from so much of this refuge.

Underground, in his workshop, though, she could almost feel him here. He'd come here nigh every evening since she had been living with him. He would tinker with his tools and work on the puzzle box he was making her, always saying it was 'almost ready.'

There it sat, upon the work desk, insides and gears no longer exposed. A metal cube, worked with complex geometric patterns and numerous interlocking panels. Prometheus had not let her get a good look at it before, always insisting she wait until he'd finished the design.

And this was the symbol of what he'd done for her, wasn't it? A gift for her, wanting naught in return, merely because he saw her pain and wanted to ease it. Or because ... because ... Why did one person go to extraordinary lengths for another? Why had Uncle Kadmus brought her the first puzzle box from Atlantis when she was a child?

Pandora traced her fingers along the ridges of the box, wondering at its intricacies. It was hard to even focus ...

A hot tear fell from her eye and splashed upon the desk.

Gods!

She rubbed angrily at her eye. Gods, she wasn't going down that road.

Well, at least she would solve the box, clear her head, and get back to figuring out how to reach him in Tartarus.

She pushed at a panel and found it slid to the side with a simple nudge. Another, and then another. Huh. Though Prometheus had concealed the gears within, segments of the box could twist and turn, creating a design of almost endless permutations.

End upon end, she rotated the panels, time melting away as she mused at the masterpiece. Another panel slid into place, then she could twist the middle ring on the bottom. That seemed to unlock rotation of other rings.

She'd never seen—nor imagined—such a complex puzzle. Was there only one solution or were there a thousand? Or was the entire thing one big diversion meant to entertain without actually having a—

As she twisted the box once more, the top slid open, exposing a circular panel that rose up. And then the World itself shifted. Air currents popped, followed by her ears. A wave of vertigo ensnared her, bringing her to her knees. Light around her bent back on itself, as if she was caught in a collapsing bubble.

Then a flash of darkness.

PANDORA OPENED HER EYES. It was no longer night. And she was no longer inside, but rather kneeling by a dirt road. A warm ocean breeze swept in from the north.

North. The ocean should have been south of the Aviary.

And this ... Pandora turned, looking around herself. The whole landscape had changed. The box—and what a box!—had transported her to another island?

That seemed utter madness.

From down the road, a stream of people rapidly approached. There were donkeys hauling carts and men and women and even children, arms laden with bundles, all scrambling toward her at a half dash. Some cast furtive looks over their shoulders as if the Furies pursued them.

Where in Hades's vile world was she? What the fuck was going on?

"Hey!" Pandora shouted at a woman scurrying down the road. "What's happening?"

The woman looked at her as if she were utterly mad. "You haven't heard?" Her accent was a bit off, a strangeness to her words. "Khione landed to the south, come to claim the island from Helios. She and her war band are heading this way, and the only refuge will be inside Helion." The woman actually grabbed Pandora and ushered her along. "Now move your arse lest you find out what an army does to a woman out alone."

Though her feet continued to carry her—the refugees seizing her like a riptide—Pandora's mind staggered from what she'd just heard.

Khione ... Khione ... As in Kalliope's play about the siege of Helion?

A cold having naught to do with the supposed Winter Queen had wrapt around Pandora's chest. An impossibility.

Khione. As in the Ambrosial War ... which had transpired some four thousand years ago.

INTERLUDE: PROMETHEUS

1570 Silver Age

Kratos's fist smacked into Prometheus's temple. The impact sent blinding whiteness surging through his vision, drowning out all other sensation. When hints of clarity once more seeped into his vision, Kratos and his sisters were dragging him down stairs he had last descended long ago, when Zeus had damned Kronos and his followers to the same fate Prometheus would now endure.

Despite himself, despite his foreknowledge of this and the ages spent preparing himself, a gasp of despair escaped him. This Fate he would have paid most any price to avert. Most prices, but if there was a way around it that did not betray Pandora or the future, he could not see it.

His end had always led here.

Bia chortled in manic delight. "Remember the last time we came here together? Oh, what times we've had together, haven't we now?" Styx's daughter jabbed his bruised ribs with one finger. "Ah, you didn't even see what lies beyond, though. Ooo, hehe. It's glorious, I tell you."

Not deigning to answer her, Prometheus held his tongue, focusing his mind inward. He would need the retreat of deep meditation to survive this. He would withdraw into the palace of his memories and find solace in the moments he had stolen from eternity. He would sever any awareness of his corporeal form and thus endure whatever ravages were visited upon it.

He would ... fool himself. Pretend the tongues of agony would not lap at his heels.

The siblings carried him down into the cavern deep within Olympus.

There, across the breadth of the cavern, lay the hateful Tartarian Gate, an archway cut into rough stone and leading into another tunnel. A tunnel to a place that was not a place, beyond all Realms.

"There are demons there," Zelus said, seeming almost to speak to herself. "Formless abominations from before the dawn of time. They shift and writhe and ..." The Titan shuddered, in some perverse amalgam of horror and ecstasy. "They wriggle up inside you."

Kratos and Bia shoved Prometheus forward, sending him staggering toward the Gate. For an instant—only an instant—he debated trying to struggle against them. Though the orichalcum fetters suppressed his Pneumatikoi and the Art of Fire, leaving him essentially mortal, he *might* have still escaped.

But he had seen the ambit of Fate, and this was his. He had to pass through the torment if the future was to have even the fragile chance he'd hoped to give it. All of it, his interminable life, would amount to naught if he refused to accept this.

Besides, maybe this was justice, long denied, for his own misdeeds. He had manipulated and killed, and even those crimes paled in comparison to those who had died as a result of his actions and inactions. All-consuming oceans of pain and death fell at his feet in the name of his gambit against Fate. So perhaps he owed those who had suffered because of him this retribution.

When Kratos grabbed him once more, Prometheus did not resist.

The Titan pushed him through the archway. And the archway pushed back, the air turned viscous, the pressure like wading through a quagmire. Then they pulled free and Prometheus's ears popped. His skin tingled as if a multitude of invisible ants nibbled every inch of his flesh.

Kratos's sisters followed, and the three of them guided him downward, descending deeper, not through Olympus—for they had left the Mortal Realm behind—but into the atramentous wasteland of Tartarus, the binding wall of the World. The only light in the tunnel came from the torch Zelus bore, and, oh, how Prometheus longed to be able to reach for the flame and immolate these sadistic cretins.

Down and down they plodded, until a faint incandescence lit the passage ahead. Unable to suppress his dread, Prometheus shut his eyes for a few steps. Kratos and Bia were guiding him anyway. Was he truly about to suffer this? Was this real?

He had betrayed the so-called Elder Gods, or so Nemesis had accused him. This was the end that choice had brought him to.

When he opened his eyes, the cavern ahead had come into view. Fell light emanated from tornados of flame and iridescent fulgurations in vast expanses of emptiness that demarcated the edge of the World. The greater cavern was actually a rim of stone encompassing the Realms, broken by flows of sputtering magma and surrounded by the first of two concentric, onyx walls. Covered in spikes and bounded with chains that ran off into jutting stone outcroppings, the walls of Tartarus glinted with infernal light and dripping blood. Those walls bent, in convex arcs, seeming to warp if looked at, twisting into impossible geometries.

The twisting summit vanished into the staggering blackness that engulfed Tartarus. But it was what lurked between the two walls that truly boggled the mind with profound foulness, and Prometheus had no doubt some degree of Zelus's derangement had come from first-hand experience with the horrors. Demons, as she said, spawned in Khaos, and bound within the World by these walls.

His captors dragged him toward a cyclopean pillar that rose outside the wall. Spiralling stairs encircled the column, and they followed that path, round and round, while Prometheus clenched his jaw lest he release any other sign of despair. That satisfaction, at least, he would deny them. He would not plead nor make vain struggles as he knew they would delight in.

At the terminus, a spiked chain joined the column, the links each bigger around than a person. The chain ran up to the top of the black walls, which was clearly how the siblings intended to get him up there. The idea of leaping off flashed through his mind. A fall from high enough would kill even a Titan. Not him, though. The Fates would not allow his death, no matter how he longed for it.

They marched him up toward his damnation, and he could not resist. The chains seemed to squirm beneath his sandals as if alive with the tainted foulness of this prison. As if they were part of the writhing torment encompassing the whole of the cosmos.

As they ascended, the air grew thick with cloying shadows and smoke billowing up from lava flows, until they gasped for each breath, and Bia broke into wet coughs. Still, they pushed him upward, past curving spikes jutting from the wall, any one of which was the size of a house. Up, past more chains, to crest the wall itself.

Despite the appearance of onyx, it had an almost fleshy give beneath his sandals, leaving no doubt this boundary was *alive*. Prometheus only dared to hope it was not conscious. The expanse of this inner wall stretched long, but—for what he could only assume was further perversity—his captors guided him to the far side, hundreds of feet across.

There, Kratos held him, allowing him to gaze on in horror at the caliginous tracts between the two walls. Within the infinite shadows, he beheld the squirming masses of formless entities. Ever shifting, their very natures seeming inchoate, as flailing appendages formed and unformed upon bloated, amorphous bulks throbbing with prurient need. Amid them opened a sea of eyes and mouths and sex organs, all as transitory as the rest.

Any given entity continuously vanished into the endless dark of the Khaos bound within the walls, making it impossible to gauge their numbers or size. Impossible, yes, but he knew them as manifold, and each an enormity onto itself.

Behold the abject horror of the Ontos.

"They feast upon our souls," he rasped.

"Oh, yes," Zelus purred. But she had no idea what he meant, thinking, no doubt, he feared merely for *his* soul, for having come here. As if these abominations would not claim *all* souls in time.

With degenerate sensuality, she stripped Prometheus's clothes, even as Kratos hammered his fetters into a spike upon the wall. The wall itself rippled at the assault, and Prometheus imagined he felt it shudder in discomfort.

Zelus stroked against his manhood and he fitted her with a glare. Abruptly, her knee snapped up into his groin, sending him toppling to the ground. The force of it doubled him over in all-consuming agony. Such that it took him a moment to even realise Bia had wrapt barbed chain lengths about his wrists, further tethering him here, looking out over the ocean of tenebrous Khaos.

"Zeus says you cannot die, *Epimetheus*," Bia taunted. "So he'll test that by sending a bound harpy to come and eat your liver." Curled up in a ball against the pain in his groin, Prometheus could not even wince. "I wonder what will happen? Will it grow back?" She snickered. "If so, I suppose the harpy will have a fine supper every night, won't it?"

Kratos blew on some whistle, perhaps intended to summon the Storm spirit Bia had mentioned.

Prometheus shut his eyes, retreating inward. He had known this was coming. Had prepared for it.

As he fell into himself, their voices faded into oblivion.

Those with trained minds, especially those with the Sight, could learn to reenter their pasts. To live them afresh, within the palace of memories. And Prometheus had a palace overflowing from his interminable life. He had been so many men, passed so many years.

Enough he might—almost—ignore even the pain the harpy promised.

Almost.

PART III

In those days Atlantis was yet known as Hesperides Island. None can say how Lord Atlas tamed the ancient drakon Ladon, but he did so, and through Ladon, claimed Hesperides Island and renamed it after himself. This affront —history records—the other great Titans could not bear, knowing an interruption in the flow of Ambrosia would cost them their immortality. War, then, became the only recourse. War for the Ambrosia.

    — Kleio, Analects of the Muses

15

ARTEMIS

200 Golden Age

An unnatural blizzard bombarded the woods on Helion, no doubt choking the city as well. Artemis's father's men probably couldn't even risk riding forth to hunt for where this witch Khione might lurk. Crouching beneath a cypress tree, Artemis raised an arm against the pounding snows and shivered.

Word had come that war had broken out between the Titans. A shame for the people, but it was her chance to prove herself just as worthy as her brother. Helios seemed to think, just because Artemis's Phoebid nature had dominated—with her ebony hair and silver eyes—she could never be worthy as his heir. No, he wanted someone with his golden eyes, like her twin. Or maybe he just wanted a *boy* child.

But it wasn't Apollon stalking these woods, hunting for the Titan who laid siege to Father's city. It wasn't Apollon who would win this war for Helion. No, Artemis had spent the better part of five decades in constant training, and she doubted even her father could match her talents at Pneumatikoi.

She allowed Pneuma to flow through her, collecting in her senses. Perspicacity, masters termed it. Her eyes sharpened until she could make out the fur of a rabbit scrambling for cover even through the curtain of snow separating them. She could smell the animal from twenty feet away. She could even hear the crunch of ice as it hopped.

Grinning, she rose and slipped from beneath the tree, stalking through the woods, bow in hand. She nocked an arrow but didn't draw. With Pneuma-enhanced strength, she could shoot even in this weather, but not far. The wind and elements would snatch up her arrow before it had crossed much distance. She would need to be close to Khione. Close enough she would probably only get one shot.

But if she made it, if she killed the Titan Queen, even Father would have to favour her.

Pushing through the snow, she hunted. Khione would not have come alone, of course. Freezing the city would not allow her to claim it without a war band. Artemis just needed to find them and, if she could, catch Khione separated from the others.

Before long, her teeth began to chatter from the cold. She could flow a little Pneuma into Tolerance, but she would need every breath of her power to confront the Titan and her warriors. Better to suffer a little now than deplete her reserves. Then, almost as if she had reached some invisible barrier, the snow abated. Behind her, a blizzard raged, and before her, mere flurries dusted the land. The clouds overhead actually swirled about the rest of the island, forming an iris above this one hill, showing blue sky overhead.

Unexpected.

Artemis faltered, dropping to a crouch in the snows despite the temptation to rush forward into the relative warmth of the hill. Up there lay the cyclopean ruins of the old city. Had Khione chosen its broken colonnades to house her warriors, keep them fresh while the rest of Helion was worn down by her foul weather?

If so, it changed a few things.

Still crouching, Artemis crawled forward until she could make out the marble columns and the men moving among them. She cocked her head, focusing her senses.

"How much longer we gonna wait?" a man asked.

"If you think you're weary of it," another answered, "imagine how Helios's poor bastards in the city feel. Give it another day and they'll be begging to surrender."

Artemis sneered. They would see who begged.

She took a breath to settle herself, picturing herself drawing in more Pneuma. She allowed it to flow through her like water coursing through canals. Opening the sluice gates, focusing the flow powered numerous Pneumatikoi. Alacrity to enhance her reflexes and running speed. Lightness to manipulate her gravity. Potency for superhuman strength.

Grasping her bow and arrow with one hand, she broke into a trot, racing up the hill, covering the distance as fast as a galloping horse. The instant she reached the closest column, she leapt up onto it. Lightness allowed her to run along its surface nigh forty feet, to reach its capital. She caught the lip with her free hand and heaved, flinging herself atop the column. She landed in a silent crouch, then leaned forward, peering down at the warband below.

No obvious sign of any females. If Artemis got closer, maybe she could feel the other Titan's Pneuma, but from up here, she was too far above. Instead, she scanned the men Khione had brought with her. A single sentry was posted at each of the four cardinal directions, none of whom seemed to be much on guard. Perhaps they justifiably imagined no one coming here through the blizzard.

They were, however, far enough out ...

She nocked her arrow and sighted the sentry closest to her. Her enhanced senses allowed her to pick out a gap between the man's helm and cuirass. She loosed. Her arrow took him in the neck and he fell, unnoticed by his companions. In quick succession, she took out the remaining three sentries.

Below her, another man pissed on the column, too lazy to make his way to the latrine ditch. His mistake.

With a brief influx of Pneuma to toughen her bones and muscles, Artemis drew a knife, then dropped down behind him. He started to turn—midstream, the nasty bastard—but she moved far more quickly than he could have hoped to, slitting his throat and darting behind another column before his body had hit the ground.

She stalked amid the colonnade, her blade making quick work of man after man. A dozen were dead before the first cry of alarm went up, a body discovered. Artemis leapt onto a column, kicked off it, and used the momentum to fly into the courtyard, landing amid a startled group of six mortals.

"Titan—" one of them started to cry, an instant before her knife cut his throat.

They reached for weapons, tried to swing at her. But with the Pneumatikoi of Alacrity, their movements seemed comically languid, as if they flailed at her from underwater. She ducked under a blow, ramming her knife into the man's armpit, then jerking it free only to drive it into the eye of another. Her kick shattered a man's knee. She caught him as he began to fall and flung his body as a missile at a pair more of men who tried to close in.

Her remaining adversaries continued to attack, but to them, Artemis must have seemed a whirlwind of death. She twisted out of the way of their blows with ease, cutting down one after another. Even as the last in the courtyard had fallen, she had snatched up her bow once more. She leapt into the air, kicked off a falling man's head, and spun, nocking and loosing while flying to another column.

She couldn't say if her arrow actually hit its mark, but she continued to bounce between the columns, nocking another, and firing into the ranks of the terrified mortals.

As expected, they broke, screaming and fleeing into the raging blizzard rather than remain here amid flying death. Artemis allowed herself a grim smile of satisfaction at their panic.

And then she felt it. The crackling force of concentrated Pneuma drawing nigh, tingling her senses. She had Khione's attention.

Maybe the other Titan could sense her too, though few had developed their Perspicacity to such degrees as Artemis. The moment she hit the ground, she dashed behind another cyclopean column, arrow nocked.

The Pneuma source drew closer.

Almost here.

Artemis stepped out and loosed her arrow. The figure she saw had hair even whiter than Kronos's brood, with skin that seemed to have its colour sucked right out. She bore a loose white peplos, completely heedless of the cold. Khione waved a hand, and a curtain of mist knocked the arrow out of midair. A flick of her fingers sent a cascade of ice shards—as big as javelins!—shooting for Artemis.

Pulse pounding, she ducked back behind the column the instant before those missiles impacted. Behind her, a chorus of cracking and crashing erupted, sounding as if the ice had even managed to crack the ancient stone.

What in the Underworld was *that*? Artemis had assumed some foul sorcery had allowed Khione to summon this blizzard, but no Titan she'd ever heard of could do what she'd just witnessed. Pneumatikoi allowed one to manipulate energy in their own body. Not generate ice javelins.

A breath, and she increased the flow of Pneuma to her Pneumatikoi, then stepped out, another arrow nocked. Again, she loosed.

Again, a surge of misty coldness seized the arrow mid-flight. Khione slammed a fist into the ground and ice crystals erupted along it in a cascade streaming for Artemis. It was all she could do to leap onto an adjacent column, kick off that, and flee deeper into the colonnade.

Wispy laughter chased her. Khione was *enjoying* this.

A sudden thought struck Artemis like a blow. What if she was not the hunter this day?

Rather than peek around again, she darted behind column after column, focusing on the pulsing heat of Khione's Pneuma in her mind. All she had to do was outmanoeuvre the other Titan.

Of a sudden, boreal winds whipped through the ruins. Whatever force had held back the storm from this place had been withdrawn. Blinding snowfall obscured Artemis's vision outside the covered porticos. If Khione was trying to conceal herself thus, it seemed to confirm she didn't realise Artemis could sense the very throb of her life.

She allowed herself a grim smile and continued to edge toward that Pneuma, keeping columns between her and her prey. She *also* had to assume Khione herself could see through the snowstorm, which meant Artemis needed stealth to get around her. The vicious weather would prevent her from running up any more columns, either. Maybe that had been Khione's main intention.

Arrow nocked, Artemis stalked round and round, ever closer. Blowing out a breath, she stepped between two pillars, drawing a bead upon the source of Pneuma. She loosed. Immediately, she took off at a dead sprint, racing for the other Titan.

A wild gale caught her arrow and instead of landing in Khione's torso it gouged her arm. The Titan screamed. Briefly. Artemis collided with her, her fist slamming into Khione's side with enough force to hurl the woman bodily through the air. Khione flew almost ten feet before crashing into a column, then tumbling onto the rime-coated marmoreal floor.

Artemis started to leap at her, then realised with her Lightness Pneumatikoi held, the winds would fling her about like a leaf. Instead, she raced forward, pulling her knife once more. Before she closed, Khione had gained her feet. Clearly, with such speed and ability to ignore pain, she had mastered some Pneumatikoi herself.

A xiphos of ice formed in her hand and Khione lunged at Artemis. She had not expected a swordfight—especially armed with a shorter knife—and all Artemis could do was deflect and fall back. Further blades of ice erupted from Khione's flesh. Shards of it wormed their way free then launched themselves into the air at random angles.

Once more pressed, Artemis dodged around both the projectiles and Khione's ice sword. The Titan wasn't bad but had clearly not focused overmuch on martial disciplines.

Artemis, however, had. She waited until Khione overextended, then stepped inside her reach and slashed. The knife struck Khione's skin but barely scratched it, as though Artemis had hit a bronze cuirass. Pneumatikoi of Steadfastness.

Rather than fall back, Artemis grabbed the other woman in a

pankration hold and twisted, slamming her down into the ground. Icicles burst from Khione's skin, gouging Artemis's arm. The knife clattered onto the stone. Khione struggled, a match for Artemis's Potency, if not her technique. Artemis shifted until she managed to wrap her legs around Khione's arm and pin it.

With her free hand, she grabbed an arrow from her quiver and slammed it into Khione's eye.

Not easy to fortify *that* into bronze.

The Titan spasmed beneath her and a wave of cold sent Artemis tumbling over backward, clutching her arms around her chest. Her insides felt frozen solid. Her mind ceased to function. It took all she had to grasp her Pneuma—she'd used so much already—and send it into Tolerance. Slowly—painfully—warmth seeped back into her organs.

She caught her breath.

The blizzard had faltered, the sun beginning to poke through the clouds. Rays fell upon her face, forcing her to blink in the sudden radiance. Had that all just happened?

For a time, she just lay there, reeling. Then she turned, looking over at Khione's corpse. Beyond the Titan lay the bodies of so many of the men Khione had brought with her. They did not deserve her remorse. No, these men had come here to raze and plunder and would have murdered, raped, and enslaved had they breached Helion.

Still, caught in the moment, Artemis realised she had ended a score of lives without the barest second thought. Should that concern her?

With a groan, she rolled over and gained her feet. She would need the body to prove to Father she had been the one to accomplish this. Not Apollon, no. Artemis.

Her arrow had made a mockery of Khione's former beauty. Would it prove more grotesque to remove it and leave the gaping wound, or to leave it be and let Helios see how it had played out? After a moment's deliberation, she decided to leave it and dragged Khione by her hair all the way to the gates of Helion. Doing so required her to flow a bit more Pneuma in Potency, further draining her reserves. It would take her days to draw back in the breath to replace what she'd expended here.

At the city gates, open-mouthed guards took the corpse from her, offering her escort to the acropolis. The whole of her body ached now, and, much as she wanted to see Father's reaction, still more she longed for wine, food, and a soft bed. Maybe a hot bath first.

Helios's seneschal led her into the expansive hall with its soaring ceiling and bright-painted columns. Her father sat upon his throne, golden eyes gleaming. Others stood amid the columns, among them her glowering brother.

"So it's true," Father said, rising when Khione's corpse was cast at the base of the dais upon which his throne rested. He cast but a cursory glance at the fallen Titan before shifting his gaze to Artemis. "And *you* managed to slay her?"

Artemis stiffened. Still, even now? Even after all she had done, had she not won some measure of respect from this man? "I did."

"Hmm." Helios returned to his throne. "Well. I suppose you've earned a reward. Perhaps I can make a good marriage for you. Kronos has two sons, maybe one of them."

She wanted to spit. She wanted to scream. "I do not need a man. Neither as my *reward* nor to govern me."

Though she had let go of her Perspicacity, she could have sworn her brother snickered in the wings. Her imagination, maybe.

"The very fact you could make such a claim proves you do," Helios said with the air of dismissal.

Artemis gaped at him. It was like ... he didn't begin to see the circularity of his claims. The sheer absurdity of it left her speechless.

With naught left to say, Artemis fled the throne room.

Only when she was alone in her chambers did she allow herself to curse. A string of expletives that would have made great Ouranos himself blush.

16

ATHENE

1570 Silver Age

*H*and resting upon the slight bulge of her belly—could anyone even tell yet?—Athene stalked the halls of the Throne of Zeus. It was hard to even breathe after what Father had done to Prometheus. He had summoned all the Olympians to witness the trial, if trial was even the right word for what Athene had just seen. She didn't know whether to feel more shocked at the idea that one of their own would betray her father, or at what Father had done about it.

Her gut roiled, but surely this was too soon for nausea from the babe. Wasn't it? When did these things even begin? Before now, Athene had never much troubled herself with such petty concerns.

While she wended between the marmoreal columns and the shadows saturating the back of the palace, Hera abruptly stepped out in front of her. The queen wore the finest peplos Athene had ever seen, so heavy with embroidery a mortal woman's shoulders would have ached from it, but cut in a style that had gone from fashion two hundred years ago. Perhaps Hera dressed thus to promote 'traditional' standards. Perhaps she simply had no clue how people garbed themselves anymore.

The queen's gaze darted to Athene's hand upon her abdomen and sneered, apparently having judged the case at once. "I suppose it shouldn't surprise me a whore would wind up thick with child out of wedlock. Especially a bastard whore."

Much as she would have liked to step around Hera and ignore her —or, in fact, to punch her in the face—one did not ignore queens. Or punch them, sad to say. "Greetings, Mother."

If it was possible, Hera's gaze grew even more withering. "Do not call me that. Your mother is as much a whore as you are. I'm sure you'll find the dog around here somewhere."

Athene sketched a quick bow, just low enough to avoid making her disrespect obvious, but not so low Hera would miss its perfunctory nature. "I had best seek her out, then, shouldn't I?"

While Hera's words were not technically a dismissal, Athene took them as such and darted around another column. She had to hunt her mother, though, and when she found her, it seemed she was actually returning from the main entrance. Perhaps she had gone out for some air after what Father had just done to Prometheus.

Pensive, Athene beckoned to her mother, who nodded and drew her into a side room. The moment they entered, a pair of slaves who had been setting the couches scrambled out, as if they expected the Olympians to bite them. Or, well, Mother wasn't an Olympian, but then Men feared the goddess Hekate far more than they did Athene.

"Bring wine!" Mother called out after the retreating slaves, then settled upon a divan set within the room's atrium, reclining in the cool sunlight. Her expression was unreadable, save that a mountain now weighed upon her. She looked a woman ready to drown in her own thoughts.

"I'm sorry," Athene offered, perching upon the divan's foot beside her mother. She was afraid to even ask how her mother felt this day. Her relationship with Prometheus was complex, Athene knew.

Perhaps Mother would have answered, but she was saved from

doing so by the slave returning with an amphora of wine and two bowls. He placed both upon a table before the divan, then retreated in a half bow, scuttling like a crab.

Mother snatched up the amphora and filled both bowls with an aromatic vintage that, when Athene leaned closer for a proper sniff, seemed imported from Illyris. The added spices had a pleasant bite, and its warmth filled her so much she closed her eyes.

"You are with child," Mother said, jolting Athene back to the present. Was it the Sight that told her thus, or had she noticed even the faint bulge? Or some motherly instinct Athene could not understand?

"I am," Athene admitted, setting her bowl down.

"Unwanted."

Athene squirmed. "The father was unwanted. I will keep the child." How did she know these things? Oh, sometimes Athene caught flickers of insight when her mind drifted, that was true. But Mother, she had ways of discovering the answers to questions she ought not have even known to ask. *Seen from the vantage of dreams*, Mother had once said of her gifts.

Her mother sipped her wine. When she set the bowl down, her visage had become so severe Athene recoiled a hair. "He was here."

Yes, Hephaistos too had answered her father's summons, and Athene had made certain to keep columns between them, and to flee the room the moment Father had left. She had no desire to see him, much less to give him any chance to discern her condition. "He did not see me."

Mother clucked her tongue but nodded. "If you need help, Daughter, you have but to ask."

"I know, and I will. When the time is right."

A slight smile rose upon Mother's face. "You sound a bit like your older sister."

While Zeus had many daughters, including Hebe, his Olympian child with Hera, Athene had no doubt Mother meant *her* other daughter, Kirke. What the Heliad knew of vengeance, Athene didn't really know, but Kirke had tried to help her, and she would not forget that.

"Come," Mother said, rising. "I want to show you something."

She led Athene deep into the Throne of Zeus, into back chambers beyond where Kratos and the rest of Styx's offspring had dragged Prometheus. At first, Athene assumed Mother intended to show her the infamous Tartarian Gate, but she broke away instead, leading her deep inside the mountain, down steps cut into the raw stone.

Rather than proceed into the far depths where the Tartarian Gate lay, though, she paused before an orichalcum-banded door Athene remembered well, for Father had never once allowed her down here in her almost sixteen centuries of life. Mother laid a palm upon the door and murmured something under her breath, sounds that had the hair on Athene's arms rising. Then she opened the door, revealing a circular cavern. Along the perimeter rested a half dozen quicksilver mirrors, each framed by its own arch, which themselves represented the only cut stone in the chamber.

"The Seeing Pools," Athene breathed.

"Common folk name them thus," her mother said, "but properly they are called the Oracle Mirrors. Long, long ago, Kronos constructed these from quicksilver, though even I cannot fathom how he accomplished it." Her mother drifted around the cavern, casting furtive glances at each mirror in turn. "When we took Olympus, your father and I sought to understand Kronos's secrets. There are so many things you do not fathom about the World, its past, and its future, my daughter."

Athene moved toward one of the arches, but before she could look deeply, Mother caught her elbow.

"Your father has become obsessed with these devices. He hunts for something in the past or future, something he will not share with me. Whatever it is, it haunts him night and day. There is danger in too much knowledge, especially knowledge of the whims of Fate."

A chill sweat built upon her back at her mother's words. "Then why bring me here at all?"

"Because while knowledge has a price, it does not mean we

should not strive for it. That principle has guided my life, Athene, and as my daughter, you too have the potential for the Sight. Perhaps these mirrors will help spark the gift in you."

"Is that what sparked yours?"

Mother grimaced. "No. My method is not available to you." She squeezed Athene's elbow in reassurance. "Your father has begun to lose himself, child. I am not certain I can ever forgive what he has done to Prometheus."

Athene nodded slowly. She thought she understood, though Mother left so much unvoiced. Maybe sharing this with her was a subtle way of spiting her father for what he'd done, while helping Athene to become more like her mother. Still, she could not turn away from this chance.

With tentative steps, she approached one of the mirrors. At first, she saw naught save the silver sheen. But the surface was not flat, it rippled like water, and had depth that had earned these mirrors the name 'pools.' Vertiginous waves seized her, and Athene stumbled, feeling like she plummeted into the mirror itself.

An icy chill washed over her skin while silvery images blurred about her. A flicker, a fall, as if into the mirror.

A gasping breath as her vantage lurched into impossible angles.

⋛

A SERPENTINE NECK *wrapt around her ankle and Athene shrieked as it jerked her underneath the slavering monster. The Gígas's fist slammed toward her face.*

She twisted to the side and the blow crashed into loose scree, sending the both of them careening further down the escarpment, toward a precarious ledge that might pitch them into open air beneath Olympus.

Now, the creature leaned in, roaring at her with teeth filed into fangs, spewing putrid breath over her. It meant to actually bite her face off.

Screaming, Athene twisted the spear in its belly. The Gígas's gaping maw twisted up in pain.

Flooding as much Pneuma as she could into the Pneumatikoi of

Potency, Athene heaved with her legs. Her attacker flew skyward five feet, enough for her to roll out from under it before it crashed back down onto the slope. Its momentum sent it skittering toward the precipice below. On her belly, Athene watched as it skidded over the edge, arms and serpents flailing wild gyrations for the heartbeat before it dropped off into the mists.

More Pneuma. She needed to send more Pneuma coursing through her channels, into the Pneumatikoi of Tolerance to block the pain and get her moving.

Doing so, she had barely gained her feet before another shadow fell over her.

Oh, damn.

Athene dove to the side once more, an instant before the crashing form of another Gígas landed in the spot she had just occupied. The impact of its landing flung up a storm of loose rock, but it barely fazed the Gígas, who was already up, advancing upon her with a spear.

This one had legs and was barely warped by the consumption of Man-flesh. Only when she rose, her own spear between them, did she recognise its—his—face. Pallas, son of Kreios and father of Hephaistos, among other perverse spawn. His eyes had taken on a leonine aspect, and coarse hair had sprung up around him like a mane, but otherwise he might still have passed for an ordinary Titan.

Still, he had joined the attack on Olympus. Which meant she was more than free to kill the bastard.

But this ... she had seen this moment. The revelation dazed her, left her reeling, even as she remembered it had in her vision.

His lunge, when it came, was so fast she barely saw him move. Even with her Alacrity Pneumatikoi flowing, he was a blur, his spear thrust more like a soaring arrow. Her own spear turned the point aside, barely, but not before it struck her cuirass with enough force to part the bronze, then gouge her bicep.

Stumbling backward, Athene gave ground under the furious onslaught, careening ever closer to the same ledge she had just sent the other Gígas pitching down. Pallas roared—that too more lion-like than human—and charged in, and Athene could see why some Men had called him a god of war like her brother Ares.

Again and again, she deflected his spear with her own, only managing to keep up by continuing to give ground. She'd never defeat him like this, though. Internally, she shifted the flow of her Pneuma, draining even what she'd sent into Tolerance—and the pain hit her in fresh waves—to pour into the Pneumatikoi of Steadfastness, turning her flesh to iron.

His next blow, she allowed to take her in the shoulder. It punched through her cuirass, drove through her reinforced skin, and sent her down to one knee with sheer force. But her own swipe took out Pallas's kneecap and sent him pitching over, tumbling among the scree.

White haze danced at the fringes of her vision, her stomach lurching at the pain. It forced her to return the Pneuma flow to Tolerance just to retain consciousness. Shaking off the delirium, she gained her feet.

Pallas had started to turn over. Athene couldn't use her left arm but managed a clumsy swipe of her spear blade, nevertheless, carving out Pallas's hamstring. The Gígas bellowed in agony, all pretence of leonine might cast aside.

This bastard not only made war on Olympus ... Worse, he sired Hephaistos. What a father he must have been, to raise a son capable of such ... such ...

Panting, Athene dropped down, knees landing upon the Gígas's back. She cast aside the spear and pulled a knife, then wedged the point in between the creature's shoulder blades. "You know hunters claim lion skins as proof of their prowess ... I think I'm going to wear yours."

And she set to carving, his screams resounding off the slopes of Olympus.

DRENCHED in sweat and desperate to draw breath, Athene pitched over backwards. Her arse smacked hard upon the rocky floor, drawing forth a groan. But the physical pain faded far more quickly than the afterimages of madness which had flitted through her mind, and she caught herself casting about the cavern and cringing at the sight of the other Oracle Mirrors.

Then Mother was there, hands upon her cheeks, forcing Athene to look into her aureate gaze. Holding it there, tethered to this moment. Almost painfully, Athene's pounding pulse slowed, leaving behind an equally throbbing headache in its wake.

"What ...?"

"I do not know what you saw," Mother admitted. "The Mirrors are personal, and I cannot imagine what now haunts you. Some aspect of the past you had not known? Some vision of your future?"

The latter, for certain. And, much as it sickened her, part of her looked forward to it. Was she a monster to hope for such crushing violence?

"I'll have my vengeance," she rasped.

If her mother had any thoughts on that, they remained concealed, and the woman just patted her cheek, offering no further comment on the matter. Rather, she pulled Athene back to her feet. "Depending on how close to the surface your gift was, it is possible things will come to you again. Once woken, the Sight is less inclined to slumber."

After they exited the chamber, Mother resealed the door, once again muttering strange words under her breath with her palm upon the surface. Athene watched, dazed by what she'd seen, tingling with anticipation of when it would all come to pass.

When and how became the missing pieces of her puzzle, and she knew only the what and the why.

"He took from me ..." Athene said, her voice sticking in her throat.

Her words drew her mother up short, who turned, placing a hand upon her shoulder. "We are our choices. For someone to steal those is for them to pilfer pieces of our very souls."

The truth of that struck Athene, and she backed away, suddenly short of breath. Gasping, in fact, unable to keep wind down. With a shriek, with instinctive fury, she flooded Pneuma into Potency and Steadfastness then slammed her fist into the wall, sending spider-webs of cracks through the stone. Again. Again, roaring, her fists painting the tunnel in dust and blood. Until the screams became wracking sobs, and her mother drew her inward, holding her tight.

"He took *all* of me!"

"I know."

And for a long time, Mother just held her in the dark, a fervid beacon against Athene's side.

When she had caught her breath—and cleaned her face, for she'd not let the others see her thus—she began her ascent back to the palace.

"I'm going to raise this child," she said as they made their way back up the stairs.

"I had foreseen that," her mother admitted, casting a brief glance Athene's way. "A woman should have her mother's aid in such times." A pause. "If she wishes it."

By Hyperion's radiant light, yes. "Come with me to Kronion, Mother."

It was dark, and her mother was facing away, but Athene could have sworn a beaming smile graced the woman's face.

First Athene would bear her child, then she would see about real-ising the future.

17

PANDORA

200 Golden Age

The wave of refugees had swept Pandora up and into the city of Helion. She'd long heard tales of the place, though never seen it before. In the stories, a great Colossus had straddled the narrow inlet into the ringed bay. Here, no such monument existed. Of course not—it had not been built yet.

Her mind lurched in wild gyrations, the very World seeming upended by the circumstances in which she found herself. Had she heard some bard speak such a tale, she'd have called him a madman or a drunk. Or both. It was not so much she felt she wandered in a dream, but that a shroud that had blanketed her senses had fallen away. She at last saw the truth of life.

Cyclopean limestone walls encircled the polis, but despite their height and thickness, people pushed away from them, terrified of the Titan Khione who closed in upon the city. Even knowing how this ended—or how history recorded it ending—Pandora could not really blame them. A thin layer of snow now caked the rooftops and she felt the cold wafting off those outer walls.

Unless she missed her guess, an actual blizzard must rage outside, engulfing Helios's war bands in frozen rage. Of course, no one would allow her upon the walls to check, but she imagined what the fields must look like, encased in white. She was witnessing history unfold around her, and the thrill of that filtered the terror of her situation.

With nowhere to go, she sat in a tent pavilion the refugees had set up between the main tenements of the outer city and the cyclopean wall. Thousands of men, women, and children sat huddled here, wrapt in blankets and gazing upon their loved ones in desperate need of reassurance. Pandora could have given them that, could have told them the city didn't fall. But such words would have condemned her as a madwoman and probably seen her driven from this camp.

And what if she was *wrong*? Yes, she'd seen a play about these events thousands of years after the fact. Did Kalliope even know the full truth of these days when she wrought her play? Did she record history or modify it for dramatic reasons? If Pandora had actually somehow entered the past, was the past guaranteed to play out just as it had before, or could her mere presence change the outcome of the siege? These and a hundred more questions spiraled around her mind. Especially: could she return to her own time?

Still, it was not with total surprise she spotted the herald come amid the refugees, even before he banged his staff for attention. "The invader Khione is *dead*." Another clack of staff upon flagstone. "Khione is dead, slain by Helios's own daughter, Artemis." And once more he brought the staff down. "Return to your homes."

Pandora almost laughed. She might have to wait a while before her home became available. Atlantis wasn't even Atlantis yet. At the moment, it was probably still called Hesperides Island. Her mirth rapidly subsided, though, replaced by a tightness in her chest. Everything she'd ever known didn't even exist.

She didn't exist.

Half dazed, having not a clue what to do, she wandered the polis even as most of the other occupants of the tent pavilion began to filter out of the city. They could return to their farms and villages, though, if Pandora had her history correct, the Ambrosial War had only just begun and would rage on for some years to come. Maybe nowhere was truly safe, and that thought ought to terrify her.

Or ... or could she simply adjust a few panels on the box and have it take her somewhere else? Did she travel upon the will of Ananke, or did she, in using the box, spit in the very eyes of the Moirai? More to the point, if Prometheus's box *could* take her to any place or time, how could she begin to understand its workings? Just activating it without knowing what she was about might manage to drop her somewhere worse than this.

The gilded palace of Helion himself lay atop the acropolis, which itself sat upon a mountain at the city's heart. As the blizzard abated, the palace reflected sunlight in an aureate gleam that seemed nigh blinding from below. Perhaps the Titan lord could help her, though she couldn't imagine why he would. Her own golden eyes meant she probably carried his blood, yes, but so did innumerable others, and any Titan blood in her veins was too diluted to name her even a Nymph. Or maybe, at this point, none of the genē would even be established.

Pandora rubbed at her temples. How was she to function in a land that operated under such different paradigms?

And then, descending from the mountain, perhaps having come from the palace itself, she spied the auburn-haired Titan. Twice she blinked in an effort to reassure herself it was really him beyond the gleaming sunlight.

Maybe he was the one person who might offer some answer as to how she'd come here, or why.

Of their own accord, her legs broke into a run, a frantic dash that threw herself in Prometheus's path, panting, chest heaving.

The Titan fell back a step at her approach, his crystal eyes widening. His expression fell away almost as quickly, and he caught her elbows. "Pandora."

And if the run had stolen most of her breath, that simple name knocked what remained from her lungs like a blow from his muscled arms. He *knew* her. He knew her, some four thousand years before she'd even be born. How in Hades's infernal necropolis could he know her? How was *any* of this possible?

The question stilled upon her tongue, as if her heart was too weak to dare to ask it. Instead, she stood there in aphonic stupor, gazing at him, silently imploring him to force the World to make some kind of sense.

With a gentle hand upon her shoulder, he guided her back down the mountain. "This place is not safe. War has come here, and it won't end with Khione's death." Was that a tremor in his voice as well? He too struggled to make sense of events unfolding around him. So it was not that he had come from the future like herself ... No. Something else. "I have a home on Ogygia. We can sail there and find safety."

"The Aviary, right?" Her voice sounded like it belonged to some other person. The words seemed to come from some place outside of herself.

He glanced at her abruptly, his shock returned for so brief a moment she *might* have imagined it. "I have considered building such a place. I have not found the time, as yet."

Pandora found it hard to swallow. To hear such things only compounded the daze she'd found herself walking in since awakening on Helion. Despite the whirring of her thoughts, she couldn't formulate a coherent question while they walked.

In silence, she allowed him to guide her to the harbour, and onto a sailboat not so different from the one they'd taken out of Marsa a few days ... A few thousand years from now.

From outside the city, Pandora caught sight of lingering frost upon the cyclopean wall and the fields surrounding the polis. Already, the sun had begun to melt the aftereffects of the blizzard, but it might take days before all the snows had vanished.

Prometheus made for Atlantis—what would soon be Atlantis, she supposed. She had heard Knosós existed even in ancient times, maybe even into the Time of Nyx. Perhaps they would stop there to gather supplies before skirting the greater island to reach Ogygia. There was a strange familiarity to all this, as if she sat across from exactly the same Prometheus she had just watched get sent down to Tartarus.

As if this was already her friend, though he hadn't met her yet. But he knew her name ... Was it from his pyromantic visions? Was something else going on?

"You have so many questions writ upon your face," he said, when Helion lay many hours behind them.

So many they threatened to crush her beneath their weight. Questions of such import they made all that had passed in her life until now seem petty. Perhaps everything else *was* petty in the face of the monumental shift in reality she had experienced. While others went about their lives, thrust into their narrow perspectives, she had passed through time.

In Helion, amid the refugees, she'd managed to acquire a satchel. Producing it, she fished out the box he'd made and offered it to him with both hands, as if in supplication. Let him make sense of all of this. Oh, please let him.

After setting the tiller, he scooted over beside her and took the box, turning it one way and then the next.

"Send me back," she rasped. Part of her longed to touch his hand again, to reassure herself he was real and not in Tartarus. In this time, she might again talk to her friend, might share long conversations and games of draughts. Might have more time. But this wasn't her time.

Prometheus adjusted a panel on the box, frowning. And Pandora winced. What if he triggered it again without meaning to? "This sent you back in time," he said, with the air of one talking as much to himself as to her. "Is it based upon the Time Chamber of Vulgeth?"

He was asking *her*? She swallowed. "I don't know how you made it." Much less what he was even talking about or where Vulgeth was or any such thing.

He took that in without visible reaction. "I'll work on your box when we get to Ogygia."

"It's *your* box."

"Are you so certain of that? You are, after all, the one who used it. I would rather call it Pandora's Box."

Pandora hugged herself, hardly knowing what to say. She felt so overwrought she could make no sense of any of this. She felt like a spectator watching a drama unfold upon a stage ... save the stage kept expanding, until they all lay within its ambit.

On Ogygia, he took her not atop the mountain, but to a small cottage upon its lower slope. Everything was different, from the rocks to the trees, but Pandora was fair certain this place would one day become Marsa. The lay of the land, that didn't change. In the intervening millennia, the tiny cluster of fishing houses they had passed would become the harbour.

Compared to his Aviary, the cottage seemed quaint, with a single bedroll upon the floor, lying in front of a fire pit. Outside, Prometheus set about cooking a casserole, laced with cod and bits of other fish he'd bought from the fishermen. Once he'd folded it all together, he stuck it in a clay oven, then settled down beside her on the ground.

"I cannot fathom where best to even start," she said.

He turned his sapphire gaze upon her. She expected him to take her hand, as he so oft had done to offer comfort, but now he seemed more reserved. Ah. Because all the moments they'd shared had not yet happened for him.

"Start with whatever seems most pressing and build upon the questions that arise from that."

Pandora folded her hands in her lap. "You don't know all the things that have happened to me, though I shared them with you in *my past*. You were ..." The words stuck in her throat. After a lifetime of sheltering her heart, an exposure seemed to open it to fresh wounds. "I cared about you. I cared, and something happened."

He pursed his lips. "Your mind reels from reconciling the anachronic implications of our meeting then and now."

"Yes."

"You ask yourself, did the me you knew recall this very conversation?"

Such a question had crept in upon her while they sailed from Helion. She had introduced herself to Prometheus on Atlantis and he'd said he'd heard of her already. Heard of her from *now*? But he already knew her name, even when he found her in Helion, no doubt from his visions. Innominate dread stilled her tongue, even as her flesh prickled.

"I am asking."

"And am I to speculate about what my future self knows?"

Finally, she managed to give voice to her fear. "If you did—will have known—the implication is that my presence here may not have actually changed the past as yet."

"What do you think?"

Perhaps, that if she had managed to take some steps that might have actually altered her relationship with Prometheus, then the one from her time might not have saved her from Atlantis. Would that unmake the version of her who now sat beside him on Ogygia, four thousand years before those events?

Such weavings of her mind made their own history at least as great a puzzle box as the device he'd built. Her Box.

They ate the casserole and he invited her to rest upon the bedroll in his cottage, while he himself slept on the floor across from the fire.

THE EXPRESSION UPON HIS FACE, the roil of pain and sympathy as Kratos beat him, it woke her. Sweat had plastered Pandora's hair to her face. The better part of her nightmares had ceased since using the Box, so perhaps Morpheus had truly haunted her dreams, seeking her in her own time, while here she was beyond his reach.

But Prometheus's visage in that moment ... it tore through her heart. It carved it asunder like a knife. He'd known he was going to his own damnation. He'd known he would suffer, and he thought of her, how it would pain *her*.

Blinking away tears, she forced herself to sit.

Across the fire pit, eyes sparkling like crystals in the tenebrous cottage, he had pushed himself up on one arm and now stared at her. More sympathy, concern even.

Pandora edged her way closer to him. "I saw you ... tortured." The pain of it wracked her, left her voice quivering. "They dragged you down, said they'd cast you into Tartarus."

A slight shudder seized him, though his gaze remained fixed upon her.

"I swore I'd find a way to help you."

"Then I believe you will."

She placed her palms upon his cheeks. "Maybe you don't know what you meant to me. Will mean." Surely, she herself had not fathomed it then. Maybe not even until now. She pulled herself forward until she was straddling him, then kissed him. At first, unsure how he'd react, she merely brushed her lips over his.

Then his hands fell upon her hips and she had her answer. It was not the rhythm of her clients she fell into, but one far more intimate for its uniqueness and uncertainty. His lips massaging her own, her tongue exploring his mouth. The flush of his initial intrusion inside her, as he leaned backward, as she guided him.

There was something deeper here than she had ever experienced. Something glorious in the reign of true choice and the need, not of custom, but of connection. A soothing, heaving whirl of flesh and emotion.

She felt him convulse beneath her. His release surged into her in a coruscating wave as though some rush of energy passed through her. His crystal eyes glinted with a whorl of stars in motion. And more, in her mind's eye, she saw a maelstrom of visions, like fragments of his life. A flaming cavern drenched in smoke and lambent from lava flows. Standing upon the balcony of some twisted tower, gazing out into iridescent vapours as lightning and flame played upon one another in a dance. And a spreading of a *living* night across the sky, as if the gloaming claiming the World were a thing of writhing tentacles, lurching its way into reality.

These things, and a thousand more flashes all blurred together into mad amalgams that tried to swallow her mind and soul. All of it, his whole history, was a tempest of nightmares. An unfathomable weight borne upon his shoulders, as if all the World was his responsibility.

Physically and emotionally spent, she collapsed onto his chest, not caring that tears leaked from her eyes onto him.

The depth of him stretched so far back, so wide, she imagined no one could grasp the whole of this Titan. But she would try. She had lost him in her time. Maybe here, she could finally have something to hold on to.

18

ATHENE

1571 Silver Age

"Pandion," Athene said, when her mother offered her the babe wrapt in a bundle. "His name is Pandion, and one day he shall be king of Kronion."

Mother smiled knowingly. "You'll have to raise him as a demigod," she said.

Athene gaped at her uncomprehending.

"If you don't want to acknowledge the father, then the father cannot be a Titan."

Athene balked. It would mean Pandion would never sample Ambrosia, and though his Titan blood would extend his life, he would live and die as a mortal, unless he so impressed Father. But the alternative was impossible. Mother was right ...

With a nod, Mother left Athene to recline upon her bed. She nursed the child, then slept with her hand upon his tiny chest, soothed by its regular rise and fall. A dozen times she woke, needing to reassure herself the breaths still came as they ought.

But the child was strong, and she need not fear, she knew. He was a Titan.

In the morn, a wet nurse saw to Pandion, and Athene stretched her legs, walking along the halls of her palace in the acropolis. Father had gifted her the very polis founded by his own father when she came to adulthood, and Athene had strived to rule it well. Before granting her the city, he'd erected both this palace and a temple for the mortals to come and offer her worship and sacrifices. Every so often, the priests would bring in food and wine and goods left in the temple in her honour, and sometimes Athene would even use them, though occasionally the food rotted in the sun before it got to her.

Sometimes the citizens left new sandals or khitons or tiaras or jewellery, and when she would wear their gifts in the agora below, Athene fancied she oft caught cheers or boasting. *Look how the goddess wears the sandals I crafted for her! I left her that bracelet on my son's birth!*

Yes, she had to admit, their adoration was intoxicating, and sometimes she extended her strolls just to see if anyone would notice her garb. Now, though, she remained secluded in the palace, preferring to stroll in the courtyard.

Basking in the sunlight, she paused before the fountain, taking solace in its burbling flow. Water cascaded out of the open palms of a mermaid, flowing through her fingers onto a lower shelf of layered seashells. From there, it pitched into the greater basin, in which swam a shoal of goldfish. Athene watched the patterns formed by the falling water, and it was as if those waters massaged the whole of her aching body. As if they flowed over the expanse of her soul, soothing away all the stresses of time.

As if ... she ... was ...

§

GLAMOURED to look like any other aristocratic mortal, Athene sat in the assembly, watching as the young prince Theseus, seated beside King Aegeus, took in the assembly in his father's court. This man, the descendant of Pandion, had his ancestor's bearing, if not quite his aspect. The way he surveyed the gathered aristoi—and that pompous emissary of Minos—it reminded her of a leopard. He was more than his father had ever been, and Athene couldn't help but quirk a smile at that.

Ah, but then, she had seen this moment, hadn't she?

"The nine years have passed," the emissary intoned, with the air of a speech he had given before. "And upon this, the twenty-seventh anniversary of your crimes"—he stretched the last word with such arrogance Athene rolled her eyes—"the time has come to once again send your seven boys and seven girls to sate the beast."

Theseus rose, his chair scraping noisily along the stone floor. "No."

"No?" the emissary asked, as if the very word tasted alien to him and his tongue could not quite wrap itself around the sound of it.

"No," Theseus repeated. "No more sacrifices. I will walk the Labyrinth. Find this Minotaur. I kill it, our debt is paid. I fail, your king has claimed the son of his rival. Fair recompense for the loss of his own heir. Either way, Athenai owes no more sacrifices after this."

The men and women gathered in Aegeus's throne room gaped at the young man, as if unable to imagine their prince would put forth such an idea. Indeed, Aegeus, too, paled. Perhaps, had he suspected Theseus of such a play, he would not have invited his newly found son to this assembly.

No, but Athene had known it would come to this, long ago, and it was as it should be.

Whatever resulted in the Labyrinth beneath Knosós, Theseus had saved his polis. This was the true heir of Pandion. Athene's heir.

THREE DAYS LATER, Athene felt almost as though she had never been pregnant. Perhaps it was the extra draught of Ambrosia her mother had arranged for her, or perhaps her Titan nature, but she thought mortal women took longer to recoup. Then again, what did she know?

With Mother by her side, she walked the Long Wall that connected Kronion proper to the harbour district well beyond the main gates. She had built this wall long ago and walked its twenty-mile circumference so many times she had lost count, but it felt different now.

"I saw things again," she admitted. "This time in the waters of my fountain."

"Hydromancy is a common method of accessing prescience," Mother said, her own gaze flitting over the hills between the wall and the Aegean Sea, seeming to take in the whole expanse of this island.

"Like your dreams?"

"Oneiromancy can grant prescience, yes, but it is distinct in its own right."

Though not quite sure whether she understood, Athene nodded anyway. She had no energy for an extended lecture upon the intricacies of the Sight. What mattered was Mother seemed to confirm that both what she had seen in the Oracle Mirrors below Olympus last year and this vision from a few days ago represented a real future. Athene was an *Oracle*.

Hmm. How did her strength at prescience measure up against Apollon? Legend said he was trained by famed—or now infamous—Themis herself in the use of his gift. Probably Athene, novice that she was, had naught on the skills of Helios's blessed son.

When she fell silent, Mother glanced over at her. "Has word reached you about Merope?"

"The Pleiad?"

"She was wed to Sisyphus of Korinth last year." Oh, that much Athene knew. She had made it her business to learn of the Kreiad genos. Sisyphus was the son of Hephaistos's sister Bia, with her husband, the demigod Aiolos. "I imagine Zeus waited until she delivered a babe," her mother said, voice quiet. "Shortly thereafter, Ares smashed her head upon the acropolis steps. Some rumours claim he broke her spine before that."

And perhaps did worse before that, Athene imagined, though Mother did not give voice to such things.

For a few moments, silence reigned between them, and Athene traced her finger along the crenelations of the Long Wall. Out here, she could make out farmers' fields where they grew wheat, and there, olive trees. Sometimes, Kronion seemed peaceful.

"I know why you're telling me this," she finally said, pausing to lean against the wall and stare at her mother. "You say Father's retribution against her is already horrible. And I would not have wanted that, because the Pleiades are not my enemies. The Kreiads, however, *are* my foes. Hephaistos and his whole cursed line."

"Including Merope's newborn child?"

Athene waved that away. "I will make Pandion the first mortal King of Kronion."

"You want your son to hold authority independent of your own here?"

"Yes." Other poleis had mortal kings to attend to the prosaic needs of a city, it was time Kronion had this as well. Besides, she had seen it, in her vision. His line would produce kings and heroes for generations to come. This Theseus would walk among the polis to the utter adoration of his people. "And I want to expand Kronion's power through Pandion."

Her father might balk on learning a Titan had begun seizing territory or trade routes from another Titan, but mortals were freed from any such restriction.

"Help me achieve it," Athene said.

"As you wish."

Athene nodded, and from the look on her mother's face, the older woman knew well enough what was coming. "I want Kronion to dominate Korinth. I want Hephaistos to watch as his own spawn seizes his polis and strips his genos of all meaning."

Mother clucked her tongue, then sighed. "These schemes will not avail you, Athene."

"I've foreseen a glorious future for my line!"

The woman reached for Athene, caressing her cheek. "Be that as it may, conquering other poleis, breaking an entire genos, none of this will assuage your wrath. It will *stoke* it."

"Then let it be stoked," Athene growled. "Let it become a confla-gration that consumes him, and only in the end will he understand the price of his hubris in thinking he can take whatever he wants. Let *all* Titans learn the price!"

Though she expected to see grim resolve upon her mother's face, instead the woman closed her eyes for so long the silence grew uncomfortable. "There is much of your father in you," she said, when at last her golden gaze settled upon Athene once more. "But I understand your rage. I would not leave my child to face such alone, even if I think you are making a mistake." A sad smile creased her face. "So be it. We will strive against Korinth and its line. We will strike at them, again and again, until you alone say when it is enough. Then we will see, Athene, if the world has become what you will it."

Athene could not help but squirm, just a little, at the intimation that, despite having lived sixteen centuries, she was about to be subjected to a very long lesson.

19

PANDORA

201 Golden Age

Reclining beneath the shade of an olive tree, Pandora stroked the scraggly hair of the babe nestled to her breast. In her days as a hetaira—so long ago they seemed now—she had mixed tonics that prevented conception. On Ogygia, she could have found the herbs needed to make such things but no longer had any desire to do so.

Now, she had found something here, with Prometheus, in the year she'd lived on this island. Something a lifetime on Atlantis had denied her.

Beneath her tree, she listened to the waves lap at the shore, feeling almost too content. Such anxieties plagued her, from time to time, as if she did not deserve peace. Always, she tried to push them down. This was real.

She was really here, holding her daughter, luxuriating while her lover built them a larger cottage farther up the mountain. Still not quite the summit where he'd build his Aviary, but that would come in time, she knew.

In the late afternoon, after the babe had woken, fed, and slept once more, Prometheus made his way down the slope. A sheen of sweat glistened upon his bare chest, and he'd tied back his auburn hair.

She offered him a smile in greeting, nodding her head at the amphora of wine beside her. She might have passed it to him but wouldn't risk waking their child for aught on Earth.

Prometheus poured some wine in a bowl, sipped at it, then pushed it aside. "Have you settled upon a name for her?"

"Hmm. I think, Pyrrha." She winked. "For the fiery hair she gets from her father."

He chuckled, answering with a slight, merry shake of his head. "Well, Pyrrha it is, then."

NIGHTS, sometimes, proved harder. The nightmares had mostly abated, never mind occasional visions in which her mind imagined the torments that must befall the *other* Prometheus in Tartarus. The reminder that, for all the precious moments she shared with him now, the man she so loved would suffer unimaginable agonies in his future.

She had sworn to him she would find a way to save him.

What, then, did it mean that she made her life here, in the past, happy with him while elsewhere he languished? It meant she had broken that promise, even as she fell ever deeper for him.

She would roll over and stare at his sleeping form and think it was impossible to love someone so much as this. To see the very ambit of the World in the beating of a heart slumbering beside her. Was this tiny family of hers not the very meaning of her life?

A hundred times a night she woke to check on Pyrrha, to make sure her daughter's breathing sounded proper, that she was warm enough in her blankets. No matter how oft she reassured herself naught would happen, still she needed to see, again and again, that the child remained hale and healthy.

Now, leaning over the tiny form, she knew without doubt: this had been the best year of her life. The only time she had truly felt home since Zeus and Hekate had taken her from Tyros all those years ago.

But was she *failing* the very man who had helped her claim this life?

❧

OGYGIA, it seemed, had once belonged to Atlas before he left to conquer Hesperides Island and ignited the accursed war that yet raged on. It had not come to these shores, though certainly many Titans had tried and failed to claim Atlantis from Atlas. The bodies of those who had attempted it continued to pile up.

Prometheus had told her, some months back, that Atlas was *like* a brother to him, though not actually, in fact, related to him by blood. Either way, he took no part in the war, save occasionally conferring with other Titans who came and took his counsel. In these cases, he would meet them in private, most oft upon the mountain summit, where he would one day build the Aviary.

On one such day he asked Pandora to take Pyrrha for a walk and she agreed, despite a drizzle of rain falling over the island. It was best, she supposed, to grant him his discretion for his guests. Moreover, he seemed inclined to conceal Pandora from them, as though some of these Titans might pose a threat to her. Thus, from behind a tree in the light woods surrounding their cottage, she watched him escort yet another such Titan up the slope.

It had to be a Titan, for both her height and her luxurious amaranthine himation raised against the weather. Prometheus took females up there oft enough, and Pandora knew another woman might feel the bitter twinge of jealousy at that. How could a Titan male not lust after the grandeur and superlative grace of Nymphs? But Prometheus had never given her the least reason to distrust him.

In his eyes, she saw the refraction of his soul. That soul was many things: haunted and brooding and, perhaps, burdened by guilt. But it was true to *her*, of that she had not the least doubt.

So she watched her lover take the Titan up the slope, noting by the set of her features the war must not go well. It never seemed to.

Once, Pandora had asked Prometheus why so many came to call upon him. "Most seek Oracular insight. Some hope I will actually fight by their side, believing I aided Ouranos in ending the Time of Nyx."

"Did you?"

"After a fashion."

He was always like that. Perhaps it was his nature to make himself into another, living puzzle box, or perhaps he did so because he knew she could not resist him thus. Either way, she prodded with her questions, moving a piece of his enigma at a time, ever searching for his hidden centre.

Such were the games they played in daylight.

And at night, she writhed in the half-light, envisaging the ruination of his flesh and soul in Tartarus.

"WHAT IF WE COULD CHANGE IT?" she asked one morn, while they sat upon a rock overlooking the bay. She worked her tongue around an olive pit, just the way Uncle Phoenix had taught her. Pyrrha rested in Prometheus's lap, looking out at the waves along with them, blessedly quiet for a moment.

"You mean alter the future."

"Just don't side with Zeus in the first place. You helped him win the Titanomachy. You helped him end this Golden Age by destroying the entire Ouranid League. Do you *really* think the World better off under his rule than it was under the hegemony?"

Prometheus, too, popped an olive in his mouth. When she'd told him of her uncle's olive lessons, he'd readily joined her in the morning routine. "Better off ... Such an interesting question. As if we might abort the flow of history and allow it to stagnate in one moment for all eternity."

Pandora scoffed. "Because history must move forward regardless does not mean the unfolding that happened resulted in a beneficial transition for anyone."

"A society that remains mired in place without progress begins to wither."

Ah. So he did not so much believe his arguing points as he did enjoy the act of debating her. "A move toward tyranny doesn't qualify as progress. We surrendered a flawed oligarchy for an insane autocrat." She paused, softening her face. "He hurts you. He hurts me, and he hurts so many others, playing with lives like pieces on the draughts board. He does not, so far as I can see, move toward any greater aim than his own gratification. And all the while, he demands we worship him as a god, as though his ego needed its flames fanned."

Now Prometheus grimaced, if only for an instant, then stroked Pyrrha's brow with one thumb. For a long time, he held his peace, staring at the waves. He'd told her once that most Oracles required a medium to harness prescience. For him—for pyromancers—that was flame, though others could see things in the tides. Cleromancers read cast pebbles, tiles, or bones. It seemed, in her estimation, what one really needed was a sufficiently complex system through which the Oracle could fall into a trance and access some hidden part of themselves.

As Prometheus was no hydromancer, he could not be reading the waves. Rather, he must flounder in the shifting currents of his own thoughts. Pandora could empathise with such a situation.

After a time, she reached over to trace her fingers along the back of his hand, and he looked up at her. "Some think the Moirai, the Fates, mere metaphor for the forces that govern our lives. But they are the arbiters or emissaries of Ananke itself. They weave all our lives as threads within a greater tapestry. Suppose you could change the past, pluck a strand, and alter the picture. Could you do so with any certainty of not unraveling the whole of the tapestry in the process?"

She sniffed. This was what it always came back to, a war in her mind. If she prevented Prometheus from siding with Zeus and thus stopped Zeus from winning the Titanomachy, the sixteen centuries since then would not have happened. She could never predict the course of events that might have followed. Maybe their world would enjoy a continuing Golden Age, would not fall under the thumb of a despot. Europa might have lived a happy life in Tyros. Pandora might have grown up in Agenor's court, remained Europa's ward, perhaps even wed when the time came.

Of course, she never would have met this man whom she loved so much it hurt.

The weight of that knowledge—that all the good in her life ensued as a result from all the bad—clenched around her very soul, threatening to crack it wide.

Like any such conclusions, her line of reasoning only led to more questions. "If we cannot or dare not change the past and thus the future, why would you even ever build a Box that would allow for time travel?"

Prometheus sighed, his shoulder slumping. Oh, he had mulled this over long as well, hadn't he? "I can only imagine I will build this in the future because you gave it to me now."

His answer slapped her like a blow to the face. It left her gaping in voiceless abhorrence, unable to tear her gaze from his eyes. At least, not until he pointedly looked down at Pyrrha.

"We have a daughter," he said simply.

And there, like a clarion, it rang through her mind. She had given him the Box to study. He used it to invent it. Because he knew this moment, because he loved her, because he loved their daughter. Pandora gasped at the sudden pain in her chest as her lungs seized up, unable to draw breath after the weight that had fallen upon her like some cyclopean monument.

This had all always happened.

His hand grasped her shoulder to steady her, but it wasn't enough, and her vision dimmed at the fringes.

HER SWOONING HAD LASTED but a moment, though its source stalked the corners of her mind in constricting circles, round and round, with ever deepening implications. What if Prometheus sided with Zeus because that was what had led to Pandora being here now, allowing their love? Allowing Pyrrha's very existence?

If so, then he had never intended the Box to *change* the past or future, but rather to create the blessed moments of his own history. He had fulfilled his own past. Had seen her in Atlantis and known the time had arrived for him to begin the creation of this loop.

Pyrrha held against one shoulder, Prometheus had helped her back to their cottage and eased her down by the fire pit.

"You deal with it better than I imagine most would," he said, once he'd settled the babe down for a nap. Because he could read the whirring of her mind writ plain upon her features. Because he had gone through the same deductions in his own mind already.

"I cannot use the Box to stop Zeus from damning you." The words eviscerated her. They felt ripped straight from her guts.

The moment she had opened the Box, everything had changed forever. Or naught at all had changed in the least.

"I don't think you can change events that brought you to this moment. And I think if you tried, the Moirai would not take kindly to having their tapestry mangled."

"I am powerless." Or she was powerless *here*, in the past. But that didn't mean she couldn't help the Prometheus from her time. Couldn't keep her vow to him. And once she did, he'd know it was safe to reveal what he knew of this shared past together.

The Prometheus of now watched her face, eyes darting back and forth. His nod confirmed he'd not only read her intent upon her visage, but that he agreed.

The only question was, could she take that step? Could she walk away from the life she had now, with him and Pyrrha, and move into the uncertain future with no guarantee she'd ever find a way to reach him?

"I'm still working to refine the design," he said, as if in answer to her question. As if to offer her a respite from making the impossible choice. "We want you to have as much control over when and where it sends you as possible."

Pandora gnawed on her lip. Though his work bought her time to linger here, she could not do so indefinitely. She'd made a promise, and regardless, she owed him everything. This life she so cherished was a lie unless she earned it. Unless she proved worthy of him. And she could not do that here.

She could not be worthy unless she was willing to risk everything to save him.

Though it might stretch through eternity and shape days four millennia from now, this moment still could not last forever.

20

PYRRHA

219 Golden Age

For more than half a year, Pyrrha had wandered the poleis of Elládos. She had stayed in Korinth for a time and found welcome in the courts of Kreios and Eurybia. The Titan lady had retained her as a mathematics tutor for her son Pallas, though Pyrrha had soon found Pallas's arrogance grating. The man thought he had little to learn from 'a haughty Nymph,' and Pyrrha had barely restrained herself from laying a curse upon the pompous arse.

It had been Enodia, who had taken up residence by the harbour of Lecheae, who had dissuaded her. "Vengeance, if it must be taken, should be reserved for reasons far less petty than idle words of young men without hair upon their stones." The mental image had done more to soothe her nerves than the words themselves, and Pyrrha had left Korinth and wandered the lesser poleis and the small towns dotting the peninsula.

Sometimes, Enodia met her in the wilds. The sorceress had the Sight herself, and thus, like Papa, always seemed to know just where to find Pyrrha when she wished. Whether Pyrrha sheltered with kindly farmers or slept in lean-tos in the forest, Enodia would show up some nights, offering some morsel of arcane training.

"Necromancy is a sub-discipline of the Art," Enodia told her, when they sat in a forest glade beneath a waxing moon. "We evoke ghosts, most oft to interrogate them and thus divine secrets about the forgotten past. Sometimes the dead even know about the future."

"How?" Pyrrha demanded.

To that, Enodia shrugged. "The dead pass into spaces the living cannot understand. They perceive that which is beyond us, and sometimes, in hateful necropoleis out in the nebulous Roil, they gather and speak. You would shudder to learn the depths of what is whispered in courts beyond this world."

Still, the nights when Pyrrha found herself alone far outnumbered those when her mentor appeared. Sometimes a fortnight or longer she would spend with no one to talk to save villagers who could not have begun to understand her. She saw things they did not. Almost unbidden, the Sight would come upon her, and she would find the fallen stalking her. Here, a woman murdered by her husband after he learnt of her affair. There, an eight-year-old boy who drowned in the river and forever followed his oblivious parents around, desperate for answers they could not give. The villagers would sometimes fall into despair when ghosts lurked nigh, but they would call it malaise and think they needed more wine to cure it.

The dead wanted her to save them, but Pyrrha had no such power. Was she to confront the bereaved parents and tell them their dead son wandered the Earth in torment, desperate to touch them when they could not even see him? If she had thought it would somehow help the child, she would have done so in an instant, but Pyrrha no longer believed the dead could be released.

Thus, in the end, she learnt the boy's name, Agapetos. Using necromancy, she summoned him into a circle deep in the woods and looked hard into his face. Her skin tingled with his presence, crawling with his regard.

"Why am I here?" the child demanded.

Pyrrha wasn't sure if she wanted to laugh or sob. "Because your presence in this village torments both you and your loved ones. Because ... all I can do for you is to help you move on."

Thus, she incanted in Supernal, calling up the forces of the Roil. The child fell into a crouch, whimpering and wrapping his arms around his knees. The sight of it almost had her stopping. Before she could decide, the umbral ground beneath Agapetos turned aqueous. The boy shrieked as he sank. Tenebrous hands lurched from the new-formed mire, seizing the soul. With gut-churning slowness, as Pyrrha stood there watching in mute horror, they dragged the child into the depths. The last to vanish were his tiny, twitching fingers.

Pyrrha fell to her knees and retched. Finally, after catching her breath, she wiped her mouth with the back of her hand. Nyx! Had she made aught better? She had envisioned those necropoleis Enodia had mentioned. Had dared to believe the boy might find some final rest ... But that had looked more like the Roil had *devoured* him. And the parents? Could they live now?

Pyrrha had no answers.

And Enodia did not come.

WHEN SHE CAME TO DELPHI, staring up at the tiny fort upon the lower slopes of the Olympian Mountains, it felt she dragged the weight of a bireme behind her. So much wandering, and still she had no true answer as to who she was or her place in the World. Her Sight felt more curse than blessing, and despite the power, she had never found her mother. Even necromancy had failed to summon the woman's soul, who, like the boy, must have moved on, beyond the Penumbra.

Pyrrha had seen this place in dreams. A dozen times in the past months, her dreams had shown her the fort upon the mountain and, more disturbingly, the tunnels beneath them. Atramentous depths that called to her, and she began to dread she knew what lurked down there.

In the time following the end of the Ambrosial War, while Pyrrha was yet a young child, the Titan Themis had founded the polis of Delphi here. According to legend, she was among the greatest Oracles of the World, and she called others of her kind to her for training. Was Pyrrha an Oracle as well as a medium?

Was that her answer? Certainly, she had experienced strange dreams, and Enodia had implied that both gifts were aspects of the same Sight. Considering Papa was an Oracle, perhaps Pyrrha was too. Perhaps, through Themis, she might refine her abilities further.

Or this she told herself as she made her way up the slope and to the fort. Far below, she spotted a port, but she imagined the Titan would live in the acropolis, as Titans were forever wont to do, looking down upon mortals from high above.

Outside the fort, she paused. Cyclopean walls surrounded Delphi, the stones larger than any three Men could probably move. Had actual Cyclopes built this fortress? Had Themis somehow conscripted the flesh-eating monsters to such work? Perhaps the Titan would grant her the answer.

Papa had mentioned Themis on occasion and apparently considered her a friend, though Pyrrha had seen her only once, just before she founded Delphi, when she had called upon Tethys in her court. She remembered a dark-haired Titan of noble bearing who had insisted upon speaking to Tethys in private.

The town within the fort was sparse, composed mostly of the agora, the acropolis, and a handful of shops and manses for the aristoi. Pyrrha wandered the streets at leisure, while her mind ran over what she would say to the Titan. Was it best to play upon her friendship with Papa? Was she assuming too much in thinking them friends? She racked her brain, trying to remember exactly what Papa had said of Themis.

Always fair, always striving for justice.

But what did such even mean? By now, Themis would most likely have heard of Pyrrha's ... well, she refused to think of it as a crime, so call it her *actions* against Poseidon. Would the Titan consider Tethys's banishment of Pyrrha justice?

Among such musings, she reached the acropolis and Themis's palace.

A short steward greeted her with a stiff nod. "Who may I say is calling?"

"Pyrrha, daughter of Prometheus, come to see Themis."

The steward remained expressionless, not even his voice affecting the least emotion. "The Oracle is in the catacombs beneath the mountain." The way he said it made it seem she spent all her time down there. "Head down to the harbour, then follow the dirt path to a square arch carved into the mountainside."

A tinge of familiarity shot through Pyrrha and left her skin tingling.

As if his words were a dismissal, the steward turned and disappeared back into the palace. Pyrrha huffed, suppressing an urge to put the man in his place. Antagonising him would avail her naught and might well make her getting aid from Themis harder. Instead, she made her slow way back down the mountainside.

These mountains, named for the highest peak of Olympus, were famed for being almost impassible. Some claimed Gigantes—Cyclopes included—lurked in hidden caves and valleys, ready to prey upon the unwary who plodded over these ridges. While she could not say what, something about these mountains radiated a kind of power, thrumming beneath her feet. Was that why Themis had chosen this location?

Far below, she found the path the steward mentioned. The dirt was already hard packed from so many pilgrims come this way seeking a prophecy or advice from the Oracles of Delphi. At the terminus lay the mountain, with more cyclopean stones forming an arch leading into a vault. A triangular gable above the arch lay empty, allowing the fading sunlight to stream down upon the inner chamber. Pyrrha passed through the arch into that chamber, finding it hexagonal. Within lay three more similar arches, each leading into a tunnel. Only one was lit, with torches stuck in sconces illuminating a passage.

The obvious path. Ducking through the archway, Pyrrha peered down the tunnel. Within lay alcoves set with sarcophagi cast in shadow by the sporadic torches. With a grimace, Pyrrha made her way deeper inside. Who was buried in these halls? Dead Oracles? Older persons of import? None of her lessons had ever mentioned any great fallen civilisation here. Was it possible ... could these tombs date to the Time of Nyx?

Further inside, she passed openings into other unlit tunnels. Though she gazed inside, she could make out little in the shadows beyond, save that some of those tunnels seemed much wider and dug out of natural stone rather than carved cyclopean blocks. Caverns hollowed out long ago, no doubt, and Themis had connected to them with her newer vault. But why?

Pyrrha hesitated on one threshold, tempted to snatch a torch and go exploring. Doing so might have offended the Oracles, though, so instead she moved on, following the lit passages. Eventually, she came to another hexagonal chamber deep within the mountain. Other tunnels led off from it, but her attention was drawn to Themis, who sat upon a stool within a circular diagram, peering down at a cloudy pool of water. Around the back of her seat, steam vented up through grates, obscuring the Oracle.

"Pyrrha," Themis said.

Pyrrha started. "You remember me?"

Themis's eyes glinted. "Of long ago, I knew you."

"I ..." Pyrrha swallowed. She had come all this way and still didn't know what to say. "I am lost. I am tormented by visions from the Underworld, yet I find myself *compelled* to look. I have lost my parents and my home, and now I lose myself. I need a reason for ... for everything."

Something washed over the Oracle's face. Not sympathy, but understanding, perhaps. "Know you, far better than I, the chill of the grave that awaits. The brushing hand upon a faltering neck, the windswept cheek exposed to bitter drafts. And all around the expanse of bone."

Taken aback, all Pyrrha could do was frown. "Did that ... make sense in your head?"

Themis snorted and rose. "Do you know why I built this place here?" She had been wondering. "In the murky depths far beneath the Earth coil and shift saurian colossi spawned by Echidna. The blood coursing through their veins is the most virulent of poisons, but it runs thick with puissance. Should one survive its touch, it can rarify their nature, bring out the depths of their soul."

Pyrrha folded her arms. "You speak of drakons." Once, when the sisters had not known she was listening, she heard Hera claim Tethys kept such a creature concealed beneath Thebes. That the Titan had unleashed the beast to repel Kronos's ships after Okeanus's death. "You believe their blood may enhance Oracular Sight in those who can survive contact with it."

"We call it Python, an Old One, elder spawn of the Primordials. Its shifting bulk fills the lava tubes you looked down before." The name resounded in Pyrrha's mind. A name from her dreams, of long back.

No. Not this …

I TURN WITH YOU. A nightmare almost forgotten.

Themis beckoned her to follow, and Pyrrha did, her feet seeming to move of their own accord. Was this the call of her dreams?

Themis led her back to one of the side tunnels, pausing to claim a torch out of a sconce, then handed it to her. "We keep Python well fed, so it is not likely to hunt you." Well fed? The import of her meaning settled upon Pyrrha like a weight. They offered the drakon human sacrifices.

"I scour the countryside for murderers, bandits, and rapists," Themis said, in answer to Pyrrha's unspoken question. "You know, as word has spread of it, I've found men have become more likely to keep both swords and phalluses sheathed."

Pyrrha couldn't think of much to say to that. Perhaps Themis justified the sacrifices however she could. Or perhaps she actually did offer a service to her lands. "What do I do?"

"Within the tunnels, pools of its seeping power gather. Go and have a sip. If you live, your Sight may become stronger, clearer. You may be more you." Themis shrugged. "Or turn back and flee, retreating into whatever shadows you crawled out from." With that, the Titan drifted away. Perhaps she already knew what choice Pyrrha would make.

Perhaps that was the benefit of Oracular Sight. Pyrrha, though, lingered, staring at the cloudy waters. 'You may be more you.' What did that even mean? Was the future Themis foresaw for Pyrrha the one she should want for herself? But she had not come here to turn back. That had never been a real possibility.

Grimacing, Pyrrha slunk into the cavern, keeping the torch high behind herself to avoid spoiling her night vision. She had not gone far when the sound of something immense slithering over stone in the far distance came to her. She drew to a sudden stop, frozen in place. This had been her worst idea yet. Enodia had never said aught about coming to Delphi.

Dreams of this place had brought her here, and because of them, she was now going to become food for a drakon. Huh. What if Themis had lied about the nature of the sacrifices? Oh, shit. The idea, once it had occurred, refused to leave, even as it intensified the chill sweat on her back. What if the Titan actually sent men and women into these tunnels thinking to claim draconic power, but they were the sacrifices that kept Python sated?

She felt ill.

Maybe she should have fled, taken no chance. But still, she pushed on, deeper into the tunnels.

She came to a narrowing of the passage, where the only way forward was to climb into an opening barely large enough for her. Pyrrha's stomach clenched at the thought of such an enclosed space. Of something finding her within, while she would be powerless to even move.

But she wanted what Themis had offered, wanted it with the soul-rending craving that a drunk sought for wine after long day dry. Wanted it so badly it flensed her with the need. Teeth gritted, Pyrrha climbed into the narrow space. On hands and knees, she tugged herself forward, deeper and deeper.

Prodigious, squirming shadows encircled her, almost seeming to tug at her wrists and ankles, making it feel she waded through a mire. Grunting with the effort, she pushed ever forward.

Ahead, the passage grew more narrow, and she had to turn sideways to fit. Pyrrha shoved the torch in first, then twisted, wedging herself inward. Why was she pressing on? Should she turn back?

The thought came to her, and yet her body kept moving, summoned by some ... *presence* ... deep within the mountain. She could not say how far underground she had delved, but deep.

Was this ... a dream?

Rough stone scraped her cheek. Warmth dribbled down her chin and neck. The passage forced her to worm through it, seeming to close in around her with each foot forward. What if it grew too tight? What if she couldn't turn back and got stuck in here, alone? Would she die of thirst, screaming herself raw for help that could never find her?

The vision of such hit her, and its terror actually made tears rise up at the fringes of her eyes.

And *still* she could not make herself turn back. Deeper and deeper, until the passage opened up into a wide cave, the base of which lay several feet below the opening she was in. Despite her attempts at grace, Pyrrha tumbled from her point of ingress, pitching down onto the chilled floor of the greater cavern with a pained grunt. Her torch clattered down beside her and lay there, flames dancing in front of her face.

She was lucky she hadn't singed herself.

With a huff, she rose to her knees, snatching up the torch to look around. She was in a wide tunnel, but her torchlight failed to reach both sides of the space at once. The cave was smoother than she'd have thought, with no stalagmites and few stalactites. Was this a lava tube?

Forcing herself to rise, she turned about. She couldn't say which way she was meant to go since the tube seemed to vanish into darkness in both directions. Maybe it didn't matter.

Picking a direction, she plodded onward. Her sandals echoed faintly upon the stone beneath her, her steps drawn forward though she could not have said why. Her flesh had grown clammy with chill sweat, and she cast a single furtive glance behind herself. The expanse in both directions seemed a fathomless darkness.

A sick sensation began to grow inside her gut, the feeling she was not alone down here. Some monstrous, alien intellect lurked in the darkness. Was it ahead? Behind? It seemed almost omnipresent in the tenebrous tract she had intruded into, as though she had delved so deep beneath the Earth as to reach somewhere *else*. Somewhere inhabited by a timeless mind so momentous it spread through the whole of the mountain.

With each step she took, the sensation of wrongness increased, but still her feet refused to turn back. Then came the scraping of something rough over the stone, reverberating through the tunnel, and the sensation that whatever lurked out there, she not only felt it, but it felt *her*.

... COME FORTH ...

The voice bombarded her, even as it had come to her in dreams down through her years. It had *known*. It bombarded against the inside of her skull with all the discordant force of Supernal invocations, as if able to bend reality to its whims.

Was that Python speaking in her mind? She had not dared to believe the drakon could hold such power. Ahead, she once more heard mammoth grating of scales over stone. The slithering was intermittent, as if the massive serpent only sought to reposition itself on occasion. Nevertheless, Pyrrha winced with each grinding echo.

Her fist trembled at her side. Every instinct bellowed at her to flee this place, crawl back into the tiny tunnel from which she had emerged, and never look back.

COME FORTH ... BRIGHT ONE ... YOUR MIND SCRAPES THE ABYSS ... SO VIBRANT ...

An Old One, Tethys had called Python. A creature from before time itself, spawned by the fathomless Primordials.

It beckoned, and she approached. She plodded further down the tunnel, until her torchlight glinted off a jagged wall ahead. An abrupt sense of cyclopean immensity settled upon her, as if the Earth itself reared before her, alive and aberrant, utterly beyond the scope of comprehension.

YES ...

An incandescent eye opened in the wall before her, its faint radiance adumbrating the shape of a saurian head rimmed with a thicket of broken horns and spines.

All breath ceased for her and Pyrrha's heart seized up, even as she collapsed to her knees.

The eye was bigger than she was. It looked *inside* her, scourging her soul to its pith with its alien regard. The force of it ravaged her, left her trembling and paralysed.

... DRINK AND ... BECOME ...

With painful slowness, she managed to turn her head. Then, in the recesses of the tunnel, her torchlight glinted off some liquid that seemed not quite water.

The eye shut, plunging the cavern into greater darkness once more, and the mammoth serpent slithered forward, parading a wall of endless coils in its passage.

Released from its hold, Pyrrha found she could move once more. And had dawdled far too long already. In such places, it felt she would never again look upon the light of the sun. Almost weeping, she edged her way forward until she reached the pool of it. The surface reflected her like a mirror, silvery and perfectly still.

Having no idea what would happen when she drank it, Pyrrha decided to scoop a draught up in a waterskin. With that claimed, she quickly fled the tunnel, retreating until she found the small passage she had crawled through.

Casting a last glance over her shoulder—and seeing no sign of the serpent—she forced her way out.

§

ALMOST COMPLETELY BEREFT OF DRACHMAE, Pyrrha didn't expect to find shelter within the fort. Instead, she headed into the woods beneath the mountain, found a sheltered glade, and built a small fire.

With her campsite secured, she unstopped the waterskin and sniffed the substance she claimed from those catacombs.

It had a faint acrid scent to it but otherwise seemed unremarkable. So ... Had she done all this just to toss the stuff away? Maybe she should. Themis had made no secret that some who touched the drakon essence died from it.

And Python itself was monstrous beyond words. Something so far removed from human experience as to shame conceptions of knowledge.

But within this liquid was *power*. Unmitigated, unbridled power she could imbibe and make part of herself. Everything she had ever sought could be hers with a little more strength.

So why in Nyx's dark bosom should she turn back now?

She threw back the skin and took a long swig. Thick, viscous fluid poured down her throat, its bitter bite souring her mouth. She gagged almost immediately. Gods, she needed pure water. She stood with the intent to head for a nearby brook she'd seen, but her knees gave way and sent her tumbling to the ground. Her stomach convulsed.

Darkness seized her.

Pyrrha cradled the grey-eyed babe, dabbing her finger against the newborn's hand in hopes of getting her to grab it with her own tiny digits. The girl stared at her, wide-eyed, hand half closing around her finger.

"Aww. That's it, Mama's got you. Mama's always got you."

Her midwife moved about the plush chamber around her, gathering up rags and towels. "Are you well, my lady?"

Pyrrha was perfect and graced the midwife with a smile. "Well enough, Eileithyia. Well enough, for certain."

The door was flung open before Eileithyia could say aught in answer, and Zeus billowed in, his platinum hair flowing about him.

"Well," he demanded.

"A beautiful baby girl," Pyrrha said, beaming.

Zeus, though, seemed to deflate, and he shook his head. "A girl." Was it scorn in his voice, or just disappointment?

Either way, Pyrrha frowned at him. "What should we call her?"

Zeus shrugged, apparently beyond all care for the birth now. "Whatever suits you."

❧

PYRRHA GROANED, pulling herself out of the weirdly vibrant dream. People she'd never met had felt as real as though she knew them. Was that a hallucination induced by imbibing drakon filth or a prophetic dream? She tried to rise, only to find vines had grown up around her wrists and ankles.

"What the ...?" A surge of panic seized her, and she tugged on the plants holding her without avail.

The glade abruptly began to close in around her. Shadows deepened beneath the moonlight, and her fragile campfire dwindled down to embers. The trees nearby creaked and groaned, the branches clattering together as if bestirred by a wind that did not exist.

A throbbing heartbeat resounded through the wood.

Thump. Thump.

She was still dreaming. Please, Gaia, let her still be dreaming.

Thump. Thump.

Something moaned, in the distance, and the air tasted of putrescence. A pervading sense of wrongness erupted around her, and an instant later, a half dozen tree trunks ruptured with wet sucking sounds. Virescent maws opened within them, each glinting with faint luminescence and shining pus. Figures lurched from within, yanking themselves out of the trunks in perverse mockeries of birth.

Rough, bark-like skin covered both the males and the females. Dryads and satyrs. Wood spirits.

The heartbeat quickened. *Thump. Thump. Thump.*

Pyrrha jerked against the vines binding her, but they held fast. They tightened until her circulation cut off, drawing a shriek from her. A glistening dryad scraped mucus from her face and cast it aside before crawling over toward Pyrrha, lithe and naked.

Before her eyes, more Wood spirits drifted into the grove. They drove each other up against trees and began rutting in pairs or trios. Vines and leaves and branches commingled in their orgy until the wood seemed to pulse with prurient need.

THUMP-THUMP-THUMP-THUMP- THUMP!

Despite her revulsion, the energy in the air seeped into her, her own nethers joined the throbbing that had become the World. The dryad reached her, then leaned in too close. With a rough, distended tongue, she lathered Pyrrha's face while groping at her breasts.

Pyrrha's mind screamed at her to buck and try to throw the spirit off, but all she could do was moan, her body begging for more. And beyond, the World thrummed and the Veil began to fray, as something momentous pushed against it. A sense of a consciousness older than time itself pressed in upon her, even as it pressed upon the World. Something eldritch and unknowable and utterly, completely, consumed with consumptive lust.

21

PANDORA

201 Golden Age

*D*ays went by, and Prometheus spent more and more time alone, tinkering with the Box. One day soon, Pandora knew, he would finish it, and she would be forced to use it. She would return to the future and once more be forced to face the reality Zeus had presented her with.

Which meant saving Prometheus.

The only known means of ingress into Tartarus lay beneath Mount Olympus itself. Pandora would need to either sneak in that way or find some alternative route into that forbidden Realm. Either way, the very thought of the nightmare-scape haunted her, both waking and sleeping. It seeped into her dreams, an absolute darkness she found herself wandering, and the sense that within the expanse of the black lurked monstrous intellects. And they felt her presence among them.

As her fear prickled her flesh and brought on cold sweats, she could only loathe herself for that terror. She was afraid to even *see* the torments her beloved suffered with each passing moment.

So she walked along the shore and allowed him to work. Sometimes she brought Pyrrha, sometimes, as today when the babe slept, she left her with her father. Pandora waited for destiny to catch up to her and force her to walk the path she so trembled before. She willed herself to become as the unbreakable orichalcum wall around Atlantis's citadel. Her determination would need to make her inviolate.

For she would strive with the very self-styled god of Men and lord of the World. She would plumb the depths of Tartarus and achieve what no mortal had ever thought possible: a return to the world of the living.

To occupy her mind, she sang to herself, trying to forget that leaving the now meant leaving behind her babe's childhood. One day soon, the child would laugh. Then she would walk and talk and take in the world. If Pandora returned to keep her promise and save the babe's father, Pyrrha would have to grow up without her. Pandora would miss those irreplaceable first words and steps, and Pyrrha, perhaps, would forever wonder why her mother had not been there with her.

Could Pandora return here, after saving Prometheus? And then leave the Prometheus of her own time alone, knowing his every moment with his lover would forever lie in the distant past, in memories he could never reclaim? That, too, sent a twinge of sorrow running thought her chest. Ananke had presented Pandora with impossible choices. If the Moirai cared the least for the anguish they inflicted upon mortals, she could not see it.

Musing over such until her song had begun to falter from the pain pinching her heart, she caught sight of the masts first creeping over the horizon. First one, then another and another. Those looked somewhat like Phoenikian biremes, albeit of a primitive design long out of fashion. And they came here, to Ogygia.

Had more Titans come to call upon Prometheus? No. No one sent three ships to seek advice from an Oracle.

Pandora glanced up at the mountain, but she'd never make it before they spotted her. Perhaps they already had. Many Titans had sharper senses than Men. Still, she broke into a trot, soon panting from exertion as she made the climb. Where else was she meant to go? The woodlands dotting the slope would offer her some cover, at least, and perhaps she could take shelter until Prometheus arrived.

Still, it was not like her lover could fight off two hundred foes, either. Had he seen the ships? Did he even now try to reach her?

Someone leapt over the ship's side and—before she'd gone half so far as she'd hoped up the slope—began a sprint in her direction. Titan feet kicked up a curtain of sand as a pair of them raced forward with such speed their limbs seemed to blur.

In the woods, Pandora crouched down behind a thicket. She could barely control her ragged breaths. Even as they closed in, her mind kept leaping back to Prometheus and Pyrrha. She should have tried to warn them. She should have made a break for it, hoping he would hear her shouted warnings, even if it meant these people claimed *her*.

But Pandora did naught save hide.

The first to arrive was a boy, no more than fifteen she'd have gauged, and flush with glee. His platinum hair flapped about in the island breeze, but it was his ice-blue eyes that seized her.

No. No, not this ...

Zeus. Zeus as a boy.

He was trailed momentarily by a slightly older boy who looked an awful lot like him, save for a jagged scar across his nose and the first hints of a flaxen beard about his chin.

An older man followed, platinum haired himself, with a flowing beard. Another Kroniad. He was tall, bare-chested, and well-muscled. The older Titan surveyed the island, gaze seeming to scour every tree.

The hammering of her heart must surely give her away. It must reveal her and damn her.

"I know you're here!" The older Titan bellowed. "I know who you are! I know what you are! Give me the Box and you may live."

Now, her pounding heart actually seized up, missing a beat. The

Box? How in the fuck did he know about that? How could he possibly know about that? The World once more shifted, her mind struggling to find purchase upon the compounding revelations. Others knew about her precious puzzle. Not that she had it at the moment— Prometheus had been adjusting it up in the cottage.

And these people were here for her, and for him, as well.

These Kroniads. So, this must be Kronos himself, father of Zeus and apparently this other boy. Kronos had been one of the winners of the Ambrosial War, though not so securely he managed to take Atlantis back from Atlas. Somehow, those two and four others worked out a deal to keep the Ambrosia flowing under their control.

At the moment, though, Atlas must seem his greatest foe. Perhaps he had come to try to wring advantage from Prometheus, as Atlas's foster brother. Perhaps he had actually already known Pandora would be with Prometheus.

"Last warning, woman!" Kronos snapped. "Hand over the Box, or we take it."

Even had she had it now, she'd not have dared give such a thing to him. Prometheus had made it for her, and she needed it if she had any chance of saving his future self from the torment Zeus inflicted upon him. Besides, she could not even harbour a guess at what Kronos would do with such a tool.

And her? Was that why they feared *her*? Because they knew or suspected that even Pandora, a mortal, could wreak unimaginable havoc should she learn to control a device that could send her through time at will.

Pandora kept to utter stillness. Instinct demanded she break into flight, but she could not outrun the Titans. Her only chance of escape lay in remaining concealed and awaiting her moment.

"Very well, then. Zeus, find the woman." Kronos paused. "And be careful. She is more dangerous than she appears." Huh. Well, *that* was news to Pandora. "Hades, with me, and bring the others. Prometheus offers a far greater threat still."

Hades? Fucking god-of-the-dead Hades was Zeus's big brother? That was ... that was ... Wasn't he a ghost? Oh. Her mind was muddled. Obviously, he wasn't a ghost as yet, but would become one in the way such things usually happened.

More and more Titans and Men had begun to fill the beach, surely the better part of the crews of all three ships. If not two hundred strong, close enough to make no difference.

"Isn't all this a bit overkill for one Titan, Father?" Hades asked.

Kronos cast a hard look at his son. "That depends on whether he decides to cooperate or not. You underestimate him at your extreme peril. There are few more dangerous foes in the full ambit of the World." Then he turned to the other son. "I want the woman alive, boy."

Zeus shrugged as if he'd never countenance murder. As if it were the most foreign thing imaginable. As if he would not become history's most sanguinary king.

Careful not to make the least sound, Pandora crept further and further away into the woods. She could not make for the slope or their cottage upon it. Not with all those people converging upon Prometheus. She had to imagine he would make it out of this, as she had seen him again, millennia later. Herself though ... her future was aught but certain.

She needed to get away from Zeus. So she skirted around the edge of the mountain, out of the path of Kronos's war band.

Her heart continued to pound its painful rhythm.

And once again, Zeus threatened to take from her all she loved in life.

22

KIRKE

1576 Silver Age

*S*ix years after leaving Ogygia, Kirke found herself walking off the gangplank of a bireme in Kronion's harbour. Six years since she had last seen Athene, but their mother had summoned her, and Kirke would never refuse her. She might, had Athene herself sent for her, have made some excuse to avoid this trek. After all, Themiskyra had offered promising seclusion and the chance to study the effects of the moly at greater length, with only the occasional need to venture forth and spread the Nectar.

She couldn't allow the demand for the substance to fade away completely and thus make it impossible to test future batches, after all.

Satchel over her shoulder, Kirke hopped from the plank and wended by a press of dockhands eager to unload cartons of Phrygian textiles out of Ilium. Such exotic fabrics might fetch a fair few drachmae here, where the aristoi were always trying to outdo one another with the latest fashions.

The Long Wall enclosed the harbour, and Kirke followed it toward the city proper, ignoring the maze of side streets and alleys branching off from the breezeway. At a multitude of small stalls, merchants hawked ceramics and fruits and sandals, but most were stuffs for commoners. Cheap, yes, and thus suited for those who could afford no better, but not of sturdy enough make to last beyond a few seasons of hard use.

She paused only long enough to purchase a cup of wine for an obol and chugged it before handing the cup back. A little something to fortify her nerves would not go amiss. Yeah.

Her height combined with her Heliad eyes meant some recognised her as a Titan. Many genuflected, while others gave her a wide berth, clearing the path before her. Kirke tried to incline her head at each show of obeisance, though it slowed her progress to a crawl. Zeus had convinced these people that Titans were gods, and Kirke still, even after all this time, did not quite know how to react to their deference. Did she miss being a princess of great Helion? Yeah, of course, but that didn't mean she expected *worship*.

She liked to imagine, if she succeeded in overthrowing the Olympians, these people would rise up and live better lives. Freer lives, where they need offer no sacrifices to Titans. Well, a few gestures of respect for a princess wouldn't hurt.

The city had changed since last she saw it. She passed through the South Gate and headed through the Colonnade of Justice to the agora, allowing herself to gawk just a little at the expansion of public works. Even now, artisans carved a marble facade on what she could only assume would serve as another state building. A peristyle ringed the building and Kirke delayed long enough to make a half circuit around the construction.

"It will be a mint," her mother said from behind her shoulder, causing Kirke to jump.

Slowly, she turned to take her mother in. Had Mother dreamed of Kirke's arrival on this day or merely spotted her in the market? If she knew Mother, the woman wouldn't answer even if asked. "Summoned, I arrive," she said, offering a faux grand bow.

Her mother snorted, her fiery hair billowing about her face in the wind. "Your sister awaits in the acropolis." Mother motioned her to follow and guided them through a wide stoa, then up to the stairs ascending the hill. "Do you know why I called you here?" her mother asked as they climbed.

Was that a challenge to Kirke's own prescient abilities? They had never been so great as either she or her mother might have hoped. Like Mother, Kirke could sometimes catch glimpses of the future in her dreams, but only on rare occasions. The nightmares had abated after Prometheus had handed himself over to Zeus, at least until recently, so she had to believe Zeus had redirected Morpheus to something else for a time. Either way, after being dream-stalked, Kirke had found herself with very little desire to even try to access her dream Art. "No," she answered. "Do tell."

"Your sister plans to help her son become the first mortal king of Kronion."

"She's the goddess of the whole damn city," Kirke said, squinting as she gazed up at how many more steps they had to climb. "Can't she just declare whatever she wishes?"

"If she wanted Pandion to spend the first twenty years of his reign constantly striving against attempts to subvert his authority, perhaps. That, or perhaps they would think him merely her proxy, with no autonomy at all. No, she wants the people of the city to openly choose him as their king and representative to the Olympians."

Politics. Hmm. Kirke had little patience for the subtleties of such. Not when she played a much larger game to free the soul of the Thalassa world from Olympian tyranny. Athene—whatever Kirke may have felt for her half-sister—was, in fact, a symptom of that corruption. They were all drunk on the power of the Ambrosia and mortal worship.

"Fine," Kirke huffed, pausing in the climb for a moment. As Nymph, she'd mostly only ever received enough Ambrosia to sustain her youth, not to truly fortify her Pneuma and give her the level of stamina her mother enjoyed. The problem with Nymphs—and lesser male Titans, she supposed—was that they could never surpass the lowest magnitudes of Pneumatikoi and were thus considered a waste of Ambrosia. A somewhat circular situation, if anyone asked Kirke.

Kalypso had wanted to test Nectar on themselves, but if it affected their minds, how would they be in any position to judge that? "So she wants people to choose him as king without making it obvious she has forced him upon them."

From the glower Mother levelled her way, she clearly did not appreciate the sentiment, but what did she expect? Athene wanted the people to choose a king, but only if they chose *her* king. It was an illusion that their wills meant aught. More than most Olympians offered, true, but the end result was that no one actually allowed Men ownership of their own lives.

While Kirke kept silent, slowly Mother's face softened. Perhaps she grasped Kirke's point or perhaps she merely passed over it. "I have to go away for a time, and I cannot say how long I'll be away. That's why I called you here, Kirke. Athene needs someone to help her in her ends. You yourself prompted her toward this slow vengeance she now strives for."

Oh, was that what making her son king was about? Some move against Hephaistos? And she couldn't miss the subtle barb in Mother's tone, either. "She makes her son a pawn in her schemes."

"Kirke," Mother snapped. "Help your little sister and your nephew. Do you understand me?"

"Perfectly," Kirke said, resuming her climb. Athene wanted help with her vengeance, and that posed no impediment to Kirke's plans against the Olympians and might even help bring them to fruition. Besides, it gave her an excellent excuse to linger in Kronion and test the Nectar here. With the mandate her mother had just given her, she had every reason to move among the high and low of the polis, going wherever she needed. Which meant opportunity to peddle her drug and a willing populace who might one day rise to challenge Zeus.

Still, she'd need to move with extreme caution. Spread the Nectar too fast, Zeus and his cronies might start to ask what had changed in this polis of late. Wariness, yes, but it was still too good an opportunity to pass.

"I'll help her with whatever she desires, Mother. She is my sister, after all."

❦

THE MAN KNELT *in the shadow just beyond the brazier's light, his face concealed by the gloom. With a sudden convulsion he pitched forward, catching himself on his hands. Aborted gasps escaped him, like he wanted to scream, but all he managed where pained wheezes. His flesh, what little the brazier illuminated of it, it rippled like waves, as if something monstrous flowed beneath the surface.*

Nausea seized Kirke and she reached for him. The utter madness of what she saw flensed her, left her hugging herself in wordless horror.

The man fell forward, face smacking the ground, a moan building in his chest. Joints popped audibly within him. Then, the awful, gut-churning sound of muscle and tendons ripping apart.

"No ..." Kirke breathed.

Her victim screamed, his cries so long and agonised tears glistened in Kirke's eyes.

His hip snapped, breaking apart as something bulged within it. Desperately, he tugged away his clothes, casting the torn and ruined garments aside, even as the bulge in his hip ruptured. Flesh shred in a shower of gore as some new limb protruded, dragging its way free from his innards.

Stumbling backward, Kirke collapsed onto her arse, hand to her mouth.

The limb distended, until a hoof clacked upon the stone beside her.

❦

HER DREAMS WERE HAUNTED, and Kirke could not guess at the import of such vivid nightmares, unless Morpheus again tormented her. Such were her thoughts when she joined Athene just before noon.

Their mother had not specified where exactly she had intended to head for. Not to Kirke, at least, so when Athene let slip that the woman had intended to seek out her old friend Persephone, in the cursed Underworld, Kirke had sputtered on her wine. Her coughing fits sent crimson stains seeping down the front of her khiton, and the wracking convulsions had lasted long enough to leave her flushed and breathless.

"Truly?" she asked her half-sister, while the two of them reclined in Athene's palace on the acropolis. Kirke couldn't even imagine how Mother would manage to enter the Underworld—save the obvious and unappealing way—but if anyone could do so, she supposed it was the great witch Hekate.

Athene nodded sternly, offering Kirke a woollen napkin with which to dry herself.

Accepting it, Kirke made a perfunctory attempt to pat her ruined clothes dry. The drink had been to help her drown out the return of her nightmares, not dye her khiton. "Yeah, well, maybe she should have bid a longer farewell then. I mean, sure, she bid us farewell, but for all I knew she was planning to visit Neshia or something, not leave the whole Mortal Realm behind."

"Maybe she did not wish to trouble you," Athene said, earning herself a withering glare.

Kirke thought about reminding Athene she had a couple thousand more years life experience than her, but what good would it have done? Olympians talked down to Nymphs as a matter of course, probably unaware they even did so. She might also have mentioned that Mother had trained her in the Art, while Athene herself knew precious little of truths beyond this fragile mortal world. But pointing that out would have earned her naught.

Instead, she slipped from the divan and onto the floor, trying to ensure no stains spread to the furniture, then poured herself more wine from the amphora. "Anyway, it's fine, I'm fine. *She'll* be fine." She hoped. "Pff. Hades probably isn't even mad." Sure. "So what is it you hope to accomplish, exactly? I mean, make Pandion king, yeah, fine, but he's five years old, so maybe not quite ready for the reins of power. The public might be more inclined to elect a king who has his adult teeth in. Just a guess." She sipped the wine, watching her sister.

Athene huffed at that. "Obviously. I'm setting the stage. But I also want to see about seizing control of the peninsula. Which means, among other things, we need to weaken the closest poleis."

Kirke smiled around the bowl at her lips. "You mean Korinth."

"It is ruled by the demigod Sisyphus." Athene took a sip of her own wine. "So, tell me, sister, what exactly can you do about him?"

Kirke took another drink, as much to buy herself time as aught else. Unfortunately, plenty of Nectar combinations had produced rather extreme bouts of madness in numerous subjects, even while many of those batches had actually proved closest to actual Ambrosia in other effects. It would be easy enough to recreate such effects on purpose, though until this moment, she hadn't imagined wanting to. "You don't want anyone to see your hand in this, yeah? I ... have a means of ensuring Sisyphus destroys himself."

Athene leaned forward, eagerness glinting in her grey eyes. "What? How?"

How much to share? Kirke would not be enough a fool to think she could trust Athene to keep secrets from her father. Not about this.

"Mother taught me a great deal of alchemy back in the Golden days. I have methods." She set the wine bowl down. "But I'd need to travel to Korinth to apply them. I could be back in a fortnight, I'm certain."

Oh, Athene all but bounced up and down at her offer. "Do it."

It had, in fact, taken Kirke a little *over* a fortnight to brew the right concoction of Nectar, reach Korinth, and ensure Sisyphus's wine was spiked with it. It was amazing what disaffected and ill-treated slaves would help her do when prodded just right. But then, that was part of the problem with the Olympians. They suffered from such extreme hubris they could not even conceive of how much Men loathed them and their ilk.

And Sisyphus was a demigod—half Titan, half mortal—so, close enough.

She had not, however, lingered in Korinth long enough to see the results. Doing so might have aroused suspicion, which would have proved disastrous for Athene's mission and even worse for Kirke. Hephaistos might have seized her with impunity, and she could not imagine her father doing aught save despairing in impotent fury. Perhaps he would have sent Phaethusa or one of Kirke's other half-siblings to plead for her release, but those pleas would have fallen upon deaf ears, and Father would have let the issue lie.

Athene met her in her palace's vestibule, arms folded over her chest.

"It is done," Kirke said.

WORD CAME, some two months later, that Sisyphus had slaughtered the entirety of his guests at a symposium over some trifle. Oh, the stories conflicted about what started it, some claiming it was an argument over Urania's Analogy, while others argued it sparked from someone claiming to be able to best Sisyphus in pankration. Either way, Kirke had never imagined her actions would lead to the deaths of a score of people, some no doubt innocent.

Almost, it was enough to make her wish she had never come to Kronion.

But Athene summoned her to her private chambers, and Kirke found her half-sister staring into a basin of water as though it might talk to her. The Olympian didn't even seem to notice when Kirke entered, so for a moment, she waited, watching.

And Athene, she just kept gazing into the waters as if ... Oh.

Oh! Kirke had spent enough time amid Oracles to recognise attempts at hydromancy when she saw them. Kirke herself relied upon oneiromancy, but hydromancy was more common. Their family had a gift for the Sight, and Athene was clearly trying to refine hers.

From the vexed look upon her sister's face when she rose, it seemed she still lacked control over her abilities. Given their differences in their methods, Kirke couldn't offer much advice, nor was her own Sight all that strong.

Athene beckoned her to sit, and Kirke joined her by the hearth. When she had settled, her sister settled her gaze upon Kirke. "I was trying to see if I could view just what happened in Korinth," the woman admitted.

Ah, well shit. Trying to keep her expression blank proved a struggle. "And?"

"It appears Sisyphus has taken a draught of Nectar."

Kirke's palms began to sweat. "Oh, yeah, well I had heard about it spreading wildly in Korinth of late. One cannot be surprised, really. Men would do aught for the chance to improve their health and extend their lives, to say naught of the sexual benefits, and we cannot really blame them, now, can we? I mean they truly are very short lives, and so full of pain. If something can alleviate either issue, well then ... we ..."

Athene had fixed her with so stern a glare Kirke found it took the sum of her willpower to keep from fidgeting. Had her sister seen more in that bowl of water than Kirke had first imagined? Had the Sight revealed the nature of Kirke's duplicity? "I asked you to bring about his downfall."

"Yeah, well, he's pretty far fallen now. If the kin of those he murdered haven't burned down his estate yet, I imagine it's only a matter of time, right? That's how it goes with the powerful. People idolise them and worship them until they get a glimpse at their heroes, then they see the blemishes and suddenly, it's all, 'kill the wretches!', right? Having kin murdered gets people all riled up like that."

Now, Athene leaned forward. "How did you get the Nectar, Kirke?"

What if ... what if Athene could actually be an ally against the other Olympians? If she already knew about Kirke's actions, then Kirke's only chance here might lie in swaying Athene to her side. In making her an accomplice. "Ah, hmm. Yeah, I can adjust the dosage so it might enhance your Sight. I mean, there would be risks, you know? There's always risks with these things, but it may allow you to see more, and farther than you ever imagined."

"Nyx ..." Athene gasped. "You didn't buy, you made it." The grey-eyed Titan slumped backward. "My half-sister has been making Nectar."

And far better for Kalypso if Athene thought it was all her. Maybe the other Nymph wouldn't have to join her in Tartarus.

"It can give you your vengeance," Kirke prompted, words rushing from her mouth. "Imagine if you could know the past and future. It'd be like ... like how Oracles used to go to Delphi to learn from Themis. Only, they weren't so much learning from her as drawing strength from Python, back before Apollon slew the drakon. Well now, now, you want to refine your Sight, you either have to go through him—and we both know you won't like whatever price he charges—or through me, and I'll give it freely, sister. And you'd see everything you needed to, and more."

The thing about rage was, sometimes it blinded a person. Sometimes she couldn't see aught else, no matter how close it was. Maybe that was why the sly grin spread over Athene's face. Maybe she imagined herself feeding that rage with Oracular visions that would allow her to outmanoeuvre the Kreiads at every turn.

And maybe, just maybe, the Nectar would even do that.

It too must carry a price.

23

PANDORA

201 Golden Age

*N*estled in the boughs of an old oak tree, Pandora watched a young Zeus pass beneath her, almost choking on her own rage at this vile creature. This boy who would grow into a monster that spread suffering in his wake like a trail of snail slime. This arrogant, solipsistic abomination who thought the whole of the cosmos existed in service to his petty desires.

She could change all that with a knife in his throat.

Zeus trudged about the forest, hunting for her, no doubt imagining what torments he might visit upon her while not quite violating Kronos's decree she be brought in alive. Yes, Pandora could fair see the whirring of his twisted mind as it envisaged her broken flesh, pliant beneath his grasp.

Maybe Prometheus was wrong. Maybe the chance to undo the totality of suffering wrought by such a blight upon history was worth whatever price she'd pay for changing the Fates' designs. In fact, fuck the damn Moirai. That they would weave a fate that hinged upon the existence of such rank evil meant they were themselves, if not outright evil, so apathetic as to amount to much the same thing. Should she offer obeisance to goddesses of Fate who worked their will by permitting such egregious breaches of all decency?

Raping, murdering Zeus had made himself king of the World. And Pandora would not stand for it.

Nor could she, however, contend with the Titan in any sort of physical confrontation. He was faster, stronger, and tougher than any Man, even if he had not yet developed his ability to harness lightning or command the winds. And for all she knew, he already had those abilities, even as a teenager.

Instead, she set upon gathering up vines from the wood and twining them around her wrist. She'd read of snare-making, though of course had never tried it. If she could catch his ankle up, it might distract him long enough for her to strike. Oh, she had only a simple knife on her, not a dagger meant for war in the least. But driven up under the chin, it would end even a Titan, of that she had no doubt.

So, she needed but catch him off his guard long enough to close the distance and land the blow.

Her lover had warned her this course would mean they never met, that her precious Pyrrha was never born. To kill Zeus now would mean he and Hekate would never abduct Pandora, would never kill the Pleiades—and that Pandora would never travel back in time with the Box. Everything she knew and loved would unravel. She knew it for truth ... and still. How many thousands, tens of thousands, would flourish in a life in which Zeus never ascended to the throne? Prometheus would never languish in Tartarus, Europa would never find herself dragged from Agenor's court.

The thought of losing Prometheus and Pyrrha ripped her soul to pieces, even as she worked. As if she contemplated driving her blade into her own throat as well as Zeus's. But wasn't such a sacrifice worth it? How could she truly relish her happiness if she knew she had bought it with the suffering of countless generations more? With the torment of her own lover in the future?

Was she to make that choice, to condemn so many others for her own sake, she would be guilty of the same selfishness as Zeus himself. This path was all that lay before her. A chance to make the World better, even if it cost her all that mattered most.

So she cut vines, setting the snare just as old diagrams had shown. Pandora had never thought to need such skills, but then, she tended to remember almost aught she ever read. And she read quite a lot.

A stick crunched behind her and she froze. He'd found her! Not daring to breathe, she turned about, looking over her shoulder.

It was not Zeus who stood there, however, but a woman. Or a Titan in a woman's shape. Clad in an aureate breastplate with a matching helm that concealed all but her vibrant blue eyes, the woman stood there, glinting in the radiance of the setting sun. Golden-hued wings stretched out behind her, filling up the space between the trees.

The only winged Titan Pandora had heard of was Nike, though stories had not mentioned this gilded armour. Or the sheer presence of her, one that stole thought and breath and demanded rapt attention. Demanded, in fact, that one prostrate oneself and beg forgiveness for all missteps.

That last Pandora refused to do. She would not kneel or beg. If Zeus had sent another of his lackeys to apprehend her—or Kronos had, perhaps, in this time—she would meet her fate with dignity.

"Who are—" she began.

The woman surged forward with the speed of a peregrine falcon, snared Pandora's peplos with one hand, and heaved her around backward. The World whooshed by as Pandora flew out from the tree line. She hit the grass with an *oomph*, rolled a dozen times, and crashed onto her back on the mountain's edge.

Her vision dimmed even as her stomach clenched.

Pandora could do naught save moan. Every muscle in her body felt bruised, and she could only pray no bones had broken.

Groaning, she tried to sit. A single beat of the Titan's wings carried her across the distance between them. The golden-armoured figure landed in a crouch before Pandora, caught her up again, and heaved her to her feet.

"You would think to thwart Ananke?"

Pandora gaped, and not only from the pain lancing through her sides and head. This creature *knew*? She knew what Pandora had intended for Zeus?

Catching her bearings at last, Pandora realised they had reached a plateau on the mountainside. The ground beyond dropped away nigh a hundred feet to the sea. She might survive a dive from this height, might escape thus. *If* she could clear the rocks that broke the surf just off the island.

Rather than look and risk giving away her plan, Pandora kept her gaze locked upon her golden adversary. Had an agent of the Moirai come to stop her from attacking Zeus? Did that mean she actually might have succeeded in changing the timeline?

The Titan seized Pandora once more, this time using one hand to heft Pandora off her feet by the back of her neck. She carried Pandora several steps thus. The realisation hit and hit hard. Her attacker intended to cast her off the cliff, using the very means of escape Pandora had intended as the method of execution.

Shrieking, Pandora seized the knife from her belt and jabbed. The blade clinked off the aureate plate as though she'd struck orichalcum, not even leaving a scratch. Her captor caught her wrist with her other hand and twisted. Fresh jolts of pain shot through Pandora's whole arm, and the knife tumbled from her numb fingers. She kicked out, her sandal smacking into the woman's greaves with no effect whatsoever.

She was actually going to die now. She was going to die, not because of Zeus or some agent of Kronos, but because she had refused to heed Prometheus and tried to change Fate. The realisation settled in her throat like a lump.

Her captor dropped her, and Pandora stumbled, arms gyrating as she tried to steady herself and keep from pitching backward over the cliff. Falling onto the rocks thus meant certain death. "Please," she begged. Dignity be damned. "Please don't—"

A beat of the woman's wings sent a gale rushing over Pandora. It hurled her backward, far out over the cliff. The rush of shrieking wind stole her screams. She flailed as she fell. And as the sea surged up to meet her, she just managed to twist around and fall feet-first instead of landing on her back.

The ocean still struck her like a Titan's fist.

THERE WAS blindness and saltwater scorching her throat and sinuses and twisting and something that rushed past her and swept her up in a grip as strong as any Titan.

Then more darkness, gasping, retching up seawater. Moans and pain.

And finally, blinking, an almost full moon above her while she lay on her back upon the deck of a ship. The vessel heaved with each synchronised pull of numerous oars.

A man knelt beside her, naked, and peering into her eyes. Not a man. His own eyes were like pearls, opalescent and alien. Gills flapped on the flesh of his neck, and small fins twitched upon his forearms.

A merman.

Pandora sucked down a painful breath, trying to push away from the alien creature before her. Her throat felt scraped raw, as if she had swallowed fire rather than water.

"Sirsir, bring her here," a woman's voice commanded.

The merman hefted her up as though she weighed no more than a child. Clammy, webbed fingers fell upon her shoulder and guided her forward, giving Pandora a chance to take in her surroundings.

She stood upon the main deck of a bireme, one circling around Ogygia. Was this one of Kronos's ships? Most of the crew at the oars seemed Men, perhaps some Titans. Other warriors stood about the deck, peering into the night. Apart from them stood a cluster of other naked men and women. Mer, working with or for her new captors.

The creature, Sirsir, escorted her to a Titan female with eyes as blue as the sea and hair as black as Pandora's own. Once there, the mer shoved Pandora forward a step. The Titan stared at her with such an indomitable aspect and Pandora found herself squirming under that gaze. Only after a moment, when the woman looked away, did she notice the male behind her.

That was ... the boatman. Enki. Well *damn* ... And if he had lived so long ago, any doubt he was a Titan was erased.

"Well," the woman said at last, "who are you?"

Enki claimed to have known Prometheus a long time. 'Off and on,' he'd said. Perhaps his own private joke.

"I'm Pandora."

The Titan woman looked at Enki, who glanced at Pandora and shrugged. So he didn't know her yet. At least some people had some respect for causality.

"And what, Pandora, were you doing in the sea?" The lead Titan demanded.

The truth—that some agent of the Moirai had assaulted her for trying to change the timeline—would cast her as a madwoman, but perhaps a half-truth would serve. "Kronos's forces attacked the island. I suspect in an attempt to capture Prometheus. I fell from the cliff while attempting to escape their assault."

Another heavy look passed between Pandora's captor and Enki. Then the Titan looked back at her. "I'm Tethys. It was my Telkhines who fished you from the sea rather than let you drown."

Pandora glanced over at the mer, Sirsir, who still stood closer behind her than necessity warranted. "Thank you."

The mer's eyes nictitated, the gesture more unsettling for the opalescence of the orbs. How had Tethys gained command of these watery gods? Pandora pushed it from her mind. Tethys demanded her immediate attention, regardless of who or what served her. Tethys, progenitor of the Tethid genos, had abandoned the Elladósi world around the time of the Titanomachy.

But from the Ambrosial War she would arise as one of the greatest Titans in the World, helping to found the Ouranid League and thus earn her own bloodline. In fact, Europa's own ancestor, Io, was a Tethid, who had thus introduced the genos into Phoenikia. Or would do so, thousands of years from now.

"Have you naught else to say, mortal?" Tethys demanded.

"I need to return to the mountain," she said, watching for Tethys's reaction.

A scoff answered her. "A mountain you just fell off fleeing a war band led by the most ruthless Titan in the Thalassa? Unless we secure Kronos, any attempt to return to Ogygia would mean your probable death."

Yes, there was truth to that. But still, she could not leave. "My daughter is there. In danger."

Tethys folded her arms. "All children are in danger until this war is done. Still, Kronos's soldiers are more like to harm mothers than babes. Are you so ignorant of the ravages of the war you cannot imagine what they'd do to you should they catch you there?"

To say more meant gambling on just how Tethys felt about Prometheus. He had remained neutral in the war, true, but some—as apparently Kronos—might still think him a threat because of his connection to Atlas. And Tethys? Would she want to use Prometheus's lover against him? But without Tethys's aid, Pandora would have little chance of rejoining him or Pyrrha.

She allowed herself a step forward, an effort to demand Tethys's attention. "The child is mine *and* Prometheus's."

At that, Sirsir chittered something in some foreign tongue, and Tethys cast another look at Enki, her expression concealed from Pandora. When she looked back, her visage had become as implacable as the sea she loved.

"Hold her," she said.

Before Pandora could even react, Sirsir's webbed, cold fingers seized her biceps. "No! I have to reach them."

Tethys laid a hand upon Pandora's cheek, a hint of gentleness in her caress. "If you are his lover, he'll appreciate me *not* allowing you to kill yourself. You cannot return to him until we have Kronos."

Pandora jerked her arms side to side to free herself. She might as well have tried to push over an oak tree with her bare hands for all the mer moved. "You cannot do this." It was the kind of petulant objection indignant fools raised. Because, of course, Titans could do aught they pleased. But Pandora had suffered abduction and captivity as a child and would *not* allow herself to suffer it once more. Not again. Not *again.* "Release me!"

That earned her a roll of Tethys's eyes and a few snorts from those close enough to hear.

"Be still," Sirsir said, his voice suddenly deep as the ocean. It reverberated in her skull and dragged her mind through a watery haze. She felt her arms go limp and, for the life of her, couldn't even remember why she'd been trying to struggle. "Follow," the mer commanded.

And, of course, she did, as he guided her to a bench amid the oarsmen. After she sat, she blinked, the mire in her head starting to thin. Sirsir raised a warning finger in front of her face. A webbed, clawed digit that left her squirming at the sight of it. Perhaps thinking her cowed, the mer then set about fastening a bronze manacle to her ankle.

Pandora forced herself not to whimper. Similar fetters bound some, though not all, of the other rowers about her in this part of the ship. Slaves forced to serve in the bireme at Tethys's pleasure.

But the oar for this bench remained locked in place and Sirsir made no move to force her to attend to it. Just as well, as she doubted she could have kept rhythm or maintained it without someone else to join her.

Instead, she busied herself looking about her new prison. Some few men around her leered at her, licentious thoughts writ so plain upon their faces as to prove almost comical. Looks Pandora had seen all too oft, but at the moment, had not the least interest in emboldening. Rather, she favoured the gawkers with such a disdainful stare the most of them looked away. Men like these wanted to see a woman writhe in discomfort at their attention. They couldn't handle one who returned the challenge.

Most of those about her, though, seemed too sweat-drenched and overwrought by their backbreaking work to give her the least notice.

Soon, the drums started up again, and the oarsmen began their labor once more, their small respite over.

On some of the oars, blood stained the wood, where men's blisters had ruptured. How long had Tethys pushed these poor bastards?

The Telkhine had saved her life, without doubt, but Pandora could not let herself forget one truth. Tethys was still a godsdamned Titan. The race of Man still lay prostrate beneath her plodding sandals.

Some things never changed.

And perhaps not even the Golden Age had offered so much better times than those Pandora had left.

INTERLUDE: KADMUS

1550 Silver Age

When the sun set upon Tyros—late this time of year— the symposium began. First, the feasting upon seasoned cod and a myriad of sweet breads. Then, the drinking. Kadmus had attended Elládosi symposiums and the similar ones on Atlantis as well, but Phoenikians were somewhat more relaxed in their pastimes. No symposiarch to enforce how much everyone must drink or any such thing, nor were the rules against women of the house attending quite so strict.

In a way, Kadmus found the structured Elládosi method endearing, as if those people demanded even fun be had within the bounds of propriety. Everything must be taken seriously in such poleis, especially recreation.

Here in Phoenikia, it was different. Guests from around the city poured into the palace, thronging the chambers, the atrium, and the garden. In many such locations, musicians plied their trade.

In the courtyard, he saw Europa playing the lyre. She'd taken it up as a child and he, for his part, had toyed with it just to prove he could, though he'd never had her talent for it. Only a year apart in age, she'd always insisted on studying the same subjects as he, and he found he could do naught save return the favour.

When she finished a song, he sat on the stone bench beside her. "May I?"

"Of course," she said. "I have to check on Pandora anyway. I left her inside with Kassiopeia." She paused. "She's solved that puzzle box a dozen more times already."

Kadmus offered her a smile and strummed at the lyre. A few chords told him he was out of practice. The looks of those nearby told him they noticed it too, which actually brought a mischievous grin to his face. On the sea, men sang songs, oft ribald enough to make Dagon himself flush in his home beneath the waves. One in particular—about a trio of lonely mermaids—came to mind, and Kadmus played the melody, wondering if anyone at such a party might have the least idea what they were listening to.

Were he to sing a single refrain, he might manage to mortify even his indulgent father. Kadmus amused himself imaging the look upon King Agenor's face should he hear of it.

"I know what you're thinking about doing," Phoenix said, stepping out from behind some of the guests watching him.

"I'm living moment to moment," Kadmus answered.

"Unless you want them to be your last moments, I'd suggest you keep lines about mermaid problems from passing your lips."

Well. At least someone could tell what he played. With just a hint of reluctance, Kadmus set the lyre aside. Phoenix motioned for him to follow, and they strolled the gardens, away from greater throngs of drunken guests.

His brother offered him a jug of wine and Kadmus took a swig. Huh. The very same he'd just brought from Atlantis.

Phoenix grinned at the unspoken comment and reclaimed the jug for himself.

"How has Byblos treated you?" Kadmus asked, peering up at the stars. A clear night. A perfect summer.

"Well enough, and her princess even better. Zeus's envoys still attempt to pressure us, though."

"Bah." Kadmus nearly spit in the bushes as he passed them. "The Titan King of Elládos thinks he's king of the whole fucking World."

"True enough." Phoenix took another drink before handing the wine back. "None dared stand against him." And his blood ran through both their veins, through Io. Bastard Titan. "He forces us to take care in their waters. We cannot risk antagonising him too far."

No, especially not if it meant Zeus might turn Poseidon against Phoenikian ships. Would Dagon protect them against Poseidon? Maybe near to Phoenikia itself. Maybe. Certainly not in every foreign trade route they had so painstakingly claimed.

Phoenix abruptly drew up short and fell to one knee. It took Kadmus a moment to see why and follow his brother's lead.

Beneath a cedar stood two Titans. Nike, come back again for the first time in five years and ... who was that beside her? Kirke, wasn't it? A direct daughter of Helios.

"Goddesses," Phoenix rasped. "We did not know you were among us."

"Are not all welcome at this symposium?" Kirke asked, voice more timid than Kadmus would have expected. As if it was almost a real question. As if she sought permission for her presence here.

"Of course they are, my lady," Phoenix said.

A sudden thought had Kadmus's stomach dropping, twisting, ready to retch up all that wine. What if Nike had returned for Pandora? If she took the child away now, after five years, it would rip Europa's heart from her chest. Kadmus could fair see the utterly broken look upon his sister's face at such an event and almost choked at the sight in his mind.

"Hello, Kadmus," was all Nike said, though.

She knew his name? Titans seemed so far above Men, it always came as a shock to find they paid the least attention to lowly mortals. This goddess who, in legend, had led the gods to victory in the Titanomachy more than fifteen centuries ago. She knew his name. Cared enough to address him.

"My lady," Kadmus said, lowering his face.

When he looked up, Nike and Kirke had moved on, caught up in their own whispered conversation. Titans, here, though they seemed to hold little enough interest in the drinking.

"Did you know they were in Tyros?" Phoenix demanded, pulling Kadmus to his feet.

"No." And he could not imagine it portended well. But Nike said naught of the child, so maybe he'd been wrong. Maybe Pandora was not her daughter, or at least she was not here to take her back. Or maybe the girl was Nike's child and even the Titan could not help herself from looking in on her. Hmm, yes, that would make sense. She could never raise her, never acknowledge her—Zeus could do as he wished, but females, even female Titans, could have no bastards— but still could not quite push Pandora from her heart.

Which probably meant Europa was safe from heartbreak.

"Perhaps we ought to inform Father he has such distinguished guests," Phoenix said.

Yes, perhaps they should.

And Kadmus imagined that, when word got out that Titans walked among them, none of the guests would find the symposium quite so uninhibited as they had moments before. For who could take their leisure under the gazes of living gods that might punish imagined slights with generation-spanning curses or bottomless cruelty?

KADMUS STOOD by his father's side, one hand resting upon the back of the throne as he leaned in whispering, telling the man of their new guests. King Agenor's face no doubt remained impassive, perhaps even smiling at his guests, but Kadmus could feel the tension seep into his father's shoulders, see the subtle tightening of the king's grip upon his armrest.

Titans in the palace. The very lords of the World, the living gods themselves, had come calling upon them.

Whatever the man might have said in response vanished as a

collective gasp passed amid the gathered throng in the throne room. In a wave rushing outward from the gates, men and women dropped to their knees, bowing at the newest arrival.

Kadmus's own knees wobbled. Had he misjudged Nike? Had she now come to take whatever she thought her due? Dare they stand against her if she laid claim to the child?

There, across the hall, Europa knelt, holding Pandora's hand as if the child had come from her own flesh. And perhaps she *had*, for Pandora seemed carved out of the very heart of Kadmus's sister. A perfect babe, brilliant and full of life, and so much more real than anyone around her.

It was not, however, Nike who strode through the gates, but Zeus himself, platinum bearded, icy blue eyes flashing, and trailed by his attack dog, the Witch-Titan Hekate.

Even mighty King Agenor rose at Zeus's approach and prostrated himself before this foreign Titan king. And how could Kadmus do aught save mimic his father's gesture, dropping to his knees in obeisance to the god before them.

Still, he stole a glance at the two new Titans in their midst. Four Titans in one night. Yes, he had seen more than that in the streets and palaces of Atlantis, but this was Tyros, and their ilk did not so oft come here, Dagon be praised.

Kadmus's throat had closed up on first entrance of the god. His palms had grown clammy, his skull felt too small for the pounding within it. All awaited the whims of the Titan who had slithered into the palace like a dragon, implacable and unfathomable. Why *him*?

Stalking the hall, Zeus surveyed the prostrated mass before him as if it were his due, as if it were only natural. He was, after all, not a mere Titan but an Olympian, and he thought *all* he saw his due. So had he claimed Io of Argos two centuries past and she had fled, his seed in her womb, to these lands where she became Kadmus's distant ancestor.

And now Zeus was *here*.

The witch spoke something into the Olympian's ear, and the Titan flashed his teeth before his gaze settled upon Europa. Like a blow to Kadmus's gut. No ... Such could not happen. Such could not be borne.

"I will have the girl, Europa, as my pallake," Zeus declared.

Kadmus's father stumbled to his feet. "My lord! Surely you might choose someone else. My daughter is the sole princess of Tyros and destined for—"

"For a good many nights upon her back," Zeus snapped.

No.

No, fuck that. Perhaps cutting the Titan's balls off might abate his ceaseless lusts. Kadmus rose and strode boldly toward them, intent to interpose himself between the Titans and his sister. "This is not Argos," he spat.

His brother Phoenix, though, said even less. Growling, the man snatched up a small amphora and charged.

Zeus turned on him, eyes growing cloudy. For an instant, it felt like all the braziers in the room dimmed. Like the air filled with a pungent aroma, the too clean scent that followed a storm. Lightning crackled along the Titan king's fingers, tumbling over his digits, like a performer's coin trick.

Knowing it was in vain, still Kadmus opened his mouth to shout a warning to his brother.

Zeus's hand shot forward and a bolt of lightning ripped from it. So white its luminance seared itself into Kadmus's eyes. So loud it stole all other sound from the room, leaving naught save a ringing in its wake. The bolt bodily flung Phoenix back through the hall, hurtling him a dozen feet through the air.

Prudence demanded utter submission before such unthinkable, inconceivable power. Wisdom dictated *any* course, save the one Kadmus's body now took, shoulder slamming into Zeus's gut. It felt like running into a stone wall, and yet the pair of them came toppling down, tumbling onto the floor.

No sound, save the ringing, but as Kadmus rose, he saw Pandora's open mouth and flailing hands, clutching at Europa, as Kadmus's sister tried to guide her away. He saw as Hekate grabbed both of them by their wrists and began dragging them toward the atrium.

Roaring—starting to just hear his own voice—Kadmus pounded a fist into Zeus's face. That, too, felt like he punched solid rock. The Olympian glared at him, clearly over being dazed.

Then an explosion from outside shook the very foundations of the palace. Dust poured down from the ceiling, and columns trembled. Even Zeus seemed stunned, hesitating. The clamour cut through any delirium that had followed the lightning, and Kadmus could see and hear again.

Before he could land another blow, Zeus heaved him upward. The World lurched, rushed past Kadmus as he flew, seemingly weightless. Then he collided with a pillar in midair. The impact snatched away all breath. An instant later, he fell, crashing ten feet onto the ground.

That blow stole his very sight.

So many moments one wanted to forget, but they seeped into the ocean of the whole, joined its flow, even as they forever polluted it with their filth.

At first, the basement under the Temple of Demeter seemed pitch black, and Kadmus had to navigate with a hand upon the smooth stone of the wall. Soon though he caught sight of a flickering light in the distance, as if someone had lit a candle down a long hall. The chill he had felt on climbing up Demeter's palace redoubled here, as did the sense of having stepped into some other world, almost as though one might find a gate to Hades's domain in this place.

As he drew closer to the light source, he realised he had entered not a basement as he had believed, but a tunnel carved into the mountain, a place awash in umbral dances and the hum of something not quite of the Mortal Realm. Foreboding gripped him and a memory of words Harmonia had spoken about things beyond this world, the very thought of which set him to trembling.

Eventually, he found the illumination came from a torch set into a sconce, far from the stairs he'd descended. As he drew nigh, the sound of drums reached him, reverberating through the tunnel, making it seem as though a slight quake shook this world. Suddenly overcome with vertigo, Kadmus steadied himself against the wall. A nameless dread began to coil along his spine, shortening his breath. He glanced back the way he'd come only to find shadows now moved there, like figures shifting just out of his vision, flanking him, though no one could have possibly moved around him in the narrow confines of the tunnel.

He grabbed the hilt of his xiphos. "Are you the Children of Gaia?" he demanded.

Then the wall of the tunnel warped, seeming to turn malleable, and a figure stepped out of it, snatching his wrist in a grip rock-like in both texture and power. Kadmus's stomach dropped out from under him, the dread that seized him so profound it stole thought and breath, both.

The entity before him looked somewhat like a Man, but shorter, reaching only Kadmus's sternum, and misshapen, as if its spine had twisted back on itself. It had swarthy skin of a texture almost like the stone it had emerged from.

"Kabeiri, they call us here," the figure said, its voice warped and grating upon the ears. The Kabeiri bent Kadmus's wrist back until he yelped in pain, giving over any attempt at drawing the sword, and finally jolting his mind into working once more.

Then there was a half dozen of the creatures, grasping him, dragging him further down into their chthonic world.

THE EARTH itself seemed to obey Kabeiri command. For, when they had brought Kadmus into the depths of a cavern from where he could look into a precipitous ravine, before he had time to even gauge its depth, stone grew from the ground to encompass his ankles, forcing him to remain standing. Kadmus yelped, tugging at heels that wouldn't budge in the least.

Sheer disbelief seized him, stopped him from reacting as they took his xiphos and his cuirass, leaving him but the exomis tunic he wore.

This was impossible. The thought echoed through his mind, round and round, utterly in defiance of what he beheld before him.

More of the bent, warped creatures danced around him, beating drums of taut skin, which—Kadmus could not suppress the intuition —might have been made from Man-flesh. So perverse and alien was the display, it felt more like standing outside himself, watching the procession.

The Kabeiri hammered a discordant rhythm upon their drums, chanting in a language that seemed to make reality itself bleed away, leaving the air thick and viscous and humming. Harmonia had said, on the ship, that beyond even the Underworld lay a Spirit Realm. That the denizens thereof came to the Mortal Realm, slipped inside Men and wore their forms, transforming them into mer, or perhaps into these twisted beings of stone and pain.

The thought caused a knot to form in his chest. Would he not have been better off having then marched right into the domain of Hades himself? Would the Underworld not have proven less dismaying than this corruption of the Earth?

What had Demeter meant, in her accusations of his crimes? Was he not justified in taking any course to save his sister? Or did he lie to himself to think thus, denying the indignation he would have felt if someone used such rationale upon him?

They did not, however, leave him overlong with the torments of his mind.

Whilst most of the Kabeiri continued to beat their drums, a pair of them waddled toward him and began a more direct torture. Despite his protests, his cries of wanting but to learn from them, they wedged slivers of rock under his fingernails. When his screams at that dwindled, they forced a stone rod into his anus, and Kadmus wept for shame and pain, hours after the incident ended.

He wanted to curl into a ball and hide from the world. He wanted to cast himself over the precipice and end his misery. But he could not move, could not even lie upon the ground to rest his body or soul.

And then an image came, of an innocent woman, bound to a mast, for days on end.

ॐ

A DELIRIUM between sleep and waking madness had claimed Kadmus, and his mind seemed to leave his body, flitting about the cavern to the delighted cackles of the Kabeiri. Though they said naught of the sort, his disembodied mind drew from them the impression that, in breaking his body, they would open it up for one of their kind to crawl inside and take root in this world.

It was the ultimate culmination of all his misfortune. To lose not something so mundane as his life, but his very sense of self and have his body put to use for the whims of another. Taken by those with power simply because they could.

Just as Demeter had claimed. As Kadmus had failed to understand, then.

Failed, in his wretchedness. Ba'al, what had he done?

"Forgive me," he rasped, into the darkness, knowing full well that naught that dwelt here could even fathom such a concept as forgiveness.

Here, in the bowels of the Earth, on the threshold of somewhere else, there was only the simplest of questions: Who had the most power?

And here, in this place, the answer, equally simple: not Men.

ॐ

HARMONIA DID NOT RESIST as he escorted her back to the bireme, even willingly swam out to it when they reached the shore. His crew pulled her aboard having no idea whom they'd brought amidst them.

Perhaps by accident—though Kadmus doubted it—one of the

men tugged her by the peplos, managing to dislodge the garment and expose one of her breasts. Harmonia backed away and covered herself, though she seemed more irked than abashed. Or perhaps she simply concealed her true feelings well, refusing to allow mortals to see her discomfited or afraid.

It was petty of him, of course, taking her, when she had no part in Europa's abduction. Kadmus's sister would have been ashamed of him for such base vengeance, and the thought of her reaction to what he had done had his cheeks flushing. Gods damn it all! Was he to now release Harmonia and look twice the fool?

No.

No, and perhaps Harmonia might yet help him, for she seemed to know things she ought not. Either way, her calm—and the knowledge of what Europa would say—only redoubled the heat in him. He grabbed her wrist and dragged her astern, away from the rest of the crew, then shoved her onto the deck.

A tiny yelp escaped her, then no other reaction, save a slight sadness in her eyes. Disappointment? Not fear, though. Still not fear, and somehow that made him want to scream. What in Dagon's deep was wrong with her? What was wrong with him, for so wanting to see terror in her eyes? This whole affair had become skewed, as if a riptide had seized him and refused to let him go.

Growling, Kadmus knelt beside her. "These men would hurt you in an instant if I told them to." In fact, they might do so unless he strictly forbade it.

"Would you hurt me? Would that fill the vacant hole in your breast? Is that a moment you would treasure?"

Kadmus recoiled. "How do you know what words are shared between a brother and sister alone? Are you an Oracle?" His pulse was racing. He felt a chill on the back of his neck, and yes, a hollowness inside in his chest. This was not happening. She could not know these things.

Harmonia rose to her knees, bringing herself eye level with him. Her eyes were the colour of ochre, flaked with darker specks, and they held him such that his breath caught. Was this some Titan trickery? Some godlike grace that could break the very will of a mortal? "Would you know the depth of knowledge that lies deep within the Earth? Would you hear the whispers of Gaia?"

"I ..." He was losing himself, of that he was certain. Becoming enraptured in the power she wielded, and her uncanny insight. Could Zeus have planned all this? No. The Titan would have simply killed him had he known himself pursued. Still, Harmonia was manipulating him.

Before he could fall further under her spell, Kadmus blinked, turning away. He clutched his fists at his sides and banged them against his thigh. What madness did she play at? He would *not* be dissuaded, not turned from his course, no matter where it might take him.

"Bind her to the mast!" he snapped at no crewman in particular.

Perhaps a night tied upright like that would loosen her tongue. Perhaps that would serve to get her to spill her secrets.

THERE IS an impetus that drives the soul in times of emotion, Kadmus decided. An undeniable force that leads one to swear to any course, no matter how rash, whilst in the grips of passion. Oaths that, upon reflection, reveal their impossibility.

Such as the oath to bring Europa back, no matter what. Or his promise to himself on leaving Lesvos that he would search every last island in the Aegean should he have to. Faced with the vastness of the sea and hundreds of isles to search, such a promise now seemed the vain, petty indulgences of an incensed child.

The last, Skyros, had proven as profitless as all the others, and, on returning to the bireme, he could not help but note the despondency washing over the faces of the crew, like men staked to drown in the rising tide, losing hope one gasping breath at a time.

Islands of barren rock and atolls with settlements barely worth calling villages. Fishing towns and trade hubs. And none had seen

Zeus in months. How much time had now passed since he'd left Tyros? A fortnight? Perhaps more.

The days bled together in a cavalcade of endless sea, sleepless nights, and haughty promises he could not keep had he a lifetime to do so.

Now, his steps had no spring as his sandals thumped upon the gangplank. Every boarding had become akin to trying to scale the slopes of Olympus itself in an effort to ascend to the heavens.

A man offered him an amphora, and he took a swig from their dwindling stores of wine, polishing off the last of the vessel. After handing it back, he paced around in front of Harmonia.

Days strapped to the mast—released for but moments a day to relieve herself—had left her lips cracked, her wrists blistered around the ropes. The misuse of her pristine flesh somehow failed to abrade her beauty, a thought that sent a fresh spark of vexation running through Kadmus. How dare she endure this, when all who had come to save Europa began to falter? How dare this Nymph bear her torment in silence and still remain graced with such allure?

How dare she ...

Hardly knowing what he was about, Kadmus wrapt his hands around her throat, pressing his thumbs against her jaw with just enough force to shove her head back. Fingers just beginning to dig into delicate flesh. "I am denied the prize I seek, over and over, Nymph." He swallowed, suddenly parched despite the wine. "I am left adrift now, in this sea. And I find myself thinking, petty though it is, if I shall not look upon my beloved sister again, if she is forever lost to me, then perhaps my only recourse is to take someone from Zeus forever."

Her throat quivered, ever so slightly, and Kadmus hated himself for the satisfaction that offered. "You're not going to kill me, Kadmus." Her voice, despite her bondage, retained its musical aspect and a softness he could not endure. That, and a certainty, as if she spoke not of her desire to live, but of an acute knowledge of Fate, of something beyond the ken of mortals.

His hands slipped from her throat. Had she seen through his

bluff? Had he been bluffing? Even he wasn't sure anymore, damn it all. How far would he have gone to save Europa?

He swallowed, shaking his head. "Y-you spoke before of secret knowledge."

"The whispers of Gaia." The Nymph's voice was intoxicating. Could she work her spells upon his mind even while so bound? If so, best he walk away now. Best, in fact, he gag her, or even throw her overboard in offering to Dagon. "Would you like to hear them, Kadmus?"

"What is Gaia? That's not one of the Olympian Pantheon. Some obscure Elládosi deity?"

At that, she giggled. "Wine."

After a moment of incomprehension, he bellowed for another amphora and tilted it so that she drank. When she'd slaked her thirst, he sent the rest of the crew away. "What is Gaia?"

"The oldest of gods, or among them. The Elder Goddess of the Earth itself. She speaks to us in whispers, if you will listen. And, on the rarest of occasions, through the voices of her Children."

What madness was the Nymph on about? Kadmus had never heard tale of any such thing, and he'd studied a great deal about Elládos and its gods, both for political reasons and as a pastime to share with Europa. "Is Demeter not your Earth goddess?"

"Release me. These bindings chafe and we both know I'm not going to dive into the sea to escape."

No, but then, the bonds were intended to torment her into revealing where her father might have taken Europa. Kadmus watched her face—those eyes!—a moment, then resolved to untie her. Released, Harmonia rubbed her wrists, even as she slunk down on the deck with a sigh.

A Titan, yes, but also a woman in physical pain, nigh overcome with fatigue, and surely in the grips of some fear as to what these men would do with her. Oh, Dagon, how he wanted to hate this Nymph, this daughter of his enemy. Denied access to Zeus, how could Kadmus not wish to revenge himself upon the Olympian's kin? But maybe not Harmonia. She knew more than she had revealed, of that he had no doubt, but she had about her also an air of innocence, an aspect of beguiling purity. Such things made him want to rub soothing balms upon the rope-born abrasions on her wrists, to offer her comfort and succour. To touch her with gentleness.

But then, whether he wished her harm or no, still, Kadmus must do all within his power to save his sister. He owed Europa that. So he knelt before her once more and took her chin between his thumb and forefinger. "Give me something I can use, Nymph. I beseech you, help me now." He swallowed. "Or I will have no choice but to have you bound once more, and this time I'll have you stripped naked and tied upside down until your blood wells in your head and your skull feels ready to burst from it!" He realised he began shouting, became short of breath, and paused. "So, please, tell me where to find my sister."

Whatever Harmonia had expected, it clearly had not been such a threat, for at last her eyes widened in real apprehension. She watched him, perhaps trying to judge whether he might truly carry out so monstrous a threat upon her. A question not even Kadmus himself was certain of the answer to.

Several breaths she sat like that, before swallowing. "I cannot say where Father would have taken her."

Kadmus lowered his eyes. Damn it. Was he now compelled to follow through on his ultimatum? If he did not, no further threat he ever plied her with would hold weight. Yet ...

"I can, however," Harmonia abruptly added, "tell you about the secret knowledge and the whispers of Gaia. The hints of what is to come."

He looked up at her. "How does this help me find Europa?"

"You wanted to know if I am an Oracle."

His throat was so dry. "Speak." For her life depended on it.

"Demeter has ruled the city of Thebes since Tethys fled this sea long ago."

"Common knowledge."

"Ah, but you, I think, don't seem to realise she is the head the Cult of Gaia, at least the one in Thebes."

Kadmus folded his arms. "Why should I care about such things? Small cults hold little interest."

"Even if they offer members uncanny insights?"

Well, that was interesting. "You *are* an Oracle, then? Given powers by this Gaia? And Demeter?"

"Demeter may serve Father, but she is no great ally to him. She will sympathise with your plight. You have heard, I'm sure, of the legend of the loss of her daughter, Persephone."

Indeed, though he'd thought it mere fancy. "That Zeus's dead brother Hades dragged her bodily into the Underworld, yes. Am I to believe such a thing?"

"The world is deeper, older, and more abstruse than Men would care to believe. Persephone was yet another of Zeus's bastards, and Hades took her to punish his brother for his crimes."

"Your *father's* crimes," Kadmus snapped.

"My father's crimes, yes. Did you know Persephone was taken not long before Zeus himself took Io?" Harmonia leaned forward. "Coincidence, perhaps. Or maybe the Fates work interwoven threads, all of us caught up in a loom we cannot see."

"I wouldn't give a broken fishbone for this talk of Fate. I want to find my sister. If these whispers of Gaia have answers, that's all that matters."

Harmonia frowned. "If anyone can help you, it would be Demeter. She hears the deep whispers, and she blames Zeus for the loss of their daughter. My father ... is complex and not well loved even by the Olympians he himself appointed as the Gods of Men. Maybe least of all by them."

"Nor much loved, I think, by you." Harmonia refused to reveal what Kadmus wanted to know, true, but her words certainly indicated an animosity—or at the least an apathy—between her and Zeus.

"I spend my days hiding from my father's wife because he decided he could not resist laying with my mother, whether she willed it or no. Do you imagine I relished life alone in Zeus's bastion, isolated and forbidden from even calling upon either of my parents in their dwellings? Do you think life so very easy for Nymphs, Kadmus?"

Her reprimand stung more than it ought to have, and he flushed. Had he judged her too harshly? He must have, surely. An urge to comfort her, to say something to assuage her suffering and his guilt surged up in him, choked him. But who was he to offer comfort to her, least of all moments after he had just threatened to have her tied to a mast upside down?

Instead, he rose. "Perhaps life has not treated either of us so well as we might wish." He looked to his crew. "Fetch her something to eat!"

❧

ROUGH HANDS SHOOK HIM AWAKE. Someone shouting his name.

Phoenix?

Kadmus opened his eyes to find the brazier light lancing through them like actual blades and immediately shut them once more. "Oww." His stomach lurched, wanting to retch.

"Get up!" his brother shouted.

When Kadmus dared peek once more, though, it was Kilix, not his oldest brother who knelt beside him.

The symposium.

Europa.

The thought struck him as a fresh blow, one with more force even than being hurled into a column by a god. For this blow smashed not bone but his very soul, leaving him trembling in such abject horror as to dim even the agony of his wounds. Was his head cracked? His ribs broken?

Such counted for less than *naught* compared to the realisation that Europa was a second Io. Zeus took Nymphs as his pallakae across the world on a whim. What import should he give the desire or honour of a mortal woman?

And then, another thought. "Phoenix?"

Kilix pulled him up—it turned out the pain in Kadmus's ribs was not *quite* blocked by the anguish of his soul—and motioned to a shroud-laden body across the hall. So caught up in his torment,

Kadmus had not even noticed the wailing women encircling the body, Kassiopeia among them.

Phoenix.

Numbness claimed him, then, settling around his neck like a noose, dragging his steps forward, through the lament-filled hall. Zeus had murdered his brother and abducted his sister. He would have his way with her for a time, probably leave her with child, then cast her aside, as he had done Io centuries back.

There was madness in the earth, now, and it had taken root, deep, infecting them all.

"Pandora?" he asked, realising she wasn't here.

"The Titan took the child too, in the chaos. Perhaps to ... comfort ..."

Europa? What comfort was a child for a woman facing such a fate? The knowledge that her adopted daughter would be there to *watch*? It sounded like perverse Titan thinking to Kadmus's mind. It was vile. Stomach churning.

Madness.

Utter and complete.

For the very World had shifted this night. It had come undone upon the seams, an unraveling of order, as chaos came bubbling to the surface.

"The wine magazine exploded," Kilix said unprompted. "Nearly got lit aflame myself."

For a moment, Kadmus stared at him, uncomprehending. Wine magazine? The amphorae? That was the explosion. So had the other two Titans arranged such a thing to cover Zeus's abduction of Europa? Had Nike done it?

Then another thought. "What in Ba'al's arse were you doing in the wine magazine?" Kadmus demanded.

"Uh ... behind it. There was this flute girl. She likes her wine, you know, so ..."

Kadmus seized his older brother's hair. "You should have been here!"

Kilix shoved him, and Kadmus stumbled and fell, still disoriented and weak. Fresh red jolts of agony shot through him on hitting the ground. It took all he had just to keep sucking in breaths, to try to keep his vision from dimming too far. "Oww."

"What the fuck, little brother? You didn't do aught, and you *were* here. So if you seek someone to blame for this debacle, perhaps it is not I you best look to."

Kadmus swallowed, gritting his teeth, then struggled to his feet. "No, you were too busy thinking with your cock. Which sounds remarkably like a certain Titan king I know of."

His brother stiffened, fist clenching at his side. "I do not force myself upon women, Kadmus. Do not compare me to that creature."

"Enough!" their father roared.

Kadmus blanched. He hadn't even realised the king had drawn nigh.

"Both of you bicker like children while your precious sister suffers indignities not to be borne! Shame! Shame upon the pair of you useless wretches if you do not retrieve her!" The man fair trembled now, not only with age, but with a clearly immeasurable grief.

Kadmus flushed in shame, his tongue failing him.

"Father, surely you cannot believe we can—" Kilix began.

"Shame!" The king thrust a finger into Kilix's chest and that alone seemed forceful enough to drive Kadmus's brother a step back. "Shame!" Spittle flew from Father's lips, his words slurred. "Do not return here without her if you call yourselves her brothers! Find her!"

As if a flattened cushion, the king collapsed onto the floor in a heap, gasping and trembling. Kadmus took a step toward his father, but the man's gaze seized him, demanding he follow the command as given.

Find her.

Find Europa and return her to home, or do not dare return to this place. But who had ever reclaimed any of Zeus's pallakae? Maia, Elektra, those famous Nymphs returned to their homes when he finished with them, yes. But mortals? Mortals wandered in shame like Io, at best making their lives in new lands where they would never again have to look into the eyes of those who had once known them.

For those who had known them in the before knew them in *other* moments. Perhaps Europa was right, and life was moments, but even so, some moments demarcated boundaries in time. Thresholds one could pass in but a single direction. There was no return.

Find her.

Kilix grabbed his elbow and guided him from the great hall. It was grief-born madness, perhaps, but their father had enjoined them to retrieve their sister or not return themselves.

Outside, in the atrium, Kadmus looked to Kilix, unable to still the shudders running through him. In truth, he'd never shared the easy rapport with Kilix he did—had done—with Phoenix or Europa. But still, the look upon the other man's face told Kadmus all he needed to know. They would go, they would follow Father's command.

They would not return to Tyros without Europa.

&.

AND THERE, *in the quicksilver pool, at long last, he beheld the object of his quest. The sister he'd thought lost forever, lying abed, in labor. Her heaving cries shuddered through him as if some fragment of her agony welled up in the quicksilver and flowed into Kadmus.*

He tried to reach for her, to grasp her hand and offer some comfort, though, of course, he knew she was not really there. The liquid flowed and warped and became the World, and Europa held a son. The bastard son of Zeus.

Then his sister was walking in a throne room, a modest one compared to the palace of Demeter, but hardly unadorned, for bright frescoes bedecked the walls and tapestries depicted ancient glories.

Time kept slipping through his fingers, moments melding into one another with no space in between. His sister was holding her son's hand, and he was not a babe but a child, at least three or four years behind him. And Europa guided him to the empty throne, beside which stood Elektra.

Harmonia's own mother, and a Queen of Atlantis.

This place was ... Knosós, on the north shore of Atlantis. Elektra hefted the child and placed him upon the throne.

"Hail King Minos, son of Zeus."

More flickers, wispy moments scattered in a life where Europa refused to leave her son's side. The first time he picked up a sword or rode a chariot or sailed, she was there, watching over him, her precious demigod, whom she loved even more than she hated his father.

And in the sea of her moments, there was no Kadmus ahead, only behind.

Seeing it all, Kadmus pitched over backward, gasping, no longer ashamed to shed his tears even in front of Harmonia. Not in the face of the apogee of Fate itself.

"She's there, in Knosós, on Atlantis ..."

In naming her location, he pretended he could do something about it. Sail there, save her, bring her home. But, even if he could defy what the Fates had deigned to reveal to him here, the truth was, the sum of all her moments was a *happy* life. She had smiled and laughed and loved, despite the moments of pain that interspersed her joys, joining the sea of her memories.

And if he changed that, if he stripped away this future and destroyed those moments, he might have taken something from her, stolen it from her.

"If she willed it, do you truly believe she could not have sent word to Tyros?" Harmonia asked.

Because he had known it, even back when she was first taken: Europa could never reclaim what she had lost that night, only become anew, reborn as the spring.

All fight left him, and he could do naught save wrap his arms around himself and gasp under the gargantuan weight of destiny. Slowly, almost afraid, he looked to Harmonia. To see such things, even hints of them, must thus crush the very souls of Oracles. To behold the future and the World beyond must be an incomprehensible burden.

Having no words, all he could do was take her hand and see in her eyes she understood and accepted his revelation.

§

THE KABEIRI HAD GATHERED in a rough throng when Kadmus and Harmonia ascended the stairs once more. Neither had spoken on the climb, though he had begun to regain his strength, and part of him longed to talk with her. Still, a greater part felt as though he were drowning in his reflections. Perhaps she sensed the pensiveness that had claimed him, the feeling of being swept away in a current and beholding something Man was not meant to see. The scope of such vision left him speechless, even in his own mind. Unable to form coherent thought, save all his struggles, meant naught because rejoining Europa was never before him. Or perhaps his travails meant *everything,* for they had brought him here for an epiphany.

One of the Kabeiri strode forward, away from the others, bearing a stone spear that clacked upon the cavern floor as he trod toward Kadmus and Harmonia.

"I ask you to release him now," Harmonia said.

The head Kabeiri sneered, the expression full of more disdain than Kadmus had imagined a face could hold. "Lady Demeter commands he fulfil his Fate."

To become one of these creatures, possessed and lost? Was that the end the Fates had decreed for him? Such a destiny left him stupefied in abject horror. In his mind's eye he could see himself, bent and misshapen. Could feel the agonies of being bound in the rock returning to weigh him down until the end of time.

"I have not seen his victory," Harmonia protested.

Snickers in answer, before the first Kabeiri spoke. "You have seen the struggle, so it must unfold. Such is the will of the Fates, clearly."

"What?" Kadmus managed to ask, his voice sounding raspy and distant in his own ears. "What Fate?"

Harmonia grimaced as she turned toward him. At first, he thought she might not speak at all, so much did she seem to struggle to give voice to the turmoil within. "I told you that Tethys ruled these lands for millennia. That she protected her home through bargains with benthic powers." Harmonia glanced at the merciless Kabeiri as though they might somehow spare her whatever she had to tell him. "The last of Tethys's drakons yet lingers in a cavern far below here, haunting an underground spring. You must face and slay the monster."

Kadmus gaped at her. "A dragon? Slay a ... giant serpent that has lived here for *thousands* of years. Have you taken all leave of your senses? I am no Titan to even attempt such a feat."

Harmonia swallowed hard. "And yet you must. I have seen it, and ... Demeter has sworn that, if you succeed, she will name you king here. The first mortal king of Thebes."

Now he balked. True enough, he could not return to the kingdom of his father now, knowing Europa forever lost to them. And yes, he'd need a new home, preferably one of comfort. But he had not thought to ... had not imagined ... Kadmus's breath caught. "Why?" he stammered. "Why are you even helping me, why do any of this?"

"Because you love me. Or you shall."

An Oracle. His hand had gone to his mouth before he even realised it. She had been *waiting* for him on Lesvos, hadn't she? Knowing he would arrive, that all of this—or enough of it, at least—would unfold thus. The look on her face confirmed his unspoken question.

Fate had snared him from the very beginning. Harmonia had warned him, true, but warned him knowing he would never listen to her no matter what she said of it.

"But you don't know for certain that I *can* slay this dragon. You just said you never saw that."

In answer, she brushed her fingers along his own. So whatever love she saw in their future, it must then be born from this very moment, created by itself. She loved him because she had seen him love her in the future—which he *would*, he realised, had already begun to—but only because of the love she had first shown him.

A moment that led back to itself, over and over. One more weight upon an Oracle. One more reason he'd needed to see the quicksilver pool to begin to understand what burdens Fate asked of people like Harmonia.

Such an onus as others could never see. To not only deliver the prophecies, but to create them, to live them, bound by them, lives predicated upon moments sundered from time.

Kadmus squeezed her hand. "I shall slay this dragon, then. And you and I shall reign over Thebes if it pleases the Fates."

She smiled then. "At the least, it pleases *me*."

A SINGLE KABEIRI accompanied Kadmus into tunnels that led far below the ravine that housed the quicksilver pool. The bent and wretched spirit shuffled along in obvious pain, yet quickly for all that, making good time.

Kadmus carried a torch to light his way, though these creatures seemed to need very little illumination to keep steady footing.

They walked until he began to suspect they had actually passed down to sea level, or close to it, beneath the cliff on which Thebes proper rested. The Kabeiri had not spoken, but a question had weighed upon Kadmus's mind since they first tasked him with slaying this dragon.

"Why? It has lived here so long, and clearly you have adapted to its presence."

The spirit sneered at him—Kadmus began to suspect such was the only expression their faces were capable of. "Their blood is thick with Eitr."

As if some strange foreign word explained aught of this endeavour. Or was it yet another circular moment, forced upon him simply because it was foreseen? It would happen because it had happened?

They reached the tunnel's terminus in an even larger cavern than the one they had imprisoned Kadmus in not long ago. His torch failed to offer much more than a glimpse of the expansiveness of this cave, and Kadmus quickly gave over trying to make out his surroundings.

The spirit paused at the threshold, going no further, seeming almost frozen in place. Could it be ... afraid? Was even this creature from beyond the Mortal Realm afraid? From its belt it drew a xiphos and proffered it to Kadmus. Not the bronze sword they had taken from him, but rather one of lighter weight and darker, slate-grey metal.

Kadmus gave a quizzical look.

With a roll of its eyes, the Kabeiri snorted. "Adamant. Did you think to pierce drakon scales with mere bronze, mortal?"

Huh. Were dragon scales harder than armour?

The Kabeiri turned from him without a further word, so Kadmus gave it no more thought. Instead, he made a few trial swings with his new sword, adjusting to the weight and feel of it. One thing became immediately clear—this was the finest weapon he'd ever held.

Torch in one hand and sword in the other, Kadmus finally resolved to venture deeper into the dark expanse before him. Soon, he came upon the sound of burbling waters and followed it to the centre of the cavern. His heart began to hammer in his chest, a rhythm so loud the dragon would probably hear it. His palms were clammy holding the blade and light.

Overcome by a sudden dread, he paused, panting, desperate to catch his suddenly elusive breath. For all his bravado with Harmonia, he knew this for madness. Elládosi legend claimed dragons were the spawn of the great Echidna, some monstrous sea goddess. And he, a Man, thought to challenge one for this spring?

The scope of his hubris left him torn between wanting to laugh and turn and flee. Had he not berated himself for hastily sworn oaths about Europa? Here he was again, having agreed to tasks beyond the capability of mortal Men.

Rather than walk further into this madness, he turned. His sandal had slapped only once more on the cavern floor when he heard a sloshing, as of something immense emerging from the waters.

The instinct to freeze in place seized him, but he fought it down and turned back, swinging his torch out to the side of his head so he could see. Its light did indeed reflect off water not so far away.

But he saw naught else.

In his mind's eye, he imagined a vast serpentine bulk slithering just out of sight, circling, waiting to enwrap him in its coils. Conjured by his own mind or not, the thought of it choked him until he could barely suck breath in and out. Dread of whatever must now share this cavern with him had locked his muscles in place and he couldn't move. It was a wonder he'd not lost control of his bladder.

With an effort of sheer will, he forced himself to keep turning slowly, swinging the torch around to examine the gloom encompassing him. Every slap of his sandals sounded like a gong in his own ears, announcing his position to the dragon.

But all he saw was perpetual darkness. Did it ... actually toy with him?

Or was it possible the creature was not even here? Had his mind tormented him, filling itself with the worst of his fears?

Either way, Kadmus had no inclination to linger. Not knowing what else to do, he dashed forward a half dozen paces, bringing the spring itself into view—the waters stretched on father than he could see the end of—then spun around, xiphos ready.

Perhaps drawn by his movement, the darkness now closed in until he caught the hint of torchlight glinting upon wet, black scales, circling, almost of a height with him.

"Ba'al's stormy arse," Kadmus rasped. It was even bigger than he'd expected. Bigger than he'd like to have imagined serpents ever grew.

Nor could he even harbour a guess at how long a dragon of such bulk must stretch. For a moment he held in utter stillness on the edge of the spring.

A second source of light emerged then, on his periphery. Twin, fist-sized orbs, incandescent and filled with ancient loathing, wrath and heat pouring from the very eyes of this monster. Kadmus could make out but little of its features, just a hint of spurs and horns and fangs, as if the head bristled with teeth in all directions. A glinting, saurian nightmare he had awakened and thus enraged.

To glimpse the enormity of this thing, it stole his very self. His knees threatened to give out from under him, and he was seized by the deranged instinct to prostrate himself before the monster. As if his obeisance might somehow buy him another breath.

This moment he had seen in fleeting glimpses in quicksilver. It had always been coming to this, hadn't it?

"Come on then," he said, quivering voice giving lie to his attempt at bravery. "Is this Fate? Is this my *Fate*?"

Snakelike, the dragon's maw darted in so fast Kadmus could barely react. Barely, but then, Kadmus had been a warrior, a pirate, a soldier. Not trusting himself to time a swing, he merely jabbed with the adamant xiphos. The dragon's own movement carried its head right into the blow and the sword parted scales.

Perhaps unable to arrest its momentum, the dragon slammed headfirst into Kadmus, the impact sending him flying, stripping the blade from his grasp. The World whirled, rushing by in a breathless instant before Kadmus crashed down into the spring and found himself flailing beneath waters far deeper than he'd expected.

Blind, he twisted about underwater, trying to orient himself even as he fought against the crushing pain in his lungs. Thrashing around, he at last breached the surface and gulped down the delicious, putrid air of the cavern, catching sight of his torch, now fallen beside the spring.

A tremendous crashing greeted him when he regained the use of his senses, revealing the dragon banging its own head against the ground. It was trying to dislodge the adamantine sword it had managed to ram hilt-deep into its own snout.

Dagon's deep! How was Kadmus not dead?

Silent as he could, he swam to shore, though perhaps the monster could not have heard him regardless, given the cacophony it raised as its horns gouged rivets in the stone. Its own enormous strength had proven its downfall, dealing itself a greater, more painful blow than Kadmus might have managed.

The more it writhed and thrashed, the more it flung bits of sizzling blood about, as if the very essence of the beast held such power as to corrode like acid. Kadmus reached the shore and gaped. What the fuck was he to do now?

A smart man would have tried to sneak from the cavern, Fate be damned. Harmonia had said she saw him *fight* the dragon. She didn't see him win, so maybe he didn't have to if only—

In its gyrations, the serpent must have caught sight of him, for it reared back and released a roar that shook the cavern, flinging acidic spray from its maw, even causing a stalactite to fall crashing into the spring behind Kadmus.

The impact of the giant stone had Kadmus leaping away, which was all that saved his life as the dragon lunged for him once more. He came up in a roll.

Now his heart pounded harder than ever, pulse throbbing in his temples. But the fear had fled, driven out by his coursing adrenaline, or perhaps by the pervading sense of destiny that sat upon him. This was it, then. His final, grandest moment: glory for the ages, or death.

Kadmus dashed alongside the winding coils—dimly wondering if he could avoid being snared in those jaws a third time—and caught a spur of the dragon's spine. The creature's momentum hefted him aloft and allowed him to land on its back.

The monster immediately doubled back on itself and, as expected, made the same lunge as ever. Its single means of dealing with any prey. This time, Kadmus jumped only slightly to the side, catching the protruding hilt in midair. His weight yanked the blade loose, tearing free a great swathe of dragon flesh in the process.

Sizzling blood splattered over his face and arms, and he screamed as if lit aflame by the acid. The dragon, however, flopped upon the ground, banging its head in wild agony, even as its blood erupted in geysers.

It would hurt, he knew.

But then, maybe Fate always hurt.

He lunged in, ramming the xiphos up under the thrashing drag-on's chin with all his might. It was like stabbing a plastered wall, but the blade penetrated, and he jerked, rending a great gouge out of its throat.

More acidic blood rushed over him and Kadmus dropped his blade, falling backward as his own agony seized him. He stripped out of his sizzling exomis, screaming even as he tossed it aside. The acid had landed upon his flesh as well, now drawing up innumerable burning welts. He was going to die! He had slain the dragon and was still going to die!

In a panic, he raced for the spring and dove beneath the waters.

A thousand stinging lances of torment wracked him, as if burns covered him head to toe. But with each passing moment underwater, the burning abated more and more, until, at last, he burst to the surface, still in pain, but able to move.

Enough to lie panting beside the dying dragon of Tethys.

THEY AWAITED HIM, not in the Kabeiri cavern, for those spirits had now vanished back into the stones whence they came, but within the shadows of the Temple of Demeter. The Titan herself, holding a crown as if she had known he would succeed. More importantly, by her side was Harmonia, joy and relief and vindication in her ochre eyes.

Naked save for his sandals—having given over any attempt to reclaim his acid-corroded exomis—covered in burns, Kadmus stumbled forward, into her arms. Had she *known*? Despite her words, had she known he would succeed and they would rise as king and queen? Had she spoken otherwise for his benefit?

Maybe one day he would ask her of it. For now, he was almost afraid of the answer.

Harmonia guided him before Demeter, and Kadmus fell to his knees before the Titan goddess once again.

"I will not find Europa," he admitted.

"But you may have a home here," Demeter answered. "So many of the Olympians are weary of the politics of Earth, myself more than most."

He nodded in silent understanding. In losing Europa, Kadmus had at least found Harmonia. Demeter had lost Persephone and found ... emptiness. A hollowness that rendered all the daily necessities of governing a polis banal and petty.

"Would you take the honour?" Demeter asked. "Would you arise, the first mortal King of Thebes?"

He inclined his head, and Demeter laid the crown upon it. For a few breaths, Kadmus remained kneeling, feeling the weight of it. Of all he had passed through. Of the schemes and vicissitudes of Fate.

Then he rose and took Harmonia's hand.

Time, at last, for the birth of new moments.

PART IV

For seven years the Ambrosial War raged, Titans slaying one another in desperation to control the distribution of Ambrosia out of Atlantis. In the end, rather than see the World burn, the six strongest Titans agreed to a pact where they and they alone would control the distribution of Ambrosia. This pact ended the Ambrosial War and formed the Ouranid League that would rule the Thalassa world for over two thousand years. This time, we call the Golden Age.

— Kleio, Analects of the Muses

24

ARTEMIS

201 Golden Age

The polis of Sardeis lay on a wide plain between the sea and the mountains. Upon the mountains lay woodlands Artemis had hunted in her youth and spent a great deal of time training in, honing her senses. A part of her would have rather headed there now than toward the city's arching gate, bent on her mission.

Especially with Apollon by her side. Her golden-eyed twin had a perpetual smirk about him, as if he had done her some great favour by convincing their father to let Artemis 'attend him' on this endeavour.

She cast a wary glance at him. He no doubt thought he truly had done right by her. She was the one who slew Khione and saved Helion. She had fought for Father in the year since, defending his island. But now, it was Apollon that he sent to Phoeba to broker peace with their grandmother.

"Gratitude would not be amiss," he said, having read her ire on her face.

"Nor would humility," she snapped.

He shrugged. "No, but I thought that too much to hope for."

Petty, obnoxious little prick ...

Having no choice, really—unless she wanted to abandon any chance at earning honour—she paced along beside him as they made their way up to the acropolis. A servant moved to welcome them, but Aidos raced past him.

Their cousin almost toppled Artemis over when she threw her arms around her. "I heard you were coming!" Aidos chirped, actually hefting Artemis off the ground. She punched Apollon on the arm. "I see you brought the Heliad, too."

"*She* did not bring *me*," Apollon tried to object while Aidos pointedly ignored him.

The daughter of their maternal aunt Asteria, Aidos had spent as much time growing up in Phoebe's court as Artemis herself. Since their grandmother had fostered Aidos for years, in some ways, she was more sister than cousin, though Artemis had seen little of her in the past few decades.

Artemis saw little of most people, of late, preferring the solitude of sylvan haunts over bustling poleis like Sardeis. Everywhere she looked, servants bumbled about carrying amphorae or vases or baskets. They served foods no one here had hunted for. They pampered soft guests with perfume and oils. And they mewled before the high and mighty.

Aidos guided them around the gardens, blessedly far from the crunch of people, then paused beneath a cypress tree, kicking off her sandals as she slumped down into the loam.

Realising she didn't intend to immediately announce them, Apollon scoffed. "I must make our presence known. Some of us came here for a reason."

"Is it because Helios tugged upon your puppet strings?" Aidos asked with such feigned innocence Artemis couldn't stop herself from snickering.

Apollon didn't answer that, just spun on his heel and stormed off toward the hall.

Aidos snorted. "As if aught happens in this polis Grandmother doesn't know about." From beneath her peplos she withdrew a ceramic phial. After she popped the cap, a whiff of honeyed wine reached Artemis. Aidos winked and allowed her a glimpse of the amber liquid.

Ambrosia.

Already, Artemis's mouth watered. Her pulse quickened. "With the war, I thought ..."

"It's much harder to get," Aidos admitted. "But I heard you were coming and saved some."

Oh. Grandfather Koios was an Oracle, so it stood to reason he might have known they would arrive some time ago. Maybe even before Helios ever sent them.

By Gaia, Artemis needed that. Her skin flushed at the thought of even a few sips fortifying her Pneuma. And of ... other effects of the draught. "I don't suppose you have any men in mind?"

That drew another snort from Aidos. "Isn't Helios still claiming you're a *virgin* Titan?"

Now Artemis rolled her eyes. What the fuck was it with men and that sort of thing, anyway? Father thought it made it more likely she could find a good marriage that way. And Artemis, past sixty years old, had *definitely* spent all those decades in complete celibacy.

"Anyway, yes, I know a few discreet slaves who can get the job done." Aidos took a swig, downing half the phial all at once.

Artemis opened her mouth, reaching for it with trembling fingers. Gaia, don't let her drink it all!

Sated—in every possible way—her flesh tingling from the increased flow of Pneuma, Artemis stood in Phoebe's court. Grandmother and Grandfather both sat upon their thrones in the rear of the hall, while

Artemis and Apollon stood with their backs to the pool in the hall's midst.

Apollon, of course, insisted on standing a step ahead of her as he addressed Phoebe and Koios. "Surely you can see the mutual advantage of an accord," he pleaded. Whined, perhaps, given that Koios seemed to have about as much interest in working with their father as a leopard had in allying with a tiger. A land could support only one apex predator, after all.

"At present," Koios said, "Atlas still allows us supplies of Ambrosia out of Atlantis. Any move toward solidarity with his enemies risks our own supplies."

Apollon scoffed. "He charges you exorbitant prices and you *thank* him for it? How far, exactly, will you bend over for him, Grandfather?"

Wow. Artemis pointedly turned her gaze upon their grandmother, gnawing her lip and afraid to even witness Koios's reaction to that.

For a moment, Koios said naught at all. Then he rose. "This audience is concluded. Enjoy the fruits of a land *not* beleaguered by war with Atlas, boy."

Doubt and emotions Artemis couldn't discern warred across Phoebe's face as her husband departed.

Artemis shook her head. Apollon was far too used to everyone kowtowing to his words. The golden child of Helios thought the sun rose and set through his arse, and he had no idea how to talk to anyone not awestruck by his bluster.

When he had slunk off like the petulant brat he was, Artemis took a tentative step toward her grandmother. "Mother sends her love."

Phoebe started, then met her gaze, nodding. "How is Leto?"

Bored in Helios's court. Neglected. Relegated to the status of an ornament for the crime of having been born female. "She endures."

The look on her grandmother's face told her the woman caught the whole of her meaning. "Walk with me, child."

♨

PHOEBE, always fond of the moon, took Artemis out into the night and they wandered from the city into the plain, where the full moon shone bright and the stars twinkled like beacons in the firmament. When Artemis was a girl, Phoebe had brought her here and claimed the Primordials had given rise to all the cosmos in a time before time.

In the story, Dyaus, the Sky God, and Gaia, the Earth Goddess, had mated and birthed so much of all she cherished. Pan, the Wood God, and Hyperion and Thoth and more besides had sprung from their loins. Not Nyx, though, who ruled the Night and the stars. She was older than any of the others, and it was possible even Dyaus and Gaia were of her. Either way, though, Thoth the Moon God relieved the darkness of night, and for that, Phoebe had taught Artemis to remain ever grateful.

When she was older, Artemis dared to wonder how anyone, Titan queen or not, could know what happened before time began. Such questions had only ever drawn a scowl from Phoebe. No answers. Perhaps it was better not to ask certain things.

Now, Grandmother laced her arm with Artemis's and guided her on a seemingly aimless stroll. For a long time, Artemis said naught. How could she stand to break the peace of such a night? To spoil a perfect moment she might carry in memory for ages to come?

But she had not come to Phoebe just to take midnight walks with her grandmother or steal small sips of Ambrosia with her cousin. "An alliance with Helios might allow you to extend your influence over all Lydia, maybe even into Phrygia. Imagine yourself queen of this whole peninsula, Grandmother."

Phoebe sniffed lightly. "Koios regrets ever having consented to Leto's marriage to vain Helios. His precious daughter deserved more." Her voice seemed to imply she felt the same.

"But then, Apollon and I would never have been born."

"Yes, of course, and we wouldn't trade you. It does not mean he does not resent the lord of Helion, Artemis. Besides, it is difficult being an Oracle. He sees pain in the future, and death, and tragedy, and cannot always grasp whence such things come. So he becomes overly cautious, afraid of every turn in fortune, as if they might result in his fears."

"You don't believe his visions?"

"I did not say that. I just think we have to live as we must. One cannot thrive while in constant fear of the future."

One could not live in constant fear at all, no matter the source, Artemis suspected. But she hesitated. This was her own grandfather she might dishonour ... "Helios already negotiates with Atlas. Should they form an alliance, Atlas's trade terms with Koios might not still hold."

Phoebe stiffened, then withdrew her arm from Artemis's. "What do you suggest, child?" The woman kept her gaze on the moon, not looking at her.

"If you allow your husband to hold you back, you may lose an opportunity that might never again present itself. This war changes the whole of the Thalassa, and we cannot go back to how things were. There is only forward, Grandmother."

At her words, Phoebe wrapt her hands over her arms, as if intent to hold in emotions too powerful for her chest. It seemed even elder Titans were not immune to the ravages of the heart. To choose between a loved one and the future must have torn her apart, but naught Artemis had said was a lie. The war would resolve itself, one way or another, and the only question would be which Titans came out ahead and which came out worse than they had been before.

A soft moan escaped her grandmother. "I must think on it before I confront him."

Grandfather was stubborn, Artemis knew. Because of his visions, he always thought himself right, more informed than those around him. He would not cave easily, if at all. However this played out, Sardeis would suffer for it.

❧

IN THE PREDAWN DARKNESS, Artemis sat in Aidos's chamber while the other girl recited Phrygian poetry. Already her stomach chittered at her, demanded she beg her cousin for another taste of Ambrosia. She shouldn't be so bold ...

Shouldn't, but a person didn't always do what she should.

"You don't happen to have any more?" Artemis asked when Aidos finished a stanza.

"Poems?" Aidos asked, quirking a mischievous brow.

"Ambrosia," Artemis whispered.

Aidos blew out a breath and shook her head. "Believe me, if I did, I'd have brought it out already." She twirled a finger around her locks. "I've heard talk that the eldest of the Titans, those who have had the most Ambrosia, have Pneumatikoi that makes them like gods."

Artemis snorted. "We're not gods. They may bleed ichor, but their shit still reeks the same."

"Will we bleed ichor one day too?"

Not if Atlas continued to hoard the Ambrosia. Not if the other Titans failed to reclaim Hesperides Island or at least force Atlas into equitable distribution.

Maybe Aidos saw the look on her face. "No. You don't think we might be left ... mortal?"

"I don't know. It seems unthinkable, to be honest. I imagine if it ever came to that, the remaining Titans would throw everything they had at Atlas. To do aught less is to embrace death." She hesitated. "But that might still only ensure Ambrosia for those in power. For Titan daughters like us ..."

"Oh, they call me a Nymph these days," Aidos admitted, and Artemis winced. It meant not enough Pneumatikoi had presented in Aidos. Titan girls relegated to such status were considered good for little more than marriage alliances and breeding. That Aidos, after being named a Nymph, would share even a drop of Ambrosia— knowing it would prove harder and harder for her to get—bespoke a kindness Artemis wasn't sure she knew how to repay.

Hardly knowing what else to say, she reached over and drew the other woman into an embrace. "Grandmother will work something out. She knows what is at stake for those like us."

ɕ&

IT WAS TWO DAYS LATER, and Artemis's head throbbed like a Cyclops had stepped on it. A night's indulgence in Phoenikian wine came with a cost, even for a Titan. Which made the slobbering oaf banging the gong outside her door all the more offensive.

When she opened the door she found Apollon. No gong, so apparently he'd raised such racket with naught save fist on wood.

"What in the vile mists of Achlys do you want?" she demanded.

"We must have gotten through to Grandmother, for Grandfather has left the city. Word is he and Phoebe had quite the boisterous argument last night."

Ah. Well, Artemis had been far too drunk to have noticed an army marching through her own chambers, much less to have heard an altercation across the palace.

"She has agreed to an alliance with Helios!" Apollon blurted. From the look on his face, he clearly thought his words in the court had somehow led to this, rather than Artemis's private conversation with Grandmother beneath the moon. "We must return to Father and report our success."

Artemis gnawed on her lip a moment. Well, for better or worse, she had wrought this. She had driven the wedge between her grandparents, and now, because of her, the war would come here for certain. But maybe, just maybe, Nymphs like Aidos would get their share, thanks to Phoebe.

And once more, Father would heap the praise for it upon Artemis's twin.

25

PANDORA

201 Golden Age

A half dozen of Tethys's biremes had surrounded Ogygia, but still, Kronos had slipped through the Titan's fingers. Oh, Pandora had heard her Telkhines had boarded and sunk one of Kronos's ships while her war bands engaged in bloody slaughter of those on the island.

But neither Prometheus nor Kronos had been found, and Tethys had dared not leave Thebes unattended for long. Pandora had pleaded to be released, but neither Tethys herself nor Sirsir had even come to speak with her. And the taskmaster had offered her only the helpful advice of, "If you don't shut your mouth, I'll fill it with the shit rag."

Given that the Titan man seemed quite capable of following through with his threat, Pandora elected to shut her mouth. Through the limited view available to her, she watched the azure sea break and fall as they drew ever farther from her new home upon Ogygia. Eventually, the waters lightened to cerulean as they entered the Aegean Sea.

They passed through the Strait of Korinth. Was it even called thus at this point? Did Korinth yet exist? The city had been founded by the Ouranid Kreios, but she didn't know if that was before or after the creation of the Ouranid League. Either way, in her day, the city was still ruled by Kreiads and owned by Kreios's own grandson, Hephaistos.

Beyond the Strait, they at last came to Thebes. As they made port, Sirsir deigned to show himself once more. Without a word, he unshackled her, then ushered her above decks and over the gangplank to where Tethys herself waited, impassive stare fixed upon Pandora.

No sign of Enki, so maybe the other Titan had already departed the ship.

Sirsir left her again, diving into the sea all in silence. In the days coming here, Pandora had pondered what the mer had done to her mind. Something in his voice had hypnotised her, and the memory of it sent chills shivering through her.

"I trust you understand why I had to keep you bound," Tethys said. She waved a hand to indicate Pandora ought to follow. Seeing no real choice, Pandora complied. After all, it was rather too late to make an escape back to Ogygia. "I could not chance you trying to leap overboard and get yourself killed, nor waste resources to have any of the Telkhines rescue you a second time."

"I understood the reasons."

"Well then, I hope the journey did not prove too taxing."

Pandora glowered as the Titan led her beyond the harbour and to a great cliff, rising several hundred feet above them. A marble staircase cut into the cliffside led up to the polis above, though all she could see of it was an enormous wall peeking out over the clifftop. "I had to shit in a bucket in front of a dozen strange men. I cannot say I found the voyage the most pleasant I've ever taken."

Tethys answered with a glance and narrowed eyes. A silent

warning not to push her tolerance. "Be grateful you weren't the one who had to collect the buckets and empty them."

The climb up the stairs left Pandora breathless long before they reached the summit, and while they passed a landing halfway up, Tethys did not pause. Which meant neither could Pandora, though she saw other members of Tethys's returning crew follow with greater leisure. The Titan herself seemed to possess unending stamina and expect the same from Pandora.

"I will keep you safe in Thebes," Tethys said when they reached the stairs' end.

Pandora stood there, hands on her knees, gasping as she looked about. Twin rivers cut around the city. One, she believed, would continue south past Korinth—once it existed—while the northern river pitched off the cliffside in a misty cataract some distance away.

Tethys allowed her a brief moment to rest—or perhaps to take in the grandeur of her polis—then led her through a great gate in the wall around the city. They followed the main street to an agora, and continued on, toward the acropolis, though the Titan now reduced her pace. Perhaps she had finally realised a mortal could not handle such a climb.

"I do not know where Prometheus is at present, but I will send word across Ogygia and Hesperides Island that I have brought you here as my guest. Knowing him, he would mostlike discover your presence regardless, but the missives can only help."

So she truly intended to help reunite them. "Thank you," Pandora said, somewhat ashamed of her gasping between words. Whatever Tethys had forced her to endure on the ship, she had saved her life. And if she brought Prometheus and Pyrrha back to her, it was all worth it.

※

TETHYS LED her through the acropolis and into her marmoreal palace and its maze of columns. That the Titan bothered to offer her a tour meant she must have reconsidered how she wanted to treat Pandora. Which meant Tethys had decided she wanted something from Prometheus. Did it rankle, treating a mortal with even this modicum of respect? Did Tethys seethe beneath her impassive visage? Pandora imagined she could see a storm-tossed sea behind those ocean-blue eyes.

Following the circuit of the palace, the Titan offered tidbits about each of the wings. There, the hall from which music rang out so clear every evening, where Tethys's friend Mnemosyne had once sung in a concert that had extended from dusk until past dawn. Ah, and beyond, the corridor decorated with the grand mosaics cut from gemstones mined from the mountains of Kumari Kandam, across the Thalassa. Yes, and here, the water gardens in the caryatid-encircled courtyard, with their burbling fountains and overhanging cypress trees.

Amid the gardens, children splashed in a pond, disturbing lilies and, no doubt, fish. They seemed to range between eight and two in age. An older woman, perhaps mortal, oversaw their play, lingering beneath a cypress. Perhaps there only to ensure the play remained safe for her young charges.

"My children," Tethys said. "The oldest is Hera, the boy is Poseidon. The younger ones are twins, Styx and Perse."

The names had Pandora stubbing her sandals upon the flagstones. To save appearances, she settled on the edge of a fountain, watching Tethys's brood with a forced smile. Two future Olympians jumped about in the pond, hurling water and giggling. Zeus's own wife was right in front of Pandora, bullying her younger siblings. Poseidon commanded all the mer in the Aegean and thus controlled the sea.

The other names, while not so ubiquitous, had cropped up in occasional readings. Styx ruled some corner of Hades's domain in the Underworld, she believed. And Perse was a Nymph married to Helios.

"These are yours and Okeanus's offspring," Pandora said, not quite certain how well she'd concealed her discomfiture. She was looking at beings who demanded Men worship them as gods.

Looking at them in a time when they had probably just gotten past the age of shitting themselves, some perhaps not even that.

"Okeanus is my consort, yes. He attends the war by negotiating with Nereus of Pontus. You see, the Telkhines serve me already, but once our alliance with Pontus deepens, Thebes shall be undisputed ruler of the Aegean. Phoebe and Koios and other such Titans in Lydia and Phrygia will be forced to submit or lose access to the sea."

Her words were meant to impress Pandora with the glory of Thebes, soon to be even greater. Perhaps Tethys thought, if she awed Pandora, made her believe Thebes's victory inevitable, Pandora would then convince Prometheus to join her. What would the Titan say if Pandora were to reveal Okeanus would die in this war? That Tethys would manage to secure a position in the forthcoming hegemony, but hardly dominate over Kronos or Atlas?

None of the children paid Pandora much mind, so caught up in their own games. Which suited her well enough. What did one say to an infantile future Olympian? Instead, Pandora rose, strolling the garden with Tethys until, at last, the Titan guided her toward guest chambers inside the palace. They passed bustling servants hauling amphorae into the courtyard, perhaps preparing for further indulgent feasts despite the war.

The Titans battled for the life and soul of the Thalassa world, and Men died in droves in their names, but Hades forbid Titan parties should be impacted. Numerous walls bore vibrant frescoes depicting undersea cities and mer courts as well as coral reefs teeming with kaleidoscopic varieties of fish. Grand works of art honouring the sea Tethys and her consort so loved.

How, exactly, had she arranged for mer to serve her? Who were these Telkhines that followed her bidding? Her words indicated they hailed from Pontus, a fabled kingdom beneath the Aegean. And that Nereus, apparently, ruled there now, though Poseidon would do so in Pandora's time. Pieces of the puzzle remained elusive, and, much as she wanted to solve the picture, she feared to ask too much. She could not know how much Tethys expected her to be aware of in this time period, and a mischosen phrase might turn the Titan from a half-gracious host to a suspicious gaoler.

Almost biting her tongue, Pandora held her peace. Tethys showed her to her new chambers, these too painted in cool blues reminiscent of the sea outside. Her room had a shutterless window from which she could look out and catch sight of the waves, far, far below.

After some few pleasantries, Tethys left her with her thoughts, and Pandora sank upon a surprisingly comfortable wool-stuffed bed. After her ordeal upon the bireme, exhaustion tightened its grip upon her, and she slept.

HER DAYS without Prometheus and Pyrrha stretched on and on. Despite attempting to learn as much as she could of this time and place and the Telkhines, ennui inevitably set in each afternoon. There was a sense she could not shake that she languished here, passing time while failing to live. Had she begun to define her very existence in reference to that of her new family? Such thoughts, pathetic and weak, drove her to once more dive into her studies in Tethys's palace.

She perused papyrus scrolls and read of the Titans who lorded over this Golden Age, and how they squabbled over land and Ambrosia. She read tales of Nymphs pursued by supposedly valiant Titan lords, as if the satiation of their lusts held some inherent heroism. Most of all, she took occasion to make her subtle inquiries about the Telkhines.

Nereus, King of Pontus, had given Tethys a pact long ago. Some mer he granted to her service, in exchange for a steady stream of mortals offered up to his kingdom. What did the mer use Men for? This, Pandora did not know, though some of the palace servants believed the mer dragged their hapless sacrifices into the deep and feasted upon them, body and soul.

Pandora remained dubious.

Ten days after her arrival here, Okeanus returned and with him, word claimed, came Prometheus.

Unable to contain herself, Pandora awaited them in the vestibule, shifting from foot to foot, when she wasn't pacing about between the columns. When her lover arrived, Pyrrha cradled in his arms, his sapphire eyes locked with her own, all the rest of the palace fell away. Perhaps others stared as they embraced, as she shuddered in gasping, wordless relief at holding the two of them once more. If so, if they gaped at her wantonness, Pandora cared not a whit.

Nestled against his chest, she clutched Pyrrha's little hand.

Moments like these, one remembered truths that so far transcended petty notions of propriety. After nigh losing those who mattered most, one was forced to admit to oneself. Everything besides the people one loves comes a distant second, so far behind as to seem irrelevant and self-indulgent. Any who could not understand that failed themselves.

After she had cradled Pyrrha, after she had nursed her—and found her milk somewhat diminished, much to her dismay—and the child slept, she laced her fingers with Prometheus and lay with him. Only then, spent and reeling, could she form the words to speak of what had happened, her face pressed to his bare chest.

"The woman who attacked me bore auric armour, helm to greaves. She had great, golden-feathered wings." Pandora swallowed. "I thought she intended to kill me for trying to subvert Ananke's will. All I could think was about how you warned me but I hadn't listened. But ... Zeus had been right there and I thought, if I could stop him from winning the Titanomachy, the whole World might have been better."

"Fate is not always what we think," Prometheus offered. "The woman who attacked you sounds like Nemesis. The Moirai have many servants, but she is the fiercest of them. An assassin and enforcer of Fate."

Pandora had suspected as much, though that thought had induced more questions. "If the timeline always included me coming back to the past, falling in love with you, and having Pyrrha ..." She felt an almost imperceptible tightening of his chest beneath her, perhaps anticipating her line of thought. "If time could bend upon itself thus, did it also always include my confrontation with Nemesis?"

"You begin to apprehend the paradoxes of Fate."

So Pandora had *always* tried to kill Zeus as a child, and Nemesis had always stopped her? Which meant she was, essentially, impotent to alter the course of Fate ... Or could only do so with such a rank deviation that not even the Moirai could anticipate it. But no such course seemed to present itself, and besides, once more looking upon her family, how could she make any choice that would deny her them?

Which left her again trying to survive the turbulent present. "Kronos knew about the Box. I cannot understand how he can know about it, long before its invention. But since he does, and appears to know of me, I cannot imagine he will give over his pursuit of me." What would the Titan do with the Box, should he claim it?

Prometheus's silence spoke more than the Titan probably wished, and Pandora pushed herself up on her forearms so as to look into his eyes. "You know something of Kronos, don't you? Yet you hold it back from me." She couldn't quite keep the acid from her tone. She'd dared to think this a problem only with his future self, interacting with her past self. Dared to believe his lingering secrets a mere puzzle for her to unlock, perhaps even one he set for that very purpose. "Who is Kronos? Is he an Oracle as well?"

Another hesitation, and those sapphire eyes flitted over her face. She leaned closer, enclosing his vision, preventing any egress, and thus, she hoped, forcing him to confide in her. "He has seen a great many things, even unto the Time of Nyx, Pandora. Some few of the Titans are older than the rest and are privy to things others might not understand. Perhaps things others *cannot* understand."

With a frustrated grunt, she pushed off him and rose, wrapping her peplos about herself. "You have a talent for circumventing the question at hand."

He leaned on his elbow. "It may behoove those who seek straight answers to remember the World bends in endless curves and folds, and so-called forthright truths only serve to further obfuscate understanding with oversimplification."

Gah! Such answers made her want to scream. All the more so when she could see the truth in them. "Do not think, dear Prometheus, if I upend a brazier upon your head, it means I don't love you more than my own life."

"I am a Firewalker," he pointed out. "The flames will not harm me."

"I was shooting for the sheer impact of bronze and coal upon your skull." She sniffed. No, she would never harm him, exasperating as he might sometimes prove.

Looking at him now, at leisure in their bed, warm and safe, only served to drive home the reminder of what lay ahead for him. Which, in turn, sent her back to her prior conclusion. She could not save him here, in the past. All she could do was use the Box, return to the future, and save him from his torment then.

"I need it back," she said, the words scouring her insides. She needed to leave this Prometheus, leave their daughter, leave this precious time.

After frowning, Prometheus waved a hand at a satchel he'd dropped by the bedside. Hand shaking—she almost wished he would have said he had lost it—she fished inside until she felt the Box. The damning, impossible, wondrous Box he would build for her and create the sum of their lives from within its depths. She withdrew it and set it upon the foot of their bed, settling down in front of it.

In her crib, little Pyrrha stirred, moaning, feet kicking off her blankets for the thousandth time. As Pandora watched their daughter, an unexpected dry sob wracked her.

Damn the Fates for this!

"You do not have to do this," Prometheus said.

"Kronos will keep looking for it so long as it remains within his reach." While true, it was a flimsy excuse, as he would well know. "I cannot leave you in the situation which allowed this to come to me."

"I am not easy to kill, Pandora."

Oh, but then, it was not just death he faced in Tartarus, and the look on his face, however much he tried to conceal it, told her even he dreaded the suffering that awaited him.

He rose now, standing naked beside her, hand upon her shoulder. "If it is set correctly, perhaps you can return not so long after you left. That being the case, some few more days here will not make any difference to the future me, save in offering me more memories of this time."

Ah, an even more beautiful excuse than hers. A while longer.

Another day before she must rip out her own heart.

26

ARTEMIS

207 Golden Age

For seven years, Artemis had fought for Helion, and at last, the war had ended. The peace council had returned from Atlantis and, despite all he had done, they had granted Atlas control of the island in perpetuity, provided distribution of the Ambrosia was overseen by a new hegemony calling themselves the Ouranid League.

Great swathes of Sardeis lay in utter ruin and, rather than attempt to rebuild, Phoebe had moved a few miles further down the coast to found a new city, Phoeba. Though the Ambrosial War had only just ended, already a new acropolis had sprung up upon this hill, and below it, some few marble structures that would become an agora.

From within this agora, Artemis watched the construction up on the hill. Donkeys hauled carts of marble along a dirt road leading to the summit, the animals straining beneath the weight, indifferent to the irate shouts of their masters. Artisans from around Lydia were up there, carving blocks into caryatids and columns. Phoebe had marked out a space for a Temple of Thoth, and most of the work focused upon that and on the queen's palace.

Around her, hastily constructed stalls had sprung up, merchants peddling figs and dates and apples. Across the way, another dealer hawked textiles imported from Phoenikia, bearing dyes of rich purple and crimson. And beyond, in the harbour, ships had begun to gather.

Life, it seemed, would spring up the very moment the slaughter ended, and the merchants would come chasing drachmae as if naught had changed. As if streams of golden ichor and the red blood of Men had not stained the land and sea, no small sum of it spilled by Artemis's hands. Even death was but a small impediment to the implacable, relentless march of commerce.

Sandals fell upon the packed dirt behind her, and Artemis turned, starting at seeing her mother here. The woman so rarely managed to get out of Helion anymore. Artemis had to assume she had come to see her own mother, as she couldn't have known Artemis would be here.

Artemis moved to embrace her, but her mother held her back. "Was it worth buying your father's affection at the cost of your grandfather's?"

Artemis winced. "I don't know." Who could say such things?

"He has gone north, I hear, along the Axeinos Sea, even beyond Phrygia." Into Kimmeria? That was a wild expanse, overrun with Gigantes and closer to the Nyxlands than the sane cared to venture.

All Artemis could do was frown. Her mother was right to blame her for that. Koios felt betrayed by his wife and grandchildren, and maybe he had been. Small wonder he fled these lands. Maybe ... Maybe now that the war was over, Artemis could travel there and convince him to return. She supposed it was the least she could do to clean up the mess she had made of this land.

A marriage broken. A city razed to the ground.

But then, Atlas *had* been forced to capitulate, and the nascent Ouranid League ought to ensure Ambrosia flowed throughout the Thalassa world. All Titans, not only the greatest among them, would maintain their immortality. Surely she could claim some credit for that. Such things she wanted to say to her mother, but Leto's world was smaller. Males like Helios had *forced* it to become smaller when they named her Nymph. As small as a golden cell in a dungeon shaped like a palace.

And how could the woman not grieve for the father who had adored her and been driven into virtual exile?

"I might have expected this sort of thing from your brother," her mother chided. "From you ..."

Not knowing what else to say or do, Artemis seized her mother in an embrace, whether it was welcome or not. "I will go to find him, if I can." Maybe she would spend forever solving one woe after another. "I will bring him back. In time."

≈

A FULL MOON WAS UP, and though the Temple of Thoth remained incomplete—columns with no roof—four priestesses knelt upon the foundation, offering supplications. Some of their words were in a discordant foreign tongue Artemis had never heard. The very speaking of it made the hair on her neck stand on end, as if some wrongness seeped into the air. Something beyond this world.

The night was thick, pregnant with arcana she could not understand, though she longed for answers.

Outside the temple, she watched the priests. They poured libations over the altar in offerings to the moon. So intent was she upon the proceedings she didn't even notice her grandmother's approach until the woman was at her side.

"Is there magic in this?" Artemis whispered.

Phoebe blew out a long breath. "What is magic? There are forces we do not comprehend in the World. We offer them respect because to do less would be hubris. You can *feel* the touch of something Otherworldly close by on nights like this, I can see it in your posture. Perhaps that is the power of the Primordials."

Had the Primordials truly given rise to the cosmos in the Time of Nyx?

"And did you actually see the Time of Nyx?" Legends claimed the elder Titans had lived then, had joined Ouranos in ending the reign of Nyx and ushering in this Age. Phoebe and the other five who had won the Ambrosial War claimed to be heirs of Ouranos and named themselves the Ouranid League in his honour. But was that all posturing?

"I was too young to remember much, save we traveled here from somewhere far to the north. That and ..." Her grandmother fidgeted a little. "I recall a nightmare, as if the night sky had tried to devour the land itself. Perhaps the cycle of sun and moon had not yet fixed itself as it is now." She shook her head. "Or perhaps, those are the nightmares of a frightened child. But I believe Kronos when he claims to have seen Ouranos himself, to have fought for his cause. There are, my dear, powers in this World older than Titans. Older, deeper, and more unfathomable."

And Kronos had, after all, proved himself the most formidable of the Titans in this war. If not for him, perhaps Atlas would have become emperor of the whole of the Thalassa Sea, rather than one of the six members of the Ouranid League. Clearly, Kronos had won the respect of all others, Phoebe included.

But what did Artemis's grandmother mean by *deeper* truths? The question niggled at her, a needle worming its way through her mind, demanding answers. Just what lurked beyond this world?

"There is an order in Phoenikia," Phoebe said, then paused, finally fixing Artemis with a hard gaze. "Your father is among their number, as was I, at one time."

"An order?"

"Dedicated to uncovering these deeper truths you question at. The Circle of Goetic Mysteries they call themselves, and mayhap they have the answers you seek."

Artemis's skin tingled at the thought of it. She had sworn to go first to the Axeinos Sea and seek out her grandfather, though she dare not reveal the task to Phoebe who would surely forbid it. Still, she could not deny a temptation to seek whatever arcana lay out there. Because her grandmother was right: Artemis could *feel* a puissance saturating the World on nights like this.

"I'm curious to seek them out," she admitted.

Phoebe nodded. "Do so with care, then. Knowledge is valuable, but sometimes we learn things we might rather not know. The price of it can be steep."

Her words left Artemis shivering.

If Koios had passed into Kimmeria, he might have either crossed the western strait into Phlegra or skirted the southern shore of the Axeinos Sea through Phrygia. Artemis could not say which way for certain, but Menoetius held some sway in Phrygia, and her grandfather had once considered the Titan a friend. As such, she broke east.

Passing alone through the woodlands was easy enough for one trained in such arts, and only a hint of Perspicacity meant no beasts could sneak up on her. Oh, besides animals, she had heard chimeras haunted the lands around the Arad Mountains. She trusted her ears and nose to catch the spoor of such creatures and avoid them.

Once she scented something acrid and foul, and this she gave a berth of miles, having no desire to witness aught that might have spawned the tales mortals used to frighten their young.

She hunted for her food, swam in the rivers, ran along the banks for the sheer thrill of it, and gave over any attempt to track time. Such was the better life, one that those huddled behind city walls so oft forgot. Simple moments that made immortality worth having, and during the seven years of war, such moments had proved far too elusive.

Eventually, though, she had to break away from the sylvan paradise and follow the edge of the sea. Along its shore she walked for miles. Much as she wanted to savour the wonder here, too, winter was closing in. Daylight began to grow scarcer, the nights colder, and her progress slower.

It was thus, in the waning of autumn, that she came upon the camp. A lake of tents, it seemed, dotting around the banks of a river running down from the mountains and joining the sea. From the foundations already laid upon a hill, it seemed these people—whoever they were—had begun construction of a fortress, or perhaps even a whole new polis.

As she approached, some waved at her, apparently little concerned with a lone traveler come into their midst in broad daylight.

"I am looking for Koios," she said, addressing an ageing man who came to greet her. He was bundled in warmer clothes than her, black furs, dressed for the weather.

"Koios," the man said, bowing. Then he mumbled something in a language she could only guess at. Either way, when it became clear the only thing they shared in common was her grandfather's name, the man beckoned her to follow.

He led her inside the largest of the tents, where her grandfather sat on a bearskin rug, tossing pebbles out before him. Divining the future ... Koios spoke to her guide in that foreign tongue, and the man answered before ducking back out from the tent.

"I was expecting you," Koios said.

"You foresaw my coming?"

He motioned for her to sit, and when she had settled down before him, he fixed her with a heavy gaze. "We do not see everything we might wish."

"Oracles?"

"Mmm." He glanced down at the pebbles once more. "Sometimes we see hints we cannot unravel until it is too late. Sometimes we see events unfold clearly, but without context. Other times, we behold metaphors, perhaps constructed from our minds to parse information beyond our ken. It can be difficult to know the difference, in fact."

Artemis saw naught save differently shaped stones strewn about at random. It seemed to her that any attempt to ascribe meaning to their distribution was self-indulgent ... but then all knew Oracles did see things that proved true, after a fashion. "Sounds frustrating."

"You've no idea, child."

"And what do you see today?" she asked.

Koios frowned, sweeping up the pebbles in a single motion. "That's not what you came here to ask me."

"No, I came to ask you to return to your wife."

"I know." He glowered at her. "Trying to make up for your own actions, yes?" That hit too close, and she couldn't stop from squirming. "Well, I've seen I do return, albeit only after completing this new city. Kolchis, they call it, after me. I owe it to them to finish it."

So he wanted to return to his wife but wouldn't yet because he'd seen himself not doing so at this moment? That sounded *worse* than self-indulgent. That sounded actively self-defeating.

Perhaps he read it upon her face, for his grimace only deepened. "You asked what I saw today, granddaughter." He paused. "Shall I tell you?"

She spread her hands. What was the harm?

Koios leaned in and seized her jaw in an iron-like grip. "I saw that someday one of us, my dear, shall cause the death of the other."

27

KIRKE

1585 Silver Age

*N*ine years ago, Athene had granted Kirke a wing of the palace, and Kirke had forbidden slaves or servants from entering, going so far as to draw a tapestry over the entrance. Oh, there were only two rooms back here. Kirke's personal chambers, where she slept, read, and planned, and a windowless storeroom she had converted into an alchemy lab.

This, she always locked for fear of anyone save Athene gaining the least idea of what she worked on behind closed doors. As now, hunched over the table, once more trying to draw out extract from the moly. She was getting closer and closer, and Athene had provided her with more resources than Kirke had ever dreamed of back in Ogygia. Limitless drachmae for reagents, a large garden beyond the palace, even cover to help her sell her test batches.

Not every batch proved a step forward, unfortunately. Sometimes she thought she had made some minor incremental improvement, only to later hear one of her customers had turned to cannibalism and torn out someone's throat with her teeth. Which was *not* the desired result of a drug designed to bestow health and long life. Another time, she'd found out—to her utter horror—that sudden blindness had spread overnight among nigh three dozen people in the harbour district.

Though she had dreamed of giving them immortality, Kirke had ruined their lives, and hearing of it, she had abandoned her experiments for a month of despondency. Yeah, in such times, one had to ask if her very quest was hubris.

But always, always the work called her back. There had to be some way to achieve perfection through the moly. She had begun to suspect the blooming root might hold some connection to the great tree of the Hesperides. Perhaps the first seeds had come from that tree. Whatever the case, moly alone of all substances she had encountered seemed to have any chance of replicating the potency of the golden apples.

The lock clicked and Kirke's heart lurched. For an instant, she cast about for a sheet or tarp to throw over the table, but, of course, she had no such thing in here.

The door swung open and Athene stumbled in, bleary eyed and blinking in the gloom of the lab. Her half-sister shut the door behind her and leaned against the wall, looking for all the world like she'd just wrestled a chimera.

"I didn't realise you had your own key to this room," Kirke said. Pointless, really. She should have known Athene would have taken such precautions in her own palace. Maybe her trust in Kirke had never been absolute. "Well, anyway, I don't have aught to show you at the moment."

"I need more," Athene rasped, scratching at some crusting along her eyes. "I need to see it all."

Huh. Sometimes, people who took the Nectar just wanted more and more of the stuff. Kirke was never sure whether that result increased with different batches, or if certain people lacked the ability to regulate themselves. Whatever the case, the Olympian looked like a heaping pile of Cyclops shit. "I gave you a dose two days ago."

"Psh." Athene licked her lips, then shivered. "I needed to see things. I feel like I've got this dam inside myself, and it's so close to bursting. Almost like I can see the whole ambit of time, if I could just break open the gap a little wider. Just need a bit more of the water, is all."

Ah. Well, shit. Kirke had only a single stool in her lab, and she took Athene by the arm, easing her to sit. "What you're talking about sounds like a road to madness. You think you're one of the Moirai? You think, even if you could see the vast expanse of past and future, your mind could handle that? Athene, I gave you the Nectar to help you get better glimpses. Not to tear down dams so you can drown yourself in the flood!"

Though Kirke hadn't even seen her move, Athene was on her feet hefting Kirke off the ground by her shoulders. The Olympian's grip was a vice and Kirke yelped from the pain of it, but her cries didn't even seem to register in Athene's wild visage. "I need *more*."

"All right, all right, let me go."

As if suddenly realising she had just manhandled her sister, Athene set her down, holding her trembling hands up in warding—or horror at what she'd done. Her face had become a mask of torment and, unless Kirke missed her guess, self-loathing.

With a sigh, Kirke drew a basket from beneath the table and retrieved a tiny ceramic phial, which she handed to Athene. "Try to make it last. I need time to brew more and I'm in the midst of experimenting with some improvements."

Without a word, Athene stumbled from the lab, leaving Kirke to wonder at just what her sister had beheld when she looked into the future.

&

IT WAS A FORTNIGHT LATER when Athene, looking yet more ravaged, came to her again. She reeked of stale sweat and too much wine, and her eyes seemed unable to focus on aught around the lab.

There was little point in even forcing the woman to ask, so Kirke fished out a phial of her latest batch of Nectar and handed it over. Athene tucked it inside her khiton but didn't leave.

Kirke wanted to shake her, to shout at her that she was destroying herself. She wanted to go back, to tell herself she should never have come to Kronion and certainly never should have offered Athene a taste of this. Oh, she'd thought to save herself from Zeus, yeah, but she hadn't realised the drug would so consume her sister.

Nine years, and strong, indomitable Athene now looked more like a broken-down barn, so rotten it was easier to raze it and build anew than even think of repairing the structure.

"There's a prince come from Mnemosynia," Athene said, sounding half-asleep. "One of Mnemosyne's mortal heirs, in fact. Uh ... Pikus, is his name. I need ... someone ... to greet him. I'm feeling ... not myself."

That was akin to saying there were a few fish in the ocean. Athene was so far from herself Kirke wondered if even Mother would recognise her now. And that tragedy fell at Kirke's feet, didn't it? Yeah, she'd tried to save herself and damned her sister in the process.

"I, um ... Yeah, of course, I'll show this Pikus around the polis."

After leaving Athene, she made her way down from the acropolis, then followed the Long Wall back to the harbour. It wasn't hard to spot the Rassenian ship, with its bright green sails embroidered with the fox sigil.

"Prince Pikus," Kirke called out to the disembarking sailors. "Prince Pikus?"

One of the men craned his neck at her call, then hopped over a pile of ropes and trotted up beside her. He had a slight beard and his dark hair hung about his face in wild, sea-swept curls. "A Heliad, eh? I thought this polis ruled by Kroniads. Not that I have complaints about the company, my lady." He had a thick, pleasant accent that made her want to listen to him recite poetry or argue philosophy.

Kirke quirked a smile. That was presumptuous. "Kroniads do rule here, but I am kin to the Olympian Athene, and she sent me to greet you while she was ... uh, attending to matters of state." Her state, at least.

Pikus flashed a grin. "Her loss and my gain, I suppose." Well, rather proud of himself, wasn't he?

Kirke motioned him to follow and guided him through the harbour, wending around the bustling crowd loading and unloading. Did this place seem chaotic compared to Mnemosynia? Rassenia seemed so far removed from the politics of Elládos she couldn't help but think of it as rural, though the last she had seen the Rassenian city—a stopover when visiting her father's holdings in Thrinakia—it had become a sprawling metropolis.

"You are kin to the Muses, yes?"

"Distant aunts, yes. They are to me, I mean, not I to them." Again, that flash of white teeth and overflowing confidence.

Kirke snickered. "I met them, years ago, in Themiskyra."

The prince sniffed at that. "Ah, hmm. We do not speak of them much, you know. I think Great-grandmother has not forgiven them for going there."

Oh, well, that was awkward. Kirke snapped her mouth shut lest any other social gaffes spring forth and take flight.

After that, she restricted herself to pointing out the few interesting city buildings in the district. The harbourmaster's office, some warehouses held by various branches of the Kroniad aristoi, and the *Griffin's Beak*, a wine house that local legend claimed had served Kronos himself, though that was almost certainly a lie, as the wood would have rotted to naught centuries back.

"I could do with a cup of wine," she admitted, gauging his interest.

Pikus perked up at the mention of it, and so she led him into the wine house. The owner, Eutychios, nodded at her in recognition as she slipped onto a stool at her usual table. Few women came here, save whores and hetairai, but the establishment knew Kirke as kin to Athene and thus offered her steep discounts.

Pikus settled down across from her. "I don't suppose they have Rassenian vintages?"

Kirke snorted. "Yeah, I think for those we'll have to raid Athene's own stocks. Uh, but they've got some Argosian reds worth a sip or three, let me tell you."

The serving girls kept the bowls flowing while Pikus spoke of his far-off home. As a demigod, he was older than he looked, though he had naught on Kirke's long centuries of experience.

"Wait, you *lived* through the Titanomachy?" he gasped when she mentioned it offhand.

Kirke cast him a wistful look over the wine bowl at her lips. "I was in Helion, mostly, yeah. I remember when Artemis came and convinced Father to side with Zeus." Such was hard to forgive, especially as it had earned Artemis and her twin a place on Olympus. So self-serving.

Pikus laughed at even her most puerile humour, seeming to drink in her every tale.

In the end, they were so drunk she could barely keep her stool, sputtering from laughter, and tipsy enough the room had begun to sway like the ocean. Deciding they had best save the rest of the tour for the next day, she led him to the palace where the steward granted him a room.

Kirke passed out the moment she found her own chamber.

ALL THE NEXT day they laughed and drank, and she showed him the acropolis and the ever-expanding agora. She took him through the markets, and they sampled Illyrian wines, which he liked more than the Elládosi ones, and Phrygian ones, which he claimed tasted of donkey piss.

He had taken to calling her 'princess,' too, and every time it sent jitters running through her.

In the end, maybe that was why she did it. Maybe hearing anyone address her thus once more, after long centuries of being a mere

Nymph, had left her giddy as a child. Or maybe it was that she simply hadn't had a lover in over a decade. Certainly, Kalypso did not return her letters, and few others understood her.

Loneliness was a word easily understood intellectually, but it ran deeper than words or thoughts. It was an insidious undertow that could suck one beneath the ocean in a moment and hold a person there for what felt an eternity.

Or maybe it was that they had stopped in a wine house for three bowls of wine on an empty stomach.

Regardless, as they strolled the Colonnades, she laced her fingers in Pikus's with the impetuousness of her youth. And when he raised a brow and she ought to have broken off, still she persisted.

"My father remains lord of many lands, even still, and wealthy beyond measure. A marriage to one of his daughters could bring great weal to the House of Mnemosyne. And, you know, I'd be happy to take up life in Rassenia." Away from Athene and her madness and addiction. Living a few decades in happiness with the prince could be just what she needed—and give her a home as far removed from Zeus as possible.

Pikus's dashing smile morphed into an arrogant smirk. "Ah, yes, but not half so prestigious as a union with a child of the Olympians, now, is it? I mean, truly, do you think you buy a prince with a few drachmae and a pretty face?"

Kirke flinched from his mockery, struggling to even process his sudden turn. All his pretences of friendship had been ... what? Hoping to use her to get to Athene?

What in the depths of the Underworld had she even been thinking? She didn't need a damn husband to push her about and make demands of her. Certainly not one who could muster a look of such profound arrogance. Damn him for his haughtiness. Damn him for that adorable smile. And damn herself for never being able to control her tongue or her heart. Her eyes stung with unshed tears she could never let anyone see.

"I'm quite certain you can find your way around from here,

prince," Kirke said. Which was well, as she needed to hide her face and drink a fountain-full of wine.

BUT THE WINE did not help her shame, even knowing it was more at her own behaviour—childish, girlish fancy when she had a mission to follow—and she found herself instead stalking the streets of Kronion late at night, clinging to the shadows as if they might protect her.

It was in such gloom she noticed the scuffling footfalls trailing her in the harbour district. Her heart quickened at the sound of it. Probably she should have banged upon the door of the harbourmaster's office, for the lamp burning in the window meant he was still at work. Instead, she found herself darting down the adjacent alley, almost welcoming an altercation.

She drew up short.

Maybe her height alone was not quite enough for her pursuers to recognise her as a Titan. She couldn't imagine they would try this if they guessed the truth about her. Even a Nymph had *some* Pneumatikoi, enough to overpower mortals.

Two men followed her into the passage, silhouetted against the faint lamplight from the street. Their features were obscured by the overbearing shadows, but to them, she must have looked almost like a wraith in the darkness.

And she did not flee, which made them hesitate. She just stood there, tall and defiant—if quite a bit intoxicated—staring them down. One of them actually took a step backward, and Kirke chortled. Yeah, mocking them was foolish, but she couldn't stop herself.

"What, that's it? Here I was, thinking to myself, what an adventure I'm about to have tonight. Two big strong men coming to corner me in an alley, try to rob me—or wait, I'm a helpless woman so you probably wanted to have your way with me first, huh? I've heard some men can't get it up for a willing woman, though I'm guessing that's not an issue for you as I can't imagine you lot have too many willing women anyway. Oh! Did you forget your stones? If you want to run home and grab them, I can wait ..."

Kirke's Pneumatikoi might not have matched that of greater Titans, but pushing her Pneuma into Potency and Alacrity allowed her to cross the alley, snatch one of her pursuers up by the throat, and carry him into the main street before the other even seemed to have time to react. With a snarl, she grabbed his crotch and squeezed. "Oh, I was right. No stones, huh? Hmm. Not much of a tree there, either."

"T-titan," the other man gasped before breaking off into a run down the alley.

Kirke winked at her captive. "Guess he's gonna go grab his stones. Yeah, and when he gets back, you two can go fuck yourselves." She dropped the man and he pitched onto the flagstones, clutching his throat and wheezing.

The expenditure of so much Pneuma at once left Kirke a bit more lightheaded than she had expected, but she dare not show it.

Rather, with effort to keep her gait steady, she plodded along down the street. A few steps later she paused. A man she'd seen with Pikus exited the front of the *Griffin's Beak* and stalked around the side, perhaps for a piss. He'd told his crew about the place?

Yeah, she should definitely go home and sleep this off. That would be wise. It would be mature and wise.

Instead, she found herself peeking through gaps in a shuttered window. There, indeed, the Rassenian prince sat at a table, throwing back a bowl of wine and laughing with his mates. Probably at her expense, the bastard.

Maybe she should go in there and use a bit of Pneumatikoi on him, too. Of course, Athene might take it ill, her accosting a royal guest in her city.

Or she could ...

Kirke made her way around the back, finding the way to the servants' entrance to the kitchen. Inside, she found a pair of women, one ageing, the other younger, and similar enough in visage to have been mother and daughter.

The younger started at her appearance, her yelp causing the older to look up sharply. Both women lowered their heads once they got a good look at Kirke.

"My lady," the mother said.

Hmm. Kirke didn't much want to be recognised, but being seen as a Titan would have some edge here. "You've seen the Rassenian prince out there."

The older woman nodded, while the younger blushed, clearly as taken with Pikus's exotic accent and easy smile as Kirke herself had been.

Withdrawing a phial of Nectar—a new batch she'd not finished experimenting on—she made her way to a bowl the mother had just filled with white wine. She unstopped the phial and poured the liquid into it. The golden Nectar quickly vanished in the wine, though Kirke gave it a stir with her finger to be sure, flicking the excess off into a corner. If the Rassenians took to manic behaviour, sexual frenzies, or even trying to eat each other, well, Athene might guess at Kirke's hand, but no one else would.

The old woman blanched at what she had done, but Kirke offered her a purse. "Ten tetradrachmae," she said. Maybe more money than the woman had seen in one place in her life. "See that the prince gets this bowl."

With luck, maybe he'd wind up trying to rut with a donkey or something. The mental image was so vivid, Kirke found herself caught between grimace and grin. Wouldn't that be a story to send back to Mnemosynia?

The serving woman opened the pouch and her eyes widened, as if she had not believed what Kirke was offering until she saw it for herself. Oh, yeah, she would do it. That much money could change her life.

Much as Kirke would have liked to have stopped in the wine house herself and watch the results, she dare not risk Pikus or his men recognising her. Thus she slipped back out the way she'd come and contented herself with peering in the same window she'd looked through before. As she drew nigh, the serving girl was already retreating, having hastily set the bowl before the prince. To Kirke, the set of her shoulders and expression upon her face wrote her guilt plain as day, but the Rassenians seemed too deep in their cups to notice.

There, the self-satisfied prick sat, gesticulating in the midst of whatever tale he told his countrymen. His words sparked a fresh round of snickering, and one man spit wine from his nose. Kirke couldn't make out their words from here. Were they talking about her?

He paused his stories only to drink, then settled into his tales and mockery once more.

Of a sudden, the prince laid a hand upon his breast, then began to tug at his collar. It was working. At last it was working ...

A coughing fit seized the man, and one of his fellows rose, patting him on the back, while others leaned in with concern. In her mind's eye, Kirke pictured the prince trying to bite one of them and had to suppress her chortle.

A violent convulsion passed through Pikus and he heaved his man away, pitching over backward. People began to scream, and she heard the front door flung open, with some of the customers fleeing rather than risk being around for whatever the Rassenians would do about this.

Oh. Oh, shit. No brew of Nectar had ever outright killed someone before. Not that Kirke knew of anyway. Was it possible she'd misjudged so badly? A pang of guilt tore at her. She'd wanted revenge for his scorn, not murder. She leaned in closer, actually daring to ease the shutter open a nudge for a better view.

What if the Rassenians blamed the serving girl? Oh, what had she done?

On the floor, the prince thrashed about in utter agony. Transfixed by the sight, Kirke could not look away. The man arched his back with a strangled sob, and even as he did so, his nose ruptured, some other structure pushing its way out from rent flesh.

The man's wail became so gut-churning Kirke backed away from the window, even as the screams inside the house grew more wild. Nyx's bosom ... What had she unleashed ...?

Instinct demanded she run, but Kirke forced it down and dragged her stubborn feet back to the window. She had to know what had happened. She owed it to him, she supposed.

Inside, the prince's now blood-splattered clothes lay in an empty heap. No, not empty, for something thrashed beneath them. All of his men had backed far away, none daring to approach. A sleeve fluttered. Then a woodpecker burst free of the garments, darting about the wine house as if seeking some egress.

Kirke slapped a hand to her mouth, reeling. She'd ... she'd turned him into a fucking bird?

28

PYRRHA

219 Golden Age

The writhing World shifted and shifted again, and Pyrrha was hefted up upon a bed of roots and vines, carried into the orgy unfolding around her. Two dozen Wood spirits—dryads and satyrs alike—were enmeshed in the throes of passion. A coarse tongue was in her ear, vines wrapt around her breasts, and someone was pushing inside her nethers.

The land bent and shifted, the forest buckling inward until it became a sphere enclosing her.

Dazed, she felt it, some alien presence slithering up inside her. Maybe it was the satyr's hot seed. Maybe it was her own soul surrendering even as her body pleaded for more. Either way, she knew she was giving over, allowing them to break her will. She knew it, and she still could not turn away. She *needed* the completeness this world offered.

How tired she had grown of the Mortal Realm.

The satyr atop her leered, its face a frenzied mask of passion, its gyrations so wild as to move beyond animal need and into something monstrous. Abruptly, it lurched over backward, fletching sprouting from its splattered eye.

Pyrrha shrieked at the appearance of an arrow in its head and flung the Wood spirit off her.

The sudden violence cast her spiralling down from the hysteria that had claimed her and revealed the orgy in its awful splendour. A warping of the world as something utterly *other* had seeped in, and the denizens of that Realm, seeming more plant than person, writhed in copulation that melded them into a single throbbing entity.

Gagging, Pyrrha scrambled backward on her arse. Strong hands seized her arms and dragged her from the glade, and it took a moment before she even knew what was happening. Her rescuer was a tall, silver-eyed woman, a Phoebid probably, with a bow in one hand. She snatched Pyrrha's wrist and pulled her away, darting through the dark wood as if she could see concealed root and rock.

Pyrrha's feet kept catching on a hundred hidden obstructions, but the Titan's grip on her wrist didn't allow her to fall. Behind her, vines and branches lashed out like grasping fingers, reaching for them. On and on the woman yanked her forward, until at last they burst through the tree line.

Though she wanted to collapse from exhaustion—dozens of scrapes now covered her—the Titan forced her to press on, albeit at a slower pace, only allowing her to stop when they reached a stream. Panting, Pyrrha fell to her knees on the sand and splashed water upon her face.

"What in the whole of Gaia was that?" she rasped, droplets running down her cheeks.

The other woman slumped down beside her, tossing her bow aside. "Not Gaia, I think. It felt like something from another world. Something of a Primordial." She rubbed her hands together, looking far away. "Pan, perhaps, the God of Wood. Dryads and satyrs are his ... hmm ... supplicants, I guess."

Pyrrha shivered, rubbing her arms, suddenly realising she wore naught save the tattered remnants of the peplos the spirits had torn from her. "Thank you." She grimaced and shifted, even knowing any attempt at modesty was utterly pointless under the circumstances. "Um, I'm Pyrrha."

"Artemis."

Huh. Wasn't that the name of one of Helios's brood? Hadn't she won some famous battle in the Ambrosial War? "What were you doing here?"

Artemis quirked a brow as if to return the question. Then she sniffed. "My brother is training with Themis and I escorted him here. I went into the woods to hunt and felt something ... perverse. You're lucky I came along, though. Those dryads almost had you as one of them."

Without doubt, and, at the time, Pyrrha had welcomed it, as if they had saturated her mind with their essence. Saying that aloud, though, would make her sound a madwoman. Instead, she clutched Artemis's hand in thanks.

THE TITAN, as it turned out, had a small cottage a few hours' walk from Delphi. Artemis led Pyrrha along a route through the wilderness, one that allowed them to reach the house without encountering anyone to witness her state of undress. Inside, the Titan offered her a tunic more suited to a man than a woman. But then, Artemis herself dressed thus, and Pyrrha was in no condition to refuse *any* clothes.

Nor a warm bed in which she immediately fell into a fitful sleep. Inchoate images plagued her, though, having her jolting awake over and over, as she saw, once more, the platinum-haired man, Zeus. She saw him squirming atop her, felt her own passion rise. She saw the two of them, descending into the depths of a mountain, looking upon a strange archway cut around a tunnel. She saw Thebes aflame, as Gigantes rampaged through the streets.

What tricks her mind played upon her, coiled up and confused by the drakon blood. What madness it prompted.

For the better part of two days, she dozed, waking long enough to indulge in a venison stew Artemis had prepared, before drifting off once more. Never had her dreams felt so real, so vivid, so intoxicatingly damning. It was as if another world had opened within her, and though it flowed, in the manner of dreams, from scene to scene without her able to parse the transitions, still it compelled her to remain.

Sometimes, it felt she was caught up in some bard's tale and could not pull herself away until she had heard the end of the story.

When she woke next, the moon was up, and Artemis was outside the house, kneeling before the corpse of a rabbit with a slit throat. The Titan had prostrated herself but now leaned backward, arms raised to the moon in supplication.

Daring not to intrude, Pyrrha knelt and watched until Artemis at last turned to her.

"Why the sacrifice?" Pyrrha asked.

Artemis settled back on her haunches and indicated the moon hovering above. "A full moon. The time of Thoth."

"What?"

"The Primordial of the Moon, worshipped by my grandmother, and taught to me. I offer sacrifices in the hopes Thoth remains pleased. Perhaps he will guide my steps, perhaps guard my fortune. Mostly, we just hope the Elder Gods do not stir and trouble us." She shrugged. "Or so Grandmother says."

"Grandmother?"

"Phoebe." Another of the Ouranid League. Artemis's bloodline was pristine, and yet she bothered with a mere Nymph like Pyrrha. The woman shifted. "She knows such things, of old."

Pyrrha nodded, not knowing what to say. How did someone like her make an answer when a war hero spoke of one of the rulers of the Thalassa as 'Grandmother'?

"I don't even know how to begin to thank you," Pyrrha ventured.

Artemis shrugged. "I dare hope someone would have done the same for me." But her voice held far more left unspoken. "If you like, I can teach you woodcraft. A paltry defence against the Otherworldly, but it might help a little."

"You're inviting me to stay here."

Another shrug. "I don't linger overlong in any one place, but while I remain here, you are welcome to it." She paused. "I'll have my bed back, though. You can sleep on the bearskin by the hearth."

Fair enough.

TWELVE YEARS HAD PASSED since the end of the Ambrosial War, and Artemis confirmed she had indeed fought a battle outside Helion, against a Titan who could control mist and snow. Artemis had no idea how that was possible, but Pyrrha suspected Khione must have been some kind of sorceress with a bound lampad. No other explanation seemed forthcoming for such power.

"I don't know," Artemis replied when Pyrrha voiced her theory. "With enough Ambrosia, we can harness our Pneuma, but not like that. Something was different about her, for certain. Or maybe not everything has explanations. Maybe there is more unknown than known in this world."

The pair of them walked the woods, searching for deer, though Pyrrha found the hunt far less intriguing than the company. She had revealed her ability to see the dead to Artemis, and her host had only nodded without apparent concern.

That sort of acceptance ... well Pyrrha had only ever experienced it with Enodia.

"Can you tell me more about the Elder God we encountered beyond Delphi?" she asked, as Artemis ducked under a low-hanging branch.

"Not really. I am no expert in such things. Once, I ..." Artemis glanced back at her. "Grandmother told me of a lodge of sorcerers in Phoenikia she had once been a member of. I had thought to seek them out, but something happened with my grandfather, and I found I could not leave Lydia fast enough. I did not bother to ask Grandmother where, exactly, this Circle was, much less pursue it. No, I found my taste for such things had evaporated like morning dew."

Circle? "The Circle of Goetic Mysteries?" Of which Enodia had also once been part. All the sorcerers in the Thalassa seemed to congregate for its secrets.

Artemis cast a sharp look at her, then nodded slowly, her face unreadable. Pyrrha wanted to ask what had happened with her grandfather, but the Titan seemed so dour now, she dared not.

⁊⁊

THE SAME EVENING, after they had eaten, Artemis decided to offer another sacrifice to the full moon. Rather than watch, Pyrrha wandered nearby, making her cautious way along the light woods. They were far from her encounter with the dryads, and she couldn't imagine finding them here.

Which was almost a shame. While the horror of what they had put her through clenched her stomach, still ... *still* she felt drawn back, desperate for more answers. Knowledge was everything, wasn't it? With understanding of the World came the power to shape it.

Wandering thus, she found Enodia crouched beneath a tree, cowled and brooding as ever. "You had a brush with a tendril of an Elder God," her mentor said without preamble.

"Artemis calls them Primordials."

"Yes, they have many titles and many names. Names, you see, hold a power of their own. They are how we see ourselves, yes, and a mask we wear to shape the perceptions of others." The sorceress turned to her. "Just as you, perhaps, should have a new name."

"What?"

"Pyrrha was a scared girl banished from the court of Thebes. You must reinvent yourself as a proud, irrepressible sorceress. A mistress of the night. You have become both necromancer and now oneiromancer. Surely you have shed your childhood guise."

Pyrrha folded her arms. "Um ... Soteria? Oh! Maybe, Propulaia?"

"Choose whatever you wish, child."

Pyrrha frowned. Crotchety old witch. "Oneiromancy is ... understanding my dreams."

"Yours, and those of others. The greatest oneiromancer of our age is called Morpheus, and he too is a member of the Circle of Goetic Mysteries. Perhaps you can learn from him if you can convince your friend to take you."

Pyrrha glanced over her shoulder in Artemis's direction. "She is afraid of something."

"Everyone is afraid of something," Enodia said, rising with a slight groan. "If you want to further your studies, you will need more mentorship than I alone can provide."

Why, Pyrrha wanted to ask, but reluctantly decided to leave it be. "I'll speak to Artemis about going to Phoenikia."

As EXPECTED, Artemis tensed the moment Pyrrha pushed about visiting either Phoeba, to meet her grandmother, or otherwise searching for the Circle.

"There is a cost to all things," Artemis said, rising, and seeming intent to stalk from the cottage on another interminable hunt.

Pyrrha grabbed her hand and pulled her back down. Or rather, Artemis allowed her to, since Pyrrha could never have physically forced the Titan into aught. "Please. I must have answers. I must know the arcana that bind the World together, Artemis. Whatever the cost, surely knowledge is preferable to ignorance?"

Still, her friend glowered.

"Did you not say you do not linger overlong in one place? Let us leave here together."

Finally, Artemis sighed, pain creasing her features. "As you say. We will go to Phoeba first, and I will see if my grandmother will answer any of your questions. But, Pyrrha, promise me one thing. Do not push too far, too fast."

"I ... promise," Pyrrha said. Maybe she even meant it.

29

ATHENE

1585 Silver Age

The haze that gripped Athene's mind clotted out most thoughts, even as the tides of the past and future blended into a cavalcade of tumbling violence. For violence seemed to crest over the waves of time, demarcating its shape, the one constant. War and slaughter, battles echoing through the ages, monsters rampaging, and within a dark sea, a still darker shadow of an approaching enormity.

She saw too many things that made no sense, and too many things that *did* make sense.

But it all ran together in a muddled roil, until she could not make one time from the next, nor even be sure if all she saw was conjured up by her fevered mind.

She saw heroes striving against the chaos of the land, and her hand guiding them—or was it manipulation? She saw gods falling, and—though she told herself it was a dream—the fall of her brother

Ares outside somewhere that looked like the walls of Ilium. She saw a thousand flickers like images cast upon Urania's cave, and wondered at their source.

"Mother," Pandion chided, his hand in front of her face. For a moment she wondered whether he'd actually had the audacity to snap his fingers in front of her, or whether she had just imagined that as well. They sat in her court room, but Pandion had apparently dismissed all the other members of the court, save for Athene's steward.

"Mother, did you even hear me? They said he turned into a wood-pecker and flew away. What explanation are we meant to send Mnemosynia for such a preposterous claim? They will think we mock them. They will claim we have abducted their heir!"

Pikus. She had sent Kirke to manage Pikus. And the witch had turned him into a bird? This sounded like a hallucination. Such things did not happen.

"Find your aunt and bring her to me," she said, rubbing at her eyes and not looking forward to any confrontation with Kirke. Perhaps she ought to take another draught before the woman arrived.

No, wait. She had taken the last bit in the night, hadn't she? She needed more, and Kirke would have to provide. Once, Athene had gone searching in her sister's lab, but there were too many phials, all different, and none marked. Kirke had warned some batches were more dangerous than others, and not even Athene was so brazen as to imbibe one at random.

Or at least, she hoped she would not be.

⚘

THE STENCH of opulence saturated the air of Babilim and nowhere more so than in the heart of this palace, with its great vaulted ceilings depicting strange conceptions of heavenly courts, and its gold-plated trim framing the frescoed walls.

Athene took it all in as the guards dragged her by the elbows, the tips of her sandals just brushing the mirror-polished tiles of the floor. No colonnade ran the length of this hall, giving the chamber a vast, cavernous aspect. Lines of braziers rimmed the path to Mithra's throne upon the dais, their flickering light failing to banish the gloom that flitted about the hall.

A dozen Immortals stood in the wings behind the throne, hands on the hilts of their akinakai. Along with them, a hundred more of his guards rimmed the periphery, ready to surge up on her with the slightest motion of their king.

The King of Kings himself reclined at ease, his face concealed in shadow, while firelight reflected off the emeralds encrusted into his sandals.

Her captors carried her within a dozen feet of the dais then drove her to her knees before the Babilimian monarch with such force the impact sent lances of lightning surging through her legs. Instinctively, she reached for Tolerance, but the orichalcum fetters blocked any access to her Pneuma. Of course, if the chains hadn't bound her wrists, she could have torn through these guards in a whirlwind. Maybe she could have even fought the Immortals, though perhaps not so many of them.

"The great goddess Athene," Mithra said, face still concealed. "Come to us at last, even as Elládos falls around you."

Athene stared defiance at the self-proclaimed king of the world. "My father will not ransom me."

Now, Mithra leaned forward, offering her a hint of his features, from his trim black beard to his intense eyes. "But it is not your father I am interested in, Goddess." With ponderous import, the man rose, giving the sensation of a river changing its course. "No, I have had you brought here for something far more momentous than Zeus's petty struggles. I have summoned you forth from the farthest reaches of this world in order to bestow upon you a gift. The greatest of all gifts, in fact, Athene. I am going to give to you ... Truth."

❧

WHEN PANDION RETURNED WITH KIRKE, Athene started awake, realising she had dozed upon her throne. Had ... had she just had a vision without even the use of water? Was that oneiromancy, or had she fallen into some drug-induced trance not unlike what the Oracle Mirror had induced in her beneath Olympus?

"Leave us," she said, her mouth suddenly dry. "Andreas, wait," she called to her steward an instant later. "Fetch us wine."

With a bow, the man left to do so.

"So ... You called for me," Kirke said, standing with her hands behind her back. "And I'm basically here. You don't look so good, truth be told. Are you sleeping enough? Yeah, it's really important to get proper rest. An overtaxed mind cannot process what it sees in the Sight, you know. I've heard that—"

"Do be silent," Athene moaned, and Kirke snapped her mouth shut.

A moment later, Andreas returned, small amphora under one arm, and a pair of bowls clutched between the fingers of his other hand.

"Kirke will not be having wine this morning," Athene said, to which her steward inclined his head, leaving the amphora and a single bowl.

"Oh, ah, I could have actually gone for a sip or three ..." Kirke began, then trailed off when Athene levelled a withering gaze at her.

"I need more."

"Yeah, clearly you've not had nigh enough yet. If you like, I could probably find a cart to run over your face, too, in case you need further abuse."

Athene poured herself some wine and decided to ignore both the barb and the Nymph's temerity. When she had downed the whole bowl, she leaned back in her throne. "Did you turn the Prince of Rassenia into ..." Athene couldn't believe she was even going to say this. "Did you turn him into a bird?"

"Well, you don't seem to think I did, so perhaps we should leave it at that and both remain the happier for it. I mean, really, 'turn him into a bird' is so ambiguous after all. It could mean all sorts of things, if you really think about it. Perhaps I, err ... well, that is, what it means, as a kind of euphemism you see, that I made him crow or some such thing. And you wouldn't really want to know about it—"

Athene flung the empty bowl at Kirke's feet, shattering it and sloshing the dregs over the woman's sandals. "Enough. You have no idea what you've done now. I was building a diplomatic relationship with Rassenia on Pandion's behalf. For all we know, they may now think to make war over this, Kirke! The sheer unbelievability of the claim those sailors will bring back may be all—if aught—that stops them from launching a fleet of ships at us."

"Yeah ... Mnemosyne retreated to the farthest shores long ago. She doesn't want war with any Elládosi polis. She doesn't want any involvement at all, hardly ... Can't much blame her." That last was mumbled, but Athene caught it.

"That's not the point!" That Kirke was right had absolutely no bearing. "You have jeopardised the peace and my son's future."

Kirke snickered. "Yeah, true. But, you know, maybe having his mother spiral into depravity and addiction won't be ideal for Pandion's prospects either. I mean, I thought you had hit the bottom of that hole, but then you just set about with a shovel and decided to go deeper, even if you buried yourself with the dirt."

Pneuma surged through Athene unbidden and before she knew what she was doing she had closed the distance between herself and her half-sister. Still, she restrained herself from striking the other woman. Her sudden rush forward with the speed of a gale ought to serve as enough reminder of the difference between a true Titan and a Nymph like her. "You must leave Kronion this very day, Kirke. You are no longer welcome here."

Her sister frowned, falling back a step. "And where do you imagine you'll get your next dose? Buy it on the street? Maybe hit up the local brothels and see if they keep some in the back for special customers?"

The woman would not stop, would she? "I have half a mind to turn you over to Father for brewing that filth! Look what it has done to me! Look what you have done to your sister!" She saw spittle from her outburst pelt Kirke's face.

Grimacing, her sister ran her palm over her eyes and mouth to wipe it away. "What you've done to yourself. I offered you a drink, yeah, true, and you decided you needed to claim the whole cellar for yourself. But you're right, you do have half a mind. Half, at best. You'll turn me in to Olympus and say what, that you've been funding and harbouring my work for the past decade? Think that will go over well with dear Papa?"

Athene stared at Kirke, aghast. Had that been part of her plan? Athene had caught Kirke with Nectar, and Kirke had drawn her in and made it so she could never use it against her. And Athene had leapt in with both feet. "Get out of my city, Kirke. I don't want to see you here again."

⚘

THE CHILLS that wracked Athene came and went. The worst of them had been two nights back, when her stomach had heaved and churned, trying to dislodge everything she had eaten in the past millennium. Pandion had sat beside her, in turns weeping or begging her to tell him what was wrong while he mopped her brow.

But how was she to tell her son she was addicted to Nectar? How was she to admit she not only used, but facilitated the spread of, a drug his grandfather had declared death to sample?

She was burning up and soaked in sweat and she was frozen solid, teeth chattering.

And, Nyx, those headaches! Like a Cyclops had smashed her temples with a club a few dozen times.

Once, she opened her mouth to beg Pandion to kill her. Only the fact he was her son had stopped her, for no child should have to suffer such a request. Even if it meant she was ripped apart in solitary agony.

Or maybe the worst of it was the question ... was her mind even her mind?

And were the things she had beheld even real?

⚘

BUT EVEN THOSE RAVAGES PASSED, and the cravings, while never quite gone, became less frequent. Pandion came into his own, and the mortal aristoi elected him their king, as Athene had foreseen. As she had arranged, in fact, with subtle prodding, bribes, blackmail, and a decade of driving away or dissuading potential rivals.

The visions had helped with that, and Kirke had planted no few seeds herself, despite her intimations that the whole election was a sham. Maybe it was, but her son had basked in radiance from it, and that meant everything, in the end.

So she'd ordered a new palace constructed for the mortal kings, one not far from her own, and while work began on it, they had planned his coronation. The aristoi came, even from Thebes and Argos, and, yes, Korinth too, to see the first king of Kronion.

All gathered in the agora, a throng of aristoi, with commoners far behind them. Athene marched through the Colonnade of Justice, a gilded laurel crown resting upon her palms and a trail of agonises following behind her. Them, and Demeter herself, come from Thebes, along with Kadmus and Harmonia.

At the far end knelt Pandion, admirably composed, face lit with understandable pride. Her son. Her boy, almost fifteen now, and cresting into manhood. And Athene had seen the long line of champions and heroes that would spring from him, governing this city for centuries to come.

It was something to be proud of. Maybe it was even enough ... to let go of the past.

Athene pushed the thoughts down. She would not allow Hephaistos into this solemn moment, and the Titan had not been fool enough to attend. No, and she would not bring him here herself.

Reverently, she set the laurel crown upon Pandion's head. "Rise, King of Kronion."

Her son did so, then turned to take in the gathered throng and spread his arms wide, sparking cheers and applause that echoed through the agora. "Not Kronion, Mother," he said, when the clamour had at last died down. "Kronion was named in honour of your grandfather Kronos, who betrayed the world, and we have long since surpassed him. From this day forth, this polis shall bear the name Athenai, in *your* honour, Mother."

Despite herself, Athene felt blood flush her face. Olympians did not name poleis after themselves as the Ouranids had, and yet Pandion had declared this, in full hearing of the public. All she could do was let her hand alight atop her boy's head and take the gesture as he meant it.

Then, among the faces of the crowd, she caught sight of her mother's own golden eyes, smiling. When Mother saw her looking, she nodded at Athene.

This was it. A perfect moment, and all her striving had brought them here. Pandion was king, her mother had returned—and how could Athene not have feared when Mother had gone to the Underworld and lingered there?—and all was as it should be.

Only ... what had her vision meant? In the months since, she had oft asked herself this question. Babilim was a city in Kumari Kandam, but hardly one worthy of note. That, she had to assume, would one day change in the future.

A GRAND FESTIVAL was held in Pandion's honour, and people of Kronion—of Athenai, she supposed—flocked to the streets and clogged the Colonnades. On a rock outcropping of the acropolis, Athene walked with her mother, looking down on the polis below. While the footing was precarious, she had little fear of losing her balance, even without relying upon Pneumatikoi.

"You saw Persephone?" Athene asked, not looking back at her mother, who seemed no more troubled by their vantage than Athene.

The silence dragged on long enough Athene finally glanced back. "I saw her," Mother said, her voice far away and so heavy with burden Athene dare not ask further about her time in the Underworld.

Such a thing, passing among ghosts and wandering in the shadows, that was not for her in any event. Once, in her youth, she had asked her mother whether she ought to pursue sorcery, as Mother had taught Kirke.

"I think that is not your path, and now, knowing all I have learnt, I would not send anyone down that road, least of all one I love as a child." Her words had haunted Athene, especially for their implication that, while she would not condone Athene studying the Art, it was now too late for herself and Kirke. As if there was no way back from such depths and one could only ever delve deeper into the forbidden truths.

Truths like that which this Mithra had promised her.

Well, that was a problem for another time.

"You have made your son king, and now Sisyphus is dead and the Kreiad genos reeling." Mother laid a hand upon Athene's shoulder. "Tell me your vengeance is complete."

Hmm. There was a part of her, now, that wanted to believe that, though her visions had also revealed her flaying Hephaistos's father. Sometimes, in the dark of night, she latched onto that image to help keep the flame of her hate stoked.

And just as Hephaistos had bound her in orichalcum and left her powerless, so too would she find herself chained before Mithra. "He stole my strength, Mother." It would happen *again*. "He stole my honour. Stripped my choices from me and made me his slave. How shall that ever pass? Would the great Hekate tolerate such indignities and wave them away? Would she relegate such things to the past?"

With a groan, her mother slumped down upon the rocks, drawing Athene to sit beside her. "Do you really believe I have suffered no indignities in nigh four millennia of life? Do you think I hold my position on Olympus, such as it is, without having to let lie old grievances?"

Her mother's words burned in her. Almost ... almost tempting. "He and his line must suffer."

"You can be more than this," her mother said, eyes hard. "You can be *better* than this vat of boiling vitriol, Athene. I have seen you as a champion of Man, a protector of heroes." Heroes like Theseus, going

after this Minotaur, whatever that was? There was truth to her mother's words, and they spoke to her but ...

"His line must suffer," she repeated, wondering if she was trying
to convince Mother or herself. She set her jaw. She would see it
through, then attend to the future. "Hephaistos has a daughter, does
he not?"

Her mother sighed, nodding. "Yes, he does, a young woman in
Lydia. Her name is Medusa."

30

PANDORA

201 Golden Age

*I*n the fish-shaped tub, Pyrrha cooed, murmuring nonsense while Pandora wiggled her fingers in the water, creating eddies to amuse the child. She and Prometheus sat on the floor of their room, lounging upon a whale mosaic. The better part of a month had passed since his return, and their conversations now, precious though they were, had begun to amount to the same as Pyrrha's nascent attempts as speech.

Nonsense to entertain and placate one another. Emotions given voice, even without thought.

"You could stay a lifetime, really," Prometheus said with the air of a man who knew better. "You could go back at any time."

"I could," Pandora said, her own words cutting her chest open. "I could, perhaps whelp a few more babes, maybe wait until silver threads through my hair. Then I ought to be in the best possible shape to scale the slopes of Olympus and confront almighty Zeus. I was thinking, once our grandchildren are born, I will perhaps challenge him to a bout of pankration on his throne room floor. If I can pin him, he must surely release you."

"Wrestling him may not be the answer. Perhaps something more indirect."

Every laugh that wrinkled Pyrrha's face was the most wondrous, most agonising instant of Pandora's life. What mother could leave their child behind? How could she ever contemplate such a course? It was inhuman to be forced to this, and she could not forgive the Moirai for whatever part they played in placing her in such a situation.

Fate had twisted her in knots and sliced her to ribbons. And like a fool, she lingered here, somehow believing Ananke would suddenly turn benevolent and take mercy upon her.

But then, weren't all people fools in the face of destiny?

෨

FROM HER WINDOW overlooking the sea, Pandora spied the ships closing in upon Thebes's harbour, though she had no view of the harbour itself. From this distance, she could not say whether these were the same ones that had assaulted Ogygia just under two months ago, but she suspected so. The island of Kronion formed the Strait of Korinth, which meant the northernmost shore of Kronos's homeland lay but a short sail away from Thebes.

It was a wonder it had taken him this long to find them. The question now was, had he come for Tethys ... or for Pandora and her Box?

Her fingers tightened upon the window's lip as the ships closed in upon the city that had become her new home. How was it Zeus and his kith forever seemed to deny her any semblance of peace? From the court of Agenor in Tyros, to the citadel in Atlantis, to Ogygia, and now here. "May Hades feast upon your liver," she whispered at the ships.

Then she grimaced. Hades was probably on those ships, after all, and brother to Zeus. Well then, let them all descend into the Underworld and rot.

Pushing off the window, she strode across the room, swept Pyrrha up from her crib, and raced through the halls. Already, the palace was awash in panicked servants dashing about as if aught they might do to prepare would help them weather a Titan assault. A trio of warriors in full panoply charged past her, forcing her to push up against a column, just to avoid them.

By the time she reached the courtyard, Okeanus was there, standing before the fountain as his men raced around to prepare. The bushy-bearded Titan lord had skin tinged so faintly blue she almost wondered if he held some kinship to the mer. Servants helped him strap on his own armour, one lacing greaves, two more fussing with a dolphin-encrusted breastplate while Tethys paced around him, his xiphos clutched in her anxious hands.

Was this the very hour of his famed death? Could Pandora stop it? But then, she knew better. She'd tried to change the past, tried to slay Zeus, and all she'd gotten for it was being thrown off a cliff by Nemesis. If she could change the timeline, it would not be through any easy course, nor a few words to these Titans. Okeanus would never listen to her, and Tethys would only think her a foe if she tried to convince her that her consort might die down by the shore.

Prometheus strode into the courtyard, darting around a caryatid and racing to Pandora's side.

She grabbed him with one hand, the other clutching Pyrrha close. "This is because of me, isn't it? All those who will suffer and die this day do so because I came here, and Kronos hunts the Box."

"We cannot know that with absolute certitude," Prometheus said, though his eyes told another tale. A fear Pandora had the right of it, and chaos would ensue, with the blame falling upon their shoulders.

"Does he know his own future?" she demanded. "Is that why Kronos seeks the Box, to change the result of the Titanomachy?"

"Again, who can say how much he knows? He might have divined his end. But even had he the Box, still he is bound by the same threads of Fate as the rest of us. Ananke's grasp is not easily evaded."

Pandora winced. How very true, but, like herself, Kronos had the motivation to go to any lengths to *try*. "If the Box is gone, he may leave Thebes in peace."

"He might ..." Prometheus swallowed, looking for all the World like he wanted to say more. To offer a thousand reasons for her not to go through with this. Instead, he withdrew the Box from his satchel and proffered it to her.

Looking at the thing again, now, it became too real. Too heavy. She faltered, staggering under the weight of its import. This was her last moment with Pyrrha, and the last time this Prometheus would see her for thousands of years. Eyes glistening, she looked down at the babe in her arms. Not crying, not having any idea what unfolded around her, Pyrrha gazed up at her, replete with innocence.

Pandora kissed her daughter's forehead. "I'm so, so sorry I ... I have no ..." Blinking, she rubbed her eyes with the back of her wrist. Not like this. She would not leave Pyrrha with a memory of her mother weeping over her. That the babe would never remember this mattered naught. What mattered was the moment. And she held Pyrrha so very tight. "I will see you again, I swear it. No matter if I must defy Ananke, I will see you, precious child."

Though it destroyed her, she slid the babe into her lover's arms, then took the Box he still held out to her.

"I made what adjustments I had time to," Prometheus said, voice seeming drawn out over a loom, stretched to breaking. This was killing him, too. "Still, it is infinitely complex and relies, so far as I can tell, upon the intuitive abilities of the user."

"You built it for me," she said. "So shouldn't it take me where I want to go?"

"One would think."

Shouts had rung up outside the city, and, when she looked about, she realised Okeanus was already gone. He had gone down to the harbour to lead his troops against the assaulting forces of Kronos. He had gone to die.

Her gaze returned to Prometheus, and now even he, imperturbable as he was, stood with unshed tears glinting in his eyes. "I will take care of her, I swear," he promised. "I will give her the best life a child can enjoy in such times as these."

"I *will* see her again." One more promise to one more loved one she could not live without. And when she had fulfilled her promise to Prometheus, she would find a way to uphold her vow to their daughter. Not even the Moirai would stand in her way.

Lest anyone notice her—unlikely though that was in the course of a battle—Pandora slipped from the water garden. She passed more scrambling servants carrying wooden planks. They intended to bar the doors from the inside and hold back the tide of Kronos's forces. No such planks would stop true Titans, though they might hold back Men.

Pandora slipped from the main hall, pausing before a fresco depicting some cephalopodic, dragon-headed monstrosity lurking within an undersea chasm. What would possess any artist to depict such a thing, she could not imagine, but its too-numerous incandescent eyes seemed to watch her through the painting.

Her lover had trailed behind her, their child in his arms. His mouth was ajar, though he seemed unable to form any more words. What was left to be said, after all? She must do this, and he must convince Kronos the Box was gone.

With a breath to steady herself, Pandora began to twist the pieces of the puzzle. Intuition, Prometheus had said. Her own instincts ought to guide her, for he had built this for her. So all she needed to do was trust herself.

And open the puzzle.

Once more, the World thrummed, and her ears popped. She wobbled in place, braced herself against the wall, then stumbled as it vanished when light collapsed inward. Everything changed.

Flailing from the sudden removal of the wall beside her, Pandora pitched over sideways and landed upon a muddy bank. The late afternoon sun glinted off a waterway in front of her. As she pushed herself up, any doubt of her location vanished. The hints of aquama-rine striating the marmoreal walls that rose up from the canal, those she would know anywhere.

Atlantis.

The Box had really brought her back. Small ships and boats wended around each other in an intricate dance to navigate the canal. Some aboard the boats stared at her, perhaps mistaking her for a common prostitute down here seeking custom. Unwilling to let anyone see it, she stuffed the Box inside her satchel.

The earthen wall across the way meant she stood in the middle ring, looking at the acropolis island. Just beyond her location, a mighty bridge spanned the water, the deer reliefs announcing she gazed up at the underside of Taygete's Bridge, though she'd never spied it from down here. Across from her, marble stairs offered a return to street level.

Pausing only to brush the mud from her peplos—the garment would look rather archaic, she supposed, but it was all she had—she climbed the steps. For a moment, she had to just stare in rapt wonder at the glory of the city. Though she could not see aught of the grandeur of acropolis island beyond the earthen wall, still, even the middle ring glinted like a marble mountain worked with a thousand intricate ridges.

She allowed herself a moment to take it all in. It felt like another lifetime when she had lived here. Another Pandora, in fact. While she could not say she missed this place, as *such*, still, it remained thick with memories for her. Not all of them terrible, she supposed.

But she did not belong here now. For the moment, she needed to focus on a way to reach the gate to Tartarus beneath Zeus's palace. Spoken aloud, the obstacle would have seemed insurmountable. For who could breach the most secure location in the scope of the World? But she would, of that she had no doubt. There was no room for fail-ure. Not in this.

To find the way forward, though, she needed time and informa-tion. As much knowledge as possible. Though the Pleiades were gone, the acropolis itself had a fine library. If Pandora could flatter or inveigle her way in, maybe she'd find a way to reach Tartarus without dying in the process.

At the threshold of Taygete's Bridge, she faltered, though. A woman striding across, a Nymph, met her gaze, and the other woman's eyes widened. That was the Oracle Brizo. The Oracle stumbled backward a step, hand going to her mouth. At seeing Pandora? Why would she even recognise—

A tremendous rumbling reverberated through the polis, like the growl of a momentous drakon waking beneath the city. Pandora cocked her head to the side, not quite certain what was happening. Brizo fell back once more, shaking her head.

Dust and loose debris trembled upon the ground, and just in front of Pandora a flagstone edged upward. A tremor had Pandora swaying in place, steadying herself with her arms.

Then the land bucked like a ship caught in a tempest.

A wave passed under the ground. All around it, the stones rent themselves asunder, heaving skyward, ripping great gorges open. Sulphuric vapours and geysers of seawater erupted from these fissures, grasping toward the setting sun.

The cacophony of destruction drowned out the screams of the population, though Pandora saw the utter terror that washed over the entirety of Atlantis as though they were a single organism. She saw it writ plain upon Brizo's face as their gazes locked once more. No, not mere dread of mortal danger, but the abhorrence of a foreknown doom.

With a grinding shriek, Taygete's Bridge pitched inward. Brizo vanished into a crunch of stone raining down into the canal.

Turning to run, Pandora screamed herself, though she couldn't hear her own voice. A rushing, panicked crowd jostled her and sent her stumbling. A cluster of legs slammed into her, sending her satchel skidding away, and she threw herself forward, fingers grasping it. It skittered forward, just out of reach.

Another wave seized the island, this one even more calamitous. The geysers that had erupted in scattered patches now spilled over into one another. From her knees, Pandora watched the fissure flense through the city, and beyond, through the whole of the island.

The land adjacent to her tipped over at an angle, spilling hundreds of fleeing refugees into the rapidly expanding gorge. Beyond, upon Evenor Mountain, flashes of lightning illumined a jet-black cloud that had encircled the peak. Bright, galvanic arcs that seemed ready to blow apart the very bedrock of Atlantis, even as these quakes swallowed the city.

More and more of the flagstones cracked, great sheets of terrain turning nigh vertical.

As Atlantis literally split in half.

And Pandora had no idea what had happened to her satchel.

Scrambling, she managed hands and knees, stumbling forward through the surging crowd who fled in all directions. More knees jostled her, sent her sprawling once more. The land continued to heave, and a stone gave way beneath her.

With a shriek, Pandora fell a half dozen feet to where a flagstone had settled below street level.

Oh, fuck. Not like this! Not like this, after everything!

A woman wearing a crimson khiton hopped down beside her, offering a hand. Pandora grasped it and was hefted to her feet. She met the other woman's gaze.

It was *her*. She was looking in a mirror at another Pandora.

And the other Pandora held the Box in her free hand. "We don't have much time."

EPILOGUE

221 Golden Age

The combination of pyromantic insight and a few well-placed questions meant Prometheus could track most people down, even if they wished not to be found. And Pyrrha had not exactly concealed herself in the courts of Phoeba.

Built in the wake of the Ambrosial War, the city had already begun to flourish. Great walls encircled all save the harbour, and that bustled with biremes and, beyond them, a veritable fleet of fishing vessels. Even a Nusantaran dhow graced the edge of one pier, its crewmen unloading wicker baskets of exotic goods. Most Nusantarans didn't venture beyond Phoenikia, but perhaps these men thought to try their luck at greater profit by avoiding any intermediator in trade.

Leaving the harbour behind, Prometheus made his way into the city proper and toward the acropolis, finding, despite his desire to see his daughter, that his feet kept bringing him to pause at local merchants. Even after his long life, he was not immune to trepidation at a potentially painful reunion. Not even he.

It had been three years since he had seen Pyrrha. Sometimes, it felt longer. Sometimes, it felt he had seen her mere days ago.

Or perhaps that was because he so oft sought after her in the flames, staring for hour upon hour into the flickering patterns, hoping for a glimpse of his daughter. Or her mother.

His pyromancy told him she delved into arcana that ought to have been left alone. There were things she could not understand about the cosmos, about the Elder Gods, and about the Art. Things he could not bring himself to tell her. What parent could burden their children with truths that would shatter their innocence and steal their peace from them?

So he wandered colonnades, searching for new sandals he did not really need. He paused to buy a handful of succulent dates and watched the afternoon drag on. Watched the people mill and bustle, caught in the currents of their lives.

But there was no averting his purpose here.

So, at last, he climbed the path to the acropolis and entered the court of Phoebe. Her marmoreal halls were rimmed by a wide peristyle, with smooth columns crested by a circular capital. While he had glimpsed this place in visions, it was the first time Prometheus had come here since the city replaced Sardeis, and seeing it in person was different.

A servant—an ageing man with the air of one who thought himself above most who came here—met him at the threshold with a curt bow. "Whom may I announce?"

"Prometheus."

The servant's manner shifted into effortless obeisance on hearing a Titan had arrived. "My lord, of course. Please come this way." The man beckoned, then guided him into Phoebe's throne room.

The space existed behind her main hall, separated by more unadorned columns and set upon a slightly raised dais rimmed by benches. The Titan and her husband Koios—recently returned from exile, as Prometheus had foreseen—both sat upon golden thrones.

The armrests of Phoebe's throne were engraved to look like leopard heads, while Koios sat upon a more plain chair, having apparently acknowledged his mate's preeminence.

"Prometheus," Phoebe said, her eyes twinkling with amusement.

He drew into a deep bow. After countless lifetimes wandering the World, one learnt to cater to the vanity of monarchs, even if their reigns proved as transitory as everything else. Such courtesies cost him naught and oft earned him goodwill. "Lady Phoebe."

"What brings you to this court?" she asked, though she knew full well his purpose in coming. Like his feigned obsequiousness, it was all a game, true, but refusing to play along with the mummery would avail him little.

"Word has come my daughter remains a guest in your hall. I should like to look upon her, as it has been too many years."

"Indeed," Phoebe said, eyes still smiling. "She has become a boon companion to my own granddaughter and the two of them oft vanish into the woods for days at a time." A pause, as if she thought to test him.

Very well. He could play. "But she is not away at present."

Phoebe broke into a true grin, leaning forward. Like Prometheus, her paramour was an Oracle. Perhaps she played with him thus, striving to know just how much he could see. Koios was adept at divining the future, true, but Prometheus suspected he himself was by far the stronger Oracle.

"No, I believe she is here somewhere," Phoebe said, then looked to Koios. "Why don't you check on our granddaughter?"

Koios's gaze had not left Prometheus's face the whole time, and even now, he rose without so much as a glance at his queen. Perhaps he had known all along how this would play out. The Titan drew up beside Prometheus and beckoned him to follow, making obvious attempts to conceal any expression.

Wending around the columns, Koios guided him out into the courtyard. Perhaps Koios had foreseen Prometheus's coming, but he could not have seen overmuch. Oracular Sight tended to interfere with the Sight of other Oracles, and Prometheus *had* seen this moment, reaffirming his belief he was the stronger Oracle.

Tired of the games, Prometheus grabbed the Titan's elbow and spun him around to face him. "You know the path Pyrrha has begun to follow."

Koios pulled free from Prometheus's grip, his feigned smile slipping into an arrogant smirk. "You mean delving into the Art? I may have noticed such things." A nonchalant shrug. "Hardly a surprise, and even Phoebe has dabbled, of course."

Oh, but Pyrrha already pushed it farther than Phoebe had ever dared. "The queen may do as she wishes. You knew Pyrrha was my daughter and I would not have approved, and you *could* have taken steps to discourage her and Artemis from walking these precarious roads. But you stood by and did naught."

Koios snorted. "As if I am responsible for your issue, Prometheus."

"You attempt to abrogate responsibility for those you could have helped with the claim, 'it is not my problem.' But we all bear the burden of the future we create, through action or inaction. Choosing to ignore the problems of others *is* a choice, Koios, and one you will regret."

The Titan's smirk now became a glare. "Do you dare threaten me in my own court?"

"Call it a prophecy."

Koios recoiled, his look so stricken Prometheus had to wonder if he had just somehow confirmed one of Koios's own foretellings. He would not be the first Titan undone by his own foreknowledge of the future.

Prometheus stalked away from the other Oracle, knowing full well where to find his daughter. He slipped around the courtyard, and into the water garden where Pyrrha and Artemis both lounged beside a pond.

Pyrrha read from a papyrus scroll of love poetry while the other woman inserted snarky or lewd remarks every few lines. For a moment—too brief—Prometheus listened to the joy in his daughter's voice, the simple pleasures. For that instant, he dared to let himself believe the dark depths she had explored in his pyromantic visions were mere products of his fears. That she had not delved into sorcery. That the girl lying on her back, snickering at mediocre verses, was the sum of his daughter, still innocent.

But then, as he had told Koios, everyone had a responsibility to help those they had the power to help. And, wherever Pyrrha had gone, it was not too late for her to turn back. So he moved to let his shadow fall upon the women, and both looked up abruptly at him.

Artemis frowned while Pyrrha stiffened, his daughter clearly more embarrassed at being observed than the other Titan.

"Well," Artemis said. "I believe Aidos was looking for me earlier. Perhaps I should check in on her." Without another look, she rose and departed, and Prometheus sat down beside Pyrrha.

His daughter scooted up against a tree and tossed her scroll aside as if ashamed to have even taken a moment for such things. "What are you doing here?"

Prometheus knelt and took her hand in his own. "I have seen things."

"You were spying on me." An accusation, and it stung.

"I cannot help but have concern for my own child."

"I'm fine," she said, snatching her hand away. "Thank you for asking." There was bitterness in her voice. Did she blame him for her exile? Had he failed to do enough to spare her that?

He sighed. "You are not fine. You deepen your studies in the Art."

"Yes." She made no effort to deny it.

"Pyrrha, sorcery abrades the *soul*. You cannot practice the Art without it destroying the person you are inside."

His daughter scoffed and fixed him with a hard look. "Sorcery abrades the soul? Well, so does *life*, Father. It scours and scourges and takes and takes until we are but nubs. Shells of our former selves. Does sorcery harm us? Perhaps, but so does training as a warrior, and you do not dissuade any from that course. We pay for power in pain and blood, but at least we gain some semblance of control over our lives!"

"Pyrrha, you cannot—"

"My *name*," she interrupted, "is the sorceress Hekate."

AUTHOR'S NOTE:

"... the distinction between past, present and future is only a stubbornly persistent illusion."

   -Albert Einstein

THE IDEA of fate and free will, a major theme throughout the whole of the Eschaton Cycle, comes to the forefront of *Tapestry of Fate* through the conceits of time travel and prescience. What would it mean to see the future—and the implication there is *a* future—or to travel through time, affecting it without changing it? Pandora is forced to ask these questions as she begins to see the scope of a so-called block universe, where all of time exists already.

Historically, Pandora's box was a jar, but was translated during the Renaissance as "box" and this became the iconic representation of the artefact. So why use the box here? A puzzle box, besides falling in line with the modern usage of "a Pandora's Box," lent itself much more naturally toward the time travel puzzle present in the story.

Pandora herself, in traditional myth, is the scorn-worthy *woman* (the fallen Eve) responsible for the hardships of *men*. What's interesting is, some evidence exists that, in older, pre-hellenistic traditions, Pandora may have been a goddess, a giver of gifts (her name means "all giving"), with the later story inverting her nature from blessing to curse.

Which brings us to the emergent theme of the patriarchal nature of these societies. Emergent because, when I started out, it had not been an intended focus, but as my plotting moved forward, the necessity of it became apparent. I began intending to tell the story of Pandora and her daughter, and realised, soon, that one could not look at such a story without the context of the inherent sexism of the ancient world. The blatant unfairness of life offends the sensibilities, from Titan oppression of Man, to man's oppression of women.

If you've enjoyed this book, I encourage you to join the Skalds' Tribe newsletter and get access to exclusive insider information and your FREE copy of *The Moments of Kadmus*. **I generally send every week or every other; I promise not to mail more often than that.** No spam, no selling your email address to marauding warlords, none of that.

Join me here to grab a free novella and stay connected with me: https://www.mattlarkinbooks.com/skalds/

Thank you for reading,
Matt

PS Pandora's journey continues in the *Valor of Perseus* ...
https://books2read.com/valorofperseus

Join the Skalds' Tribe newsletter and get access to exclusive insider information and a selection of *FREE* books to kickstart your Matt Larkin library.

https://www.mattlarkinbooks.com/skalds/

ALSO BY MATT LARKIN

Tapestry of Fate

The Gifts of Pandora

The Valor of Perseus

The Inferno of Prometheus

The Madness of Herakles

The Threads of Theseus

Heirs of Mana

Tides of Mana

Flames of Mana

Queens of Mana

Gods of the Ragnarok Era

The Apples of Idunn

The Mists of Niflheim

The Shores of Vanaheim

The High Seat of Asgard

The Well of Mimir

The Radiance of Alfheim

The Shadows of Svartalfheim

The Gates of Hel

The Fires of Muspelheim

ABOUT THE AUTHOR

Matt Larkin writes retellings of mythology as dark, gritty fantasy. His passions of myths, philosophy, and history inform his series. He strives to combine gut-wrenching action with thought-provoking ideas and culturally resonant stories.

Matt's mythic fantasy takes place in the Eschaton Cycle universe, a world—as the name implies—of cyclical apocalypses. Each series can be read alone in any order, but they weave together to form a greater tapestry. Want a place to start? Check out *Darkness Forged.*

Learn more at mattlarkinbooks.com or connect with Matt through his fan group, the Skalds' Tribe: https://www.mattlarkin books.com/join-the-skalds-tribe/

For Juhi. For believing.

I want to offer special thanks to all the amazing people at Kickstarter who helped me bring this to life:

Regina Dowling, Rachel Strehlow, John Van Mulligen, Mary K Cordray, Dale Russell, Matthea Ross, Bryan Lash, Diane Youngblood, Dyrk Ashton, Jon Auerbach, Dan Zangari & Robert Zangari, yesterspectre, Shannon Leigh Broughton-Smith, Eskil, Juhi Larkin, Tristan Amant, Debbie Mumford, Suzan Harden, Rebecca Kellogg, Judy Lunsford, Kari Kilgore, Curmudgeon of Phoenix Rising, Lee Sharp, Rebecca Hiatt, Jon Wasik, Lee, Henry C Eggleton, Danny van Giersbergen, Ashli Tingle, Stuart renz, Brad, Joseph, Ron Arons, Al Burke, Caleb Monroe, Emilia Pulliainen, Michał Kabza, A.P Beswick, Thomas Colgrave, Jeremy Irwin, Connor Whiteley, Scott Smith, Bryan, Sarah Polk, Duane Warnecke, Govinda P. G. Embleton, FireflyArc, Jason Hays, and Braedon Bourassa.

Thank you all,
Matt

Milton Keynes UK
Ingram Content Group UK Ltd.
UKHW012117161023
430729UK00004B/59

9 781946 686640